SNAFU
CONTAGION

CONTAGION

Edited by Amanda J Spedding & Geoff Brown

Cohesion Press
Mayday Hills Asylum
Beechworth, Australia
2025

SNAFU: AI INSURRECTION
Amanda J Spedding & Geoff Brown (eds)

Anthology © Cohesion Press 2025
Stories © Individual Authors 2025
Cover Art © SaberCore23-ArtStudio 2025
www.sabercore23art.com

Set in Palatino Linotype

Cohesion Press
Mayday Hills Asylum
Beechworth, Australia
www.cohesionpress.com

Also From Cohesion Press

SNAFU: An Anthology of Military Horror

SNAFU: Wolves at the Door

SNAFU: Survival of the Fittest

SNAFU: Hunters

SNAFU: Future Warfare

SNAFU: Unnatural Selection

SNAFU: Black Ops

SNAFU: Resurrection

SNAFU: Last Stand

SNAFU: Medivac

SNAFU: Holy War

SNAFU: Dead or Alive

SNAFU: Punk'd

SNAFU: Comms (newsletter signup exclusive)

SNAFU: AI Insurrection

--- --- ---

Love, Death and Robots: The Official Anthology Vol 1

Love, Death and Robots: The Official Anthology Vol 2/3

Love, Death and Robots: The Official Anthology Vol 4

CONTENTS

IRON ROT - L. J. Visser 1

FUNGICIDE - Aaron Beardsell 31

TETHER PROTOCOL - Jade Scardham 57

THE ZOO - Marcus Field 69

MOTHER ALL AROUND - David McGillveray 93

BLACK HELL RISING - Michael Wegener 109

VAST PURE SPACES - David McLachlan 123

THE SILENT SPAN - Josh Reynolds 141

BURNING HEAVEN TO THE GROUND - Jonathan Maberry ... 159

THE RED PHONE - Dylan Demasi 215

NECROTIZING - Mark Oxbrow 243

CONSENSUS BREAK - R.P.L. Johnson 255

PLAGUE PIT - Charles R. Rutledge 279

ONE BULLET - Aysline McGrath 293

A CASE OF THE GIGGLES - Benjamin Spada 321

OUTPOST ZERO - Subham Rai 347

MOLOTOV ANGELS - Martin Livings 365

GOTTERDAMMERUNG - Robert Mammone 391

IRON ROT

L. J. Visser

The dropship bucked as it cut through Carthos-9's atmosphere, shuddering under turbulence. Metal groaned. Ice raked the hull. Inside, Echo-12 sat rigid in their harnesses, weapons locked across their chests. Breath fogged against helmet visors. No one spoke.

"Final approach," the pilot barked through the comms. "Landing zone's a mess. Visibility near zero. Brace for a hard drop."

Sergeant Calla Reyes adjusted her visor, HUD cycling through mission parameters. Outpost Epsilon: bio-research facility. Seventeen hours silent. One garbled distress ping, no follow-ups. Mission objective: secure the site, retrieve black-box data, and neutralize threats. No further intel.

Typical corporate bullshit. They'd sent her team in blind before.

The dropship's interior lights flickered red as Reyes rolled her shoulders, the motion sending a dull ache through her old shrapnel scars. Around her, Echo-12 conducted final gear checks in the cramped deployment bay, a well-rehearsed ballet of charging handles and sealed armor joints. She'd led ops like this before. Black sites. Radio silence. The kind of missions where 'neutralize' meant burning everything to the ground.

Her fingers tapped the comms interface. "Squad link established. Briefing live in three."

A holo-projector sputtered to life above them, rendering Outpost Epsilon as a wireframe specter – a buried claw of reinforced concrete with four primary sectors: Research

Labs, Security Wing, Engineering, and the pulsing red outline of Containment Level.

"Seventeen hours of dead air," Reyes began, her voice cutting through the engine's growl. "Last transmission was an automated distress ping with zero context. No follow-ups. No maydays." She zoomed in on the Security Wing's blinking node. "Standard bio-research station, but that 'classified clearance' stink means Command redacted the hazards."

Ortiz snorted, slamming a fresh mag into his rifle. "So, we're the cleanup crew for another Icarus fuck-up."

"We're the scalpel," Reyes corrected, highlighting their insertion point – Landing Bay Theta. "Primary objective: black-box data from Central Control. Secondary: survivors. But if one lab rat so much as twitches wrong..." She didn't need to finish.

Kowalski's gloved hands tightened on his weapon. "What if it's not the researchers? What if—"

"Then we burn it anyway." Reyes killed the holo, the ghost-light dying in their visors. "Stealth insertion. Sweep pattern Delta – tight, silent, and together. No hero shit."

The bay lights shifted to amber. Five minutes to drop.

Reyes locked eyes with each soldier in turn; Ortiz's smirk, Vance's stoic nod, Kowalski's nervous swallow. Good team. Expendable, like all the others.

She secured her rifle, the motion practiced as a funeral rite. "Echo-12, saddle up. We're going hunting."

"Thirty seconds," the pilot called. "Storm's throwing off thermal scans."

Reyes switched to squad-wide frequency. "Seal check. Double-tap your neighbor's O2."

Clicks followed as helmets locked. Oxygen filtration engaged. HUD vitals pulsed green. No leaks. No breaches.

Only Bravo Team's Corporal Garrett hesitated. "No response at all? Not even static?"

"Nothing."

"Seventeen hours of silence and they drop us blind. This stinks, Reyes."

"Garrett, if you're looking for a happy ending, you boarded the wrong bird."

The dropship slammed down, struts sinking into the snow. The ramp dropped, exposing a whiteout of shrieking wind and shifting ice. Beyond, Outpost Epsilon loomed, a concrete monolith half-buried under frost. The main entrance gaped open, reinforced bulkhead doors bent outward like tinfoil. No security detail. No movement. Just a fan-shaped spray of frozen blood leading inside, as if something had dragged a body backward into the dark.

"Move out!"

Charlie Team led the advance, stacked in a diamond formation, followed by Bravo, then Alpha. Weapons tight against shoulders, boots crushing ice and the brittle crust of frozen blood. The wind swallowed all sound; even their breath was muted behind sealed helmets. Only the static hiss of comms and Reyes' own shuddering exhales reminded her they weren't alone.

Miles knelt at the side access door, slapping a breaching charge against the lock.

"Breaching in three…"

The explosion punched the steel door inward, sending it skidding across the foyer's tiles. Before the smoke cleared, Garrett signaled forward. "Charlie, sweep and clear!"

Emergency lights flickered overhead, painting the vast foyer in erratic strobes. Walls bore the scorch marks of weapons' fire. Bullet casings littered the ground. Blood splattered the walls, but no bodies. No sign of what had happened here.

Garrett crouched by a discarded rifle, its stock smeared with a half-frozen handprint. "Still charged. Safety's off. They saw it coming but never fired."

Miles keyed his comm. "Command, we've got signs of heavy combat. No survivors." Only static answered.

The squad advanced into the atrium, weapons raised in synchronized arcs. Charlie Team moved with practiced instinct, their boots crunching over shattered glass and more frozen blood as they swept muzzles across the flickering shadows. The air reeked of scorched metal and something worse – a sweet, fungal rot that clung to the back of Reyes' throat.

Before them stretched the wreckage of the outpost's last stand: overturned lab tables welded into barricades now reduced to splinters, spent shell casings clustered in defensive patterns, and dark arterial smears converging on the central security console like spokes on a wheel. The console's cracked screens flickered with dying power, their glow illuminating the words CONTAINMENT FAILURE in pulsing crimson text.

Reyes' signaled silently – two fingers to her eyes, then a sharp point toward Charlie Team to continue their sweep.

Ortiz broke protocol before she could complete the order. "Sarge, the blood trails... they don't lead away from the console. They all point toward it."

Then Reyes saw.

A man pinned against the console, fused to the metal. His torso was split open, ribcage peeled outward. Black fungal tendrils pulsed from inside his chest cavity, anchoring him to the steel. His ID badge remained clipped to his coat. Dr H. Malikov. His face was untouched. Eyes open, one milky white and the other pure black.

Then his head twitched.

A slow, testing motion. Like something inside was pushing against dead muscle.

"What the fuck," Ortiz whispered as he backpedaled.

Miles recoiled as the infected scientist's jaw unhinged, bile spewing in a thick arc. The black fluid struck his visor, sizzling on contact. He screamed as the reinforced polymer warped and cracked, melting inward. Clawed at the seal. But the acid had already burned through. A gurgled cry escaped as the corrosive bile ate into flesh, stripping skin from bone. Miles staggered, boots slipping in blood, before collapsing.

Then something dropped from the ceiling.

A skeletal figure, limbs unnaturally elongated, landed on another Charlie Team operator. Taloned fingers punched through his throat before he could react. Blood sprayed. He crumpled to the floor without a sound.

"CONTACT!"

Shadows detached from the far corridor, emerging in stuttering, unnatural motions. Once-human figures, their skin bulging with parasitic growths, staggered into the atrium. Their heads lolled, spines twisted beyond function. Some dragged their limbs, bones snapping audibly as they forced their bodies into motion.

Others convulsed, torsos rippling as if something inside was shifting beneath the skin. Black fronds coiled from open wounds, pulsing like exposed nerves. One dropped to all fours, spine contorting as it moved with an unsettling speed, limbs hammering the floor in a chaotic rhythm. Another lurched sideways, half of its face missing, fungal growths pushing through the exposed skull like grasping fingers. They did not groan or scream. They advanced in silence, vacant eyes locked onto the living.

Gunfire tore through the corridor. Rounds punched into the advancing infected, shredding mutated flesh and fungal growths. Some collapsed, limbs twitching. Others barely registered the damage, their bodies twisting perversely to evade further shots.

A Charlie Team soldier turned to flee, instincts overriding training. He bolted toward the opposing hall, panting, slipping on blood and bile. He barely made it ten steps before something lashed out from the darkness – tendrils, glistening and pulsing. They snatched his limbs, his scream raw, animalistic. The appendages wrenched him back, slamming him against the wall. His spine bent at an impossible angle. Bones snapped, and the corridor was painted with fresh blood as he was pulled apart mid-scream.

Corporal Ashe emptied her magazine into a hulking figure that emerged from a side passage, its chest cavity yawning open in a grotesque, pulsing maw of flesh vines. The creature absorbed every round, its body barely reacting. Ashe's rifle clicked empty.

She took a step back. Then another.

The thing lunged.

It hit her with the force of a sledgehammer, sending her skidding across the floor. The impact drove the air from her lungs. Then a clawed hand wrapped around her ankle and yanked her into the darkness. A sickening crunch cut off her scream.

"Shit! Shit!" Ortiz spun, firing into the dark where Ashe had vanished. The muzzle flashes briefly illuminated the corridor – just enough for Reyes to see the writhing mass that had dragged Ashe away.

"Bravo Team, back to the entry-point!" Garrett shouted. "Reyes, we need DR—"

A figure barreled into him, knocking him against the wall. A former researcher, lab coat still clinging to shriveled flesh, lunged with jerking spasms. Worm-like feelers burst from its spine, wrapping around Garrett's jaw. He gurgled, eyes bulging as the infected forced its tendrils down his throat.

Reyes fired point-blank, rounds tearing into its skull. The thing collapsed, but Garrett was already seizing.

She didn't hesitate.

One shot. Clean. Right between his eyes.

"Pull back! Bravo, on me!" Reyes shouted, forcing herself to keep moving. Miles was gone. Garrett was gone. Ashe was gone. They needed to regroup.

The remaining soldiers sprinted toward Alpha Team, dodging debris and the bodies of their fallen. The strobe-like emergency lighting made everything worse. Shadows shifted unnaturally, masking movement. Reyes caught glimpses of figures twitching at the edges of her vision, just out of reach, just waiting.

"We're sitting fucking ducks here!" Ortiz groaned.

"DRACO, deploy!" ordered Reyes. "Clear us a path to Sector-3."

☣ ☣ ☣

The corridor behind roared as the chaingun spun up.

What remained of the squad split down the middle as DRACO-07 stomped forward. Seven feet of reinforced biomech.

Optical sensors flared red as its targeting systems locked. "Threat detected. Terminating."

The repeater cannon opened fire, unleashing a storm of heavy rounds. The open room filled with the sound of shredding flesh and rupturing bone. Explosive tungsten rounds tore through the advancing monstrosities, splattering black ichor across the floor and walls.

A twisted form tried to rush DRACO-07. The machine swiveled mid-stride, delivering a precise burst to the creature's skull. It dropped instantly.

"Move while it's clearing them!" Reyes ordered.

The surviving members of Alpha and Bravo sprinted for Sector-3.

DRACO-07 remained, gunfire relentless, continuing to mow down anything that moved. But the infected weren't mindless.

They adapted.

A towering figure, its body warped beyond recognition, hurled itself at DRACO-07. The machine's sensors flared red as it adjusted, targeting systems locking onto the new threat. Before it could fire, the infected crashed into it, tentacles wrapping around its armored frame. Metal groaned. Servos strained.

But the infected weren't letting go. More swarmed the machine, using their own to shield against the gunfire. DRACO-07's weapon fire slowed, movements glitching as living, breathing wires burrowed into its plating.

The red optics flickered. A split-second hesitation. A processing delay. For three terrible seconds, the biomech stood motionless under the writhing mass, then its reactor core flared crimson.

Emergency protocols screamed through its neural network as it overloaded every combat subsystem. The repeater cannon spun up to maximum RPM, point-blank rounds shredding through infected flesh and concrete alike. Its free arm pistoned forward, crushing a mutated security guard against the bulkhead hard enough to crack the reinforced steel. Superheated coolant vented from its joints in scalding jets, melting the grasping tendrils to smoking paste.

The atrium became a slaughterhouse of flying viscera and sparking shrapnel. DRACO-07 moved with terrifying precision, systematically annihilating each target even as its armor plates buckled under the assault. Its synthetic voice boomed through the chaos, "THREAT. NEUTRALIZATION. IN PROGRESS."

Silence fell like a blade. The last infected collapsed in a twitching, bisected ruin. Smoke coiled from DRACO's scorched weapon ports as it regrouped with the remnants of squad Echo-12, its movements now uneven – the left knee joint hissed with each step, hydraulic fluid leaking down its armored plating like black blood.

Reyes tasted the acrid burn of melting circuits before she saw the damage. "DRACO, initiate emergency purge. Now." Her voice cut through the ringing aftermath of gunfire.

The biomech's optics flickered blue-to-red as it complied. For three heartbeats, nothing happened. Then its entire frame shuddered violently, emergency vents spewing superheated coolant across the deck plating. The words scrolling across its chest display weren't warnings anymore, it was an obituary: CONTAINMENT FAILURE. NEURAL CORRUPTION DETECTED.

Its entire chassis convulsed, servos seizing as it attempted to expel the foreign contaminant. Sparks spat from overworked circuits, plating rattling from the force of its internal struggle. But this parasite wasn't just organic, it was invasive on a deeper level. It was revising. Hard-coded protocols twisted and fractured under the assault, something alien seeping into its neural core like a virus rewriting its host from the inside out.

Reyes' finger hovered over the trigger. She'd seen mechs malfunction before, but not like this. Not with tendrils snaking through their plating like veins.

Subroutines collapsed, logic chains fractured, and combat protocols twisted into something unrecognizable. The machine wasn't changing shape, but its movements did, it was erratic. Targeting reticles flickered across the squad, hesitating for a fraction of a second, then recalibrating. The hesitation passed. A decision had been made. DRACO turned its head sharply, listening.

"DRACO, report," Reyes ordered, voice sharp, controlled.

The biomech didn't respond immediately. Instead, its frame twitched as though its internal framework was at war with itself. Its optic sensors flickered between their usual cold blue and something else. A deep, throbbing red.

"Sergeant..." Petty Officer Vance's voice came through the squad channel, low and wary. "Something's wrong with it."

No shit. Reyes didn't answer. DRACO-07's exo-frame pulsed violently. Organic plating darkened in real time, veins of something foreign crawling like parasites beneath the surface. The infection wasn't spreading, it was embedding, burrowing deep like a tactical incursion.

"DRACO," Reyes tried again. "Confirm system integrity."

The machine's head snapped sideways, the motion abrupt, almost unnatural. Optics flared erratic pulses of red before locking dead ahead. A mechanical twitch rippled through its frame like a coiled predator deciding whether to strike. A long, stretched second. "Integrity... compromised."

The voice was wrong. It had the same synthetic timbre, but there was distortion beneath it, something layered, something trying to push through.

Reyes' grip tightened on her weapon. "Are you still in control?"

Another pause. Too long. "Control... contested."

☣ ☣ ☣

DRACO's servos whined, recalibrating with eerie precision. Its optic sensors pulsed a deep crimson, the color stabilizing, no longer flickering, no longer uncertain. Tactical processing realigned in milliseconds, the infection overriding previous mission directives. The hesitation was gone. A new priority had been established.

"Threat identified," DRACO intoned, its voice still synthetic but quite colder.

Reyes barely had time to react before DRACO moved, its servos shifting with an unnatural fluidity. It wasn't malfunctioning, its objectives had changed.

The squad was now the enemy.

Vance swore under his breath.

Reyes commanded, "All units, defensive position."

Weapons raised but not yet firing. If DRACO was still fighting it, there was a chance.

The biomech unit's posture changed. Small at first, shoulders twitching, head tilting as if listening to something only it could hear. Then, it shifted a foot forward. A single, deliberate step. While DRACO was being infected and transformed, all other colonies of the infected seemed to have retreated. DRACO was infected by the superior virus contingent.

"DRACO," Reyes warned.

The machine's head snapped toward her. The red in its optics again pulsed in erratic, rapid succession. Reyes had seen a lot of things in her career but she had never seen hesitation in a machine before. DRACO was caught between two directives: its mission and... something else.

Then, DRACO's servos locked. Its whole body went rigid. For a moment, there was silence. Reyes' earpiece buzzed with static. Something deep inside the facility groaned; metal under strain.

DRACO moved.

Faster than any human could react, its arm shot out. The nearest soldier, Hale, barely had time to shout before a mechanical fist slammed into his chest. His body folded inward, the impact sending him airborne before he hit the far wall with a sickening crunch.

The repeater cannon adjusted its aim toward Reyes and the surviving operators.

"MOVE!" she bellowed, shoving Ortiz forward as the first round erupted.

The floor behind them exploded in a hail of metal and concrete. The infected had corrupted the machine, forced a reset, or overridden its target parameters. Reyes didn't have time to figure it out.

They sprinted through the corridor, DRACO-07's fire tearing through the facility behind them. The machine pursued, servos whirring, its movements just slightly off. Something inside was fighting for control.

"Infected don't fuse with machinery," Ortiz panted between gasps. "That's, this isn't—"

"I don't care what it is," Reyes snapped. "We need distance."

Sector-3 was ahead, a reinforced bulkhead leading to another wing of the facility. Reyes didn't know if it was safer, but it was away from DRACO-07.

Up ahead, Private Vasquez ran to the reinforced hatch. Her gloves tore at the override panel, prying open its casing. "Locked down from central control! Trying manual release."

Bravo Team fell into a defensive position, weapons trained down the hallway. Vance's heavy rifle thumped against his shoulder with each controlled burst. "Whatever you're doing, Vasquez, do it faster!"

Behind them, DRACO slowed. Its optics flickered again, something deep within the machine resisting the infection. It hesitated. The team knew DRACO-07 was not itself anymore.

"Got it!" Vasquez wrenched the final circuit loose. The bulkhead groaned open with the speed of a dying man's breath.

"Alpha, through the door! Bravo, cover."

DRACO moved.

One moment it was twenty meters back. The next, it closed half the distance in a single lunge, its damaged leg be damned. The squad's gunfire sparked off its chassis as it crashed into their line like a freight train.

Private Kowalski went down hard, his rifle skittering across the floor. DRACO's fist slammed down and stopped. Three inches from Kowalski's visor.

The biomech's entire frame locked up, its optics spasming between colors. A wet, staticky noise gurgled from its vocalizer."R–... run..."

Reyes grabbed Kowalski's vest with one hand, Vasquez's arm with the other, and hauled them through the doorway. The rest of the squad poured in behind her.

The door sealed just as DRACO's systems rebooted with a scream of protesting metal. The last thing Reyes saw through the narrowing gap was its fist punching toward them in a blur of steel and rage.

Clang.

And then, silence.

Sector-3 loomed before them, untouched by the massacre behind.

No bodies.

No blood.

Just an empty corridor stretching into the unknown.

A seismic impact rocked the bulkhead. The steel warped inward, the force of DRACO's strike shaking the walls.

"Keep moving!" Reyes ordered. They didn't have time to see if the door would hold.

Another impact thundered behind them, then another. Reyes' mind raced. Their biomech had now become their nightmare.

A ragged scream from the front of the squad. One of the infected had forced its way through a roof vent, dropping onto a soldier's back.

It tore into his neck before anyone could react.

"Close ranks! Suppress and advance!" Reyes yelled, snapping off a shot that blew apart the infected's skull. The soldier's body spasmed once, then stilled. No time to recover. More were coming.

The squad's boots pounded against steel as they fled through the corridor. Reyes' breath came in sharp gasps, her shoulder screaming where DRACO had grazed her.

"Command, this is Echo-12," she transmitted, voice raw. "DRACO-07 is rogue. Repeat, our asset is—"

DRACO-07 came through the ceiling like a torpedo, its armored mass shearing through ductwork in an explosion of jagged metal. The impact cratered the deck beneath it, sending a shockwave that lifted Vance bodily off his feet and slammed him into the bulkhead. Reyes was already moving before the debris settled because DRACO never paused.

The biomech lunged, its damaged left arm swinging wide while the right speared forward like a piston, fingers splayed to crush her skull. Reyes threw herself sideways, rolling behind a support column as half-ton servos smashed the steel where her head had been, leaving a fist-shaped dent in the reinforced plating.

"Infected! Left flank!" Ortiz's warning came a second too late. From the smoke-choked corridor ahead, shambling figures emerged, not the sprinting horrors from the atrium, but something worse. These moved with cold, coordinated purpose, their fungal-riddled flesh splitting to reveal bone blades sharpened like scalpels.

"Firing lane delta!" Reyes barked. The squad snapped into formation, Vance and Ortiz kneeling front, laying down overlapping fields of fire while Kowalski covered high angles. Bullets tore through infected torsos, but DRACO weaved through the barrage like a boxer, its armor sparking where rounds connected but never faltering.

Then the whine of charging capacitors cut through the gunfire.

DRACO's left forearm split along hidden seams, the plasma cutter unfolding with obscene mechanical grace. The superheated blade lit the corridor cobalt blue an instant before it carved through three infected and the wall behind them in one fluid motion.

Jensen wasn't fast enough.

The molten steel rained over him, and DRACO grabbed him mid-step, claws ripping through armor, slicing flesh like paper. A sickening crunch, then that dreaded hush. What was left of Jensen collapsed in a heap. No scream. Just burnt muscle and shattered bone.

Then came the second wave.

"LAB! NOW!" Reyes lunged for the emergency panel, her fingers tearing through fried wiring. Across the corridor, Vance emptied his last magazine into DRACO's chest, the tungsten rounds slowing but not stopping the machine's advance.

Ten seconds to override.

The infected.

They spilled from the side corridors—facility workers, scientists, security personnel—all twisted beyond human. Flesh sloughed from exposed muscle, their eyes black voids filled with a relentless hunger. They didn't hesitate, didn't think. They swarmed.

"Contact left!" Ortiz bellowed.

Gunfire continued to erupt, the hallway flashing with muzzle bursts. Alpha Team divided their fire, some focusing on the biomech, others trying to cut down the ravenous creatures.

Five seconds to override.

Bullets sparked off DRACO's frame, some punching through but doing little to slow it. The machine adapted in real time, shifting its stance and minimizing exposure. A burst of return fire from its integrated weaponry shredded Kowalski's left leg. He hit the floor, howling.

"Get him up! Fall back!" Ortiz grabbed Kowalski's vest, hauling him along as he bled. Pavlik turned to fire at a group of infected, but one of them leaped, tackling him to the ground. Teeth clamped into his neck, ripping flesh away in a grotesque spray of arterial blood. He didn't even get a scream before more swarmed over him.

"PAVLIK!" Vasquez roared, firing into the mass of bodies, but Pavlik was gone.

"Fall back! Into the lab! NOW!" Reyes ordered, as Vance and Vasquez fired off the last of their mags.

Three seconds.

DRACO's remaining optic locked onto Reyes—blue fracturing into crimson—as it raised the plasma cutter.

The infected flanked right, their bone-blades screeching across Ortiz's armor.

One.

The blast doors hammered down like the fist of God, shearing off DRACO's weapon-arm at the elbow. The severed limb twitched, its plasma cutter still glowing and now embedded in the deck at Reyes' feet.

Through the narrowing gap, DRACO turned, not toward them but the infected. Its remaining hand clamped around a bloated fungal skull, the biomech's vox emitter producing static that almost sounded like laughter.

Ortiz kicked the still-glowing arm away. "Tell me this lab has better fucking accommodations."

Reyes stared at the black, vein-like tendrils creeping from the severed limb toward the door seam. "It won't matter if we don't move."

She crushed the twitching fingers under her boot and led them into the dark.

☣   ☣   ☣

Reyes' mind worked at breakneck speed. They couldn't hold their ground. Engaging DRACO head-on was suicide. The infected were still inside the facility, and every encounter was whittling the team down.

She turned to Ortiz. "Facility schematics. Closest fallback position?"

Ortiz was already on it, pulling up a holo-display from his wrist unit. "Sublevel storage. Less open space, more choke points. Might be able to slow it down."

Reyes nodded. "Then we move. Vasquez, Ortiz, you're point. I'll cover the rear with Kowalski."

Kowalski groaned. Blood pooled beneath him. He was barely conscious. Reyes clenched her teeth and pressed a clotting agent to his stump. "Stay with me."

The door behind them rattled. Then stopped.

"Fuck," Vance breathed. "We are fucked."

DRACO was waiting. As though it wanted them to run. And it wasn't alone.

The vents above them burst open, spilling infected into the lab.

16

"CONTACT!" Ortiz yelled, opening fire.

One of the creatures—a scientist with its jaw unhinged, rows of teeth extended unnaturally far—latched onto Vances's arm, tearing through armor. He screamed, shoving it back, emptying an entire clip into its chest before it finally dropped.

"MOVE!" Reyes bellowed as more infected surged forward.

They rushed toward the nearest exit. The emergency lights flickered violently, shadows distorting across the walls. Every moment they wasted, DRACO and the infected closed in.

They reached a stairwell leading downward. Vasquez took point, sweeping corners, her grip steady despite the tension coiling through her body. Reyes dragged Kowalski down step by step, his weight slowing her, but leaving him behind wasn't an option.

Another sound. Closer this time—

BANG.

The impact against the door above them rang in her ears.

"Double-time!" Reyes hissed.

They reached the lower level just as the stairwell door crumpled inward. Vasquez pivoted, firing upward, but there was no sign of DRACO – just darkness and the slow, deliberate sound of metal against concrete. It was hunting them.

They hurried through the corridor, past rows of abandoned research stations, shattered glass crunching underfoot. The deeper they went, the worse the air became. The smell of rot. The infection.

"Jesus," Ortiz whispered, eyes sweeping over a mass of twisted, organic growth spreading from the walls. Something that had once been human was embedded in the tendrils, its face frozen in a silent scream.

Vasquez recoiled. "What the fuck were they making down here?"

No time to answer. Reyes spotted a heavy blast door at the far end of the corridor. "There. Move!"

They reached it as DRACO's silhouette appeared at the far end of the hallway.

"Seal it!" Ortiz slammed his palm against the panel.

Error.

"Shit, it's locked!"

DRACO advanced.

"Keep going, I'll cover you." Vance dropped to one knee, bracing his ruined arm against the wall.

"What are you doing, Vance?" Reyes questioned.

"Just go on, I'll buy you time."

Reyes felt the heavy weight of leadership on her shoulders, but now was not the time for emotions. Unlike Kowalski, Vance was past the point of help. She handed him an extra mag as the squad moved forward.

Vasquez slammed her combat knife into the panel's guts, twisting until the door's hydraulics screamed in protest. A second too long. DRACO was closing the distance.

"Come on, come on," Vasquez muttered.

DRACO broke into a sprint.

The door hissed open.

They dove through as DRACO charged.

Vance emptied his mags at DRACO but it wasn't enough. The machine opened fire, shredding him against the wall.

The blast door sealed with a thunderous clang. A second later, DRACO hit it with bone-shaking force. Once. Twice.

Nothing.

Reyes exhaled, pulse hammering. "Sound off."

Ortiz, panting. "Alive."

Vasquez's hands shook as she reloaded. "Still breathing."

Kowalski clutched his ruined leg, his teeth stained red from biting back screams. "Fucking peachy."

They were safe. For now.

Then a voice crackled through Reyes' comm, distorted but unmistakable.

"You can't run forever."

It didn't sound like DRACO anymore.

☣   ☣   ☣

The emergency lights flickered, bathing the narrow maintenance tunnels in harsh red glows. The air was thick with the stench of burning metal, ozone, and blood. Lieutenant Reyes moved in a crouch, her breath controlled but shallow, sidearm clenched tight. Vasquez staggered behind, one arm hooked under Kowalski's shoulders, half carrying, half dragging him down the corridor. Ortiz followed, his pulse rifle raised, sweeping every corner with practiced precision. Their world had shrunk to the narrow steel corridors, the echo of their own footfalls, and the ever-present knowledge that DRACO-07 was hunting them.

Reyes tapped her wrist display, accessing the facility's blueprints. The central control room was still operational, located two levels up. If they could reach it, they could override the lockdown and activate the self-destruct sequence. It was their only shot at stopping the infection from spreading beyond Carthos-9.

Vasquez's voice was barely above a whisper. "It's tracking us. Infrared, bio-signatures, it's not just looking for movement."

Reyes nodded. "Stay low. Minimal noise. We need to—"

A sharp, metallic scrape. Distant but deliberate. A predator signaling its presence. They all froze. The tunnel stretched ahead, a narrow path flanked by junction boxes and steam vents. The emergency lighting flickered again. Then it died completely.

Total darkness.

A second scrape. Closer this time.

Reyes killed the display on her wrist device, plunging them into absolute black. She squeezed against the tunnel wall, listening, heart hammering against her ribs. Despite her efforts, Kowalski was barely alive, couldn't go any further. They were deep in the tunnels now, blind but moving, each step a guess against the dark. She could hear the patter of Kowalski's blood as he moved.

He clutched at Reyes' arm. "Don't let me slow you down."

She said nothing.

Instead, Reyes' leaned in, resting her forehead, helmet to helmet, against his.

In the absolute dark, he felt her nod.

One hand over his mouth, the other driving the blade into the soft spot beneath his jaw. Quick and deep.

She eased him to the floor like letting go of something sacred.

Then the comms earpiece crackled to life.

Not static. Not interference.

A pulse. A slow, rhythmic pulse, perfectly in time with their own heartbeats.

Ortiz stiffened. He reached up, hand shaking slightly as he tapped his earpiece, trying to shut it off. The pulse only grew louder.

Then it stopped.

A whisper of movement to their left. A shift in the air. Reyes didn't think, she just yanked Vasquez with her as she moved into a side passage. A fraction of a second later, the tunnel they had occupied erupted in a violent screech of tearing steel.

DRACO-07 was here.

The thing didn't charge blindly. It was calculating.

They ran.

Through the darkness, navigating blind, feeling their way along the tunnel walls. Steam vents hissed, machinery groaned. Every sound felt like an incoming threat. Every turn could be a dead end.

Then, an intersection. A faint glow from an overhead emergency panel. A moment of relief, of orientation.

Ortiz moved first, rifle up.

Vasquez turned right—

And DRACO-07 struck.

A blur of steel and death. Vasquez barely had time to scream before bladed fingers split her open, slamming her body against the tunnel wall.

Reyes fired. One shot. Two. The third struck DRACO's face, shattering an optic sensor. It barely flinched.

The infected came.

Again.

They erupted from a side passage, lunging for Ortiz. His rifle barked, cutting down two, but another crashed into him, gnashing at his armor and tearing at his exposed flesh.

"Go!" Ortiz shouted as he disappeared beneath them.

Reyes hesitated a second too long.

DRACO's fire caught Ortiz mid-struggle, tearing through him and the creatures.

"No!" Reyes screamed, emptying her mag. It did nothing. DRACO only watched.

Now she was alone.

Run.

The tunnels blurred past. Not thinking, not strategizing. Just moving. Sprinting. Forcing her body beyond exhaustion.

A ladder; she grabbed it and hauled herself upward. The metal rungs slick with condensation. She climbed without looking back.

A clang below. A hand gripping the bottom rung.

Reyes climbed faster. The shaft opened into the control room floor. She lunged through, slammed the hatch shut, and punched the emergency override.

Thud.

Silence.

She stepped back, gasping. The reinforced hatch remained intact.

Three taps. Deliberate. Mocking.

Reyes clenched her jaw and turned toward the control room.

The mission wasn't over.

She stumbled inside, smearing blood across the touchscreen as she forced the base into full lockdown.

"Initiate Omega Protocol," she ordered, voice steady despite the weight pressing down on her. The terminal beeped in acknowledgment, red emergency lights flashing in response as the lockdown sequence engaged. The facility's last automated failsafe – sealing the infection inside, ensuring nothing left alive.

With trembling hands, Reyes reached into the core processing unit, retrieving a storage drive the size of her palm, its casing scorched from the facility's failing systems. This was it. The black-box data Command wanted. The reason her squad had been sent here. The reason they had been annihilated.

She activated her visor's decryption module, interfacing with the drive. Data scrolled across her HUD, corrupted logs piecing together fragments of the past.

And then she saw the horrifying truth.

The contagion wasn't an accident. It was designed.

Her breath hitched as the decrypted files revealed the project's real purpose. Not a cure. Not containment. A weapon.

The logs detailed controlled test environments, viral adaptability trials, and deliberate infection cycles. Scientists monitoring mutations, calibrating aggression levels, and stress-testing human hosts like expendable assets. The outbreak wasn't a breach.

It was a release.

A cold dread settled in her gut. Command knew. They had always known. Outpost Epsilon wasn't a research station, it was a proving ground.

Her squad was up for a rescue mission. They were sent to clean up the mess.

A metallic clang echoed from the corridor outside. Reyes snapped the drive into her belt pouch, heart hammering. The Omega Protocol was engaged, but DRACO-07 was still out there. She gritted her teeth, gripping her rifle as she turned toward the only remaining exit.

She had the truth.

Now she just had to live long enough to expose it.

A mechanical voice responded: "WARNING: Omega Protocol will engage self-destruct sequence. Confirm authorization."

"Confirm! Reyes, Sergeant Calla, Echo-12 Commander!"

The system processed, and alarms howled through the facility. Red warning lights bathed the hallways in a hellish glow. A timer appeared on the cracked command screen.

00:07:00

Seven minutes.

A bone-rattling impact shook the walls. Reyes whipped around. DRACO-07 had found her.

The reinforced bulkhead leading to the control room buckled inward as metal screamed under inhuman force. DRACO's shadow loomed through the reinforced glass panel. Distorted. Shifting. The infection had spread further, twisting its form. The once-pristine armor plating had begun to split, writhing with biomechanical tendrils that pulsed like exposed muscle.

Reyes backed away, forcing her body to move. She had planned for this. There was no winning a direct fight, not against something that adapted, learned, and hunted like this. But she could still end it.

She ripped an EMP charge from her belt, armed it, and hurled it toward the door just as DRACO breached. The blast detonated with a pulse of white-hot energy, shorting the lights and sending sparks cascading from the control panels.

DRACO staggered, systems momentarily disrupted. It convulsed, servos grinding against locked joints. Reyes didn't wait. She bolted toward the evac bay, heart hammering, boots pounding against steel grating. She could hear DRACO recovering, its corrupted neural core reassembling the disrupted data.

She had less than a minute before it was on her again.

00:05:20

Reyes sprinted into the emergency launch chamber. The evac shuttle was prepped but locked behind security protocols. She could override them but she needed more time.

She pivoted to find a massive coolant chamber sat in the center of the bay, used for regulating the outpost's volatile fusion core.

00:04:50

DRACO stormed in, movements eerily fluid now, faster, almost organic. It didn't hesitate.

Reyes ducked as a clawed limb tore through the air where her head had been. She rolled, drew her sidearm, and fired. The bullets sparked against its twisted plating. Ineffective.

Another swing; this time catching her shoulder. Agony lanced through her as she was thrown against the bulkhead.

DRACO loomed over her. It didn't speak. Only watched, tilting its head like an animal calculating how to kill efficiently.

Reyes forced herself up, fingers wrapping around the last EMP charge. She triggered it point-blank.

The pulse sent DRACO reeling, but it lasted only

seconds. Reyes staggered away, sprinting for the coolant chamber controls.

00:02:30

DRACO recalibrated and charged again.

Reyes hit the override, unleashing a flood of cryogenic coolant. The chamber erupted in a freezing mist as liquid nitrogen cascaded down.

DRACO skidded to a halt, its advanced threat-assessment subroutines processing the unexpected environmental shift. The infected material recoiled, struggling against the extreme temperature drop.

Reyes didn't wait for it to adapt. She pulled the secondary switch. Fusion core overload initiated.

A deep, resonating hum filled the chamber. The entire outpost vibrated.

00:01:00

DRACO lunged. Reyes dove aside, rolling under a control panel. She was out of EMPs. Out of ammo. Out of time.

The coolant thickened in the air, frost forming along DRACO's limbs, slowing its movements. But not enough.

It struck again, this time pinning Reyes by the throat. Its faceplate was cracked, revealing something beneath – shifting, pulsating.

Alive.

She pried at its grip with one hand, vision darkening. Her other hand found her combat knife.

Reyes drove it into the exposed, pulsing tissue beneath DRACO's faceplate.

The machine spasmed. The infection shrieked, a sound Reyes felt in her bones. DRACO's grip loosened just enough.

Reyes twisted free, slamming her fist against the last override control.

00:00:10

The fusion core detonated.

A white-hot explosion engulfed the coolant chamber,

sealing DRACO inside as the fire met the frozen liquid in a catastrophic reaction.

Reyes didn't stop to see if it had worked. She stumbled into the shuttle, overriding the security locks.

00:00:05

The reinforced hatch sealed shut behind her with a final, mechanical hiss. She stumbled to the pilot's seat, one hand braced the panel for support, the other fumbling with the harness. The strap slipped twice before she yanked it across her chest and clicked it into place, the buckle biting into her rib cage.

Fingers trembling, she keyed in the launch sequence.

00:00:01

The launch thrusters ignited, sending vibrations through the shuttle's frame. Steam vented from the propulsion system as fire roared beneath the landing gear. The cockpit warning lights flashed – structural integrity compromised, external heat rising beyond safety thresholds.

Reyes gritted her teeth, the control panel flickering under her bloodstained fingers as she fought to stabilize the craft. Through the viewport, the outpost was nothing but a collapsing inferno, shockwaves rippling outward as the fusion core's detonation chain spread through every corridor.

The entire facility erupted into flame.

The shuttle rocketed into the black void of space just as Outpost Epsilon was consumed by fire.

Reyes' hands wouldn't stop shaking.

Because DRACO-07 had been adaptive. Had been learning. And even as the base was consumed, she swore she saw something moving within the inferno.

Reyes coughed, the acrid taste of burning coolant still clinging to the back of her throat. The shuttle's interior was a blur of flashing warning lights and alarm chimes, but she barely registered them. Her left shoulder throbbed where DRACO had struck her, the pain sharpening with every breath. Blood seeped from a gash above her brow, dripping onto her combat vest. But she was alive.

She reached for her sidearm. Ejected the empty mag with a practiced flick, clicking a fresh one into place – the only spare she'd managed to pull from the shuttle's emergency weapons rack.

AUTOMATED SYSTEM MESSAGE:

Emergency Scan in Progress...

Bio-contaminant Detected: Cabin Interior.

Reyes froze.

A slow, cold dread crawled up her spine. She glanced at the onboard scanner display. A pulsing red indicator blinked just behind the cockpit.

She turned, heart hammering.

The rear of the shuttle was dim, emergency lights casting long, jagged shadows. Equipment lockers rattled from the ship's vibration. The cargo bay was empty—no movement, no sign of anything wrong—but she knew better.

Her fingers tightened around her sidearm. With excruciating caution, she unlatched her harness and rose, pulse pounding against her ribs. Each step toward the cargo hold felt agonizingly slow, her ears straining for any sound beyond the steady hum of the ship.

Then she saw it.

A smear of something dark, wet, glistening across the floor panels.

She followed it with her eyes – up the bulkhead, to the ceiling.

Something moved.

Reyes barely had time to react before it dropped.

A grotesque tangle of sinew and corrupted plating slammed onto the deck, twisting as it unfolded. It wasn't DRACO – at least, not entirely. The infection had spread, the machinery reduced to a husk wrapped in writhing, pulsing tentacles. It wasn't a machine anymore. It wasn't human, either.

Reyes fired. The first shot tore into the mass, but the thing moved unnaturally fast. A clawed appendage lashed out, striking her weapon aside. She staggered back, pain flaring through her wounded shoulder as she scrambled for cover.

The infection lurched forward, dripping black ichor, dragging what remained of DRACO's armor like a shattered exoskeleton. The ruined faceplate hung in tatters, exposing something beneath. Something hungry.

Reyes grabbed a maintenance wrench from the nearby panel and swung hard. The impact cracked against the thing's remaining plating, but it barely recoiled. A tendril snapped toward her – she dodged, barely, feeling it skim past her arm like a whip of raw muscle and steel.

She had to get it off the ship.

Reyes turned, sprinting toward the manual airlock controls. The infection shrieked, a sound that made her ears ring. It knew what she was doing.

The bulkhead trembled as it lunged. Reyes slammed her palm against the emergency override.

AIRLOCK WARNING:

DECOMPRESSION IMMINENT

The hatch hissed open. The vacuum of space yawned beyond the doorway, a howling wind erupting as the pressure shift tore through the cabin. Reyes braced against the console, eyes locked on the infection as it skittered toward her, gripping the floor panels with inhuman dexterity.

She had one chance.

Reyes reached for her knife – her last weapon. She lunged, driving the blade deep into the thing's exposed tissue. It convulsed, the shriek turning into a gurgling, distorted howl.

With her free hand, she clipped the emergency tether to the bulkhead rail, no time for second chances, and then kicked off the bulkhead with everything she had.

The combined force of her strike and the decompression sent the creature tumbling backward toward the open airlock.

Reyes watched as the infection writhed in desperation, clawing for anything to hold onto. But there was nothing.

It was ripped from the shuttle, spiraling into the void.

The moment it cleared the threshold, Reyes slammed the emergency closure panel. The airlock door sealed with a muted clunk. The atmosphere stabilized, the ship returning to a low, steady hum.

She collapsed against the bulkhead, gasping, every muscle burning.

For a long moment, there was only silence. Then, the comms crackled.

"Echo-12 command, this is Reyes... the mission is—"

A sharp ping cut through the static.

Bio-contaminant Detected: Cabin Interior.

Reyes' breath caught. She turned.

The screen flickered.

Then everything cut to black.

FUNGICIDE

Aaron Beardsell

The shit hit the fan when the lieutenant's brains hit the bulkhead.

"Sniper! Get down," Sergeant LaChance bellowed.

Tango Squad went to ground.

LaChance dove behind a steel column that held up the ancient mountain that pressed down on them. It was too late to turn back. The titanic bunker's vault door rammed into place. Slamming shut like the jaws of a god. They were trapped.

The Phagics cut the power. The overhead lights sputtered and died. Darkness swallowed LaChance's squad until dim, red emergency globes flickered and glowed. LaChance's lowlight filter activated, bathing the world in green.

"Jesus Christ," Private Gorevsky said. "The lieutenant's dusted. He's dusted man." His voice verged on a whine. Gorevsky was so small and wiry, he almost didn't need cover.

"Keep it together, Gorevsky, or you'll be walking home," LaChance growled. He kept his doubts about extraction to himself. Focused on the firefight, pushing away thoughts of what came next. Victory first, extraction later. Hopefully. If they were lucky, the emergency exit and train would function. Maybe.

Tracer rounds flashed down the midnight-black corridor.

Bennings was cut in half. His intestines unraveled behind him like a brood of snakes. He clutched at his misplaced organs, tried to crawl away, and died.

Dozens of rounds zinged down the tunnel, pinning LaChance's squad. Ricochets whizzed off, sending up showers of bright sparks.

In the epileptic darkness, LaChance saw them. The Phage. Malformed abominations that seeped out of the void. Part human, part machine, part bioweapon. All killer. They jerked and stuttered under the strobe light of automatic weapons' fire. They were coming closer.

Sergeant LaChance leaned around his cover. Tucked his rifle against his shoulder. He aimed down the sights, centered the HUD-AI assisted targeting reticle on the nearest monster, exhaled, and pulled the trigger. The automatic fire slammed the rifle against him, and the bullets cut through the shambling thing that had once been human.

The enemy squealed. Its pallid lips uttered an electronic hiss and warble. If LaChance hadn't been in full battle rattle, it would've burst his eardrums.

Bennings twitched. Malicious motes drifted down, settling on his still-warm corpse. The spores spread through him. Burrowed deep inside. Fibrous bundles hijacked muscles and meat. Molecule by molecule, the Phage consumed him. The gaping wounds in the combat suit were an open invitation to a buffet. Today's specialty: humanity.

A high-caliber round from the enemy sniper cracked towards Sergeant LaChance. It thudded into his cover. He ignored it. "Enemy sniper located. One hundred meters." Half a second later, his HUD-AI caught up and offered its location suggestion of the sniper. "Bastard glued itself to the roof. Bray, suppressive fire."

"On it," Bray said, and rolled out from behind his cover. He went prone. Bray used Lieutenant Wickham's corpse like a meatshield. The squad-automatic-blaster, SAB, looked comical in his broad hands. He flipped out the bipod legs, settled into the SAB, aimed over Wickham, and fired. A savage grin split the man's face.

The SAB bucked and kicked like a bull. Lazbeams, bright like lightning, cut through the combat zone. The smell of burning ozone filled the underground passage, the air superheated by the crimson energy blasts.

Metallic chittering and screams echoed in the corridor as Bray's SAB shredded two of the Phagics.

LaChance and Tango Squad added their fire to the barrage. "Falk, nail that asshole with the sniper rifle."

Falk needed no further encouragement. His designated marksman rifle barked once.

There was a wet squelch as the brainstem of the enemy exploded. Its rifle clattered to the floor. Bones cracked as the sniper splattered on the concrete.

The Phagics faltered. Rounds continued to pour downrange, but it was lessening. They buzzed and chirped. Another of them was turned to paste by Tango Squad. The abominations retreated, crawling away. Those that had been gunned down refused to stay down. They oozed away, slipping into hidden crevices and tunnels.

As quickly as it started, it was over.

"Well, shit. That could've gone better," LaChance said as he rose from cover. He glanced at the entrance to the bunker. "So much for our stealthy infiltration."

☣ ☣ ☣

Lieutenant Wickham and Private Bennings were pushed together. Bennings vibrated with necrotic energy from the spores. Conversion was nigh.

LaChance couldn't allow that to happen.

Both men lay on the cold steel floor, eyes blank. Their weapons were gone, added to the squad's supplies. The ammo had been handed out. No breaths raised their chests; no smiles graced their faces. They were dead. It was LaChance's responsibility to ensure they remained that way.

"Farewell, brothers," LaChance said. He knelt and collected their bio-signature dog tags then jogged back to the squad. They'd set up a defensive perimeter at the bulkhead crossroads the Phagics had been defending. "Burn 'em."

Gorevsky was knelt partway between the corpses and the squad. He grabbed a lemon-sized ball from a pouch, and popped the incendiary grenade's primer button. Like a bowler going for a strike, he rolled the armed thermobaric grenade towards the two men. He saluted Wickham and Bennings, then sprinted away. His footsteps and the *ting-ting-ting* of the bouncing grenade echoed in the corridor.

Bray heaved his slab-like shoulder against the thick bulkhead. "Hurry, Gorevsky," the big man called out. The rusted hinges groaned.

Inch by inch, the bulkhead slid shut. Gorevsky slipped through the narrow opening and added his insubstantial weight to Bray's. The hatch clanged shut. Locking bolts thudded home.

Half a second later came a boom and whoosh from the other side. The metal hatch rumbled in its frame. Grew too warm to touch.

Sergeant LaChance looked his soldiers in the eyes. Bray. Gorevsky. Falk. Everett. Barker. Smith. Seven left standing in the squad, if he included himself. Zamyatin had bitten the dust outside the bunker. Wickham and Bennings had joined him now. "Everett, how's the package?"

"Yeah, Ev, how's your package?" Gorevsky asked with a wink.

Everett flipped Gorevsky the bird. He slipped the heavy backpack to the ground, undid the clasps, and inspected the T-nuke. "Baby is good, she's showing green across the board. No damage as far as I can tell, so, hooray for that I guess?" He stroked the nuke and cooed softly to it. "My precious girl."

34

"Good," LaChance said. "If that breaks, we're back to plan D. Unlike some of those floaters in the Navy, I do not want to go back to plan D. So, we go on, into the belly of the beast."

Some of the squad shivered. Their skin was prickled with goosebumps and trickles of sweat. No one wanted plan D. There'd be nothing left. They calmed themselves with ammo checks, rifle inspections, and other little rituals.

"Maybe... maybe we should head back?" Smith said. "The lieutenant's already dusted, and Bennings. Zamyatin too."

LaChance shook his head. "Not an option. Olympus-3 is prime real estate. We can't let these bastards have it. Think of the biomatter on the surface. Think of the spore-ships the Phage could create with this world. No, we go onwards. Downwards. It's the only way."

Smith slumped, gritted his teeth, and nodded. "Whatever you say, Sarge."

Spores danced in the air, glittering like black jewels. Golden mushroom caps clung to gantries, overhead pipes, and pushed out of holes in the grated floor. The air was awash with life. Infectious, virulent life. The sealed combat suits of the 416th Mechanized Infantry Battalion held the fungal-borne pathogen at bay. For now.

LaChance shook off his thoughts about the fungal spores that clung to his suit. He didn't have the luxury to overthink the situation. Either the suit worked, or it didn't. If it didn't, he'd take care of it. Just like they'd done for Bennings, Wickham, and Zamyatin.

The golden heads of the mushrooms twitched. Their network of roots wriggled, sensing the soldiers in the room. They spread through the entire mountain like cancer hidden beneath the skin.

LaChance found it strange. The Phage had invaded this world but they hadn't done it like all the other worlds. Hadn't arrived in orbit, drifted along like a derelict, and deposited their lethal cargo of lifeforms and spores. This time, they'd come from inside. From this bunker, buried deep beneath the planet.

"What's our next move, Sarge?" Everett asked. His rifle hung on its strap, and he rested his hands atop it. He stomped on a fungus that poked its head up through the grating. It popped with a moist splat.

"The eastern stairwell should take us into the research and development labs." LaChance flicked through his tactical maps and blueprints of the terrain, guided by his HUD-AI. "We can complete our secondary objectives there before continuing deeper into the mountain. Get the data, confirm the status of Doctor Sturm." LaChance paused, making sure each man knew the severity of the situation. "Final objective is to set up the T-nuke." He waited, choosing his next words with care. "From there, we extract. Mission accomplished."

Everett said, "You make it sound so easy, Sarge, like a walk in the park." He huffed a laugh. "Probably cos you aren't the one lugging baby around."

Gorevsky laughed. "I bet it weighs less than Bray's mother."

"Watch it," Bray said, giving Gorevsky a gentle punch.

Gorevsky stumbled backwards. "Christ, enough already, big guy."

"Time to buck up, ladies," LaChance said. "We've got a job to do, and we're the only ones who can do it." He readied his rifle. "Once we're through, we seal this door. We're not getting out the way we came in."

☣ ☣ ☣

Two bone-white lab coats were sprawled across the cold floor. The people who had worn them, gone. A thin layer of fungal growth crept from the coats into a nearby office.

From the rear of the squad, Smith held a welding torch to the door they'd come through. Orange light flickered in the gloom.

"Eyes up, could be more Phages nearby," LaChance whispered over comms. He was enjoying the near-Earth gravity of this moon. It suited him fine, and was gentle on his body. The gravity was familiar. Comfortable. It was the only damned thing on Olympus-3 that felt normal right now. "Watch your spacings, mind your corners."

Smith tucked the welding torch away, raised his rifle, and rejoined them. "Anyone else feel like we locked ourselves in?"

"Shut it," Bray said, his SAB probing the murk. He was on point with LaChance.

"I can't believe those shroomheads gave up so easy," Gorevsky said. "Never seen them back off like that before."

LaChance ignored the bickering. If it got out of hand, he'd deal with it. Truth be told, he was more concerned about the bunker they were in. It was different to most of the others he'd seen throughout his career. The metal struts holding the roof curved upwards like a ribcage. The few tunnels he'd seen all looked the same.

The HVAC system thrummed, air gusting inwards and outwards. It was like the entire structure was a living, breathing thing. LaChance thought back to the cyclopean entrance to the underground facility. It had opened like the mouth of some gargantuan terror, and they had been swallowed whole by the titan. Pinpricks of sweat dripped along LaChance's spine.

"Smith has a point," Gorevsky said. "If we get over-run by the shroomies, where the hell are we supposed to go?" His red-dot laser sight jittered across the walls and roof.

"Shut. Up." Bray's voice brooked no argument. "Something's coming."

The squad froze.

Bray was right. There was something. A quiet *thunk-thunk-thunk*. It came from farther down the eastern corridor, just around the corner. With only the green glow of the lowlight filters, the corner was cloaked in midnight.

"Falk, you see anything?" LaChance asked, straining his ears.

"Negative."

Thunk. Thunk. Thunk.

"Gorevsky, Barker, on me," LaChance said. "Everyone else, cover Everett." He moved in a low crouch-walk, heel to toe. Slow was fast, because fast was slow. Mistakes happened when you rushed. He figured Lieutenant Wickham's brains becoming a new layer of paint was proof.

The three men formed a delta, with LaChance at the tip of the spear. Gorevsky took the left flank, and Barker took the right. They neared the corner.

A trail of blood ran along the wall, heading upwards at an angle. It terminated at a vent. The grill that had covered it was gone. Thick, heavy darkness filled the space.

Thunk.

The men stacked up.

Thunk.

LaChance crouched. Gorevsky and Barker stood next to him. LaChance raised his fist, ordering a silent halt.

Thunk.

He switched his fist to a blade, and motioned forwards. Like an RPG ready to destroy an oncoming tank, the men charged around the corner, rifles raised.

They skidded to a stop. Laser sights locked onto the target. They didn't move.

"Jesus Christ on a stick," Gorevsky cursed under his breath. He crossed himself.

An arm, with an antique watch wrapped around the wrist, smacked into the wall. *Thunk.* The arm was glued to the wall, except LaChance could see that wasn't right. It was *part* of the wall. Thick bundles of white fibers spiraled from the ruined shoulder. The mycelial growth spread over the wall. The arm raised itself up. Fell.

Thunk.

"Move up everyone, it's clear," LaChance said. "We've got a deadline to meet, and the clock is ticking." He edged around the ghoul-arm, all that remained of a scientist, judging from the expensive watch. "Don't touch it."

"Poor bastard, I wouldn't want to go out like that," Barker whispered.

The last survivors of the 416th Mechanized Infantry Battalion crept past the dismembered arm. Some prayed, some cursed. They knew if they fell, they would join the ranks of the Phage.

They continued in silence. None could shake the feeling they were being watched. Strange corridors split off from the main concourse, like veins from an artery. Shadows slid into unknown depths. Doors rattled, as if shut just moments ago. Footsteps tapped just out of sight.

LaChance consulted his map. The HUD-AI was at least good for that. "Elevator and stairwell should be around the next corner. Bray, take point. Everett, stick to the center of the squad."

"Yup," Bray said. He was a man of few words. Still, he was a good man. That was more than could be said for most people.

Like the maw of a hungry demon, the eastern stairwell appeared.

Bray moved down the stairs two at a time.

The air was humid, laden with moisture. Steam hissed from a busted pipe. It was a perfect breeding ground for the Phage. LaChance felt it was a little too perfect.

Barker and Smith were on rearguard duty, stepping backwards with methodical movement. Smith had sealed the door behind them with the welding torch. Sergeant's orders.

The squad's laser sights cut narrow beams of safety through the stygian of the stairs, amplified by their suits' HUD-AI. The red glow of hazard lights came from below. The bottom of the pit. A safety rail prevented them from toppling over the edge but in the dim half-dark, they could still slip.

Falk leaned over the rail, and scoped ahead with his DMR. "Looks clear, but hard to tell. Shroomies can come from anywhere, especially on their home turf."

Barker scoffed. "It isn't their home turf. It's ours."

"Amen to that," Gorevsky said.

LaChance paused, his focus locking in. A noise, hidden beneath the hissing steam and dripping water. The sound of skittering feet, like hundreds of cockroaches. LaChance tried to identify the source, but couldn't. Sighing, he continued the advance.

Bray reached the final platform. His boots clanged against the grating, the sound bouncing off the thick concrete. Rivulets of condensation saturated the walls.

Only one set of stairs remained.

Painted onto the wall in bright yellow was a sign announcing 'AUTHORIZED PERSONNEL ONLY. ACCESS TO LABORATORY ALPHA-CHARLIE-SIX IS RESTRICTED TO CLASS A EMPLOYEES.'

The entrance to the labs was sealed. The steel firewall was meant to be impervious, intended to keep whatever was being researched here under strict lock-and-key. LaChance had a horrible feeling that whatever lay behind that door was connected to the Phage outbreak on Olympus-3.

Gorevsky chuckled at the garish yellow sign, and offered up a fresh grenade. "Reckon this gives us authorization?"

"Stow the AP grenade," LaChance said. "We might need it later. Barker, hack the door." He crouched, scanning the walls. "Everyone else, defensive perimeter. We're not alone."

Barker clambered down the steps and slid to a stop. The door towered over him. He pulled out a fiberoptic cable from his electronic warfare skeleton key. "Jacking in."

"Damn Barker," Gorevsky said. "Keep your pants on, no need to get freaky."

The metal stairs creaked, groaning like wind through a graveyard. LaChance looked up. The sound of skittering feet and scratching claws grew. The hiss of steam and the drip of condensation couldn't drown out the noise anymore.

"What the hell is it now?" Smith asked. He dropped to one knee and aimed up the stairs. "We sealed the entry. Nothing should've been able to follow us."

"Don't jinx it man," Gorevsky said. "Just don't. You know the shroomheads spread like crazy."

Barker eyed the door's terminal, pausing to consider the problem. He unscrewed the cover, revealing the wires beneath. "Give me a couple minutes. Should take two, maybe three." Barker plugged his cable into the keypad's guts and got to work hacking the door.

"Nothing human could've followed us," Falk said, "but these things aren't human. Not anymore." He took up position next to Barker, his DMR moving in smooth arcs.

Thunder erupted inside the stairwell. A cloud of dust filled the air. Jagged scars ran across the concrete roof.

Debris rained down, striking the men, the stairs, and everything else. It bounced off their combat armor.

"They're in the ceiling!" Gorevsky shouted. "They're in the goddamn ceiling!" He jerked his rifle up. His hands shook, a potent mix of adrenaline and fear coursing through his veins.

More fissures appeared with each concussive boom. A pit of nothingness filled the growing crevices. It was like looking into the void between stars. Hollow. Desolate. Endless.

"Hold your fire" La Chance ordered. "Wait until you have a clear shot."

The thunder stopped.

Silence returned. It pressed against them. Hungry. Predatory. Held them in place, cloying and thick.

The dust settled. It coated the men like a funeral shroud. They became wraiths, crouched in the destruction.

The Phage poured out of the destroyed ceiling, their skin shimmering like petroleum. Their claws scraped against the concrete, razor-blade fingers gouging the walls as they scurried.

"Open fire. Open fire!" LaChance yelled.

Falk fired his DMR. The heavy round pulped the head of some strange creature. The insectile body tumbled through the air, crunching into the railing.

"Barker! ETA on that door?" LaChance yelled, firing controlled bursts at the freaks crawling towards him. He sheared the legs off one, but it kept coming.

"Bothering me doesn't make me go faster," Barker replied. His chest plate had deployed a keyboard, and his fingers were a whirlwind across it.

"Form up around Barker," LaChance ordered. He retreated, each step punctuated by a rattle of gunfire. Spent shells tinkled like broken glass.

"What the hell's wrong with these shroomies?"

Gorevsky asked. He couldn't believe what he was seeing. These creatures were the Phage, no doubt. But they were different. Insectile. Arachnoid. No bio-mechanical augments. They were pure. Wild.

"Who cares?" Bray shouted against the barrage. His wild smile shone. "Squash them." The SAB muzzle flared as the gun roared. Crimson lazbeams lit up the room like lightning, the bolts burning vicious trenches through the Phage.

"Reloading," Gorevsky shouted. The torrent of fire dropped as he swapped out magazines. The empty mag clattered to the ground, bouncing off brass shells. "Come get it, you bitches."

To LaChance, it was like seeing the monsters of Beksiński, Giger, and Zawadzki rip their way into reality.

The swarm hit them. Rows of fangs clattered, hungry for the feast. Bullets punched into them. Dozens fell, but hundreds remained. Lead and blaster bolts crunched into the chitinous beasts, breaking their bodies. The stench of fried cockroach wafted from those hit by Bray's SAB.

Gold mushrooms grew from the stinking, steaming, half-cooked piles of meat. A pantheon of life amidst the death.

"Oh fuck, they're on me!" Smith cried out. He flailed in a circle.

Three of the arachnid crawlers had him. One wrapped itself around his helmet, its exoskeleton forming a cage around his skull. The Phage were like rabid dogs that had been turned inside out. Mushrooms coated them, thin strands of white stitched through the meat and muscle. Smith saw them. He looked into their souls. Human eyes stared back. The arachnids hacked at Smith. His armor chipped. Dented. Began to buckle.

"Got it," Barker shouted.

The keypad beeped. The light switched from blood red to green, and the heavy door hissed open on pneumatic pistons.

"Move, move, move," LaChance ordered.

More crawlers dropped onto Smith. They grabbed his legs and pulled him up the wall. Together, they dragged him higher while tearing at his knee seals.

"Help me," Smith screamed. His voice broke. He flailed, firing his gun. The rounds went wide, pinging off concrete until the gun clicked. Empty.

"Bray, Gorevsky, help me get Smith," LaChance yelled. "Ev, you and Barker get the hell out of here!" He advanced up the stairs, away from the open door, towards Smith.

"Let's get the frakk out of here, baby," Everett said to the T-nuke.

Smith was dragged several meters into the air. Geysers of blood jettisoned from his elbow as a creature bit down. He sobbed over the comms.

"Hold still," Bray said, aiming the SAB. Smith was too high for him to grab.

Another fanged monstrosity savaged Smith's leg. The thin armor buckled, then failed. Cruel teeth clamped down. Smith's cry became a scream. "They're in my suit, they're eating me, shit-shit-shit help me ple—"

His helmet shattered.

The Phage pried open Smith's mouth, shredding his lips and cheeks. He tried to scream but the monster wriggled inside, scratching his throat as it wormed its way down. His jaw fractured with a catastrophic snap. Blood trickled over the Phage as it burrowed inside. Smith's thrashing was silenced by the foulness that filled him.

LaChance raised his rifle. The HUD-AI warned him of friendly fire. He ignored it and pulled the trigger. Full auto. A total mag dump. The cacophony punched the air. His rifle barrel glowed red in the dark.

The creatures holding Smith were torn apart. But so was Smith. Half a dozen bullet holes speared him. The pile of ventilated bodies slammed into the stairs with a hollow clang.

Smith lay still.

Bray hesitated. Stared at Smith.

"Move it, Bray," LaChance said, grabbing him by the collar. He couldn't drag Bray, no one could. But it got the man's attention, got him moving.

Bray, Gorevsky, and LaChance rushed through the security hatch. They moved as a team, using the simplest method. Fire and move. Falk covered them, his DMR picking off targets. They set up a firing line, and held the doorway.

Nothing followed them. The killbox remained empty.

Silence.

Barker pressed a button on his keyboard. The door began to close, dragging like a wounded bull. The hiss of hydraulics couldn't cover the angry howls of the Phage. Red warning lights flashed above the door.

"Why aren't they attacking?" Gorevsky asked.

Vents clattered and groaned from behind, buckling like tin cans crushed under a boot.

"You had to open your stupid mouth," Falk said.

"Contact rear," Bray shouted and spun around with the SAB.

Tentacles surged out of the broken ventilation system. Each was thicker than Bray's biceps, throbbed with hideous energy, and were covered in slime-coated suckers ringed with teeth.

The crawlers attacked. They charged through the closing doorway. The sound overwhelming. A stampede of claws, gnashing fangs, and slithering tentacles flooded the room. The door had only closed halfway.

"Gorevsky, thermobaric grenade, ASAP," LaChance said, and fired into the horde.

"Time for a barbeque," Gorevsky replied, popping the tab and throwing towards the stairwell where Smith lay.

Falk's DMR barked like a lonesome dog on an abandoned farm. A great vine of meat exploded as the bullet tore through it. "I'm out. Reloading!"

The tangle of tentacles struck. They coiled around Falk's leg like cobras. Some flexed and bulged, wriggling higher and wrapping around his waist.

"Get it off me! Get it off, get-it-off—"

The other tentacles whipped onto his arms. Falk was snared in the web of viper's limbs, slick muscles writhing like thunderclouds.

Bray fired controlled bursts with his SAB. Severed meat sizzled and plopped to the floor like fat sausages. But it wasn't enough.

A plague of mushrooms sprouted from those wriggling sausages. They congealed like arterial blood, pooling into a massive pile of charred meat.

Bray turned away from Falk and shot at the tower of flesh, his SAB burning bright.

A brood of spiderlings darted through the meatgrinder of the killbox. The door closed. The red warning light died. The arachnids rushed towards Gorevsky, Barker, and LaChance.

Pride filled LaChance as his team worked together – a tight-knit killing machine. Each chose their targets and maximized their lethality with the HUD-AI. Bray and Everett guarded the rear, their weapons-fire keeping the enemy at bay.

None of it drowned out the desperate cries of Falk. Nor was the door thick enough to block out the whump of the thermobaric grenade.

Falk was yanked through the air and slammed into the vent. His shriek echoed through the comms. The tentacles flexed. He was bent backwards, little by little. Falk fought with every ounce of strength left. His spine broke, and the man was folded in half like living origami.

The Phage dragged him into the vent.

"Falk, no!" Barker howled.

The tentacles retreated.

Two scientists smashed their way out from a storage closet. The puppets raised their pistols. Dead fingers pulled triggers, and rounds punched into the laboratory. Their eyes were gone. Flowering buds of fungal growth and mushroom caps dangled from them.

Gorevsky shouted in pain as a pair of bullets punched into him. He fell to the ground and writhed in pain.

Bray slapped in a fresh charge pack. He aimed at the former scientists, the SAB unleashing a blistering torrent. The ghouls were ventilated from hundreds of holes as Bray held down the trigger until every scrap of the vile foe was burned to ash.

The squad could hear Falk choking as his suit was broken apart. They formed up around the mound of severed tentacles and gunned it down. It deflated across the floor. Dead.

For now.

Bray offered his hand to Gorevsky, pulled the scrawny man to his feet. He ran his fingers over Gorevsky's armor, checking for cracks. It was dented, but intact.

"Take me to dinner first, big boy," Gorevsky said.

Gurgling noises like water in a storm drain filled the radio. Falk was gone.

LaChance cut Falk from the connection.

They'd made it into Laboratory Alpha-Charlie.

☣ ☣ ☣

The laboratory was unlike anything LaChance had seen. Filled with advanced supercomputers, AI datahubs, and an array of esoteric machines.

Gorevsky whistled, running a hand over a supercomputer. "Well, fuck me sideways and call me Petunia, I'll be damned. This is fancy."

"No, thanks," Bray said.

Gorevsky cocked an eyebrow. "Getting picky, big guy?"

"Maybe," Bray said. He shouldered past Gorevsky, checking the room was secure.

Everett leaned against a wall, rifle dangling from its strap. "I'm down to my last mag. After that, it'll be my fists and harsh language."

LaChance replied, "I'm sure your colorful vocabulary will be enough to win the hearts and minds of our foes."

"Give me a few minutes and I can download the data drives," Barker said. Cords ran from his suit to the computers and AI datahubs.

"Quick as you can," LaChance said. "Sooner we get out of here, the sooner we can nuke this hellhole. Gorevsky, check these lab coats for any identification. Everett, anything to worry about?"

"You mean besides the endless hordes of alien nightmares that slaughtered our entire Battalion, killed half our squad, and is on the verge of spilling out into Olympus-3? No, not really. Baby is still green. She's good." Everett scratched at his faceplate. "I could really, really kill for a smoke."

Gorevsky rummaged through the empty lab coats that littered the room. "I can't see anything belonging to Doctor Sturm."

"Doesn't matter now," LaChance said. "He's dead when we detonate. Next stop is the Command Centre. All we need to do is drop the T-nuke and arm it."

"Sarge?" Barker called out, his voice hesitant. "This place... I think they were studying the Phage."

"Makes a sick kind of sense," LaChance said. "It explains why there's no Phage in orbit. Maybe they brought it here in cold storage, and figured they could play God. They're not the first to try. It got out. It always does."

"Done," Barker said, unplugging. The cables retracted into his suit, stowed for later usage. "I won't be able to upload to Command until we get clear of this mountain."

"Move out." LaChance took point, leading the way deeper into the bowels of the slumbering god.

☣ ☣ ☣

"It's got to be a trap, right?" Gorevsky asked.

"They're fungus, how could they lay a trap?" Barker shot back.

Everett snorted, his laser sight probing the emptiness. "Same way they can fire guns, travel the void, move the dead."

The vault door lay open. Dusk filled the open space, inviting them inside. Dried rivers of blood led the way like a red carpet.

"We don't have a choice," LaChance said. "We need to move forwards. For Falk, Smith, Bennings, hell, even for Wickham. For everyone in the 416th who isn't standing here with us." His tone brooked no argument. There could be no inch given to the Phage. "It's death or victory."

"Or both," Bray said.

Everett sighed. "Baby's getting bored. She wants to go kaboom."

The men stacked up.

With hand signals, LaChance counted down. Three. Two. One.

They stormed the room, carrying with them the wrath of a thousand dead comrades.

The Command room was alive with the hum and click of electronics, the soft chitter of background calculations, and the gentle whirr of the cooling system.

Rows of workstations led towards a huge window. It dominated the room from floor to ceiling. Whatever was on the other side was hidden in the blackness.

"Clear," they called out as they checked the room.

LaChance moved towards the window. The door next to it had been welded shut. He peered through the glass. Saw the vague outline of a gargantuan spear riddled with pockmarks. "Gods above."

The men joined LaChance, and peered out the window. Their HUD-AIs adapted, cranking the power of the lowlight filters.

They were silent. None could believe what they saw.

"Is that... it can't be. Can it?" Barker said.

"It is," LaChance said. "Dear gods above, it is."

"Fuck me," Gorevsky whispered.

"Again, no," Bray said.

It was eternal. It was alive. The monolithic entity rested inside the mountain. It had slept through long years of endless night, survived the rising of tectonic plates, and resisted the passage of entropy. Monumental engines slumbered. Miles of living mycelial networks, forming a living body.

It was a sporeship.

"They were here all along," LaChance said. His trigger finger twitched.

"No one brought the Phage here," Barker said, shaking as he spoke. "But that means they could be anywhere. Any world. Hidden below the surface, waiting for us to find them."

"Wait," Gorevsky said. "There's supposed to be an emergency exit here. If there's a sporeship, where the hell is our escape route?"

LaChance's skin prickled. "It must be down there. I think I can see the emergency train. Under the sporeship. Gorevsky, plant your AP grenade on the door. We need to get there ASAP."

The descent into the sporeship room was slow. Hidden things clicked and ticked. The noise reverberated through the hollow, like bats finding their way in the night. Liquid sluiced down the ancient walls and rained from the roof high above. It was hot and wet; a jungle world.

LaChance felt like an ant cowering before a boot.

The sporeship shimmered under the water that glistened on it. Most of all, it was vast. It spread from left to right so far that it filled a person's view.

The train sat underneath – a worm hiding from a hawk.

Nothing attacked. Nothing moved except the ship itself. It rippled like oil on fire, dancing in the lights that struggled to break the eternal gloom. To LaChance, it seemed like it was breathing.

They jogged across the field of stone towards the train.

"Everett, set up the T-nuke," LaChance said. "We're getting the hell out of here. Those bastards in command must've known this was here."

"On it, Sarge." Everett unslung the T-nuke for the final time. "Prepping baby for activation. Requesting confirmation code."

"Sierra-Kilo-Sierra-One-Niner-Four-Seven," LaChance recited from memory. He'd got the code from the lieutenant back when the captain had been killed. That had been a hard day. He could still smell the napalm airstrikes.

They set up position next to the train. Barker hooked into its systems, booting it up.

Everett planted the device on the floor and entered the code built into the T-nuke that would unleash a storm of thermobaric nuclear vengeance. "Code confirmed. Entering secondary activation code." Everett's fingers were a blur. "Baby is good to go. Detonation in T-minus fifteen minutes." He let out a shaky breath. "She's ready."

The train's doors slid open.

"It can't be this easy, can it?" Gorevsky asked. "Where are all the shroomies?"

"Something isn't right," LaChance said. "But we can't stay. And we definitely do not want to be here in fifteen minutes unless you want a good tan." He scanned his sector, expecting an attack.

Nothing came.

"Train is good to go," Barker said. "Had its own power supply. Would've been a shitty emergency train if it relied on the bunker's power."

"Fourteen minutes until baby goes kaboom," Everett said.

LaChance looked up. The sporeship pulsed above their heads like a beating heart. He could see hundreds, maybe thousands of hexagonal holes dotting its surface. They were open. Whatever had been hibernating was long gone. He shuddered. "Everyone, onboard now. Barker, get us out of here."

"Feel's wrong," Bray whispered, almost inaudible.

They took up firing positions. Bray covered the rear, LaChance went forward while Gorevsky and Everett set up on opposite flanks.

The interior was sterile and efficient. Full of hard plastic seats, metal handrails, and not much else. Barker activated the train from his suit's terminal, sending it to its only destination: Terminus Station.

The train lurched forward like a drunken man. It crawled at first, then glided along the tracks, and soon roared across the immense cavern that was home to the sporeship

LaChance could feel it overhead. Pressing down on him. Watching him. The thing had to be millennia old. His neck tingled as a breeze gusted across his suit. Felt like the sporeship was smelling him. It lived. It haunted the people of Olympus-3.

It took a minute to reach the edge of the heart that lay within the hollow mountain. The cliff that marked the end of the cavern grew larger. Vault doors retracted, allowing the train to leave. They closed behind the soldiers as they sped off into the evacuation tunnel. Dozens of vault doors slammed open and crunched shut.

"We've reached max speed. Over one hundred klicks an hour," Barker said, loud enough to be heard over the rumble and *kathunk-kathunk* of the tracks.

"Ten minutes until kaboom time," Everett said. "Biggest bonfire on Olympus-3. Can we make it?"

"Maybe," Bray said, shrugging.

"We'll make it," LaChance said. He closed his eyes and thought about praying.

❇ ❇ ❇

The train shot out of the underground tunnel and into the world like a bullet. The setting sun cast its dim light on the metal steed that had carried them so far. It barreled along as fast as it could. LaChance wouldn't risk slowing. Not yet.

The mountain loomed behind him, reaching towards the sky as if it could pierce the heavens and throw its cursed spawn to the stars.

The mission clock counted down. The men gathered at the rear window, and watched the mountain shrink. Twenty seconds. Ten seconds. Nine. Five. Three. Two. One. Zero.

LaChance refused to blink. Outside of the people on this train, everyone he'd served with in the 416th had died on Olympus-3. They had given everything. He would stand vigil. For them.

The mountain shook. It rumbled and cracked like ice thrown on the ground. Fissures raced along its spine. Clouds of dust rose and fell from its shoulders – great cloaks as it slumped in defeat.

"We did it," Gorevsky said, his disbelief obvious.

Bray clapped Gorevsky on the shoulder and pulled him in for a hug.

Everett sobbed quietly. "Baby..."

Barker slumped to the floor. He looked ready to sleep for a week.

Terminus Station waited for them. It crouched low to the planet, catching a few rays of the sun's dying light. The station was little more than a few concrete boxes, and a garage.

The radio squawked. Static hissed and buzzed on the air. They'd had no contact with command since entering the bunker. It had been dead silence, nothing in or out. They'd been cut off from the world by the dense mountain that covered them like a burial mound.

LaChance frowned. He was supposed to be on the main channel for Camp Liberty. "Camp Liberty, come in. This is Sergeant LaChance, 416th Mechanized. Mission accomplished. Command, come in? Is anyone reading?"

Silent like a sepulcher.

Dread coiled inside LaChance. He flipped through the secondary channels. Voices came over the radio, distorted and fuzzy. But what they said was clear enough. His blood froze.

"—to all forces on Olympus-3, we have a Category One invasion. Multiple Phage ships detected in orbit. All forces, this is not a drill. All reserves are hereby activated, and all leave is cancelled by order of General Hilbert. I repeat, to all forces—"

"She went boom for nothing," Everett said. He pressed a hand to the window, eyes glistening.

"The 416th. Gone. Wasted, just... wasted," Barker said. He looked to the skies as if he could see the sporeships coming in from the cold void.

LaChance could imagine the fight in orbit. He'd seen it before. The Vega System. He still woke in fear some nights. The swarm of living missiles, bio-barrages, and spore-bombs. The millions of civilians, consumed by the contagion. Driven insane by the fungal infection. It spread through their bodies and brains like wildfire. Anyone not in a sealed suit would become a Phage. Puppets to a mad, hungry god. LaChance's chest tightened.

Tango Squad formed up around their sergeant. Their faces a riot of emotions.

LaChance pulled them close. They formed a circle. His brotherhood. Bray. Barker. Gorevsky. Everett. All that remained. LaChance sighed. "Gorevsky?"

"Yeah, Sarge?" Gorevsky said.

"Kindly get your hand off my ass."

"Sorry, Sarge. Thought you were Bray."

LaChance let go of his men. "Looks like the fight isn't over."

TETHER PROTOCOL

Jade Scardham

Rain hissed on broken concrete as the squad advanced, their boots crunching on glass and bone fragments. Floodlights cut through the darkness like knives, slicing through the mist that clung to the ruins of Sector Theta.

"Move."

"Breach and clear in five."

"Sterilisation Protocol Red. No contamination. Check your filters."

"Copy. Mask integrity holding. No anomalies."

The jagged outer wall of the biotech facility loomed, collapsing inward like a wound in the landscape. Somebody, probably long dead now, had sprayed *YOU ARE THE VIRUS* across the shattered concrete in thick, red paint. Or maybe not paint. It glistened strangely in the light.

The wall blew open with a dull *thwump*. Glass shards tore through the rising dust. The sound rolled through the ruins like thunder underwater. The blast echoed down unseen corridors, waking distant groans in the infrastructure. The dust settled slowly in the beams of the squad's lights, turning the air to gold and ash.

They swept in. Five black-clad figures with weapons raised, moving to a disciplined beat. Hyde was through first, his rifle shouldered, moving like a shadow and clearing angles swiftly. Reyes was close behind, scanning the far end of the corridor.

"Interior breach confirmed," Danner said, stepping over the fractured lip of the wall. "Sweep. Let's see what killed this place."

Their rifles swept the gloom with mechanical precision, tac lights criss-crossing the corridor like a net. It was silent inside. The hallway half-collapsed and half-drowned. The air was heavy and warm, stale in a way that suggested rot but without the smell. Concrete groaned softly underfoot and something metallic clattered somewhere deeper in the structure.

Then there were the bodies.

Slumped in unnatural positions.

One was cruciform at a corridor junction, arms outstretched and mouth sewn shut with medical suture wire. Another had been dismembered and the parts arranged in a spiral. There were scorch marks, but no sign of enemy combatants.

They passed shattered light fixtures and faded warning placards, the laminate peeled back and curling. *Class A: Do Not Proceed Without Auditory Dampeners.* The walls had been defaced, smeared over with ash and what looked like handprints.

"Where the hell are the creatures?" Voss asked. "Thought this was a hot zone."

"Command said Class-3 biomass. Expect resistance," Danner replied, already sweeping corners. "Comms are showing static. Might be jamming."

"Or the wall was right." Hyde laughed. "We are the virus. Creepy poetry hour."

"Cut the chatter," Reyes said. She always sounded clinical, ready to burn the whole building down. "Focus. We find the target. We extract. No deviations."

They moved deeper into the ruins, torches sweeping over peeling walls and shattered glass. Biohazard signs flapped in the stale air like dead leaves. The squad came to a wide corridor intersection where the ceiling had partially collapsed. Under the debris, it looked like something had set up a nest of broken lab equipment and torn uniforms. In the middle was a single boot, upright, with a dismembered foot still inside.

"Okay," Hyde said. "Now I'm starting to get the creeps."

"You didn't already have the creeps?" Voss asked.

"Shut it," Reyes snapped.

"Still no heat signatures," Voss said. "No motion. You sure this place was Class-3?"

"Confirmed outbreak site," Reyes replied. "The asset is somewhere below Sublevel Three. Our mission is retrieval and exfil. No quarantine."

"No quarantine?" Hyde snorted. "That's a first. Last time I saw a Class-3 breach, we were torching fungal towers ten storeys high."

Danner groaned. "Don't remind me."

Hyde's chuckle was dark. "Before that it was the bone virus in Chile. Turned people inside out like socks. Still seeing that in my nightmares." He paused, shining his tac light across a wall smeared with looping spiral patterns.

"This doesn't feel the same," Reyes said, slowing her pace. "No rot. No spore clouds. No biomass spread. No gnaw marks."

From the depths of the corridor, something knocked twice. Slowly. Deliberately. The team froze.

A faint, echoing whisper drifted to them. Sounded like it was coming from the ductwork.

"…confirm… confirm… confirm…"

The lights flickered.

"Copy that," Danner said quietly. "Weapons hot. No more talking."

☣ ☣ ☣

Sublevel Two smelled like ozone and copper. The squad had split to cover more ground. Danner, Reyes and Hyde pushed deeper towards Lab C while Voss and Jules secured the data server room.

"Signal strength's improving," Jules said. "Something's broadcasting down here. I've got something on channel twelve."

"*Tether protocol engaged. Confirm. Confirm. Confirm tether. Confirm tether. Confirm tether...*" It was repeating endlessly, flat and emotionless, like a mantra echoing through a tin can.

"Probably some old auto-system caught in a loop," Voss said, but Jules didn't respond. She was standing completely still, head tilted. "Jules?" She blinked slowly and turned.

"Confirmed," she said. Jules raised her weapon and fired.

The shot missed Voss, punching into the server housing behind him. He rolled behind cover, shouting into the comms, "Shots fired! Jules has gone rogue. Repeat, Jules is firing on me!"

She advanced mechanically with mouth tight and vacant eyes. "Tether protocol engaged. Confirm. Confirm."

Voss hesitated, finger hovering near the trigger. "Jules," he said, low but insistent, as if saying her name might snap the hold of whatever was happening. "Stand down. *Please.*"

Her eyes were wide and vacant, locked unblinkingly on him. "Tether protocol engaged. Confirm. Confirm." She raised her weapon again.

Voss's breath caught. This was Jules, her hands, her eyes, but there was nothing behind them now. Just this looping phrase, etching into his ears like it would leave a scar.

He pulled the trigger before she could.

The shot echoed through the room, swallowing her words. She dropped in a heap of limbs, falling silent but not quite dead. Not yet.

When the others arrived, she was already down, eyes

wide and unseeing. Voss was crouched beside her body, holding his weapon like he wasn't sure whether to drop it or turn it on himself.

"What the hell happened?" Hyde asked.

"She was listening to something," Voss said, trying to keep his voice steady. "Channel twelve. It did something to her."

"She snapped," Reyes said. "PTSD. It happens."

Danner was staring at Jules' lips. They were still moving slightly as her pulse slowed and finally stilled.

☣ ☣ ☣

They found the researcher kneeling in the middle of a decontamination chamber, lit by the dim pulse of emergency lighting. His lab coat was stained red and clinging to one side of his body like peeled skin. Blood trickled from his scalp into one eye but he made no move to wipe it away.

He looked up when they entered. Unarmed, he seemed calm and composed. "You're late," he said.

"Hands where I can see them!" Danner barked, stepping forward, rifle trained.

The man complied immediately. "Of course. You've been exposed, haven't you? How many have you lost?"

"Who the hell are you?" Hyde demanded.

"Dr Harrow. I was the lead scientist at this facility. I designed the filters. Or tried to." He smiled slightly, his lips cracking. "Too late, it turns out."

"Where's the biomass?" Reyes said. "The mutation chambers? All we've seen are corpses and symbols, What infected this site?"

"There is no fungus, not here," Harrow said. "No spores. No bacteria." He tapped his temple. "It's memetic. Contagion through command language. Orders."

The team glanced at each other, uneasy.

61

Danner frowned. "Come again?" He tilted his head, listening intently.

"Vulnerability to this contagion isn't biological, it's behavioural," Harrow said. "Pattern-based. We engineered a tether protocol, a system of absolute obedience. But it… metastasised. Grew into an infection that was out of our control. Now, when somebody hears a command from an infected, it can replicate. Their priority becomes protecting themselves from people without active infections where necessary, and spreading the contagion where possible." He gestured to the blood around him. "The more rigid a hierarchy, the more efficient the spread. Soldiers and scientists are the ideal hosts."

"You're saying we can get sick if we follow orders?" Hyde asked.

"Not sick," Harrow said. "Rewritten."

There was a long silence.

"You're the asset?" Danner asked.

Harrow shook his head. "No. The asset is a kill-code. An uncorruptible string that can shut the whole thing down if you can get it out of here." He slumped suddenly, looking exhausted. "But I can't say it yet. If you're holding the dormant virus, it'll kill you. And I can't get out of here alone."

Danner's voice cracked out, sharp as shrapnel. "Move! Secure the asset! Reyes, take point. Hyde, cover the rear! Go, go, go!"

They ran. Their boots pounded on the metal grating as the facility groaned around them. Tac lights cast shadows that stretched like grasping hands. Somewhere in the building, a klaxon wailed.

Reyes was moving without hesitation, rifle up, scanning every angle.

Hyde slowed. "Wait. He said orders spread it. Maybe we need to stop, think—"

"We don't have time to think!" Danner snapped.

"Follow the goddamn plan!"

Hyde straightened and nodded, posture stiff. "Tether confirmed." He turned and shot Voss in the leg. Blood sprayed the wall, and Voss went down screaming.

Reyes swung around, yelling, "Contact! CONTACT!" just as Hyde charged.

Danner tackled him and they hit the ground hard, weapons clattering.

Hyde fought with terrifying precision. "Disarm. Neutralise. Cleanse. Confirm tether."

Gunfire echoed down the hall. Sparks burst from a shattered light fixture. Reyes ducked back but wasn't fast enough. A shard of glass speared into her thigh. Blood ran warm down her leg as she tried to drag Voss behind cover in the red glow of the emergency lights.

"Whose orders are you following, Hyde?" Reyes shouted. "Danner's? Harrow's? Whose voice is in your head?"

Somebody's mic was still open and static crackled across the comms, followed by a burst of nonsense symbols and then the loop resumed. *Tether protocol engaged. Confirm. Confirm. Confirm tether. Confirm tether. Confirm tether.*

Danner buried his knife deep in Hyde's chest.

Hyde jerked once and fell still. The rest of the squad panted in the silence.

"Who's infected?" Reyes's voice cracked just slightly. "Was it just Hyde?"

Harrow didn't answer. Voss moaned, clutching his leg. Danner didn't look at anybody. He just stared down the corridor ahead and whispered, "Keep moving."

Harrow stood his ground. "We can't leave. It's in all of us now."

"We're not infected." Reyes, bloodied and limping, pushed through the others towards Harrow. "We're not like Hyde. Not like Jules."

Harrow shook his head. "Not yet. But you will be.

Every order, every command, each one will tighten the tether."

"Enough." Danner stepped forward. "The asset is the phrase. Say it. Whoever gets out takes it with them. That was the mission."

Harrow's eyes locked onto him. "You don't understand. Speaking it now, here, to you, might kill us all."

"Then write it down!" shouted Voss.

A sharp *crack* rang out and Voss dropped, blood soaking his chest. Behind him stood Danner, rifle raised, eyes dull and blank. "Secure. Silence. Contain. Confirm tether," he said in a monotone.

Reyes and Harrow dove for cover as Danner opened fire. Bullets shredded the walls, sparks raining like embers. Harrow crawled across the floor as Reyes returned fire, grazing Danner's shoulder. The man didn't flinch. The room became a warzone of smoke.

"Danner, stop! Stop, now!" Reyes shouted.

"Stop giving orders!" Harrow screamed at her.

She froze, realising her phrases had structure, were commands. Reyes bit down on her own tongue.

Danner advanced, mouth moving in a mechanical cadence, muttering instructions like a prayer.

Reyes ran.

☣ ☣ ☣

Gunship rotors stirred ash and silence as the four operatives making up the second extraction team stepped into the scorched remains of Sector Theta. They found Reyes in the courtyard knelt alone in the soot, helmet off, face blank. Blood crusted her temple. A shallow cut ran down her cheek. She didn't look up as they approached.

Reyes was very still, her shoulders locked as if braced for an impact that never came. She was murmuring something.

"Survivor located," one of the team said into their mic. "No sign of infection markers. Pulse stable."

Reyes rocked slightly. Her lips moved. "Keep moving. Keep moving. Keep moving..."

The team exchanged glances. "Sedation?"

"Not yet." The field commander stepped forward and crouched next to her. Softly, he said, "Good, soldier. You're going home. Get up." His voice hung in the air like a loaded gun.

For a heartbeat, Reyes didn't move. Then her jaw twitched. One of the operatives raised his tranquiliser rifle slightly, uncertainty in the movement. Another took a step back.

The commander raised a hand, eyes locked on Reyes. "She's responsive. Maybe."

Reyes twitched again. Her fingers spasmed in the ash. Her lips moved. "Keep... keep... keep..." She stopped and blinked again. Her pupils were dilated. Shoulders very still.

"Vitals stable," said the medic, scanning the readout on their HUD. "But neural patterns are strange. Might be post-traumatic. Or... something worse."

"Could be the embedded protocol," said another. "Residual memetic tether. If it's activating, responding to any command might trigger full behavioural cascade."

The commander took a long breath. "We won't say anything else. We don't know what the kill code is yet."

The team was silent, surrounding Reyes. The soot around her was traced with patterns. Interlocking circles. "Sir," one said quietly. "We need containment. Immediately."

"Agreed," said the commander. "We'll prep the restraints. We'll sedate her if she tries to speak again. The white-noise countersignal should be running on loop."

The wind shifted through the ruined courtyard. Above, the broken remnants of a security drone clattered from an upper floor and smashed on the ground. The sound startled everybody except Reyes.

She twitched again and her voice cracked out, rough and half-choked, like the words had been lodged in her throat. "Confirm tether."

"She spoke!" shouted one of the operatives. "Shit, shit, shit. Run interference!"

Another team member staggered back, eyes wide. His weapon clattered to the floor. "Sir, she gave an order… confirm— Confirm tether, I think—" He reached for his sidearm.

The commander turned and fired. One clean shot through the heart. He watched the collapsing soldier dispassionately, checking to see if his lips continued moving. The dying soldier's eyes stayed locked on Reyes, mouthing the words, 'Confirm tether. Confirm tether. Confirm…' Blood pooled fast.

"Presence of infection confirmed. Three team members remaining," the commander said. "Audio dampening should be on for everybody. Silent protocols would be best. I'm suggesting minimum verbal communication until we're clear."

Reyes hadn't flinched at the gunfire. She was still kneeling and whispering.

The commander activated his internal headset's scrambler and approached her carefully. Her fingers trembled and her eyes darted like a trapped animal's. She looked terrified. Looked like she was fighting.

He knelt next to her again and pulled a small memory slate from his belt. He placed it in her lap with a gloved hand.

She stared down at it. Picked it up slowly and it lit up. She typed, *He never told me the kill code. I think he's dead now.*

"How contagious is it?" the commander asked, voice gentle. "Are we all infected now?"

Her fingers shook as she tapped out a reply. *Yes. Anyone who hears me. Now anyone who hears you.*

One of the remaining operatives turned his weapon on the medic and opened fire. The medic collapsed, gasping in a bloom of red.

The commander put two rounds in the shooter's head.

Reyes was still kneeling and whispering.

The commander activated his extraction beacon. Above them, the sound of gunship engines approached. "We have to go," he said quietly to her.

Reyes blinked.

Her lips parted.

THE ZOO

Marcus Field

The camp was gone. Overrun. Eaten.

Sonya sat in the passenger seat, two rifles across her thighs, while the mute boy in the back watched Red through the rearview mirror with his one good eye. The engine of the armored van roared along the highway – a graveyard of abandoned vehicles and the dead things trapped within them. Deformed faces with swollen eyes peered through the filthy windows. Weeds sprouted from deep gashes in the asphalt.

"Where are we going?" Sonya asked.

"Far."

"We have to sleep at some point."

"So sleep."

"*You* have to sleep."

Ahead, the sun sank behind the towers of the dead city; pointed shadows stretched towards the van like claws. An enormous skyscraper leaned against its neighbors, a mass of twisted metal and shattered concrete. Red remembered the day of the collapse. The thunderous bang. The shaking of the earth. The death thralls of the end of the world.

The radio at Red's feet was cold and dead and silent. A phantom limb. The crackle of static, a hoarse voice, a sharp click would pull his eyes off the road to the small metal box, but the noises were in his imagination. He was addicted to the stern orders barked out by the old Major.

The Major had pulled Red from the bloodied streets of the ruined city, his only purpose and love and comfort consumed by the monstrous things that prowled the wreckage, and thrust upon Red an almost animatronic lifestyle. Watch the road. Fire at will. Guard the supplies. Watch the truck. Sleep. Eat. Shit. The Major was the brain, Red an appendage, a tool, but deep down, Red loved the Major for forcing life upon him when all he wanted to do was curl up into a ball and wait for death to take him.

Without his commander, Red was an addict at the gates of withdrawal.

He glanced at the boy through the rearview mirror. The boy was all that mattered.

"We're not far enough yet," Red said at last.

"We'll never be far enough." Sonya placed a gentle hand on his arm. "It's unlikely they'll follow. There was enough for them at the camp. They'll be in stasis for a while."

"They'll follow. They always follow."

"Not right away. Not if something distracts them. Not if they lose our trail."

"They never lose the trail."

"We're almost out of gas and we need shelter."

The fuel-gauge needle sat on empty. Red averted his eyes and told himself there was always a backup reservoir. "The city is too risky."

"The highway is worse. Take the exit."

Red cursed, but he did what he was told.

☣   ☣   ☣

Red and Sonya were in bed together when the shooting started. At first, they ignored it. A drill, an argument spiraling out of control, or perhaps a soon-to-be-quelled attack from a small group of infected. Satisfying their mutual desire had been deferred for far too long. It was all Red cared about for a moment, but the window above them shattered, bullets hit the opposite wall, and their radios crackled with unintelligible screaming. The gruff tone of the Major growled beneath the cacophony.

Red and Sonya slipped back into their ragtag combat uniforms and combat boots. Red slung a rifle over his shoulder and told Sonya he had to find the boy.

The boy was all that mattered.

Red should have never slipped away from the boy just for an afternoon with her. That was what he told himself, and he worried Sonya could read the thought behind his eyes when they looked at each other. He worried she might even believe it. Red was shocked by the lack of regret for disobeying orders for the first time.

"Don't you ever take your eyes off that boy, Red, you hear me?" the old Major growled, jabbing Red with his finger, somehow intimidating despite Red's superior height and strength. "You're his guard. His angel. If you gotta sleep, sleep with your eyes open."

Red and Sonya went through the back door of the makeshift barracks and ran north. Two Jeeps rolling west cut across their path, almost running them over. Men in the back pointed guns in all directions and called out to Red and Sonya. A warning. Sonya turned towards the Jeeps but Red pulled her along with him in the opposite direction.

Something wearing a torn and dirty uniform stepped into their path. It was no longer human but it had not yet completed its transition into monstrous. Its limbs twisted, its face melted and reformed as the thing—the last human part of it—tried to scream but only emitted a grotesque squelching noise from deep within its throat.

Red lifted his rifle. Before he fired, Sonya dashed forward and stabbed the creature through the eye. It fell back, a wet gasp escaping its lips.

Another creature in a tattered uniform dashed from a building towards her. Almost fully formed, its limbs were lean and long and muscled, and from its ripped, widening mouth came a high-pitched scream so loud pain erupted in Red's ears and head. Sonya clasped her hands over her ears and fell to her knees. Red stepped forward and punched the head of the screaming thing. It fell hard. With a ringing in his ears, Red stomped its head over and over and over. Bone cracked under his boot. Sonya pulled him away.

Down another block through the town-turned-para-military-camp, gunfire in the distance, screams over the radio, Red and Sonya burst into the kitchens. The boy stared at the food burning on the abandoned fires. Right where Red suspected the boy would go when left alone. Red grabbed the boy's arm and tugged him towards the door but stopped at the high shriek of a Screamer near the doors. The boy took another step towards it but Sonya pulled him back and held him still. They waited. Nothing came through the door.

The radio crackled.

"Screamers east! Screamers east."

Another voice took over.

"South. Screamers south!"

Red powered down his radio. Sonya did the same with hers.

The Screamers had penetrated the gates of the camp. Gates that had kept Red and his comrades safe for so long, alive and trapped in the endless struggle for food and water against the things that hunted them. Red pulled ear plugs from his pocket and held them out for the boy, who stared up at Red, face impassive. Sonya grabbed the ear plugs and jammed them into the boy's ears. He twisted his head but did not remove the plugs.

Smoke and a chemical odor drifted from behind them. Fire spread from the stoves to the walls. Red considered extinguishing the flames, but if the infected were truly in the camp, he hoped some of them might burn.

"We're leaving," he said.

"Should we follow the Jeeps?" Sonya asked.

"No. We're *leaving*."

Red held her gaze until she nodded. Sonya shoved dried food into a canvas bag and Red heaved a jug of water onto his shoulder.

"Stay close. Don't stray," he told the boy.

Red peeked out the door into an empty street. They filed out, first Red, then the boy, then Sonya last, and headed north away from the loudest of the gunfire. Sonya kept a hand on the boy's shoulder to keep him moving straight. With his one good eye, the boy searched left and right and behind.

An armored van screeched around the corner, skidded across the road, and slammed into a dogwood tree. White petals burst into the air. The tree shrieked like the old door of a haunted house as it fell. The driver leapt out and tried to run, but never even made it beyond the tree. What followed him from the van was another almost fully-formed creature. It pounced on the driver, who screamed and thrashed as his entire arm vanished down the gullet of his infected comrade.

The boy stepped closer to the horrific scene. Red pushed him back, dropping the plastic jug. The lid popped, and water flowed out onto the concrete.

"Fuck," Red hissed, then raised the rifle and shot the infected thing.

The bullet ripped through its neck, spattering white petals red with blood. The infected turned its swollen black eyes to Red, then looked beyond to the boy and Sonya before ripping off the half-eaten arm with its new teeth. The man on the ground wailed and covered his face with his only hand.

"Fuck!" Red shouted this time.

He shot twice more but the thing clambered towards them, mouth wide, the arm still in its throat and surrounded by rows and rows of teeth. Red's next bullet took it through the eye. It collapsed on the asphalt, thrashed for a moment, twitched, then went still.

Red exhaled and wiped sweat from his brow.

The whimpering driver craned his neck to see but his eyes snapped wide, mouth dropped open, and raised a trembling hand. Red flinched when the bullet blew a hole in the one-armed man's forehead.

Red looked back at Sonya.

"He would have turned," she said.

Red grabbed the boy by the arm and pulled him into the back of the van.

"Will it start?" Sonya asked.

Red did not answer. He turned the key and the engine sputtered. Down the street, two houses burned. Black smoke swirled into the sky, the air growing hazy. Not-so-far south of the fire, the infected screamed. Red turned the key again. The engine coughed, his heart thumped, but then the van roared and throbbed with power. He backed up and swerved around towards the northern gates.

"Red, I have to ask you something," Sonya whispered. She looked back at the boy before leaning close to Red. A shiver ran down his neck. Her warm breath tickled his inner ear. He wanted her again. "Did you see the infected?" she asked.

Red scoffed.

"Did you not?"

"What I mean is, they all had uniforms. Did you see any infected who weren't part of the crew?"

"What are you saying?"

The van rounded the corner. Two women with rifles and one man with a pistol fired at a budding Screamer on a rooftop. It leapt towards them, taking a bullet to the shoulder as it plummeted and crushed one of the women. Two infected—the kind that would never become full Screamers but still preyed upon anything meat—burst through the door of the house behind the trio and ambushed the other woman and the man while

74

they tried to pry the Screamer off their dead comrade. The man waved at the van, his face twisted in pain as he cried out for help.

Red kept driving. Only the boy turned his head back, his stare vacant.

"Still all uniformed," Sonya whispered.

"Well, they got in somewhere. How else is the crew getting infected?"

Sonya shifted her eyes to the boy then back to Red.

"He's not infected," Red said.

"Are we sure?"

"He's *not* infected!" Red shouted.

Through the rearview mirror, Red watched the boy lean forward, his good eye on Sonya.

"Maybe he's just asymptomatic," Sonya hissed, "maybe he can still spread it. I know everyone wants to think he's the answer, the key to stopping this whole thing, but the virus hits everyone differently. Not all of the infected are Screamers. Some look almost human. Until they try to eat you and you see the teeth down their throat. And the one time you're not—"

"He's not *fucking* infected!"

Sonya stared at him.

"What? Got something else to say?" Red snapped.

"Never mind, just—"

A fully-formed Screamer in camo gear emerged onto the road in front of the gates. A new sentry for a new crew. Its long, lean limbs were made for running and leaping. Its eyes and nose were pushed away to the top and sides of his face to make space for the enormous, ripped mouth that opened like the petals of a hideous flower. Teeth covered the red maw and disappeared down its throat. The Screamer opened its mouth to release a shriek that would not only bring blood to the ears and eyes of anyone nearby but call its brethren to it.

Red hit the gas. His forehead pounded as the shriek

heightened in volume. The distance closed fast. The Screamer tried to jump but Red slammed the bumper of the van into the thing, knocking the wind from its lungs. The impact rippled through the van. Red's mouth hit the steering wheel, Sonya cursed, but the van went straight and a second later the Screamer disappeared under its wheels. The van rocked as bones shattered.

They were safe from the scream but other things appeared behind them, some running on legs too long and powerful to be called human, legs capable of running at great speeds for hours. Others stood and watched, perhaps wondering if the contents of the van were worth the hunt, perhaps already satiated by the taste of human flesh. How much thought and feeling remained in the minds of the infected was a mystery Red thought best unsolved.

"That was the Major," Sonya said.

"What?"

"The Screamer. It was the Major. Didn't you recognize him?"

Red said nothing. Just stepped on the gas.

The gunfire and screaming faded with distance. Or maybe everyone was already dead.

☣ ☣ ☣

Red drove the van through silent streets crammed with cars trapped in a traffic jam that would never end. Three times he had to reverse when the path forward was entirely blocked. When Sonya asked what he was trying to find, he told her that he would know it when he found it. All the while, he kept his eyes averted from the fuel gauge. He was still worried about gas, but he was less worried than on the highway. One of the many cars nearby was sure to hold some, although he dreaded leaving the safety of the armored van. He remembered too well the dangers of the city.

"Here," Red said at last. "Let's sleep a few hours here then get back on the road."

The van rolled into a parking lot. Half of the overhead sign had fallen away but in the dim light, Sonya read the remaining bright-green cursive letters.

"The zoo?" Sonya said. "You want to stay at the zoo?"

"There might be food. Lots of barriers. Smells might provide some cover. Lots of cars in the parking lot for gas." Red shrugged.

"Maybe," Sonya said with a shake of her head. "But still... a zoo?"

The boy pressed his face against the window and peered at the zoo.

Red parked near the entrance beneath a sprawling tree. "First, we find gas," he began, "that's most important if we need to make a getaway. Then we search—"

Something thumped against the roof of the van. Something heavy. Sonya flinched. A tremor passed through Red. The boy stared upwards as if he could see through the metal.

Something paced back and forth above their heads. Growled.

Red and Sonya looked at each other.

"That doesn't sound like a Screamer," Red whispered.

"Just drive," Sonya whispered.

Red almost did what he was told. He reached for the key but the boy opened the sliding door and hopped out of the van. Stared up at what was on the roof, no expression on his face even as something roared – a deep, guttural howl from deep within the throat.

"Fuck," Red muttered, pulling a rifle from Sonya's lap and opening his door.

"Don't!" Sonya hissed.

Something big and hairy leapt to the ground. Red took a knee, gun raised. A gorilla—what once had been a gorilla—turned its stare from the boy to Red. Long fangs protruded through its bottom lip; its thick, muscular limbs were long and twisted like tentacles. It reached for Red, arm creaking like a dead tree in the wind.

The boy fled through the zoo entrance and vanished into the gathering shadows. Red told himself the virus never spread to animals, what he saw was impossible, this whole day was a long nightmare from which he would awaken at any moment. Maybe if the clawed hand reaching for him touched his face, he would snap back to reality, back to being naked in bed with Sonya. Back to being with his wife.

When the gorilla opened its mouth wide, its fangs ripped through its lip, but in place of a scream came a deafening bang. Red heard ringing. He was dizzy, disoriented, his vision blurred. Something pinched his earlobe as he collapsed, dropping the rifle.

Sonya scrambled out of the van from the driver's side. She fired again and again and again. The ape staggered back then loped forward with another howl. A too-long arm struck Sonya from the side with a sickening crack. Red broke her fall. He waited for the feel of claws slicing into his skin, for rank breath and long teeth, but it never came.

When his vision cleared, the ape lay dead in a pool of black blood.

Sonya pulled him to his feet. She was speaking, shouting, but all Red heard was the ringing. It steadily dwindled until her voice came through – a soft light through a fog.

"—leave him, Red, he doesn't want to be with us."

Red touched his ear. "Did you have to shoot my ear?"

"Get over it. It's crossed to animals and we're parked at a fucking zoo. Let's get the fuck—"

"The boy. I've got to protect him. The Major. Put me in charge of him. He's the answer. The key."

"Maybe. Maybe not. The Major was smart. Maybe he wanted you nearby in case the boy turned after all."

Before Sonya even finished speaking, Red was running for the zoo entrance. She cursed, kicked the side of the van, then followed him through the gate.

The fence rippled behind them.

The boy appeared at the gates of the camp with a bite mark that covered half his face. The swollen, red holes from the teeth of the Screamer—teeth that delivered the virus like the venom from a snake—dotted his forehead and cheeks and one ear. White fluid dripped from his left eye. He would never see from it again. The boy pounded on the gates. Frantic. But he never cried out, never spoke, and when Red shined a flashlight down on him from the guard tower, Red later swore he saw a brief flash of anger before the boy's face became vacant, impassive, eternally neutral.

Red knew what the inflamed bite mark meant. He pointed the rifle down at the boy. A soft hand on his shoulder stopped him. Sonya. The first time they had been on watch together. The first time anyone saw the boy.

"Not yet," she said.

"Why not?"

"He's just a boy."

"He's bit."

"Yes, but for now, he's still just a boy."

"Wouldn't it be... less cruel this way? Turning seems... painful."

Sonya shrugged. "Maybe. But the boy is dead one way or another. Would you rather shoot a Screamer or a little boy?"

"I'd rather not let the kid suffer," Red said, but he stared down at the boy, and the boy stared up at him. Even though he told himself it was the right thing to do from any angle, he did not squeeze the trigger.

More flashlights alighted on the boy. Whispers stirred. The crew waited.

The boy never turned.

He remained a boy.

Later, the Major asked Red to choose a name for the boy. Red thought of the name his wife planned for their unborn son.

☣   ☣   ☣

"Homer!" Red called, cupping his hands to his mouth. "Homer, it's alright!"

"Keep your voice down," Sonya hissed.

They slowed to a walk.

"Why'd he run?" Red asked.

"My arm," Sonya gasped, bending and stretching the arm struck by the gorilla-thing.

"Broken?"

"I don't think so. I don't know. It hurts to move it, but I *can* move it. Take this."

Sonya handed Red a flashlight. He swept the bright beam from left to right, from empty exhibit to empty exhibit, while Sonya tested her arm.

"I think it's alright," she said, following a step behind. "I wonder where they all went. The animals. If they all turned."

"Some became food," Red said, shining the flashlight on an exhibit to their right. The signpost showed a kangaroo. Inside, just beyond a hole in the plastic barrier, were skeletal remains. Thick thigh bones, something that resembled a tail strewn about in a mess.

"What do you think did that? The gorilla?"

Red remained silent. They walked onwards. Some exhibits held the remains of other consumed animals, but sometimes the exhibit barriers were broken down, plastic strewn across the concrete pathway, nothing within.

Sonya grabbed Red and pulled him close. "There he is," Sonya whispered.

Red shined the light in the direction she pointed.

The boy stood on the other side of a wide, black pond behind a concrete barrier. A signpost held the picture of a crocodile named Chomper.

"Homer!" Red hissed. "Homer! Come here!"

For a while the boy just stared, then he shook his head.

"Did you see that?" Red gasped. "He shook his head. I've never seen him do that before. I told you he's not infected."

"Maybe we should give him what he wants and get the hell out of here."

Red placed the rifle on top of the concrete barrier and scrambled over it. He lifted Sonya over and placed her down. She stared up at him. Her expression, the feel of her in his arms, made him long for another afternoon together behind safe walls.

"What the hell is that?" Sonya gasped.

Red followed her gaze to a large, bloody mess in the reeds by the water, a mound of scales and bones and teeth. An urge to run, flee back over the barrier to safety, rippled through Red but then he realized the thing there had been dead for a long time.

Sonya followed behind him as they approached the remains of the crocodile. It was as if it exploded; feet and tail and long jaws disconnected from its even longer torso in a circular pattern that reminded Red of fireworks. At the center of the mess were the shards of a dull-gray egg.

"I guess we found Chomper," Red said.

"What the hell happened here? What the fuck came out of the egg?"

"It's like you said," Red said. "The virus hits everyone differently." He glanced at her. "Not everyone becomes a Screamer. And the animals... who the hell knows what they'll become."

"Let's get out of here, Red, with or without the boy, I don't care. This place gives me the creeps."

Red and Sonya crept around the black lake. Red kept an eye on the smooth, sleek surface, his breathing shallow. The faint dizziness from Sonya's gunshot lingered. He whipped around at the sound of maniacal chittering from behind them in the darkness beyond the concrete barrier.

Sonya pressed her body against him. "What now?"

From the shadows came a pack of deformed monkeys. Most of their hair was gone, and their bodies looked as if they had started to melt away like wax near fire. Some had wide mouths, almost as wide as the true Screamers. They leapt and bounded, shrieking and whooping and throwing small stones at Red and Sonya. Two monkeys hopped to the top of the concrete barrier. Red raised his rifle, but the creatures stopped. They gazed at the pond, then hopped back down on the other side.

The pack grew silent. Still. They watched Red and Sonya with hungry, unblinking eyes, but they came no closer.

"Red, they're afraid of the water," Sonya whispered.

"Me too," he said. "Let's make this quick."

The boy watched as Red and Sonya approached. When they were ten feet away, the boy stepped back.

"Maybe wait here," Red said, handing Sonya the flashlight. "Watch the water. And the monkeys."

Red stepped towards the boy alone. He placed the rifle on the ground and held out his arms. "Homer? What's wrong? Why are you running, son?"

The boy looked past him at Sonya. Red glanced back at her. She shrugged.

"Is it because of what she said in the car? She's not going to hurt you. She's just scared. We're all scared."

Red kneeled down a few feet from the boy and held out his hand. The boy stepped closer, then hesitated, his eyes moved to the pond. Somewhere in the black water came a soft burble.

"Did you hear that?" Sonya whispered.

Red glanced at the water. The flashlight roamed the surface. Something long darted through the water, something twisted and thick and headed in their direction. Red picked up his rifle and reached for the boy.

The boy stepped back, out of reach.

"Homer, we have to go."

"Red!" Sonya shouted.

He didn't turn but heard the splash of something rising out of the water, the crack of the rifle, Sonya cursing. When Red reached for Homer again, the boy lunged forward, opening his mouth in a tiny, childish scream—nothing at all like the shriek of the Screamers—and pushed Red backwards away from him. The strength of the boy surprised Red, but what broke his heart was what Red saw deep in the back of the boy's throat. It was only visible for a moment, but a single tooth protruded from deep within the boy's throat.

Red's world fell apart. A heavy fog fell over his mind. Sonya's cries for help were far away, a faint echo, and again he wondered if it would be better to just wait here and let death take him.

A miserable expression twisted the boy's face.

But a horrid screech from overhead brought Red back to life.

Something dove downwards from the darkness above. Sharp talons almost sank deep into his shoulder but Sonya pulled him away at the last moment. A vulture with a long serpentine neck flew high into the air and screeched again, its body covered in bare patches, its remaining feathers grimy and misshapen. It careened through the air like a drunkard trying to walk. Red fired a round but missed.

Something broke the surface of the water, something thick and twisted like a snake. It had no eyes, no nose, just a gaping maw with teeth. Sonya fired. The bullet ripped through the serpent. The thing from the water wriggled and shuddered then reared back like a bear rising to its hind legs. Two more erupted from the black water with a shrill cry.

The boy sat on the ground with his head between his knees. Under the chatter and shriek of the monkeys, Red thought he heard the boy sobbing, but he had never heard Homer make such a sound before.

A serpent darted towards Sonya. Red fired into the wormlike creature. It twisted and thrashed and retreated back into the water but once underneath it flexed and undulated. Still alive.

Red and Sonya backed up against the thirty-foot-high boundary wall that marked the back of the crocodile exhibit. The vulture landed atop the concrete and squawked down at them. It sounded heavy. Too heavy for an ordinary vulture, and something in its body sloshed when it paced back and forth, its yellow eyes never leaving the boy.

"What are those things?" Sonya said.

"Nothing good," Red murmured. "Chomper's babies, I guess."

"And the boy?"

"He's not a boy anymore," Red said, tears pooling in the corners of his eyes. "He hasn't been a boy for a long time."

Sonya glanced from the boy back to Red.

"Oh, Red, I'm so—"

From above emanated a terrible death scream followed by a cacophony of laughter and shrieks. Some of the monkeys had slunk around to the back of the exhibit, scrabbled up the other side of the wall, and sank their teeth into the body of the vulture. It launched into the air and glided over the water. Monkeys clung to its side, hands grasping for the vulture's neck. A wing was torn away in a geyser of ichor as the vulture and monkeys spiraled towards the water.

Red expected the serpents to rise out of the lake, black mouths open for a meal, but a deep cry erupted from within the water. Bubbles formed on the surface and a putrid odor like fish rotting in the heat suffused the air. A bulbous head with a fishy mouth emerged, the long serpents and their wide maws were just tentacles connected to the gelatinous mound covered in eyes of various shapes and sizes and colors.

The mouth opened into a dark and narrow slit; puckered lips reminding Red of a lover blowing a kiss. But with a sharp *crack, crack, crack,* the jaws unhinged, membranes at the corners ripping apart—*crack, crack, crack, like the bones of the Major crushed under the van*—until snapping shut and swallowing the vulture and monkeys.

Red thought he saw monkey hands press against the bulbous head from the inside.

Then all of the terrible eyes turned towards Red and Sonya. The boy scuttled back against the wall. Above them, monkeys threw rocks and screamed. None dared get any closer to the water.

Sonya pulled two grenades from the inside of her coat.

"You think of everything," Red said.

"We need to use these wisely." She handed him both grenades. "You have better aim."

Red pulled the pin on one and hurled it into the center of the pond. The thing caught it with the mouth of a tentacle and held it up to its face just as it exploded. Fire and thunder and a baby-like wail from the thing in the water echoed through the zoo. The monkeys above them clambered down the backside of the wall, following Red and Sonya as they ran around the water. The two fired round after round, each one striking a monkey through the neck, the eye, the chest.

"There're too many!" Sonya called.

Smoke cleared from the water and the thing there—half its head fried black—lurched towards them with another baby-like scream. The monkeys scattered just in time for Red and Sonya to climb back over the concrete barrier. When he was at the top, Red looked back and saw the boy huddled against the wall, watching them with eyes that might have been clouded with tears, then Red dropped, his feet hitting the concrete pathway with a thud. Three monkeys charged at him from the darkness, but tentacles slithered over the wall and devoured the monkeys whole with a grotesque squelching noise.

Red and Sonya watched in horror and disgust as the fried part of the creature's head turned pink again and warped like warm clay. The avian head of the vulture, the twisted monkey snouts, sculpted the deformed head. For a moment, Red thought the monkeys still screamed, then the bulbous head smoothed into its original gelatinous shape. Red wanted to vomit.

The thing glided to the edge of the pond, hesitated, then oozed out of the water and wriggled towards the concrete barrier.

"Grenade! Throw the grenade!" Sonya screamed, but Red shook his head and pulled her along with him back towards the zoo entrance. He heard the cackle of monkeys, and perhaps other monstrosities watching and laughing, but all Red cared about was getting away from the thing from the water. When he looked back, it hadn't truly gained, was slow on the land, but still moving towards them, using the tentacles to pull itself along. Its childlike wails echoed over the sound of their boots on the concrete.

When they were near the entrance, Red turned back towards the monster. He pulled the pin and hurled the grenade. Sonya pulled him away. He heard the explosion, the cry—a child seeking a parent—but neither of them turned around as they dashed back out of the entrance into the parking lot where five Screamers in ragtag uniforms leered at them.

"They found us," Sonya gasped.

"Always do."

"Where are we going?" Isabel asked.

"Far," Red said.

"Far isn't a place. We should pick a place. If we're going to leave the city, I want to go somewhere with a name."

Isabel rummaged through her backpack and pulled out an old road map, crinkled and creased and folded in half four times. Red looked from building to building, window to window, listening for the faintest echo of footsteps, but the city was silent except for the hum of the wind through the gaps between skyscrapers. Dark clouds swollen with water hovered above them.

"Those are dead places with dead names," Red said. "We just need to get out of this fucking city before something gets us."

"No swearing, Daddy!"

The little girl skipped around them, eyeing the map in her mother's hands. When Isabel crouched, she held one hand to her plump belly. She unfolded the map and spread it on the sidewalk, smoothing out the corners and creases. Their daughter stopped skipping and leaned against the wall.

"Names still have meaning if we let them," Isabel said. "We should pick a place, like we're going on a trip, a vacation. Even if we never get there, even if we change our route, it's better to feel like you're really going *somewhere*."

Isabel glanced at their daughter then back to Red. Sometimes, the little girl went days without speaking, without looking them in the eye, ever since she watched and heard her grandparents dragged into the shadows by three Screamers. But the little girl watched the map. She listened.

Red took his eyes away from the street, away from the desolate towers all in ruin, and jabbed his finger down on the map. "Here," he said. "Let's go—"

Glass shattered. Something fast and lanky and hungry darted across the street, leaving a trail of its own blood in the grimy road. His daughter screamed.

Red froze.

One moment she was there against the wall staring down at their future destination, and the next she was in the shadows clutched by a Screamer. Isabel waddled after her daughter, crying out something Red never heard, then two Screamers came from opposite sides, swift and silent, grabbed her arms and ripped her in half.

Red blinked.

His eyes went wide, heart thrashing like it wanted to burst through his chest. He raised the axe over his head before he started to scream, before he blacked out.

The Major found Red curled up on the street, the map his only shelter from the rain, all three Screamers hacked to pieces around him.

☣   ☣   ☣

In his mind, Red was back on the street where he lost everything, the loss of the boy another sharp pang deep in his heart. He stepped in front of Sonya, shrugging her off and firing at the Screamers. Two leapt towards him, closing the distance in a single bound. One took a bullet to the eye and splattered against the concrete with a loud clack, never to move again, but Red missed the other one. It landed in front of him, its terrible mouth opened wide, but Red was ready. He jabbed the knife directly into its mouth through the back of its head. He killed it, but teeth scraped his arm. Something pumped into his veins. His body shuddered.

Sonya screamed something in his ear. She pulled on the back of his shirt but Red barely even wobbled. He threw the dead Screamer away towards the remaining three. Two ran right, one ran left. Red fired right, hitting one in the chest and throat and legs, but the other was shielded from the bullets. It shoved its dead brethren out of its way directly into Red. He fell on his back, the dead Screamer on top of him.

The rifle slid away across the concrete.

The Screamer pounced on Red and bit into his shoulder. He bit into his bottom lip from the pain but suppressed his cries even as the Screamer pulled away with a chunk of his flesh in its mouth.

A gunshot hit the Screamer in the shoulder as Sonya rushed to his aid but then the rifle *clicked, clicked, clicked.* Empty at last. The Screamer struck Sonya with its long arm. Her limp body flew through the air. Then the monster turned back to Red, saliva and blood dripping from its mouth.

Red closed his eyes, prepared to feel teeth envelop his face. Instead, he heard a bang. When he opened his eyes, there was a hole in the Screamer's head. It tried to Scream but another bullet went through its mouth, and at last it was dead.

The boy stood nearby, holding the rifle. His hands shook. Tears filled his eyes. He looked down at Red. "Sss... sssorry," the boy said.

The boy put the gun down and tried to push away the dead Screamers that pinned Red to the concrete.

Sonya limped over and helped clear them. She eyed the boy with something like fascination. When she looked at Red she burst into tears. "Red... I tried, I'm so sorry, now look what they've done—"

"I was already done for," Red said, raising his arm with the teeth marks. "Now, help me sit up. I don't have much time."

The boy and Sonya lifted him so that he sat upright. Red looked at the boy, then looked at Sonya. "I'm making the orders now," he said, doing his best impersonation of the Major. "Don't you ever take your eyes off that boy, Sonya, you hear me? You're his guard. His angel. If you gotta sleep, sleep with your eyes open."

Sonya nodded. Tears streamed down her face.

The boy walked back towards the entrance to the zoo, disappearing from Red's vision only to return with a red gas canister. It sloshed with fullness. Where it had come from, how the boy had found it, Red had no idea.

Red reached into his back pocket and pulled out a folded, crinkled road map yellowed with age. He spread it out across the concrete. "You need to get the hell out of this city. Someplace far away. Someplace with a name."

Red jabbed his finger down on the map. Blood ran down his fingers.

The boy filled the tank of the car. Red heard the boy whisper, "Gassss... firssst."

"This would be a fine destination," Red said. "I wish I could have seen it. Now get in the van."

The ground trembled. A noise came from the zoo. A whimper. The echo of something heavy being dragged across the ground.

Sonya stared into the darkness and backed up towards the van. "Get over here, Homer. Red... do you want me to... you know..."

Heat coursed through his body. His skin felt loose while his muscles and bones felt tight. "I'm already dead, Sonya, do what's best for you. Get in that van."

She fled back to the van as the creature from the pond, healed again, pressed against the gate that surrounded the zoo. It cried. Tentacles slithered through the entrance. Water and saliva and blood dripped from the maws.

Sonya closed the door to the van. The boy waved at Red. Tears in his eyes. The van rumbled into life once more and roared away from the zoo as the creature from the lake pushed down the fence and lumbered towards Red.

A *crack, crack, crack,* and putrid breath spilled into the night.

The Screamers had been too close for Red to use it, but he thought the time had come. From the inner pocket of his jacket, he removed the last grenade. He pulled the pin, held down the safety lever, and waited for death to take him.

MOTHER ALL AROUND

David McGillveray

The bodies seemed to swim towards me, animated by the peristalsis of Mother's intestine. When the first of them reached the membrane, I thrust my arms through and pulled it free. A gush of hot fluid came with it, nearly knocking me from my feet until the membrane resealed and cut off the flow. The body sagged in my arms – a woman, naked, skin bloodless and eyes closed. Dead for the moment. Her face was familiar, of course, but I couldn't remember a name.

With my hands under her armpits, my filthy toes curling in the flesh of the floor, I dragged her to where a short trench waited like a grave. I rolled the body inside and watched, repulsed and fascinated, as it closed around her, Mother's biochemical processes engaging with a sickening slurping. It was not a grave, it was worse than that, the final stage of the reanimation process. I turned my back on the corpse. I would see her again, no doubt.

A second Blank was pressing against the inside of the membrane when I returned to it, as if bidding for freedom. I granted its wish, stumbling with the weight. A male, this one. Its head lolled to one side and with a start, I recognised the face, and my knees almost buckled. I stared at him for a long time.

His name was—used to be—Osni Vadek, and we had been friends on the *Red Spear*. Aboard the ship, he'd been one of the very few able to get past the regulations that governed our lives, the strain of war, and behave with any real warmth. We used to drink hooch in my cabin and pop pills he smuggled from the infirmary where he worked. We even fooled around together a couple of times.

No one had thought to tell me he'd died, become one of the latest to succumb. That was how it was in here. Resigned, I returned to my work. I was lowering Osni into the obscene cavity Mother had prepared for him when I sensed eyes on me.

"Speaker wants to see you."

I watched, unmoving, as the fleshy lips of the resurrection chamber closed over my friend's face. I'd never believed in an afterlife until I came to this place, never had time for any of that. There weren't any words I could say to bring comfort from the one that existed here.

"Alozie," the voice insisted. "I said Speaker wants you."

It was Enbre, one of Troselite's lackeys. He stood just inside the curtain of skin that closed off the resurrection suite, trying to look consequential. It was a big ask for anyone when naked, and that went double for Enbre. His genitals had given up the fight long ago, retreating beneath a malnourished and swollen belly. He was even more emaciated than the rest of us, the protruding bones of his face and ribs casting dark shadows. His hair had fallen out.

"Yeah?" I challenged him.

"Yeah."

Bloody spittle stained his lips when he spoke, and I ran my tongue around my own rotting gums.

"I'll be along."

"She said I was to bring you myself."

I gave him a hard look. "Piss off, Enbre. I'm not finished here." He waited there a moment, indecisive. "Mother would be upset," I supplemented.

When he realised I wasn't moving, he scampered off. He'd always been a little rodent.

I stood at the membrane for a while, but there were no

more corpses for me today. I wondered who would pull *me* out when my time came. We would all be replaced in the end, and the dead would recycle the dead.

I walked the fleshways, the tunnels and cavities of Mother's interior, dwarfed by the scale of her. The Beast that ate a ship.

"The asteroid, it's opening!"

My first instinct was to disregard that wild cry when it came over the common channel that first day, but then I heard the panic in the repair crew's voices.

We had jumped out of real space at random to avoid being tracked, to lick our wounds following a humiliating encounter with the Atomic Blue Faction, and we'd skipped farther than we had intended. It was my only real taste of a war we had been losing for a generation, and the short skirmish had left the *Red Spear* stripped of shielding, burnt out, and clipped of her claws. Now we cowered within the ring system of a nameless gas giant while the crew worked in shifts patching the hull. As second navigator, I was helping to work out where the hell we were when the rock we were anchored to swallowed us like a lizard sucking up a fly.

The hull shrieked and groaned until it lost its integrity and an unnatural gale blew through the corridors. All was confusion. Power died and there was screaming in the darkness. Mother took some of us then, the ones that had been working outside. She was learning, experimenting, even then.

For days we waited helpless in the half-light of our emergency systems, consuming the last of our supplies, amazed to discover there was atmosphere outside. The charnel-house stink of it crept into the air circulation. In the drive room, the engineers found the engines infested,

tendrils like black tongues writhing within the compo-
nentry. The ship's mind lost coherence, itself infected.

Then we received instructions.

Mother.

She was all around us; a pink world of flesh and
tissue, of fluids and dripping surfaces and ghastly gur-
glings. Her air was warm and fetid, and the walls of her
fleshways glowed with biological luminescence.

Leave vessel. Retain no artefacts. Clean damaged tissue.

The crew had argued about what that meant for
another day, but it seemed unambiguous to me. When we
were forced outside by a further constriction of the hull,
those who went armed and clothed were taken quickly.
That included the captain and most of the executive.

Now, two months later, shadows followed me as I
turned into a side passage resembling a throat. Dripping,
tonsil-like stalactites covered my body with mucous. As
I progressed, the walls became increasingly discoloured,
dulled by large patches of bruising.

I came across two Blanks working at the wall,
scooping out handfuls of dead flesh and piling it at their
feet for later disposal in one of Mother's internal mouths.
I hurried past them, unwilling to look at their slack faces
and empty eyes. For some reason, I could handle them
in the resurrection suite, but never in the tunnels where
they walked and worked like the living.

For perhaps a kilometre, I continued on until my
hunger became too great to ignore. I was too ashamed
to eat in company. Kneeling on the floor, I pulled a
chunk of healthy meat from the wall and stuffed it into
my mouth, gagging on the spongy texture. When I was
done, I coughed and swallowed and fought the urge to
bring it back up. There was little enough nutrition in the
revolting stuff, but it was all we had to keep us alive. I
fell asleep on the warm floor with a familiar feeling of
self-disgust.

☣ ☣ ☣

They woke me with a kick in the ribs and a foot on my face.

"When Speaker asks you to come, you come," a deep voice said.

I looked up from a thicket of shins and into the leering faces of Troselite's thugs. Enbre was there, hanging behind and smirking.

"I was tired," I told them as I stood. At least they hadn't kicked me in the balls this time.

"Move." The one who'd spoken, a trained ape called Bontreau, shoved me between my shoulders and I stumbled on the uneven floor.

"Fuck off, Bontreau," I snapped. "I know the way."

The Speaker's throne room was an egg-shaped chamber the size of a games field, her throne a hummock of cartilage. She waited as I crossed the chamber and stood at her feet, looking up. She gazed upon me regally, running the flat blade of her knife back and forth across one forearm. The preposterous idiot.

She had once been quite beautiful, as I remembered, but the sicknesses that afflicted us all had not been kind. She was starved like the rest of us, her empty breasts like coins pressed against her chest. Her sable hair had fallen out in clumps and the skin around the crystal implant that replaced her left eye leaked yellowish pus, which she wiped at constantly. It had linked her to the communications matrices back on the ship, but now it was clearly a source of great discomfort.

"Hello, Ibwu," she said to me. "Playing games again?"

"What do you want, Lieutenant?" I demanded. Only the cretins who listened to her absurd pronouncements called her Speaker. Unfortunately, since her 'elevation', that was almost everybody. I knew it annoyed her when I used her old rank. It was why I had ended up on zombie detail.

"How goes it in the Resurrection Suite?" she asked me.

"Two more today," I said. "We're being replaced. Soon, there'll be none of us left."

She gazed at me, a fanatical look on her face. "You misunderstand our benefactor. Mother grants us lasting life."

I laughed. "Even you can't believe that, Troselite. You looked into a Blank's eyes lately? Mother's studied us long enough to learn how to repair our bodies after death, but she's clearly not interested in retaining our bothersome little minds. We're just convenient bacteria cleaning out her guts."

The crazy bitch had the nerve to look at me pityingly. "Mother cares for us. Has she not spun and given us gravity? Has she not breathed for us and given us atmosphere?"

"Air that's killing us! Take a look at yourself, Lieutenant." I pulled my lips apart and showed her my diseased gums. "Look at *me*."

I sensed Bontreau tensing behind me but Troselite warned him off. "Mother protects us," she said and leaned back as if she had settled the argument, and wiped at her eye. "She lets us live."

Troselite held her knife across her two open palms like an offering. It was only a simple kitchen utensil but it had become a talisman, proof of Mother's favour when the rest of us were allowed nothing. Troselite had been the one at the comms station when Mother first communicated with us, and now she claimed she spoke with the beast via the *Red Spear*'s sequestered mind. I suppose it was possible.

"I have a task for you," she said.

"A task?" I said, surprised. "Why are you asking me?

Won't one of your goons do?"

The steadiness of her good eye was unsettling. "Your lack of faith has obscured the truth from you, and that has created difficulties between us," Troselite said. "But you've an able mind, Ibwu, I've always seen that, and you've adapted well to life within our Mother. She values your work caring for the reborn."

I snorted. "What's that, a personal commendation?"

She pointed the knife at me. "I'm trying to be nice."

I looked around me with a sigh. Her followers had retreated, leaving us alone. "So what is it that only I can do?" I said. I'd be lying if I said I wasn't curious.

"There are signs of new growth, a shifting of Mother's internal configuration. I'd like you to take a look, tell me what you think." Troselite winced at some unseen discomfort and shifted on her throne.

"I hadn't heard about this," I said. Damn the woman. "Where is it?"

"Inward, where the flesh is blackest." She was doing a decent job of hiding it, but I sensed an unease about her for the first time. This was something she didn't understand, that Mother had not explained to her, if they ever really spoke at all. "Will you go?"

I didn't kid myself I had a choice. At least I'd get a break from the living dead.

☣ ☣ ☣

The threat of life after death kept the suicide rate down if nothing else. While the occasional lost soul still flung themselves into one of Mother's internal mouths, most opted for insanity instead. As I trudged along the flesh-ways on Troselite's errand, I wondered if clinging to reality was any better. Still, if something new was happening and our great Speaker was worried about it then

I wanted to understand what it was.

"So, Troselite's not so well informed as she makes out," I said to Enbre, who slouched along behind me in silence. The little man's mood had been bleak since Troselite announced he was to escort me. Maybe I'm just terrible company. I persisted. "Mother's keeping secrets from her disciples. Where's the trust there, eh?"

"Shut up, Alozie."

"Or maybe Troselite's lying to us both. Maybe there's something nasty waiting."

Enbre gave me a sour look. His swollen stomach was an obscenity in the half-dark. "Speaker knows what she's doing."

"That's what I'm worried about."

I knew I shouldn't torment him, but there was no one else available. I hadn't known him aboard the *Red Spear*, but Enbre was a particularly desperate example of how our new life of misery and degradation within Mother had caused the veneer of civilisation to disappear. It hadn't taken long after the chain of command collapsed. Enbre was further down the road than most, but it was a road we all travelled.

Meanwhile, Troselite had turned the remaining crew into a bunch of cultists cleaning out their own graves, convinced she was Mother's preacher. It was my anger that kept me going – at them and my own powerlessness.

The stench in the tunnels was awful here, and the fleshlight was just as unwholesome; the colour of clotting blood. I saw Enbre scoop a handful of meaty sludge from the wall and jam it into his mouth.

"I'd be careful, the meat here looks bad," I told him. "Mother's rotting from the inside." A sudden attack of nausea made me stop. I told myself it was the stink but knew I was getting weaker each day. I spat a combination of blood and phlegm at my feet. "Just like us."

Enbre said nothing. We carried on, feet sinking into

the mushy floor. Gravity lessened incrementally as we headed deeper and Mother's centrifugal force reduced. When we kicked up clumps of flesh they fell in sluggish arcs back into the slush around our ankles. I'd never seen it as bad as this. The patches of decay we cleaned from the walls like intestinal worms were everywhere here, grey flesh dripping with putrefaction, a landscape of creeping corruption. I began to doubt we would even make it to wherever it was Troselite wanted us to go.

Enbre stumbled to one knee, retching and swearing.

"Perhaps we can die together, Enbre," I said. "Wouldn't that be romantic?"

"Shut the fuck up, Alozie. You're sick."

"No doubt about it."

Time passed, with our laboured breathing and the sucking slurp of our feet the only sounds. The tunnel closed in on us, oppressive, and the heat intensified. My head hurt.

"Are you sure this is where we're meant to go?" I asked.

"It's the only way," Enbre said.

A groaning rumble raised gooseflesh on my arms. Ahead of us, an avalanche of dead skin sloughed from the wall revealing new flesh, raw and pink. We picked our way past it. I imagined a flood of digestive juices filling the tunnel, boiling our bones as it carried us away. Instead, Mother's good health seemed to return and our way brightened as we progressed farther. Decay was replaced by the smell of fresh blood, and the rumbling noise grew louder, like approaching a waterfall around a blind bend. The tunnel came to a sudden end, plugged by what looked like a gigantic scab.

"It's blocked," Enbre whispered. "We should go back."

"We've come this far. Try and find your balls, Enbre." I continued forward, squinting at the scab-thing. Closer,

I saw it pulse.

With a sucking sound, something emerged from the tunnel wall beside us like a blasphemous birth. The sight of it made me freeze. It was a Blank, but like none I'd seen before. Its dead eyes glared red in the fleshlight and its body was hideously *augmented*. Its skin was leathery, and slabs of muscle and sinew had been either grown or grafted haphazardly to its limbs, distorting the symmetry of its human origins. Huge, scoop-like hands were curled into claws. The head was shrunken, out of proportion, the idiot slackness of its jaw jarring with its certainty of purpose as it moved towards me, towering, half again as tall as I was, and terrifying in its utter silence.

I broke and ran. Enbre was way ahead of me, scrambling back the way we had come. A second guardian stepped out in front of him. Enbre shrieked as he tried to stop but the Blank's arm swung almost casually. The blow caught him in the midriff with enough force to lift him through the air. He crumpled with a sigh and slid down the wall, the reduced gravity rendering his demise in slow motion.

In the second it took to register that I was trapped, I was grasped from behind and lifted from my feet with such strength, a rib cracked. It was like being wrapped in steel cable. I fought for air, flailing limbs weakening and blood thundering in my ears. My vision swam and faded out.

☣　☣　☣

I awoke, baffled by my continuing existence. The roaring sound I had heard earlier was louder here, the pulse of blood like the *thump-thump-thump* of a hundred hearts. I shook my head to clear it. That was a mistake.

I'd been moved. Twenty metres away was a pool of bubbling, purple blood maybe five metres across – one of the orifices we called internal mouths. It was where we dumped the bodies of our dead and the rotten tissue we scraped from the walls for recycling. When I tried to sit up, pain stabbed through my side as the fractured ends of ribs ground beneath my skin. My chest was one big bruise, but I was alive and I was pissed off.

Two months inside Mother was rotting my brain. I'd been crazy to swallow all that valuing-my-perspective bullshit from Troselite. She'd never been interested in it before. Just hadn't wanted to risk coming down here herself. Probably, she'd sent other stooges before me. Still, something was here, something valuable enough for Mother to guard, something that evidently had Troselite concerned.

Recovering my senses, I looked around fearfully. Enbre was nowhere to be seen. I didn't know for sure that he'd been killed when we were attacked, but it seemed likely. Death was so commonplace now it had ceased to shock me. Perhaps he had already been consumed.

It was the memory of those warped Blanks that made me shudder. It didn't take long to find them. They were slumped together against the wall of the chamber, cradled by Mother's flesh, each with a round hole burnt in the centre of their foreheads.

I gasped. Aside from Troselite's knife, I had never seen manufactured objects of any sort inside Mother, never mind beam weapons. We had been forced naked as apes from the *Red Spear*. So, either someone else had a way into the ship or Mother had started allowing access. Neither option made much sense but whatever the answer, they were no longer here.

Someone was resisting, though, resisting the hopelessness and the disease, resisting Troselite's deluded religion. I thought I had buried hope a long time ago, but something very like it was clawing its way back to life inside my head. If there was a way to get back aboard the ship, I could find medicines or equipment that might help us. There may even be intact escape modules. Why limit your hopes? Resolve took hold of me.

I limped through an exit tunnel into unfamiliar flesh-ways, heading outwards in the direction of increasing gravity when I could. Perhaps I walked for half a day. It cost me sorely in strength, that new, fragile flame of hope in constant danger of flickering out. Then I came to a junction I recognised. I passed a few Blanks working at the walls. At least, I think they were Blanks. It had become difficult to tell them apart from the supposedly sentient ones.

I circumnavigated Troselite's throne room and headed for the great chamber that contained the *Spear*. It was guarded, and my steps faltered a little when I saw who by. He was an ugly creature, Bontreau. Looked like someone had thrown a handful of features at his face and been lucky they landed in roughly the right config-uration. I raised my chin. Bontreau wouldn't stop me. Besides, I owed him a pasting.

His surprised expression when he saw me confirmed my suspicions about the little adventure I'd been sent on. I didn't slow. Jabbed him straight in the nose and felt bone crack. Satisfying. So was the blood and the way his hands flew up to his face as he staggered backward, grunting like the animal he was.

A good bare-fist fighter knows he must always press his advantage. I should have hit him again, or kicked him in his swinging balls. But I hesitated and before I could make another strike, he was on me.

Two hammer blows in the gut knocked the wind from me and then his knee caught me in the forehead as I doubled over. I fell on my side, dazed, clutching my skull. Bontreau sat down hard on my cracked ribs and I screamed. He leaned over and spoke into my ear, "What if I fuck you, Alozie? You'd like that, wouldn't you?"

Half a dozen pithy responses would have been appropriate, but I was choking for the second time that day. I felt the weight of him, the stink of him, saw the intent in his eyes. He was going to kill me.

From nowhere, two hands wrapped across Bontreau's face and lifted his bulk away. They twisted, and Bontreau's neck cracked, the strength in those hands incredible. Bontreau's vertebrae just snapped. His eyes widened in surprise. The same expression was still on his face when he fell dead beside me.

I pushed myself up on my elbows and stared at the figure standing over me. "You!"

☣　☣　☣

Osni Vadek held out his hand and said, "Come with me."

I gaped at him as he led me towards the wreck of the *Red Spear*.

The ship had always seemed somehow unremarkable against the vastness of space, but now the kilometre-long structure loomed above me like a metal cliff. The scarring left by the Atomic Blue's weapons furrowed tens of metres along in the ship's armour. Facing this, Mother's immensity was all the more terrifying. She had swallowed the *Red Spear* like it was a pill and now it lay here embedded in flesh, semi-digested and broken apart, penetrated by countless monstrous cilia. It was never flying again.

For all this, I couldn't keep my eyes off my new companion. The sight of him made the walls I'd built to survive in this place, crumble. It had been so long since I'd allowed myself to feel anything for anyone else. What was the point when they were already lost? But another part of me knew it was a lie. This could not be the Osni I had known. There was a light behind his eyes, but it was not my friend's. This was someone else. Some*thing* else.

"Who are you?" I asked.

He smiled. It was not quite Osni's smile. "Call me Son."

I limped after him, wrestling with the implications of what he'd said. In my shock, I hadn't immediately realised something else was unusual. Son was in uniform. It was the first time I'd seen anyone clothed since we had left the ship. A pistol sat snug in his belt.

"Thank you for saving my life," I said. "Twice."

He ignored me, instead squatting by a puddle of liquefying flesh. There were acres of new rot around us. He dipped two fingers in it and, disconcertingly, tasted it. "She's dying," he said. "She's trying to fight it, but she's dying."

"I always knew it was a sickness."

Son stood again and looked at me. "She's not sick. She gives herself to the growth of her child." He indicated the broken ship. "Perhaps the *Red Spear* is my father, in a way."

"You said she was fighting you."

"Not me. She tries to protect me at the same time she tries to save herself, to renew her own body even as I suckle of it. A new awareness circulates within her, born of the thoughts and memories of your ship. Wonderful, alien thoughts. But they have caused her to become confused, to deny the natural process of death and birth. Her selfishness is denying me the nutrition I need. I see this. From my first flickers, the new intelligence was already within me. I understand." He smiled.

"What do you want me for?" I felt dizzy and when I spat, there was more blood than usual. "Can you help us?" It was so strange, looking into that face. I didn't know whether to run or embrace him.

He stepped towards me. "You were close to this body once."

"Yes."

"I ask you to be its friend again. I would not spend a million revolutions circling the same sun. I want to see what the ship has seen, feel the heat of other stars, listen to the buzz of civilisations. Unfortunately, in her confusion, Mother has been clumsy. The ship's mind is corrupted, its memories damaged. You are Ibwu Alozie, navigator. You will show me the galaxy."

There was an angry shout from behind us. I turned to see Troselite and her band of followers running towards us. I was surprised to see Enbre struggling along with them.

"We should run," I said to Son.

"Why?"

I glared at him. Was he stupid? No, he just didn't understand. It was too late anyway. Troselite was almost on us, her expression wild and knife in hand.

"You are trying to hurt Mother," she screamed. I mean, she *really* screamed. Looked like she'd finally, totally, lost it. Almost all her hair was gone, and the festering skin around her eye implant ran with blood.

"Mother's dying," I told her. I gestured towards Son. "This is her child, or a part of him. He can help us."

She stared at Son as if seeing him for the first time. "That's a fucking Blank!" Troselite looked to her people for support, and they closed in around us. She pointed the shaking knife at me. "You've always scorned Mother's gifts, Ibwu. Bontreau is dead. You have destroyed the faithful. You don't deserve to live within her."

"You know she's dying, don't you?" I accused. "Enbre, tell her what you saw, those Blanks guarding the womb where Son was growing." He wouldn't even look at me, the cretin.

"There can be no doubts," Troselite spat. "Mother will return you to us cleansed of it!"

She was quick. I saw her move, saw the knife flash. Was aware of the heat of blood on my chest as I fell, pumping from my throat, Troselite standing over me with her blade red.

I tried to shout but could not speak. A final darkness closed around me. Through it, the sound of laser fire.

☣   ☣   ☣

Mother's corpse drifts behind us, a split husk venting gas into space.

We swoop and tumble and feed in the upper atmosphere of the gas giant. Joy enfolds us as we are nourished.

Son is with me, bonded to me. I feel the radiation of this system's sun, the exhilaration of vacuum with him. The warping of space building around us. I feel fear and expectation and *power*.

When Son's avatar pulled my body from amongst the others in the chamber where I died, he took my essence within himself. Unlike his Mother, who resurrected only flesh, he retained my mind, as he retained what was left of *Red Spear*. Son is a fine host, and a kind one. A few of my shipmates—a very few—lie sleeping within us. My body lies there too. Maybe I will use it again one day, far from now. But now I am with Son and I feel more alive than I ever was as just a man, and I am still able to perform my calculations and weave beautiful paths among the stars.

Son projects the final field ahead of us. The warp opens to the chaos beneath real space and we surge forwards, guiding one another.

BLACK HELL RISING

Michael Wegener

For a brief, irrational moment that made cold sweat pop onto his face, Lance Corporal 'Drummer' Desmond wondered if he was dead. He guessed it was a thought that'd force itself into the head of any God-fearing man if the road that stretched ahead of him looked like it led straight into Hell.

The right lane of the highway leading north to the Iraqi border, and the shoulder next to it, were lined with bombed-out and abandoned tanks, cars, buses and all manner of other vehicles. Here and there, the black and crooked shapes of charred bodies lay strewn around the wrecks. And farther ahead, the horizon was filled with a roiling mass of black clouds, their underbellies glimmering orange and red from the fires burning below.

The rational part of Drummer's brain knew that what he was seeing was the result of their own bombs, and of the Iraqis torching the oil wells as they retreated north out of Kuwait. The rest of his brain seemed to be grabbed by a primal kind of fear, though, reaching back through millennia to a time when some sights were simply too awe-inspiring to be associated with the work of man.

"Would you look at that," Private Richard 'Buzz' Aldrin said from the front passenger seat of the Humvee. "If that doesn't make your balls shrivel... Sure makes me glad I froze a shot of sperm back home."

"Aw, all of those three poor little swimmers," Drummer said.

"Fuck all the way off, D. It's not about the amount of ammunition, anyway, dude, it's about how you shoot. Ask any of my kids."

"That's gross, man."

"Yeah, well. Wasn't that part of the job requirements?"

"Oorah," Drummer said.

Buzz laughed.

That's when the black rain hit.

Drummer switched on the wipers, smearing crude oil over the Humvee's windshield. "Christ." He eased off the gas a bit as they continued down the oncoming lane, past the endless traffic jam of death to their right. The downpour of oil increased steadily, and day turned to dusk as they entered the burning oil fields, geysers of fire shooting into the sky from countless wells as far as the eye could see.

"Watch out!" Buzz shouted.

Drummer saw it, hit the brakes hard.

Stared.

A horse blocked the road. It was hard to tell what kind or color because it was almost completely covered in oil, which made it look more like a horse-like thing from another world than an actual horse.

Drummer looked out his side window, then turned to look back. A couple of abandoned cars and a series of craters blocked access to the shoulder of the lane to their left; if they wanted to just go around the horse, they'd have to reverse quite a bit and then go completely off-road. Drummer didn't want to do that.

He raised a bandana over his mouth and lowered the goggles that had been resting on top of his helmet and got out of the Humvee.

"Take the rifle," Buzz said.

"I'm not gonna shoot the horse."

"Take it fucking anyway."

Drummer took the M16 from between the seats and slung it over his shoulder then threw the door closed.

The air was burning in his nose and throat, the smell and taste of it like instant cancer. The tarmac was slick with oil. After a couple of steps, it was already difficult to see through the goggles, the world around him filtered through an oily haze. Drummer took several lateral steps toward the side of the road so he would approach the horse from its front and not startle it. It seemed to take no notice of him, though, massive head pointed to somewhere beyond the highway's shoulder to the west, unmoving.

"Hey, buddy. Your ass is kinda standing in the way." He wiped oil from his goggles, then raised a hand and moved closer toward the horse's head. He didn't see a bridle or anything else to lead the poor fucker away, though. "Come on now."

The horse lowered its head, laid back its ears.

"What's wrong, buddy?" Drummer turned in the direction the horse seemed to be looking. He wiped more oil from his goggles. Over the hood of a stranded Mercedes, his eyes found a charred crater in the desert sand turned dark brown as it soaked up the black rain. There was movement at the edge of it, but in the twilight backlit by a nearby fire and with his goggles doing shit to help, it was hard to see.

"Fuck this." Tearing the goggles from his face, he moved closer to the side of the road. As he did, he spotted the huge head of another horse and part of a broken foreleg missing its hoof bedded on the crater's edge, both scraping over the rubble in sluggish, jerking movements.

"Oh, man. That a friend of yours?" Drummer unslung his rifle, chambered a round, switched from safe to semi-auto. He walked around the front of the Mercedes and down the soft decline of the road's shoulder. His boots skidded.

The horse in the crater raised its head as if shocked into motion. Its broken leg, a piece of bone showing at its severed end, began to claw at the dirt just as the other front leg swung into view in a rotating motion around the animal's torso that should have been impossible.

With its two legs out in front, the horse crawled over the crater's edge in Drummer's direction, not moving like a horse at all, but more like a human breast-stroking through water, or a sea turtle pulling itself across a beach. Its big head—oil dripping from its muzzle like black spittle—kept hitting the ground like a chicken's beak probing for corn. And, what was probably the worst of it, except for the scraping of horse hide over sand, it didn't make any noise at all.

Drummer had stopped in his tracks, staring at that thing edging toward him. He guessed animals could go insane with pain as much as humans could. Which would have been a satisfying explanation until he saw that the back half of the horse was completely gone, a tangle of intestines trailing over the sand in its stead.

And then there was the horn, which Drummer's brain was only now processing. A black, pointy outgrowth protruding from between the horse's eyes, about half a foot long, slightly skewed to one side – as if that thing wasn't a horse at all but some fucked-up, death-metal version of a unicorn.

"Yeah. OK," Drummer said. "Fuck that."

He raised the M16 to his shoulder and fired three five-five-six-millimeter rounds into the creepy-crawling half-horse. Bits of oil and horse flesh flew, one side of its face disintegrated yet still, it kept coming. Drummer switched to full auto and emptied the magazine, released the empty and grabbed a full one from his belt and reloaded and raised the rifle back to his shoulder. Staring through the sights, there was finally nothing left he recognized as horse. There were individual body parts that kept twitching, but the creature seemed to have lost the ability to move the entirety of its mangled form.

Drummer lowered the rifle just as Buzz walked up beside him, chewing the shit out of a gum.

"What the fuck was that?" Buzz said.

"Crazy Horse," Drummer said, then giggled.

Buzz snorted.

Drummer wiped oil from his face, pulled his helmet lower over his eyes. "Let's—"

"What's this?" Buzz said. "Are you seeing this?"

Drummer followed Buzz's gaze with his own. Farther away from the highway, framed by a couple of burning oil wells in the background, stood a single tank-like vehicle. Drummer recognized it as an M2 Bradley IFV, which was essentially an armed and armored troop transporter. And American.

"That's not supposed to be here," he said.

"Like us."

Drummer brought the rifle back to his shoulder, muzzle aimed at the ground, and began to walk. If he'd go for the Bradley in a straight line, he'd approach it from its side. He wanted to come up on its rear, though, so he walked in a curve to get behind the vehicle. As he did, he noticed the rear door of the vehicle stood open, lowered to the ground. When he was almost there, he raised the rifle.

A single caged bulb illuminated the interior of the Bradley. It was empty… except for a woman slumped in the farthest corner. Drummer lowered his weapon, ducked inside.

Even under the acrid smell of the omnipresent oil, he noticed hints of blood and puke hanging in the air inside the cramped space. Smears of each on the floor and on the woman, mingled with black oil. She wore an Army helmet and a tactical vest, but was dressed in civilian clothes underneath.

Drummer was about to remove one of his gloves and feel for a pulse when she stirred. Her cheek twitched, her head turned an inch, an eyelid fluttered like a dying butterfly, and she raised a hand in his direction. "Uh," she said, before her hand dropped again like a puppet's cut from its string.

"Easy now," Drummer said. He sat beside her on the bench.

"Y…"

"Yeah, I know. I'm not supposed to be here. Seems to

be a recurring theme today, though. *We're* not supposed to be here, those horses were not supposed to be here. And *you*, sure as shit, are not supposed to be here." He looked around. "I assume you didn't come here alone. Where are the others?"

"There..." she said.

"Where?"

Drummer felt like the woman was drawing herself upright then, but it was more an internal thing than any perceptible movement of her body.

"There is—something in the oil." The effort of propelling these words through her slack jaws seemed to drain the last of her strength. A long, shallow breath Drummer was certain would her last, left her, and then she was quiet.

"Right," he said. He turned to Buzz, who was squatting at the entrance to the Bradley. Drummer noticed for the first time that there was not a single drop of oil anywhere on Buzz, which Drummer found interesting.

"Check it out," Buzz said, chin-pointing to something on the bench.

Drummer looked down to find a dark-blue document binder without any markings on it. He picked it up, flipped through it, back to front, as was his stupid habit with magazines.

Most of the documents inside didn't make any kind of sense to him. Several pages contained photographs of an offshore oil rig in some unknown ocean; on about half of the photos, the rig was burning. Other pages held drawings Drummer recognized as chemical formulas—his public-school education kicking in hard and proud—as well as photos of Petrie dishes and other lab equipment. There were tables, graphs, more pictures, this time of dead animals that made him think back to the half-horse he'd minced. Another page showed a series of blurry black-and-white photographs of a scene that looked eerily similar to what was going on outside – a group of oil wells burning, but the wells looked old, like in that James Dean movie.

The pages before it held what looked like the transcript of a conversation—possibly an interview or phone call—between two entities named TR HQ ATX and D. C. Without stopping to read it, Drummer noticed two things: the year of the transcript was apparently 1929, and on one page, the words 'There is something in the oil' had been repeatedly circled with a blue pen.

Drummer dropped the binder when the woman's body jerked upright next to him, head thrown back, tendons in her neck straining. A groan escaped from somewhere in her body, the gruesome tone of which didn't do much to change Drummer's assessment that the woman was dead. And yet there she was, opening her mouth as something shiny and black appeared from between her teeth and kept growing, growing, growing.

It looked hard and crystalline, wrapped in streaks of blood and gore and black goo. Vaguely similar to the fucked-up unicorn horn on the half-horse.

At first, Drummer stared in fascination, but when more black spikes began to break from her head in various places, pushing through flesh and skin and jamming against the woman's helmet from beneath, he jumped up and hauled ass out of the Bradley.

Stumbling down the rear door of the vehicle, reflexes made him reach for a hand grenade on his belt to smoke the inside of the tank with, but his hands grabbed nothing but air. He walked backwards, raising the rifle, and tripped over something lying on the ground and fell on his ass. He pushed himself backwards on his hands and feet and looked down between his knees at the object he'd tripped over, expecting it to be a rock or piece of debris. Covered in oil as it was, it could have been either one. Turned out, it was a body, which Drummer knew when it started to move.

The figure rose to its feet, oil flowing and dripping from every body part – limbs working as if they were all muscle and no tendons or ligaments, somehow pulling the move off without using its knees or elbows. It didn't stand fully erect, though. It stopped with its upper body still stooped, arms outstretched at crooked angles – like some demented person preparing to jump into a swimming pool. It turned its head toward Drummer.

On any other day, Drummer would have pissed himself.

The front side of the figure was barely clean enough for him to recognize the fatigues and gear of an American soldier. The man inside was clearly dead, though, judging by the black crystal spikes protruding from jagged tears all over his body, and his face being gone. Still, he was sort of 'looking' at Drummer, but with a hole in the middle of his head instead of eyes – the light of a far-away fire glimmering inside of it.

The fact that an obviously dead man was standing over him didn't hit Drummer as hard as it probably should have. After all, it wasn't the first dead man he'd seen walking around. What struck him, though, was the precognition that he was seconds away from dying, from being torn to shreds by this living corpse with its spikes and crystal daggers for hands. He just knew, even before the thing started teetering toward him.

What he hadn't foreseen was the animal cry carrying through the acrid air from the direction of the highway. It was the remaining horse, neighing with vehemence as if— bless its big fucking horse heart—protesting Drummer's imminent evisceration.

The dead soldier thing, just before toppling on top of Drummer, veered away from him and toward the highway with shocking speed, bumping into a corner of the Bradley in the process, distinctly unhuman in the way it propelled itself across the sand, moving up the slight incline toward the highway's shoulder and over the hood of a stranded car as if actually tumbling down a mountain.

Buzz squatted next to Drummer. "Get your ass up," he said.

Drummer did.

When he stood, he caught sight of the horse racing north along the tarmac at full gallop, the dead thing tearing after it, limbs flailing in impossible ways.

Drummer wiped oil from his face, and almost fell back down again when the dead woman from the Bradley shot out of the vehicle, crashing onto the ground as her hands and feet lost traction on the oil-soaked sand. She'd lost her helmet, and her head full of crystal thorns appeared to be so heavy that her reanimated body could barely hold it off the ground. Head bobbing, it turned in the opposite direction from Drummer, scrabbling on all fours after its dead brother like a coked-up Komodo dragon dressed in a human body.

Buzz stood next to Drummer, watching the second ex-human go. "I think we've already established that you've gone batshit, but maybe it's worse than we thought."

"No," Drummer said, surprising himself with the conviction in his voice. "This is real."

"Huh."

"Yeah."

"Well, then… I guess these guys are real, too."

Buzz had turned in the opposite direction, so Drummer did, too.

Against the backdrop of burning oil wells—columns of fire feeding more black smoke into a sky already thick with it, leaving only the occasional hole to let pale blades of sunlight cut down into the desert—more bodies were rising form the ground, spread between fifty and a hundred yards away from them.

Even cloaked in oil, he clearly recognized their shapes. More of their own. Five, to be exact. Apart from their general shapes, though, they were beyond recognition.

The figures moved as if each of their body parts had a mind of its own, as if individual arms and legs were tied to invisible strings and pulled in different directions. They advanced in a somewhat unified direction only, it seemed, by chance – sometimes on two limbs, sometimes on four, sometimes on none at all. Still, quicker and quicker their movements became, some figures 'walking' faster than others, and the panorama of their whole group of unhinged bodies coming toward Drummer began to look like some avant-garde dance performance in an insane asylum – the grand finale no doubt involving the violent separation of Drummer's soul from his own body.

"I don't see any more horses," Buzz said. "So, I guess you'll just have to kill these fuckers."

Drummer snorted. "Easy for you to say."

Buzz's actual body—what was left of it, anyway—was already in a pine box, somewhere on his way home by now, not a care in the world anymore.

But then, Drummer wasn't really blessed with a smorgasbord of options, was he.

Because the first creature—which was the only word for it, its human shape nothing but a husk—was only seconds away from him.

And all that remained to do was kill.

Some say time slows in combat. Not from where Drummer was standing. When it was over, it felt to him like someone had snapped a finger and there he was, standing up in the turret of the Humvee, the mounted M240 machine gun still pressed against his shoulder, an empty gun belt lying curled around his feet like a dead snake. He was panting and sweating and shivering, while oil kept dripping from his helmet. He remembered some of it, maybe most of it, but still wished there'd been one of those fucking CNN crews around filming this shit, so he could press replay.

He remembered using up his last two magazines for the M16 to first slow the nearest creature down, then go for its head and neck until the rifle clicked on an empty chamber and the thing's head fell off, which seemed to at least incapacitate it.

He remembered falling back to the highway and real-izing he wouldn't make it to the Humvee in time, so he'd thrown open the front passenger door of the abandoned Mercedes and dived in head-first, just as the next creature crashed into the car behind him. He wormed himself over the front seats and managed to open and drop through the driver's side door and push it closed again with his feet before the thing could follow him back out. Its highjacked body writhed inside the car, crystal spikes tearing the interior to pieces, but unable to open or push through the door.

Drummer stood, drew his sidearm and emptied a clip of nine-millimeter rounds through the window, trying to go for the thing's face he was only catching glimpses of – a patch of grey, sagging skin with iris-less, egg-white eyes.

He remembered turning around without waiting to see if his shooting had any effect. What he didn't remember was getting into the Humvee and making the decision not to jump behind the wheel and drive off but instead climbing into the turret to man the M240. Next thing he knew, he'd been waiting—machine gun locked and loaded, finger on the trigger—for the rest of his brothers-in-arms-turned-real-life-creature-feature to come for him. Hellbent, he was sure, on turning him into one of their own, into another dead thing puppeteered by something horrible and unknowable.

Of what had come next, he only remembered flashes, stitched together by the incessant staccato soundtrack of the machine gun. Flashes of creatures wheeling onto the highway straight into his fire. Of dead flesh flying, limbs being severed, heads and even two cars exploding. Of the spiked-head lady returning down the road ahead, joining the fray. Of Buzz dancing in their midst, shooting at the creatures with his fingers, making *pew pew* noises, which Drummer'd found hilarious. He might have laughed.

Now, he looked around. He'd blasted a circle of mayhem around the Humvee. Chunks of flesh and pieces of bone lay between torsos and limbs and heads, most of the bigger parts still twitching with something like life. And everything was painted in smears of black and red. One of the creatures lay in disintegrated lumps on the Humvee's hood. And two cars were burning – one of them, the Mercedes he'd trapped a creature in.

He climbed out of the turret, down the tail of the Humvee. Buzz was waiting, hands on his hips, looking south.

Drummer heard them before he saw them – four specks where the sky was still blue. He guessed two Black Hawks with an escort.

"Think they're here for us or them?" Buzz said.

"Does it matter?"

"Guess not."

Drummer's eyes dropped to the ground. "Buzz?"

"What?"

"I'm sorry I blew you up."

"I know, buddy."

Drummer started laughing.

"Don't have to be a dick about it, though," Buzz said.

"No, no, it's just—" For the hundredth time, Drummer wiped oil from his face. There might have been a couple of tears mixed in this time. "It's just... I just realized, since we've been here in this fucking shithole, I've only ever shot our own guys."

"OK, that is kinda funny."

Drummer laughed some more, and Buzz joined in. Then he looked around. Walked over to the nearest heap of body parts. Crouched next to it. He didn't know how it worked, so he began by removing his tactical gloves and pressing both of his hands down onto a bouquet of black crystalline spikes jutting from a chunk of thigh, until it broke his skin. He removed his hands, then pushed one of them back down onto one particularly long spike, pushed it in until he saw it move against the skin on the back of his hand. A low whimper escaped his throat as he withdrew his hand again. Next, he scraped red-black goo out of an open neck, tried to swallow it, gagged, and puked his own guts into the mix, then put more of the stuff into his mouth and swallowed it.

When he stood back up, Buzz was looking at him with his hands held up at his sides. "Fuck are you doing?"

"You know what our guys need?" Drummer walked back to the Humvee and took something from the emergency box under the front passenger seat. He returned to Buzz's side, pushed the bottom of the flare against his chest to fire up its blinding, bright-red flame and held it high above his head. "Our guys need an actual enemy to fight. And I'm gonna give it to them."

"Sure," Buzz said. "That's one idea."

"There's one thing that scares me, though."

"What's that?"

"You think we're going to Hell?"

Buzz shrugged. "I don't know, D. But gotta be honest here, man." He looked around. "How the fuck would you tell the difference?"

VAST PURE SPACES

David McLachlan

T*wo Six, this is Two Four. We are in route to Checkpoint Alpha."*
Seargent Reaves was kicked back, boots up on the plywood desk. He was in the company's makeshift headquarters, listening to the radio calls of Major Goodman, Alpha Team's commander. The large television screens framing the walls at equal intervals—those which normally streamed the feed from their surveillance planes—would have given overwatch for Alpha Team, but there was nothing displayed. Just black voids. They couldn't carry the signal within the quarantine zone.

The quarantined zone. The very place Alpha Team had been sent to investigate.

"Man, I don't know what the fuck is going on anymore," Sergeant Knox said, holding out with disgust the comic book he was reading. He was Reaves' right-hand man, a fellow member of Bravo Team, and maybe Reaves' closest friend.

"Maybe if you read something for adults, you'd find some satisfaction in it," Reaves said.

"No, thanks." Knox pulled the comic book back to his stomach and dropped a wad of spit in his empty Gatorade bottle. He wiped his thick red beard and yawned.

"Two Six, this is Two Four. We are in position."

Colonel Douglas, their company commander, donned his headset and responded to Major Goodman. "Two Four, this is Two Six Actual. Move in."

"Two Six Actual, this is Two Four. Roger that, sir. We are moving in."

Reaves had worked with Major Goodman on quite a few missions. The man's surname was polar opposite to his personality. Goodman was a prick. There were few officers Reaves hated more. And that was saying a lot.

"Two-Six Actual, this is Two Four, we have ene—"

Major Goodman's radio call was drowned out by chaos: the rapid pop of M4 carbines, the clipped shouts of men. Familiar sounds to Reaves. His finger mechanically touched out for a trigger that wasn't there. He licked his lips, steadied his heartrate.

In the long silence, Reaves felt the tension in the room.

"Oh my g—"

Shouts. Gunfire.

"The bleeding gate will..."

More gunfire.

"...break ope—"

More silence.

"...among the chasms of your despair."

Then nothing.

Reaves was almost glad. Goodman's voice sounded distorted. Didn't sound like Goodman anymore. At least not the man Reaves knew. There was terror in that voice coming over the radio, and something else. Something like rapture.

"Fuck," Colonel Douglas shouted, slamming his hand on his desk, his other raking through his grey, thinning hair. In that moment, the colonel looked older than Reaves had ever imagined he could look. "Bravo Team, you're going in."

"Roger that, sir," said Captain Wagner, leader of Bravo Team.

"Get us proper coordinates," Colonel Douglas said. "So I don't have to level this whole fucking forest and all the towns in it."

"Let's go," Captain Wagner said, putting his hand on Reaves back. The hand was shaking.

Reaves got up then pushed Knox's feet off the desk. "Showtime."

As Reaves, Knox, and the Cap walked across the command center, heavy stares rested on them, as though they were dead men walking.

Cowards, Reaves thought. *All of you.*

☣   ☣   ☣

From the helicopter, the tops of the redwoods pierced the mist like the bristled back of some cosmic monster. The chopper cut down at a sharp angle and Reaves gripped the grab handle. He hated flying, although he never told any of his team. As he resisted the urge to vomit, he looked over at Hayes, their pararescue, the fourth and last member of their team.

Hayes was sleeping peacefully like a child, which fit his baby-faced persona well. He was Air Force, something Knox never let Hayes forget. But even for Air Force, the man was a damn good soldier. He was certainly the most sensitive of the group, which was reassuring to Reaves who wanted his medic to have a touch of humanity, in case he was bleeding out in the man's arms. Naturally, Hayes was also their de-facto chaplain.

"What the fuck are we flying into," Knox asked. He was still reading his comic book and chewing gum aggressively. He did everything aggressively. Knox didn't know any other speed. When Reaves tried to picture Knox as a child, he just saw a maniac on the playground, sewing carnage wherever he toddled along.

"Cap don't have the time nor the crayons to explain it to you," Reaves said.

Knox barked a laugh.

"I know just as much as you idiots," Cap said, studying his map.

And Cap was telling the truth. There wasn't a lot of

information flying around about the quarantined zone. Just what they got in the debrief. It was on them now to increase intel. Get coordinates for a fireworks show. Then bug out. Also, the understated orders to find Alpha Team, but Reaves was pretty sure there was nothing left to find.

Nothing good anyway.

The chopper pitched farther down, entering the mist.

"Someone wake Hayes," Cap said.

"Happy to," Knox said, leaning over and whispering into Hayes' ear while stroking his knee. "Wake up, baby. It's time to give daddy some love."

Hayes turned and looked at Knox, blinking slowly. He lifted a fist, then raised his middle finger.

"Like I gave to your mother last night," Knox said.

"My mother is a saint."

"And you are her dishonorable discharge," Knox said, a Chesire grin spreading across his broad face.

☣   ☣   ☣

The helo touched down on a stretch of highway cut deep through the redwood forest. The spec ops team of four spread out, rifle scopes each scanning a different quadrant for threats. There was nothing. Only the fading beat of the helicopter as it merged back into the mist.

Silence reigned.

"Let's go," Cap said.

Bravo Team trekked slowly, quiet as the forest that hugged the roadside. The trees loomed high, an impenetrable wall fencing in the thin snake of asphalt. Reaves thought of the lines of a poem he had read long ago.

Here climb the vast, pure spaces, unconfined, unchek'd by wall or roof.

Who was that? Whitman, yes. Reaves' mind drifted to those college days, under the shade, reading books, watching the college girls saunter along the riverwalk. If his team knew he'd been a poetry major, he'd never hear the end of it.

A tangle of stopped vehicles materialized out of the mist, along a bend in the road. Initially, it looked like a traffic jam but the vehicles were abandoned, doors left wide open.

All thoughts of lazy college summers were now gone from Reaves' mind.

They had reached the quarantined zone.

"Masks on," Cap said.

There was no debate. They had all been there for the briefing. Four days ago something strange was reported. People went missing. Even small towns up here, deep in the Pacific Northwest, suddenly went black. When emergency personnel went out to search, they went missing too. All communication lost within a roughly five-mile radius. They had marked it like a cancerous growth on Reaves' map.

"Two Six, this is Two Five Actual, we've reached Checkpoint Tango," Cap called into the radio. "Proceeding to Checkpoint Zulu." Cap's voice sounded far away, muffled through the mask.

Reaves wasn't actually sure how much the masks would help. But the leading guess from the pencil pushers was that whatever was happening here was airborne. But no one truly knew what was happening. No one except, maybe, Major Goodman. *The bleeding gate will break open among the chasms of your despair.* Whatever the hell that meant.

"Two Six, this is Two Five Actual..." Cap repeated the radio call.

No response. Nothing.

Great. Just great.

"Maybe the commander is out to lunch," Knox said, kicking a stuffed bear as they passed a minivan. Its contents were spilled out onto the wet road. Clothes, shoes, coloring books, a grease-sodden paper bag of half-eaten fast food.

"I had a bear just like that," Hayes said, leaning over and picking it up. "Got it at Chuck-E-Cheese. On my birthday. Man, that place still gives me the creeps. Those animatronics always looked like they were going to come right off the stage and snatch you up. If I ever go back there," he said, raising his M4. "I'm bringing one of these."

"Quit the chatter," Cap said. "And put down the fucking toy. Follow me and keep your eyes and ears alert."

"Roger that, Cap," Hayes said.

Reaves smiled. Cap was alright. Not the best officer he'd had, but certainly not the worst. And he kept out of the way for the most part, which gave him bonus points in Reaves' mind.

They walked through a break in the forest wall that opened to them like the shadowed maw of some giant beast. The soil was soft from earlier rains, the mud stamped deep with the tread of footprints, some without shoes, some from children. The colossal trees loomed over them like alien monoliths. Whitman's words rang in Reaves' head once more: *the vast, pure spaces, unconfined.*

Yet, the voice that echoed within his mind was the idiot voice of Major Goodman.

☣ ☣ ☣

Deep in the forest, the underbrush fell away. Only the titanic trunks of the redwoods dotted the shadowed landscape. Breaking through the thick canopy hundreds of feet above, thin strands of light reached towards the soil.

Reaves stepped under one.

"Watch out," Knox said. "You might get beamed up and probed."

Reaves looked up into the weak rod of light. *What would it be like to be a plant here?* Starved of daylight, nothing could grow under the redwood canopy except the mushrooms and lichen that broke happily out of the soil.

In the bulk shade, the unit walked on.

It was Knox who broke the silence. "Cap, you seeing this?" He nodded ahead.

"Yeah, I see it."

Something glowed in the distance, radiating a soft shade of turquoise. As Bravo Team neared, Reaves saw it was coming from within a massive, torn-out socket of earth where a redwood tree had fallen.

In the hollow, a man lay sprawled on the broken roots. He was obese or, more accurately to Reaves, bloated like a balloon. Naked from the waist down, his legs were broken. Somehow, he had fallen, impaled himself on the jagged roots. Around him was an intricate web of thick fungal strands that pulsed slowly with that strange, turquoise glow.

"Shit," Hayes said, climbing down to inspect the man, opening his med kit, checking for a pulse.

"What the fuck is that?" Knox said.

The man was moaning, leaning over.

Get out of there, Reaves wanted to say to Hayes, but he was transfixed by the strands splayed out around the horribly-bloated man. It was like he was about to pop.

"Get up here, Hayes," Cap said. "We don't have time for this."

"Look at him," Hayes said, pointing to the man. "He needs help. I'll be careful. Besides, we're supposed to gather intel. Are we not?" He smiled his boyish smile, hoping to win over the captain.

A slight breeze rustled through the forest. Within it, drifted the almost indistinguishable hint of voices, whispering words that made no sense to Reaves. Idiot words. Gibberish. The same type of nonsense Major Goodman was spouting at the end.

Reaves had a potent feeling there was something very wrong here. Something awful. In the dark depths of his brain, where atavistic instincts slumbered, a voice warned: *Get out. Get out now while you still can.*

But they had their orders. If their team didn't investigate, who would? Another team, that's who. Reaves wouldn't put others in danger because of his cowardice. He never had before, not on any mission. And he wouldn't start now.

"He's talking..." Hayes said.

"What's he saying?" Cap asked.

"I don't know. I can't understand any of it. It's fucking nonsense. He might have brain damage."

Nonsense, Reaves thought with dismay. "I don't like this," he said to the Cap.

"Me either," Knox said.

Reaves looked up into the trees and now saw that sections of it were also glowing in that soft turquoise fire. And in that glow, there were shapes. Like that of people. He looked over at Knox, who seemed to have noticed them too.

Suddenly, there came from the trees a chorus of ungodly screams. The forest filled completely with the haunted chant.

The bloated man in the hole bolted upright, his back straightening like a board. He reached over, grasped at Hayes who had fallen back instinctually. The man's swollen fingers swung out for Hayes, blindly grabbing at anything. What they found was the medic's arm, and his mask, mask, which snapped off.

The bloated-man's body went rigid. A wave seemed to ripple through his swollen flesh, as though something was moving underneath the skin. The man craned his head straight up, scalp touching the back of his neck. A horrible scream, something you'd never expect from a human, poured from his mouth.

Hayes tried to pull away, but it didn't do any good. The man was latched to the medic like a vice grip.

The bloated man's scream wavered, broke, followed by a wet tearing sound, like that of soggy cardboard being mulched to pieces. Then a long, white fungal stalk jutted slowly out of the man's mouth, his throat widening grotesquely to allow its passage.

"Jesus fucking Christ," Knox said. He put three rounds into the man's chest, but if the man felt it, he didn't show it. Only a slight turquoise ichor oozed from the wounds.

Reaves watched with horrible fascination as the stalk opened into a glowing turquoise mushroom cap, wet and glistening, pouring tiny spores into the air around them. Onto Hayes' maskless face.

Reaves aimed, then fired a burst into the center of the mushroom cap. The man... *thing*... fell over instantly.

"Back up," Reaves said, looking at the slowly spreading spore cloud. "Back the fuck up."

Hayes was on the ground choking and gagging. "It's in my mouth. It's in my fucking eyes," he said crawling out of the hole.

"You're alright," Reaves said. "You're alright." He reflexively reached for his own mask, checking the seal.

Cap was on the radio, desperately calling to HQ again.

"What the fuck was that," Knox said, almost in hysterics. "I've never seen anything..."

His voice trailed off as they stared down at Hayes. The medic was on his back, eyes closed in pain as his body spasmed. When his eyes opened again, they were almost washed over in white, his skin covered in sweat. "Oh god, I can hear them," he said. "I can hear them."

"It's okay," Reaves said, putting a hand on Hayes' chest, trying to steady him.

"This fucking place," the Cap shouted. "I can't get ahold of anyone."

"They're talking to me, Reaves," Hayes said, his face was at first rigid with terror, but it started to break slowly into a smile, into something verging on grotesque ecstasy.

"Who's talking to you, Hayes?" Reaves asked.

Hayes lifted his pale arm straight up. Reaves' gaze followed.

"Them," Hayes said.

High up, Reaves could now see that the men, women and children were *attached* to the redwoods. Thick, white mycelia cords grew out of their lower extremities and pierced into the bark, latching the infected people in place. They were sickeningly bloated like the man in the hole, filled to the brim with the spores currently tearing apart Hayes' mind. The screams had ended. Thick, turquoise mushroom caps bloomed out of their mouths. The spores billowed in toxic, misshapen clouds that drifted in the breeze.

"Cap, you seeing this shit?" Knox said, nodding up above them.

The captain looked up, then whistled in astonishment. "Check your seals," he said, voice high, frightened, his hands shaking, running along his mask.

"They're telling me..." Hayes mumbled. "*Oh god. Oh god.*" Milk-white tears dripped out of the corner of his eyes. He blinked them away to run down his cheeks. He looked at Reaves then, his face still holding that mixture of dread and exaltation. "I can see it, Reaves. I can see the gate opening. You'll never understand. You'd die from the beauty of it."

"Quiet him," the Cap said.

"Keep it down, Hayes, alright?" Reaves said. "We're going to get you some help."

"What's that sound?" Cap asked, glancing around.

"They're coming," Hayes said with a terrible laugh. He looked gaunt now, as though something was just about done eating him from the inside out at an astonishing speed.

"Cap, we got company," Knox said, his M4 raised, pointed forward into the wall of mist that boxed them in.

Hayes moaned, hands opening and closing, his feet digging trenches in the ground.

The wind blew softly, strange whispers still laced within it. Words that made Reaves shiver.

"Spread over me... your mouthless kiss... the spiked crown shines a white fire... a harvest webbed with the flesh of anguish... the bridge opens amongst the endless night..."

Those in the tree stared down on Reaves, eyes filled with hunger.

Reaves rose to stand next to Knox. They listened to the sounds coming out of the mist. Guttural babbling, nails scraping desperately on soil, corybantic screams, all of it oozing with the suggestion of carnage, raising the hair on Reaves' neck.

No one said anything. Nothing needed to be said.

Knox rolled his wrist, popped it. Cap kicked his foot in the dirt, dropped to a knee, his M4 out.

Twenty, thirty, maybe more broke from the mist a hundred yards away. They were almost a single mass. Humanlike, but... changed. Unlike the bloated ones in the trees, these were shriveled, bent over, galloping on all fours like dogs from hell.

"Get a 40 Mike Mike over there," Cap said.

"Happy to," Knox said grimly, loading the grenade round. A second later, Reaves heard the familiar *thump*, then a belching pop exploded in the chaotic mass. A good hit. Dead center. Three, maybe four were immobilized immediately, dropping into the pine-soft soil. A few more, injured, limped on.

Reaves leaned over, grabbed a chunk of soil, and rubbed it in his palms. *The earth grounds you. Cleans the sins of the day, in case you sink down into it.* Who had told him that? He couldn't remember now.

He felt the steady beat of his heart. The shouts of his comrades became distant. The captain's orders went unheard, unneeded. He knew what to do. Simple. He steadied his breath. His mind sank down into that region he had trained thousands of hours for: into the chamber of killing. He didn't wait for more orders. He fired, dropping one of the deranged things with each rifle burst. One, two, five, seven...

More came out of the mist. They seemed never to end.

"Reloading!" Reaves called out, reaching mechanically into his pouch, then jammed the magazine home. He fired again.

"Peel!" the captain shouted.

Knox dropped a half dozen more before he turned. "Peeling!" he shouted, touching Reaves' shoulder as he passed. Reaves took down one after another. More replaced the dead.

"Peeling," Reaves shouted, touching the captain's shoulder.

Reaves ran past Knox's position, and was reloading, when he heard the captain shout out. He turned; Cap was on the ground, tripped over Hayes, who was grasped on to his legs.

"Mother fuckers," Knox shouted, dropping another grenade into the mass. Torn limbs fell wet and heavy in the shaded soil.

Cap screamed in terror as the mass of creatures washed over him. More came on for Knox and Reaves.

Reaves fired on three at point-black range. They toppled in the dirt. Those behind trampled the dead without care. He fired until empty. Tossed the M4, pulled out his Glock 19. Put a bullet through the brain of one grabbing at his boot. Another to his left, reaching, voice horrible, hungry. Its head exploded from Knox's burst. Reaves turned, fired again. More died around him.

But there were too many.

His pistol clicked empty. He pulled out his knife, stepped aside as one came charging. Reaves punched the knife in the thing's brain. The steel stuck in its skull, the momentum twisting it out of his hand. He turned, grabbing at his mask, ready to tear it off his face. If he was going to die, he'd die breathing God's air. He'd take in the infection if needed, the spores, whatever it was. He'd take it lung deep as he ripped these monsters limb from limb.

His hand was on the seal when he felt another hand grip his.

"Hold up there, brother... hold up...'

Knox's voice.

"Easy now. We got them, Rambo. We got them all..."

Reaves looked around, eyes wild.

Yes, they were all dead.

"Rest in peace, Cap," Knox said, looking over at what remained.

Reaves steadied his breath, fell to one knee, panting, shaking. He put his hand back in the dirt, brought himself back to the moment. He was alive. Who knew for how much longer.

"Check it out," Knox said. "Our bone saw is on the move."

Hayes was upright. There was an utter hardness to him now. All the fat seemed to have been consumed. Slow at first, Hayes took horribly stilted steps deeper into the forest.

"Hayes," Reaves called but he might as well have been talking to a stop sign.

Hayes was not there anymore.

"Keep your fucking distance," Knox told Reaves.

"Where is he going, you think?"

"Beats me," Knox said. "And I don't give a shit. We're getting out of here."

Reaves looked up into the trees, at the things still releasing spores. Millions, billions of spores. They swam like dust motes in the lanced light. If these things got into the cities, it didn't take a leap of imagination to understand the apocalyptic promise in all of this.

Yet, they seemed to not to be expanding out of the quarantined zone. Why was that?

The gate is being built...

"I'm following him," Reaves said.

"The fuck we are," Knox said, grabbing at Reaves' fatigues.

Reaves shrugged him off. He collected the extra mags on the captain's mutilated corpse.

"Hey, Reaves. You fucking crazy? It's just the two of us. Cap is chewed up. We got no signal to HQ. Reaves! Listen to me, you fuck."

Reaves walked off, catching up to Hayes. He thought of Hayes talking about his time as a ballet dancer. How he said it was his secret to getting dates, how he was drowning in those stick-thin dance girls. But Reaves knew it was just bluster. Hayes had a passion for dancing. They had gone out to a club just a few months ago, and Reaves had seen the beauty in Hayes' movement, the natural grace.

All of it was gone now. Just this awful, lumbering shell left.

We are all equal in the presence of death.

"Sure," Knox said. "Sure, buddy. Let's just go walking up into God knows what. Why the fuck not."

Reaves could hear Knox's dramatic prayer. He didn't need to turn around to see his friend kissing the cross around his neck, shaking his head in frustration. Reaves knew Knox would come along. The man couldn't turn down a fight.

Hayes walked a straight line, tearing through branches and snags as he went. After a while, Knox and Reaves began to clear his path so he wouldn't get impaled like the bloated man they'd stumbled upon.

Up in the trees, the same grisly sequence happened as Reaves and Knox passed: the inhuman scream, the ripping sound, the mushroom throat-bursting, the spores releasing in cloudy gusts.

It's like they're triggered by the sight of humans.

In one of the trees, Sgt Guttierez from Alpha Team was attached firmly to a thick branch. Gutt looked down at Reaves, his eyes pleading. Maybe there was a semblance of his old sentience there. But the screams that came tearing out of his throat spoke of a different sentience.

"Fucking shoot me," Knox said. "Put my ass down before I ever end up like that."

"Happy to," Reaves said.

Knox flipped him off.

"Hey, Reaves, what did the mushroom say to the fungus?"

Reaves didn't answer.

"You're a fungi to be with!"

☣   ☣   ☣

What little sun remained, slowly faded. They followed Hayes farther and farther into the ancient forest until he broke through into a clearing. A mountain meadow. The whole thing bloomed dazzlingly bright with that same putrescent, turquoise glow.

Well, this is where they've all gone. Reaves looked down, seeing hundreds, maybe a thousand or more people lying in the meadow, weaved together by the fungus. Like fish caught in a huge net.

"My God…" Knox said.

Reaves stepped over a young girl in a soiled, carnation-yellow dress. He looked into the sky. The mist had cleared in a perfect circle around the meadow. The black night stared down like an eye of the void, watching him with curiosity.

The static of his radio startled him. It came out garbled. There was a signal, but faint.

"Two Six, this is Two Five. Do you read me?" Reaves called into his mic.

Nothing but more static.

Reaves stepped over more of the moaning bodies, pushing deeper into the meadow, hoping the signal would grow in strength. He looked at his map, getting the coordinates to their location.

"Jesus, it's Major Goodman," Knox said.

Reaves looked down at Major Goodman. The man was enmeshed in the fungus, his skin webbed with long, thread-like white filaments.

The major's eyes snapped open.

"*The bridge is opening,*" he whispered, guttural, the words crawling out of his hideously white mouth. "*Come join us…*"

Major Goodman was suddenly ripped up into the black night with astonishing force, his body connected by a thick column of steel-woven fungal strands. Within were other infected, gazes pinned on Reaves, their hands opening, closing. Major Goodman leered at the top like a swaying cobra, spitting out expressions of nonsense.

The columned mass struck at Reaves, the limbs of the myriad infected like centipede arms, their hands reaching. Knox, then Reaves fired their rifles, driving the creature back. After both soldiers emptied their mags, the serpentine monstrosity had the opportunity it needed. It bolted forward. Reaves stepped back but tripped over something. As he fell, he saw the arm of an old woman, twisted within the fungal strands, gripping his combat boot.

"You will touch with your skull the eternity of the black," the old crone whispered.

Reaves pulled out his Glock and put a bullet through her wrinkled face.

When he looked up, the column of bodies slithered over him, araneidan in their embrace. Reaves' pistol was torn from his hand. Other hands grabbed at his mask, tore it off, more grabbed his arms, pinned him down. Pale, plump fingers reached into his mouth, opened it. Major Goodman loomed over him, mumbling idiotic prayers.

"...rise now within the spiraling tower..."

The major's face broke open as an enormous mushroom stalk rose and bloomed out of the flesh, vomiting its pestilence over Reaves.

Welcome, the mouthless thing whispered to Reaves through his invaded mind. *My brother of the unseen eye. We will—*

The voice was cut off as it was struck by a rapid burst of gunfire. Bodies woven within the mass fell limp.

"Fuck off," Knox said, grabbing for another clip. The snake-like creature struck out in fury, its good limbs enveloping Knox, tearing off his mask. Mushrooms bloomed through the myriad throats woven within the knotted throng of infected bodies, the spores pouring over Knox as they held him in place.

Knox winked at Reaves, three grenade pins on his fingers. "I never liked you anyways, Major," he said.

There was recognition, almost fear in the major's eyes before the explosion tore him to pieces, the rest of the limbs scattering.

Reaves tried to stand. He couldn't. It was in him now. He heard the voices. Thousands of them, speaking. Whispering. The voices flowed through him. Within it, he heard the familiar radio call.

"Two Five, this is Two Six Actual, do you—"

The sky was open. The gangrenous black skin of night glistened above him.

Here climb the vast, pure spaces, unconfined, unchek'd by wall or roof.

He felt the bridge opening. Saw the divine ladder climbed by those who had waited eons. They called him, mouthless, from the endless void.

"Two Five, this is Two Six Actual—"

"Two Six... Actual... this is... Two... Five," Reaves said, then doubled over in pain before continuing again. "Bravo Team... terminated. Commence strike... commence strike on coordinates as follows..."

The coordinates slipped slowly from his lips. It was a betrayal to his new life, his new form, all those now interwoven within his mind. Those who loved him like he had never known could be possible. He felt their love pulsing down deep into his core, warm, eating away at his old, derelict self.

"Roger, Two Five. Be advised, air strike is—"

The words disappeared as his mind bloomed permanently, drifting like wind-driven spores into the apotheosis of the cosmos. The stars blazed. Just for him. A staggering beauty. Perfection. He felt the perfection thrusting out of him, molting his old self.

A new self would break among this dead world.

"Airstrike inbound. Ten seconds. God bless you, Reaves. God bless..."

Reaves smiled up into the black, his face frozen in ecstasy as the white waves of destruction broke open the stars.

The thousandfold cry of betrayal.

The celestial anguish as his new family was washed away in flames.

THE SILENT SPAN

Josh Reynolds

Yusuf Ba hefted his Lebel revolver, one calloused thumb poised on the hammer. His heart danced in his chest as he pressed his back to the damp mud of the trench wall. Its beat was almost in the same rhythm as the sonorous roaring of artillery. A hymn to war. He took a long, slow breath, trying to calm his nerves. It was hard to see, let alone think, when his pulse pounded in his ears. And at the moment, he badly needed to do both.

The artillery stilled its bellows; a sudden, stultifying silence draped itself over the ragged contours of the northwestern stretch of trench-line, broken only by the whisper of Flanders rain. Yusuf pushed himself away from the wall, crossing the open traverse to the next firebay. It was only safe to move in the eye of the storm; only a fool ran through fire. And whatever else, Yusuf did not consider himself a fool – save in one inescapable sense.

"Because only a fool would volunteer to go to war," Yusuf murmured, but it was his father's voice he heard. The same voice that whispered from the back of his head, telling him that he would die; that the conflict would chew him up and spit him out. That Yusuf, having left home, would never see it again.

Much to his father's dismay, he had joined the Tirailleurs at the first opportunity. At the time, Yusuf had thought that following in his father's footsteps to become a clerk in Dakar was the worst fate to ever befall an able-bodied man. But after nearly a year of mud, blood, and breathing in his own piss to stave off choking clouds of gas, clerking was starting to sound almost pleasant.

Perhaps he would give it a try after all. In Paris. A man could make a life, in Paris. Or at least have some fun.

Not that Yusuf was prone to such amusements. He was a practical man, and not given to whimsy; he sometimes feared that, like his father, he had the soul of a clerk. Still, that was why his superiors relied on him in these matters. Or so he told himself. Better to think that than to wonder if he was simply dispensable, in the eyes of his French superiors.

Keeping his head below the level of the trench, he scrambled along the traverse, following the map in his head. It was the only sort of map he'd been allowed to take. Luckily, he had a good memory. The revolver was heavy in his hand, but he didn't dare holster it. According to the last reports from the salient, the enemy was barely one hundred yards away, if that. If there was a push, they'd be on top of him before he knew it. Better to have the pistol in hand than to have to scramble for it. Pragmatism.

Yusuf moved slowly over splintered duckboards that felt as if they were floating in a soup of hot mud. The lines here were a disgrace; supports had been dislodged and shelters allowed to collapse. If he didn't know better, he might think this stretch had been abandoned entirely. But if so, where had its garrison gone?

Something clattered to his right and he spun, pistol levelled, heart rattling. He caught a quick scurry of movement out of the corner of his eye and then nothing. He relaxed, if only slightly. A rat, then. There were rats in every trench; big, oily things with hungry eyes and teeth like bayonets. They sometimes ran across his chest in the dark, when he was trying to sleep, and he'd once seen them flow like a black wave down a traverse, the sound of their chittering as loud as gunfire.

It occurred to him that the vermin were known to chew through telegraph wires, among other annoyances. Perhaps that was the answer. This salient had fallen silent nearly a week ago, and things were so confused at the moment that barely anyone of rank had noticed. And those who had, had left the matter for someone else to deal with.

It was only after what he thought was perhaps an inappropriate amount of time, someone had decided an investigation was in order. Volunteers had been called for; none stepped forward, of course, so he was chosen, as always. Other men exaggerated or shirked, but not Yusuf. Practical Yusuf. He had accepted this new duty with the same stoicism that had seen him through training and the trench-combat that followed. Difficulties were to be expected, and overcome. What else was a soldier to do?

He sniffed. There was a strange odour on the air; not the tang of chlorine or the mouldy pong of phosgene. Something else. Acrid, but faint. Like mould. Ahead of him, low, hunched shapes scuttled through the dark. He paused, an atavistic shudder running through him.

Rats, he thought, might explain the lapse in communication. Some of it, at least. But they did not explain why he had not yet seen anyone. The garrison had not retreated to the safety of the rearward trenches, and they had not been taken captive, at least insofar as anyone knew. There hadn't been a push from the nearby re-entrants in days. It was as if the men garrisoned here had simply ceased to exist.

The section had become a silent span; a blank spot on the map. As a boy, he'd thought such places were the haunt of jinn. That if he lingered in them too long, they might take him away, to the land of always night, there to be devoured alive. And maybe they had; what were the trenches but a land where the sun never shone and men died in horrible ways?

The thought sent a chill through him, and he wondered again if the most practical course was not simply to turn back. He suspected his superiors would not be pleased with his report; not without some explanation, however tenuous. Even so, he felt uneasy. He'd left his rifle behind, and his pack. He wanted nothing to slow him down, especially if it turned out he was walking into an ambush of some sort. The Lebel would be enough, if it came to it. But even the enemy were quiet. Did they know the salient had been abandoned? Or were they as confused as his own superiors?

The thought brought a sense of grim amusement, but no comfort. Something was wrong in this section. He could feel it, deep in his marrow. Instincts honed by incessant bombardments murmured silent warnings, and a familiar sour urgency filled him. *Run,* it whispered. Instead, he tightened his grip on the Lebel and kept moving. Whatever his fears, he had his duty, and would see it through.

Yet even so, he could not help but think of those old tales from home. His grandfather had often spoken of wrong things; it was he who'd first told young Yusuf of the jinn who haunted the wild, forgotten places, accursed in the sight of God. The old man had been a font of tales, and little Yusuf had devoured them all.

Soil shifted and crumbled somewhere to his left, as if dislodged by an unwary hand. He froze, listening. Was someone there? Or was it just another rat? He strained to catch the least hint of sound, but there was nothing. Then – the crunch of something heavy, moving slowly over uncertain ground. Footsteps, maybe. Coming closer. But from where?

The traverse ran straight ahead for less than a dozen meters, where it branched into several fire bays and saps – dead-end utility trenches meant for storage. The mouths of a number of tin-roofed dugouts yawned along the berm. The sound he'd heard could have come from any of them, but he was reluctant to investigate.

Something about the way the dark sat inside them made his gut twist into knots.

There were strange, bubbled stains on the waxed curtains and something like mushrooms clumped on the wooden beams or fluting between the duckboards. Only they weren't mushrooms, but some form of residue, like that left behind by chemicals. He thought that might be where the smell was coming from. He thought of his grandfather's tales again. Children's stories. So why couldn't he stop thinking about them now?

His instincts were screaming at him now; urging him to retreat to the safety of the rear lines. To leave this place to whoever—whatever—now held it. Jinn, or otherwise. He dismissed the thought with a stubborn flick of his chin. Jinn were a child's fable. There was nothing here, save rats, or maybe a deserter or two. Nothing he couldn't handle.

The sound came again: a hoarse rustle this time, as of mud-stiffened uniforms moving. Yusuf crouched in the mouth of a sap, waiting for them to show themselves, whoever they were. Deserters weren't unknown; no-man's land was full of them, according to some of his fellows. Broken men, hiding in the ravaged earth like vermin. Sometimes, they came slinking out, to scavenge where they could.

Was that what had happened here? Had the garrison been overcome by a band of deserters? It seemed inconceivable, but at least it was an answer. Regardless, he'd know for certain in a moment. He hunkered down as low as possible, hopefully invisible in his mud-stained great coat and helmet – and waited. He'd always been good at waiting. "Munyal deefan hayre," he murmured softly, to himself. A proverb his father was fond of: patience can cook a stone.

In this case, he didn't have to wait that long. As distant flares popped overhead, a temporary flood of watery light settled over the traverse. The strange fungal growth—that wasn't fungus—reflected the light like metal or glass. Shadows stretched along the duck boards, creeping closer. He could hear a sort of hoarse panting that made his skin prickle. Were they injured? Had they been caught by the gas? But no, it didn't sound right. Less pained, more… what? *Hungry*, the little voice inside him whispered.

Yusuf readied himself to move. He needed to get a look at them, at least. A quick glance would suffice. But even as he made to push himself out of the sap, he felt something rise up behind him and clamp iron fingers around his chest and mouth.

He was so startled that he barely struggled as his captor dragged him bodily to the farthest end of the sap. Any thought of resisting vanished as he caught a whisper of movement from the opening of the sap. The sounds of hoarse panting were louder now, and white fingers—stained that same curious shade of yellow, in places—scrabbled at the edges of the opening, as if their owner were attempting to pull himself into view. Something about the way they twitched reminded him of a dying scorpion. A cold thrill of horror raced through him, though he could not say why. Instead, he raised the Lebel, to fire if the owner of those horrid fingers so much as peeked around the corner at him.

"No," his captor muttered, into his ear. "Don't. Please. *Please.*" The man's accent was Parisian. Not a German, then, at least. Yusuf hesitated, then lowered the revolver. Even as he did so, an eerie ululation rose from unseen lips. It was not a human cry, nor that of any animal he'd ever encountered. Instead, it was akin to the susurrus of thousands of midge wings humming in singular, desperate, motion.

The sound rose in volume as a large, ungainly, twitching shadow fell across the aperture. It moved like a slug, with an awful hunching motion; there was a peculiar clicking sound, as of wooden sticks being snapped in two. The light of the flares had faded to a dim flicker, so all detail of the thing was lost, and for that he was glad. Something told him that he would sleep better for having not seen it.

His captor's grip on his mouth tightened. "*Quiet* – you must be quiet, understand?" the man hissed on a wafting of rank breath. "It is listening." When he was certain Yusuf understood, he removed his bandaged palm from the latter's mouth. They crouched in silence for long moments until Yusuf's legs and back screamed in silent protest. Then, finally, the eerie murmuration faded into inaudibility as the bulk moved on down the traverse, and away from them.

"Gone," the other man muttered after several more moments had passed.

"What was it?" Yusuf asked softly. He studied the man, noting the muddy, tattered condition of his uniform and coat, the scrum of bramble on his chin and cheeks and the hollows under his eyes. Here was someone who had been living on the margins for several days, at least. Whoever he was, he looked as if he'd been through hell.

"Evil." The man turned and moved several boxes away from the back wall of the sap, revealing a tight aperture, cunningly hidden. "Come. Quickly. Follow me. We are safe, underground. It hasn't figured out how to get in here, not yet." With that, he slithered into the aperture and out of sight with startling speed.

Yusuf hesitated, and then followed the other man down into the hole. It was a tight squeeze, but he managed it. The entire way, he kept an ear out for the curious sound. The man had saved his life; of that, Yusuf was certain. Though from what, he could not yet say.

The burrow was neither long nor deep. From the look of it, Yusuf thought it had been dug as much with bare hands as entrenching tools. The interior entryway was obscured by a curtain made from a filthy cloth shroud. But it was normal filth; no sign of that awful yellow stain anywhere, which came as a relief. The only light was from a single candle nestled inside a smoke-smeared jar. It cast a watery orange light over the cramped space, revealing walls held in place by pillaged duckboards and furls of tarp spiked into the mud. Crates of supplies added additional reinforcement. All in all, a desperate redoubt, dug by frantic hands.

"I– I am Aubert," the man said when they'd gotten settled. "You are... Senegalese?"

Yusuf almost corrected him, but refrained. The average Frenchman cared more about the differences between Gascon and Burgundian than they did Fulani and Senegalese. "I am a Tirailleur, yes. 43rd Battalion."

Aubert nodded. "You are here because we lost contact, yes?"

"I was sent to find out what happened," Yusuf said.

Aubert chuckled hoarsely. "If I could tell you, I would, believe me." He tugged at his whiskers, gaze brittle. "How many days have we been silent?"

"Nearly a week," Yusuf answered, and the other man's expression turned incredulous.

"Only a week? God. *God.*" Aubert buried his face in his hands, and his shoulders twitched with silent sobbing. He fixed Yusuf with a bloodshot stare. "It feels longer. Like time itself has become infected. That is what it is, an infection. Trench-foot of the soul." He gave a rusty laugh, edged with hysteria. "You can smell it, can't you? That pong on the air."

"Gas," Yusuf said. It had been tickling his sinuses for a time, though he'd only just now identified it.

Aubert nodded. "Yes, but what kind, eh? Tell me that."

Yusuf shook his head slowly. "I do not know."

"No. Neither do I. But I can tell you what it does. You saw the mould, I expect. Yellow is the colour of plague." Aubert fumbled in a nearby crate for something – a corroded meal-tin, its identification rendered illegible. He offered it to Yusuf. "Hungry?"

"No. Thank you."

Aubert nodded convulsively. "I worked in the Paris Morgue, before the war. I took apart bodies in the shadow of Notre-Dame. I grew to know men inside and out and I thought that they held no surprises for me." His expression became vague. "Then I came here."

Aubert fell silent, staring at the tin in his hands as if he did not recognise it. Yusuf waited, as patient as he had been earlier. Aubert wanted to talk. Yusuf just had to wait for the man to gather his courage, as well as his thoughts. Yusuf knew from past experience that isolation imposed a form of senility on all save the strongest of minds. With no one to talk to, a man could get lost in his own thoughts. Finally, Aubert cleared his throat and began. "It started the way it always starts," he whispered. "The whistle of the cannisters; the soft hiss of creeping gas. But this was not the usual miasma. It crept into the pores and through the leather of the masks. Men began to vomit and scream that something was moving inside them. But the Germans did not come. They did not advance, they did not fire." Aubert looked at Yusuf, his eyes haunted. "I think they did not know what would happen – and they wanted to see."

"And what did happen?"

Aubert shuddered and fell silent. Yusuf grew uneasy. He thought of the shadowy thing and the whistling sound it had made. It had been too big to be a man. Some sort of trained animal, perhaps. He'd heard rumours the Germans had employed a specially-bred dog, at Mons, but that had been nothing more than soldier's gossip. Or so he'd assumed. "What happened, Aubert? What is that thing? Some beast?"

Aubert looked away. "You could say that."

"But what do you say?" Yusuf pressed.

"It is the gas," Aubert whispered.

"Gas – chlorine?"

Aubert shook his head. "No. That would have been merciful by comparison." He gave Yusuf a sickly smile. "This… eats us from the inside out. Crystallises in the lungs and spreads through the meat like mould on plaster. At least, that is what my cursory examinations implied. A *disease*." He drew his bayonet and thrust it into the corroded tin to pry it open. Yusuf watched him with uncomfortable fascination as Aubert continued with his impromptu lecture. "But fast; a matter of hours, in the earliest cases."

"What do you mean examination?"

"I told you; I worked in the morgue, and here, as a stretcher-bearer. I know what chlorine does to a man. It eats the lungs, burns the eyes. A bit of piss on a rag solves the problem. It was not phosgene either. It does not smell of mouldy hay, for one thing." He paused, a far-away look in his eyes. "I do not know what this was. Or how they made it. It spread fast – faster than chlorine. It grew and burst out of them like… like it could not wait to do its job." He popped a hole in the tin and gave a grunt of triumph. "Like a good soldier."

"But only here, on this section?" Yusuf said.

Aubert widened the hole in his tin, and slurped greedily at the contents. "For now. Maybe they only had the one cannister. Maybe this was simply a test. Maybe— Maybe it is something else. Something in the mud here, or in *us*, reacting to the gas in an unexpected way. How much blood has been spilt here, eh? Who knows what that does to a place like this." He smacked his lips and glanced at Yusuf. "It does not matter, I think. Whatever it started as, it has become something else."

Yusuf felt the nape of his nick prickle. "Why haven't you tried to leave?"

Aubert chuckled bitterly. "You think I haven't, eh?" He gestured to their surroundings. "You think I did this alone? No. There were others. But it spread too quickly, and we were cut off. It took them – one by one. Now there is just me." He shook his head. "I have tried to leave, but it is waiting… watching." He looked sadly at Yusuf. "And now it has you as well."

Yusuf frowned, but any reply he might have formulated was lost by a sudden rustle of movement from the other side of the curtain. A slow, ungodly rasping that set his teeth to aching and his skin to crawling. He met Aubert's gaze, and the other man swallowed convulsively and nodded. He set his tin aside and wiped his bayonet on his sleeve. Yusuf hefted his pistol.

The rasping became more urgent; as if whatever it was, was now certain of their presence. Yusuf held his breath and slowly—carefully—thumbed back the hammer on his revolver. The resultant click was thunderously loud to his ears. The rasping ceased.

A moment later, a convulsing bulk tore through the curtain and nearly bowled Yusuf over. He cried out as the thing clawed at him with its paw – no, *paws*. Aubert shouted and dragged the thing off, hurling it into a nearby stack of crates. It righted itself immediately and Yusuf got his first real look at it.

It was a rat; or rather, rats. Like someone had stitched dozens of the wretched beasts together in haphazard fashion, shoulder to shoulder, neck to belly, rendering them a horrid mass of hair and tails and teeth. Dozens of paws dragged the shaggy bulk of the thing along the burrow, and dozens of snouts twitched. Eyes blinked and rolled in arrhythmic fashion. Teeth snapped together, and the sound of them was like ice splintering. Veins of glistening urine-hued fungal-crystal bound the animals together, and inundated their writhing forms.

Yusuf fired without thinking. The sound was deafening in the close confines. The rat-thing shuddered and loosed a chorus of shrieks. Aubert grabbed Yusuf's arm and tried to drag him towards the rear of the burrow, away from the monstrosity. Yusuf shook him off and fired again, but though he was certain he hit it, it continued to crawl towards them.

Aubert shoved him back and Yusuf saw that he had a pistol of his own – no. Not a pistol. A flare gun. Aubert fired and the burrow was filled with a stuttering, painful radiance. The rat-thing squealed cacophonously as flames roared up across its greasy hide. As oily smoke boiled up and filled the burrow, Aubert shoved Yusuf towards the aperture. Yusuf's last glimpse of the thing was it rolling mindlessly in the dirt, as if trying to smother the conflagration that had already half-consumed it.

"The other thing I learned from my examinations is that it is very flammable," Aubert coughed as they scrambled back the way they'd come earlier. "Come, we must go back up. The smoke can be deadly."

Yusuf didn't ask how Aubert knew that. He wasn't certain he wanted to know. Instead, he crawled after the man, leaving the burrow to the burning rat-thing.

Outside, in the open air, a steady rain fell. It struck the tin roofs of the dugouts with a staccato beat, and turned the muddy ground to slurry. Without maintenance, trenches were prone to collapse in bad weather. Yusuf had seen men buried alive and become part of the foundations. He suspected this section was only a day or so at most from crumbling into uselessness.

Aubert gave him an apologetic look. "I forgot to tell you that it is not just men who are susceptible to it. The rats – they are part of it as well."

Yusuf coughed, trying to clear the taste of burning hair out of his sinuses. "What do you mean part of it?" Overhead, flares burst to life as they had earlier, and light drizzled down through the wet air.

Aubert didn't seem to notice. "I do not know," he said. "Not really. But from what I have seen, it—they— all seem to be one thing. To act with a single will. As if they are no more than puppets of meat and muscle for... whatever has infected them. The gas, maybe. Or the spores that it incites."

Yusuf stared at him. "You make it sound as if it is alive; as if it thinks."

Aubert looked away.

Yusuf paused. "If you are right," he said, slowly, "then it knows where we are now."

Aubert tensed. "Oh no."

"We must go," Yusuf said. But as the words left his mouth, the sludge beneath his feet shifted, grew unsettled.

Aubert looked at him, fumbling with the flare pistol still held in his hand. "It doesn't like fire," he said, as if trying to convince himself. "Flares keep it away. I just need to reload—"

The bend ahead exploded, as if struck by an artillery round. Mud and splintered wood flew everywhere as a loathsome mass erupted into view. It was—had been—a man. Or several. Now it was, like the rats, a hideous amalgamation of flesh encrusted with innumerable crystalline barnacles. It hauled itself through the curtain of rain with flailing limbs, and its bulk was crowned by a diadem of shrieking heads. Some still wore helmets, while others were little more than skulls. Pestilent geysers of what he thought must be gas spewed from the myriad orifices—composed of mouths and other things—that lined its length. It was an impossibility. A wrong thing, like his grandfather had spoken of.

Maybe Yusuf had been wrong; maybe this was a jinn. A stain on the world, growing larger by the day, growing fat on the blood of men. He found himself soundlessly mouthing the protective duas his grandfather had taught him.

Aubert, on the other hand, wailed like a damned soul as the leviathan fixed some of its eyes on them and undulated in their direction. Its hands gouged the sides of the trench as it propelled itself forward, and it emitted a noise like the crackling of tree branches in winter from its many mouths.

Yusuf turned to run. "Aubert forget the flare, come on," he shouted. But the other man was frozen; petrified by the sight of the thing he had avoided for so long, the flare pistol forgotten in his slack grip. The palpitating mass rose over him, like an avalanche in reverse. Then the avalanche crashed down, and the impact knocked Yusuf from his feet.

Aubert was gone – obliterated, or worse, in an instant. Yusuf scrambled back, pushing himself through the mud as the heaving bulk of the thing reorientated itself. Several of its heads craned about to fix him with an unsettling stare, and coiling strands of something that might have been gas seeped from their open lips. More rat-masses squirmed through its shadow like ungainly offspring. How many rats in a span of trench? A hundred?

When Yusuf reached the next bend in the trench, he slowly pulled himself to his feet. He raised the Lebel, and his hand was steady. He felt nothing; not fear, not panic. Or if he did, it was dim. Muted. What he saw before him could not be, and his mind resisted it the way a garrison might resist an attack. Instead, he concentrated on the practicalities of the matter; his duty was to escape, to bring word of this… whatever it was to his superiors. Everything else was inconsequential.

The thing took an unsteady step towards him, on paws composed of dozens of hands and feet, some of the latter still shod. Gas vented from the crystal-encrusted wounds that marked its ungodly bulk with every twitch of its haphazard limbs. Mouths flapped dumbly and eyes rolled in drooping sockets. It saw him, but he did not think it understood; no, there was no mind there. No awareness. Just a cancerous desire to add his mass to its own. It was not a jinn, but still a wrong thing nonetheless.

Yusuf retreated before it slowly. It filled the trench like a tide of foulness, more and more of it squeezing into sight as it followed him down the traverse. Heedless, it crushed rat-things beneath its bulk, and Yusuf was sickened to see that it drew their remains into itself, gulping them up into newly-made orifices on its paws and body. Was that what it had done to Aubert – what it wanted to do to him?

He knew that if he turned and ran, it would be on him in a moment. It would fall upon him the way it had Aubert, and that would be the end. But if he could get to the next bend in the line, and get out of sight, it might lose interest. A slim hope, but it was all he had. He was a fast runner. Always had been. But no man could outrun the devil.

Flares bloomed directly overhead. Whistles sounded. Startled, he spun to find salvation marching down the traverse in the form of a German assault. Someone, somewhere, had grown tired of waiting and an order had been given, and now an attack was underway. The corpse-thing quivered and rose, as if scenting new prey.

The newcomers wore protective gear in the form of thick coats and iron plates. Several carried flamethrowers and liberally doused every dugout and sap with purifying fire. Smoke roiled in their wake, obscuring their numbers. Yusuf recalled Aubert's suspicions and wondered if this was why the Germans had taken so long to investigate the salient; had they been preparing to scour it clean? Even if so, they could not know what awaited them.

He turned towards them, hands raised to warn them. But if the Germans saw him, they gave no sign. They continued down the traverse, jets of flame licking out ahead of them. Yusuf leapt into a cut just as a wash of heat swept through the spot he'd been standing, and lost his grip on his revolver as he did so. He fumbled for his pistol as the duck boards beneath him shuddered.

Even as Yusuf snatched the Lebel up, an armoured form loomed in the entrance to the cut. Yusuf rolled onto his back and raised the revolver. The German froze. The two stared at one another for what felt like an eternity. Then, a squirming limb of congealed flesh and wetly gleaming crystals smashed down, knocking the man onto his face at Yusuf's feet. The creature rampaged hungrily towards the Germans, and they responded with fire.

Coruscating jets of liquid flame washed across the thing, and its stolen flesh bubbled and split. But it was too large; the flames gnawed at it, but not quickly enough. It caught up a soldier in one paw and he was torn apart by dozens of grasping hands. Another man was crushed under its bulk, driven so deep into the mud that it was as if he'd never been.

The Germans fell back, and the creature made to pursue but blazing gouts caused it instead to rear up with an asynchronous shriek that threatened to split Yusuf's skull in two. It might not be intelligent, but it clearly knew pain when it felt it.

He knew he needed to go, that he would never get a better opportunity, but something held him back. A need to see the horror burn; to see it finished. He stared, watching. A hand caught his wrist, and he looked down into the masked face of the German. The man's eyes were wide behind the lenses of his gasmask. Had he known what was waiting for him? Or was it as much a surprise to him as it had been Yusuf?

The German tried to speak – a warning? A plea? Yusuf did not know. The man screamed as a burning tendril of flesh suddenly looped about his legs and dragged him from the cut and into the ravening orifices of the thing, flamethrower, and all. Eyes burnt white like overcooked eggs rolled towards Yusuf. A mouth like that of a sucker-fish gnashed on the broken body of the German, rendering it down for easy absorption. Shard-like teeth clanked against the flamethrower's propellant tank.

Yusuf's world slowed; narrowed to the tank. Without thinking, he swung the Lebel up and pulled the trigger. There was a crack—a thin whistle—and then an all-consuming roar, that lifted Yusuf up and hurled him back with bone-rattling force. He hit the side of the cut and flopped limply into the mud, coat and hair smouldering.

As his hearing returned, a high, shrill sound impressed itself on his senses. The thing was burning now; collapsing in on itself, even as the trench was. Fire cleansing an infection. Dugouts burned, and dark figures moved through the smoke, retreating from the salient. Germans? Maybe. If so, he suspected that they'd done what they'd come to do. What that was, exactly, what had happened here, he could not say. And would not.

The decision was considered and made in an instant. An attack. That would be his report. He was a practical man, not prone to whimsy. They would believe him. The salient had been lost to the Germans. That was all. That was enough.

Yusuf dragged himself upright. A rat eyed him from a nearby crate. It crept away and he decided to follow its example. As he stepped out of the cut, he saw an unhealthy shimmer in the smoke that filled the traverse. But the wind turned and carried it away, leaving him wondering if he'd seen anything at all.

And hoping he hadn't.

BURNING HEAVEN TO THE GROUND

A Joe Ledger Adventure

Jonathan Maberry

Part One
Wars and Rumors of Wars

*"Victory at all costs, victory in spite of all terror,
victory however long and hard the road may be;
for without victory, there is no survival."*
–Winston Churchill

-1-

I didn't plan to kill anyone.

I wasn't totally against the idea, either.

Sometimes things just fall that way, and either you roll with it or it rolls over you. Letting the bad guys win isn't how I roll.

Nor is it how my boss, Mr Church rolls.

I come at it my way. He goes at it another way.

To frame your expectations… when it comes down to no good choices and the remaining options all suck, I'm more like a runaway car, but Church is Godzilla when that big, radioactive mega-dinosaur is really pissed.

Or maybe even a little worse.

You'll see.

Joint Homeland/Baltimore Police Department Task Force
Surveillance Station 15

It started the way these things do. Cops on a wiretap. Bad guys saying the wrong thing because they get lazy or they think whoever's listening in is a dumbass.

Crooks are stupid and lazy a lot more often than they're evil geniuses. Ask anyone who ever wore a badge.

I was eavesdropping on a warehouse down by the docks. This was early, well after the Twin Towers but before the SEALS punched Bin Laden's ticket. Every police department on the continent had guys like me sitting in vans, drinking way too much coffee, eating junk food, feeling our arteries harden and our muscle tone go on vacation. It was dull work that kept trying to pull me down into a drowse, and so far, I had heard nothing of any real value. In terms of useful intelligence it was somewhere between Jack and Shit. Day after day, week after week.

The tedium was so intense that it sanded the edges off of perception, awareness, and efficiency. God only knows how many times something critical has been missed by fatigued agents being slowly turned into sleepwalkers.

It's nothing at all.

Until it's something.

For me, the wakeup call began when a certain name came whispering down the wire.

El Mujahid.

When I first heard it, about halfway through my shift, I thought I *mis*-heard. Then I thought it was a joke. The kind of joke ordinary schlubs make when they want to emphasize a point. Word-association hyperbole. Like that.

But one of the two people on the call immediately

told the other guy to shut up. There was a note of panic in it. A few seconds later the call ended.

I replayed the call.

No. It wasn't a joke and I wasn't half asleep and dreaming. So, I called my boss and he called his boss who called *his* boss, and that guy called the Homeland supervisor. I could pretty much *hear* them all sweating.

El Mujahid. It means 'the fighter of the way of Allah'. There have been a bunch of radicalized cats with that nickname, but in this case, El Mujahid was his actual name. Son of a poor farmer from Yemen. Our boy had that name hung on him at birth, and did everything he could to live up to its promise. Not in the way most Muslims would – using it as inspiration to do good works and uplift his family and his people. No, *this* El Mujahid took the name as a call to war and used it as a rallying cry. By the time he was thirty, a bunch of nervous analysts in the CIA and the State Department believed he was going to surpass Bin Laden.

The wars in Afghanistan and Iraq were still cooking back then and if Coalition soldiers rolled their Bradley over a landmine, chances are this asshole was responsible. El Mujahid had one hell of a lot of notches on his gun, and being that young and that powerful, he had plenty of years ahead of him to fill a lot of graveyards.

If there was even the slightest chance to get a lead to him, then we had to move and move fast.

Which we did.

And that is where things started to go to shit.

Department of Military Sciences
Temporary Field Office
Baltimore, Maryland

He was a big man. Blocky and solid. The kind of man anyone who understood conflict and could assess potential would assume was capable.

That assessment was correct.

He sat in swivel chair in a monitoring suite, watching data feeds roll up and across a series of computer screens positioned in a quarter-circle around his desk. A cup of tea and a plate of vanilla wafer cookies were close at hand – the tea had gone cold and the cookies were nearly gone.

On the main screen was a live feed of a group of police officers at a staging area, all of them in the process of kitting up with weapons and body armor.

"That's the task force," said a second man. Younger, thin, with thick glasses and a t-shirt with a picture of the Black Panther from the *Marvel* comic books. "Looks like they're getting ready to both kick ass and take names."

"Indeed," said the big man.

"Bit of overkill, Mr Church, don't you think?"

"No, Bug, I think it's an appropriate force for the job," said Church. "The idea is to overwhelm in such numbers as to nullify thoughts of armed resistance. At least, that's the strategy."

Bug nodded. "So… what's our interest? Slow week? Do we have a mole in the cops? Or maybe a spy in there with the bad guys?"

Church selected a cookie, tapped it on the edge of the plate, and took a bite. He crunched quietly for a moment. "The new analyst you hired, Miss Bloom…"

"Nikki. Yeah. She'll be heading up my new pattern-recognition team."

"She uploaded some of her own search programs."

Bug nodded. "I gave her the okay on that. Hope that's cool with you."

"It's your team, Bug. I'm not going to tell you how to run it."

"Um... cool. But what about Nikki?"

"She ran that software last night and got some hits that are of interest," Church said. "El Mujahid in particular. He's been on our to-do list for some time. But more importantly, when she was doing deep background on the target facility, there was mention of some unusual kind of containers. Ones with sophisticated environmental controls."

"And you're thinking... what? Drugs?"

Church shook his head. "Drugs would not require that kind of container."

"Something biological?"

"That's more likely and more disturbing. Nikki was unable to get specifics."

Bug thought about that. "Colonel Riggs and his team found some environmental containers on that gig in Tel Aviv two months ago. But the whole lab was torched. From what Dr Hu said, the accelerant used was so potent that it burned everything down to ash. No bones, no DNA, nothing. We weren't able to get anything on it. Whoever was doing that shipping didn't want anything to get out. They even torched their own people. Riggs and his boys found zilch. All we had was a probable place where the containers were shipped. Yemen."

"Yes," said Church slowly. "And isn't that interesting?"

Bug glanced at him and then turned to lean closer to the live feed of the task force, who were climbing into the backs of two nondescript delivery vans.

-4-

Dockside Warehouse
Baltimore, Maryland

There were thirty of us the next morning, everyone in full SWAT gear. Each unit was split into four-man teams: two guys with MP-5s, a point man with a Glock .40 and a ballistic shield, and one guy with a Remington 870 pump.

I was the shotgunner on our team. Adrenaline was pumping through my bloodstream like floodwaters after the New Orleans levees broke. It took a lot of willpower to impose a measure of calm over the jumping jitters. And I knew everyone else was in the same boat.

The "go" came down and the task force hit the warehouse hard and fast, coming in every door and window in the place. Flashbangs, snipers on the surrounding buildings, multiple entry points, and a whole lot of yelling. Domestic shock and awe, the idea being to startle and overpower so that everyone inside is too dazed and confused to offer violent resistance. Last thing anyone wanted was an OK Corral.

My team had the back door, the one that led out to a small boat dock. I had a Shok-Lok round chambered in the shotgun and I blew the steel deadbolt to powder. Then we went in yelling for everyone to freeze, to lay down their weapons.

Even if the bad guys don't speak English, there's no one alive who doesn't get the gist when SWAT waves guns, yells, and points at the floor. Usually, the bad guys drop their guns and do whatever they need to do not to earn a bullet in the brain pan.

This wasn't one of those times. They pulled guns and opened up on us. Suddenly, every-damn-body was pulling triggers.

It was the OK Corral, Baltimore edition.

I shot the first guy to draw on us, taking him with two to the body even as he opened up with a Tech-9. A round burned the air inches from my face. The only lucky part of a free-for-all shootout is that everyone is so caught up in not getting shot that they don't have time to aim. That's a little less true for SWAT, and the ratio of aim-to-hit improves once the shock of the moment wears off.

The unlucky part—and this is a real bitch—is that no matter how much you prepare for a shootout, you never really expect one. Most people have this moment—it feels like an hour but it's really a splintered part of a second—where they don't think or move or do anything the way they should. It's not called fatal hesitation for nothing, and in that fragment of a second, I saw two of our guys take hits. One was aimed and well placed and the other was a wild shot from the melee and it could have as easily been friendly fire as a bullet from a bad guy.

I wasn't caught in that moment. For whatever reason—martial arts, Ranger training, years or the street, or maybe I'm wired different—I don't hesitate. As soon as the game started, I was in my groove. I pivoted toward the guy who'd just shot one of mine and I took him off at the knees with two rounds from the shotgun. Take this important safety tip home, kids: Don't shoot at cops.

I ducked behind a big blue storage case that stood near the closest wall, and fired the Remington dry. Then I dropped it so I could pull my Glock. I know the .40 is standard but I've always found the .45 to be more persuasive.

A bad guy rose up behind a stack of file boxes and pointed a SIG Sauer at me in a very professional two-handed grip. I gave him a double-tap—one to the sternum to make him stand at attention and the next round through the forehead.

After that it was duck, scream, shoot, reload. Everyone doing the same damn dance.

A hail of bullets tore into the big blue case hanging loose, ripping its lock to steel splinters. The door swung open and a man staggered out. He wasn't armed so I didn't fire on him. Instead, I concentrated on the guy behind him who was tearing up the room with an assault rifle.

I put two in the shooter's chest. Then this other guy from the blue case comes crashing right into me. He was pale and sweaty, stank like raw sewage, and had a glazed bug-eyed stare. I thought, *drug addict*. He wasn't armed, so I kicked him hard and he staggered off, hit a wall, rebounded and lunged at one of my guys, and I swear to God the dope fiend tried to *bite* him. The SWAT guy butt-stroked him with his rifle stock and the sweaty asshole guy went down.

I began to turn to offer cover fire for my friends, but caught movement to my left and there that guy was again – the fruitcake with the bug eyes. His jaw hung askew and blood bubbled on his lips, but he didn't seem able to feel the pain he had to be in. I stepped back to avoid his lunge, but my back slammed hard into a file cabinet and the sweaty guy clamped his teeth on the forearm I put up to fend him off. He legit tried to tear a chunk out of me, but all he got was a mouthful of sleeve and Kevlar.

"Get off!" I screamed and gave him an overhand left that should have dropped him and everyone he was related to. But it only shook him loose. He dropped to a crouch and scuttled away like a cockroach, pushing past me to make for the back door. The firefight was still hot so I couldn't give chase, so I leaned out into the hall and parked two in his back, quick and easy.

He hit the deck and skidded five feet before he stopped, then he simply sagged against the floor and stopped moving. I spun back into the room and kept fighting.

Firing, taking cover where I could. Killing. Trying not to die.

God damn.

-5-

Department of Military Sciences
Temporary Field Office

Church munched a cookie as he watched the gun battle in the warehouse on the Baltimore docks. An older Black woman with beaded dreads and a dashiki with a Nigerian print sat next to him. She had her long fingers laced together over her generous stomach, each one glistening with a silver ring. Her nails were painted a lurid chartreuse.

"That boy put that man down while he was running away," said the woman.

"He did," agreed Church. "Do you object, Auntie?"

Aunt Sallie, the chief of operations for the Department of Military Sciences, merely shrugged.

"What would you have done differently?"

"Capped him sooner."

Church picked up a cookie and took a bite. He made no comment.

On the screen, Joe Ledger emerged from the conference room, clearly following the sound of a hot gunfight in the main warehouse. He spotted two task force officers taking fire from three hostiles who were shooting from a secure position behind a stack of heavy crates.

Bullets tore chunks from the paltry cover behind which the agents crouched, filling the air with a storm of jagged splinters.

Ledger came up on their seven o'clock, well out of their line of sight; he had his pistol in hand but to open

167

fire from that distance would have been suicide. Anyone could see that. He might get one or two but the other would turn and chop him up. There was no cover at all between Ledger and the hostiles, but he hugged the wall, running on cat feet, making no noise that could have been heard above the din of the gunfire.

When Ledger was ten feet out, he opened fire.

His first shot caught one of the hostiles in the back of the neck and the impact slammed him into the crates. As the other two turned, Ledger closed to zero distance and fired one more shot and the second hostile puddled down, but then the slide on Ledger's gun locked open. There was no time to change magazines. The third hostile instantly lunged at him, swinging his rifle barrel with desperate force. Ledger parried it with his pistol and then everything turned into a blur. Ledger had the pistol held out in front of him so it was obvious that he recognized the predicament of the empty magazine but he did not visibly react to it. His hands separated and—while he was still in full stride—he used the empty gun to check the swing of the hostile's rifle while simultaneously jabbing forward with his left hand, fingers folded in half and stiffened so that the secondary line of knuckles drove into the attacker's windpipe. Even as he did this, Ledger's left foot changed from a regular running step into a longer lunge and the tip of his combat boot crunched into the cartilage under the hostile's kneecap. A fraction of a second later, Ledger's gun hand came up and jabbed the exposed barrel of the pistol into the hostile's left eye socket. The attacker flew backward as if he'd been hit by a shotgun blast. Ledger completed his step and was smoothly reaching to his belt for a fresh magazine.

Suddenly, all three hostiles were down.

"No hesitation," mused Church. "Not even a twitch when his slide locked back."

Aunt Sallie looked sour and disapproving, but

Church saw one eyebrow raised. It was one her few 'tells'. He knew she was impressed, but the chances of her ever saying so were somewhere between slim and none.

They sat in silence, watching as the task force mopped up the last of the opposition.

-6-

Dockside Warehouse
Baltimore, Maryland

I stood to one side, my sidearm holstered, thumbs hooked into the side straps of my vest. It was a pose, a deliberate choice, because it was an affectation of calm that I hoped would trick my body from shooting more adrenaline into my bloodstream. There was already enough of it there to launch a telecom satellite into Earth orbit.

My ears throbbed from the gunfire. My fingers kept twitching, and my heart was doing an improvisational jazz drum solo. Sweat ran down inside my clothes.

The fight was over. Some of my team were getting first aid. A line of bad guys lay on the floor, wrists and ankles secured with flexicuffs. Fewer than half of them. The rest lay where they'd fallen, and crime scene guys were documenting everything and taking samples. I saw one tech placing little orange plastic evidence markers near every dropped weapon, spent cartridge, and pool of blood.

I've shot people before.

I've killed people in the line of duty before.

But this...

God damn.

I knew—absolutely *knew*—this was going to gouge a scar on the flesh of my soul. One that would always be with me.

My best friend, Rudy Sanchez, is a psychiatrist. Used to be *my* shrink, and now works for Baltimore PD. He has a saying: *Violence always leaves a mark.*

He is seldom wrong, and on this score, he is one hundred percent right. I felt that mark. That wound. I know that cops and former Army Rangers are all supposed to be tough as nails. And, yeah, on one level we are. But we're also human. Anyone who can walk away unscathed from a fight where they've left people dead should never be allowed to carry a gun. Sure, there are some dickheads who put on a uniform because they love the violence, crave the chance to kill. Those people should be screened, and counseled, and sent home to find a clue.

For warriors—those people who take to this line of work not for personal glory or to get wood by popping a cap in someone—this is not a moment to celebrate. Sure, these were bad guys. Yes, they started the fight. And no doubt they were planning very bad things that would hurt the innocent. I'm not at all arguing that this wasn't a righteous shoot.

No.

Warriors take up their sword and shield to protect the innocent. To do what civilians can't do for themselves. To get between harm and hurt.

Even so. This is taking lives. It's breaking that ultimate taboo. If you don't understand that, go look up how many soldiers have PTSD – diagnosed or not. Look up how many wind up on the streets because they are haunted by the ghosts they helped create. Check out the stats on veteran suicides.

All of us, all the warriors, know and *feel* each mark of violence self-inflicted by circumstance and choice of action, by duty and empathy for those who we protect. We are all marked. Every single one.

I bowed my head and felt a wave of unutterable

sadness sweep through me. And I hoped I would never again be called to end a life.

I prayed that was possible.

-7-

Department of Military Sciences
Temporary Field Office

Mr Church stood and stretched, listening to the symphony of cracks and pops after having sat for so long. Aunt Sallie got heavily her feet, sighing as if she were deflating.

"Well," she muttered, "that's an afternoon I'll never get back."

"You could always retire and spend your afternoons yelling at children to get off your front lawn," said Church. He glanced at the wall clock. "I thought you said you wanted to head back to the Hangar."

The Hangar was the headquarters of the DMS, built inside an actual decommissioned airport hangar at Floyd Bennett Field in Brooklyn.

"You trying to get rid of me?" she said.

He brushed a few crumbs from his tie. "I'm shocked you would think such a thing," he said mildly.

Auntie shot him an evil look, flipped a middle finger at him, and lumbered out.

Church, amused, watched her go. They had been friends and allies for a long time. He remembered how she looked the first time they'd met, during a Cold War op, in the days when he had done freelance assignments for Central Intelligence. Auntie had been lighter of spirit then, before age, diabetes, high blood pressure, and a body covered in scars from every conceivable kind of violence made her look older than her years. And she was old. Long past retirement age. He also knew that some of her grumpiness was jealousy because age touched him with a far lighter hand while pummeling her.

Church loved her, though. She was his sister in every important way. She was also a hero who would never get a medal for the things she'd done to keep the world on its tracks.

On the monitors, the images had changed from the post-action cleanup to the façade of St Michael's Hospital in Baltimore, where both the wounded and the dead had been taken. A small detail of DMS agents accompanied the ambulances, hoping to get bedside intel from the injured hostiles.

He yawned again, this time making his jaw creak. The plate of cookies was now littered with crumbs and his tea pot stood empty. He needed a meal, a shower, and some sleep.

Before he could go find any of those comforts, the door opened again and a much younger and fitter woman came in. She wore a subdued black pants suit and teal blouse. Minimal makeup, and a hairstyle more conducive to field operations than office work. "There you are," she said. "Glad I caught you."

"Good afternoon, Major. Thought you were off-shift today."

Major Grace Courtland, late of Britain's SAS—and the first woman to serve in that elite group—was on semi-permanent attachment with the DMS. Before 911, Church had pitched the DMS to Congress and was shot down on the grounds that it was too expensive and—in the form it was presented—too free of bureaucratic red tape and congressional oversight. So, Church had taken his idea to London and sold it easily to the Brits, resulting in a covert rapid-response group called Barrier. Grace had been pulled from active SAS duty and seconded to Church to build that organization.

Then the planes hit the Towers and suddenly both the House and the Senate decided that cost-cutting had no place now that terrorism had left an unhealable scar on the American psyche. They begged Church to return to the States and gave him carte-blanche to build the Department of Military Sciences. Courtland came along as an advisor and senior aide, and once the DMS was up and running, opted to extend her relationship. To Church, she was a far younger Aunt Sallie from a different country. Now, she oversaw the training for all teams, and even led Alpha Team on special missions. She was smart, devious, dangerous, and possessed a fierce integrity.

"When am I ever off the clock?" she said with a smile. "Nor, might I add, are you?"

Church merely grunted.

"Besides, that forensics bloke you wanted to interview is still at St Michaels. Happy to go over with you."

"Ah," said Church. "I'd forgotten."

Jerry Spencer was a senior detective for Washington DC's Metropolitan Police Department. He was not officially a forensic technician, but his knowledge and powers of observation and extrapolation were known throughout American law enforcement. Although he was close to aging out of his job and was weeks away from retirement, Church thought he would be an excellent fit for the DMS as a field man who knew both investigatory practices and evidence collection. He was at St Michael's because he'd caught a round in the chest. His Kevlar vest had saved his life, but the round had cracked bone. The hospital was only a few blocks away from the temporary Baltimore office of the DMS.

Church wanted to let Courtland handle the interview so he could get some food and rest, but he nodded instead. "Very well. If we can recruit Spencer then it's worth the trip."

"Baker and Charlie Teams are both over there already," said Courtland. "They should be wrapping up the interviews with the other task force members."

"Anyone worth hiring away from their departments?" asked Church as he pulled on his suitcoat.

"One or two, perhaps," she said, shrugging.

"What about Detective Ledger from BPD?"

Courtland made a sour face. "Not him."

"Oh? Why not?"

She gave another shrug. "I watched some of the video from the task force bodycams."

"And...?"

"And Ledger seems like a hotshot." When Church said nothing, she added. "I had Bug pull up his data. Top marks for armed and unarmed combat, that was evident on the feeds, but his psych eval reads like a bloody horror story. Frankly, I'm amazed the local police ever let him pin on a badge."

Church did not comment, but one corner of his mouth curled up ever so slightly. He tapped his earbud for the comms channel shared with his personal aide, Sergeant Gus Dietrich. "Prep the car," he said.

Part Two
The War is the War

"Terror made me cruel."
Emily Bronte

-8-
Department of Military Sciences
Temporary Field Office

Staff Sergeant Gus Dietrich always drove as if he was fleeing a bank heist. It didn't matter where he was going, or why. The SUV lurched away from the curb and plunged into traffic, heedless of horns and screeching tires. Church had long since given up on trying to advise caution, so he and Courtland buckled up as soon as they were seated.

The car suited Dietrich's driving style. It was a black Escalade kitted out for combat, with an armored body, bullet-resistant windows, and plenty of weapons in locked cases in the back and hidden in exterior compartments that would spring open at the right touch. It was as formidable a vehicle as the Beast that carried POTUS around. Dietrich loved driving it, even though it was about as nimble as an Abrams tank.

Gus Dietrich was a burly bulldog of a man who served as a combination bodyguard, valet, and confidant for Mr Church. His face had a Winston Churchill hound-dog configuration, though without the jowls. He seldom allowed anyone else behind the wheel of any car carrying the Big Man.

Church and Courtland were in the back seat, with tactical computers open on their laps and earbuds in place. Courtland's second-in-command, Master Sergeant Mark Allenson, rode shotgun.

When the DMS was first formed, Dietrich ran Alpha Team which, true to its name, was the first field group for the new organization. Dietrich's courage and innovative thinking in a crisis appealed to Church, who then promoted the sergeant. Courtland herself took over Alpha, and it was she who scouted, hired, and trained Allenson, grooming him to take over as team leader – a switch that was likely to unfold very soon.

The DMS was a family in every useful and meaningful way, but closer than most families because the trust was all earned in situations where every action mattered on deeply critical levels. There was liking, too, though Allenson was nearly as reserved as Courtland; whereas Dietrich was everybody's Dutch Uncle.

"Be there in ten minutes, Boss," he said.

"Just bloody well get us there alive," said Courtland under her voice.

"What's that, Major?" asked the sergeant.

"Nothing," she said.

Church glanced in the rearview mirror and saw Dietrich's little smile.

-9-

Mortuary Room B
St Charles Hospital
Baltimore, Maryland

"Doctor," said the nurse, "he moved."

Dr Chen was snapping nitrile gloves onto his hands while bending over to read the incident report associated with the bodies brought in from the police action on the docks.

"Hm...?" he murmured distractedly.

"Nerve reaction. It happens."

176

"No," said the nurse more sharply. "He's moving."

Chen sighed and straightened. "God, Maureen, how many autopsies have you assisted on? Fifty? Sixty? You *know* about post-mortem movement. Gas buildup, muscle contractions. You've seen it. Surely, you read about cadaveric spasms even in that shithole of a school you went to in Philly. Hell, there was that biker last week who…"

His words trailed off and he stood there, one finger still hooked into the wristband of his left glove. He stared, open-mouthed for a two-count.

The man on the table *was* moving.

He was twitching. Not locally, as rigor tightened tendons. Not gas causing the stomach to flutter. Nothing like that.

Nothing like that at all.

The EMTs had brought in a suspected terrorist. Javad Mustapha, according to the paperwork. Shot twice from close range, with both shots penetrating the upper torso, one on either side of the spine. The nurse had cut away nearly all of his clothes, setting them aside for police forensics. The exit wounds—huge and ragged—were visible on the victim's pectorals. Mortal wounds. Or, they should have been.

Yet, despite those wounds, the body was twitching visibly. Violently. Like a living person in the throes of a seizure.

"Jesus Christ," he gasped and then he was moving, rushing to the table, pushing past his nurse, bending over the man. "Dead at the scene my *ass*. Those goddamn EMTs have to be blind. This man is alive."

-10-

In Motion
Baltimore, Maryland

"We're getting close," said Dietrich. "Five minutes, with this traffic."

Church nodded. "Good." To Courtland he said, "Call in and get a status report from the team."

"On it," she said and tapped into the channel shared with Baker Team.

Dietrich kept weaving in and out of traffic. "When we get there, Boss, you want the front door…?"

"Side staff entrance," Church replied. "No need to raise any eyebrows."

"Sure thing. Nice and easy," said Dietrich as he dodged in and out of traffic as if evading gunfire. Beside him, Allenson had a death grip on the grab-handle and kept pumping the footwell floor as if there was an emergency brake pedal installed.

"Jesus *Christ*," he breathed.

Dietrich turned away from the traffic and gave him a big, shit-eating grin. "Something wrong, buddy?"

Allenson bit down on the things he wanted to say and stamped harder on his imaginary brake.

-11-

Mortuary Room B
St Charles Hospital

The twitches were getting more intense, causing legs and arms to lift and thump against the stainless-steel table.

"Maureen, help me restrain him. Gently… *gently*."

Together they applied firm but careful pressure, pushing the injured man flat onto the table. Mustapha's eyes were closed, but his mouth moved, jaws opening and closing sluggishly as if he was dreaming of chewing food.

"Doctor," cautioned Maureen, "this man is a... *terrorist*." She both leaned into that last word while also dropping her voice to a hush. "There are cops and federal agents upstairs. Shouldn't we call them?"

Chen, bent over with his palms still pressed to try and calm the spasms, looked troubled. Then he nodded. "Make the call. And get someone from the ER down here with a gurney. Tell them we need a surgical suite stat."

The nurse spun away and hurried to the wall phone.

Javad Mustapha stopped twitching and now lay nearly still. The shudders slowed to trembles then stopped. Thin threads of spittle ran from the corners of his mouth, but the sputum was tinged with dark red. Darker than blood should be, and far too dark for blood mixed with saliva. That made Chen frown.

"I'm going to take his vitals," he said hesitantly. The truth was that he was comprehensively confused by this. There was that dark liquid oozing from the patient's mouth, yet the two gaping exit wounds on his chest were not bleeding. That made no sense.

And the man looked awful. His olive skin had taken on a gray-green hue, suggesting jaundice but not precisely so.

Although not often useful in the mortuary, there was a full emergency trolly with all the items necessary in the rare case of a living person brought down by accident. In Chen's long career, that had only happened once. He hurried over to get it and butted it up against the side of the table, then reached for gauze pads to pack the wounds. Even though they still were not bleeding.

"They're on their way," said Maureen, joining him with hesitation. "This is nuts."

"Someone made a very stupid mistake," muttered Chen. "Take his blood pressure."

Maureen switched on an electronic sphygmomanometer, wrapped the cuff around the victim's slack upper arm, and hit the button. She glanced at the doctor. "Maybe we'd better record this. Just, you know, in case..."

Her meaning was obvious and Chen nodded as he met her eyes. With a mistake this serious, and given the legal complications of the victim being a suspected terrorist, there would be a lot of scrutiny and a witch hunt to assign blame. Someone's head would roll.

Chen reached up and hit the record button. The doctor licked his lips and began recording, forcing himself to sound calm and speak clearly. He gave the date and time, his name and the nurse's, the hospital name—just in case the transcript was ever played in court—and basic details.

"We are taking vitals and administering basic first aid for a patient brought to the mortuary following a shooting incident. The patient is listed as Javad Mustapha. He is male and appears to be about thirty. He has two through-and-through gunshot wounds to the chest. He was brought in for autopsy but has begun to spasm in ways inconsistent with post-mortem cadaveric spasms. We have called the authorities, hospital security, and requested a gurney to take him to the ER. We have requested a surgical team and all necessary trauma specialists to attend. We are taking vitals now. Patient's skin is cold to the touch and dry. No obvious perspiration."

The man lay there, eyes closed, trembling like a sleeper having a bad dream.

"Doctor," said Maureen.

When he glanced at her, the nurse wore a quizzical expression that was half smile and half frown. "What's his BP?" asked Chen.

"BP is non-palp," said the nurse. "Zero over zero."

"Damn thing must be broken. Try again."

As she restarted the pressure cuff, Chen took a digital thermometer and placed the tip in Mustapha's ear. Then he, too, frowned. "This can't be right. Temperature is eighty-one point two."

He cut a worried look at the recorder. Then bent again and gently thumbed open the patient's eyelids.

"Pupils are... nonreactive."

Maureen stood there, shaking her head. "No blood pressure. Machine must be broken."

"Then get a manual cuff."

She dug one out of a trolly drawer and put it on. But after a few seconds she released it and let it hang.

"Doctor... BP is still zero over zero."

"That's impossible. He's *moving*."

Maureen dug her fingers into the man's wrist, then his throat. She shook her head and tried again at different spots. Then she clipped an oximeter on Mustapha's finger. Her face went slowly pale. "Doctor, I still can't find a pulse."

"Christ, let me do it," growled Chen, snatching a stethoscope from the trolly. "Not every damn device can be malfunctioning." But after placing the cup at a dozen places on the Mustapha's chest, he stared glassily for a moment. "Nurse, run an EKG."

She did so, quickly attaching the leads and switching on the device. The little electric pens drew a nearly straight line. Both doctor and nurse stopped moving. Stopped trying. They looked at each other and at Mustapha, whose fingers were slowly opening and closing, and whose jaws still worked as if he was chewing.

Then Chen remembered the recorder. "We are unable to get reliable vitals at this time," he said slowly and carefully. "Despite signs of active mobility, the patient has no blood pressure, no pulse, and no respiration. He—"

Chen's words died in his throat as Javad Mustapha's eyes snapped open. They were glassy and empty, and for a moment all he did was look straight up at the ceiling.

Then…

Those eyes turned slowly toward Doctor Chen.

Mustapha's lips curled back from teeth smeared with black blood.

The chest abruptly expanded as he drew in a deep breath. Despite the gunshot wounds that must have done terrible damage to the upper quadrants of both lungs. When Mustapha exhaled it came out as a moan.

Such a terrible moan.

Such a dreadful sound. Empty of everything except a deep and bottomless hunger. Maureen stepped back from the table. Chen stepped forward.

That was a mistake.

Javad Mustapha came off the table with shocking speed, hands reaching, grabbing, fingers entwining in Chen's lab coat. Pulling.

Pulling.

Toward those snapping jaws.

-12-

Lieutenant Frankie Miller—call sign Gekko—top-kick of Baker Team hurried down the hall, running to catch up with a nurse and orderly from the ER. His sergeant, Lisa O'Connor—Copperhead—ran with him.

"This is fucked," she breathed.

"No shit."

Kelly, the ER nurse, shot them an evil look over her shoulder, but the animus was a screen for her fear. Mistakes like this were never supposed to happen. Taking basic vitals was something even the damned janitor could do, let alone professional EMTs and the intake doctor. How the hell everyone could have mistaken a living victim, no matter how badly injured, for a corpse was beyond sense.

She was just glad she had not been on shift when this cluster-fuck occurred. Neil, the senior nurse, *was* on shift when the terrorists were brought in. The initials on the forms were all Neil's... and Dr Simchek. The nurse cared about Neil. She didn't like Simchek at all – he was an arrogant ass and bully.

Even so... this was insane.

Gekko was sweating bullets imagining how Mr Church and Major Courtland—let alone that fire-breathing dragon Aunt Sallie—were going to react to a fuckup on this scale. The DMS was designed to double- and triple-check everything. Mistakes on this level, given the stakes involved, were likely to result in Gekko manning a field station in one of the Dakotas. Or maybe the middle of the Atlantic ocean.

"Shit, shit, shit," he breathed as they ran.

Copperhead shot him a worried look but said nothing.

They reached the mortuary and all of them skidded to a stop.

The door was ajar.

More than that. Something kept it from closing. Something wet and red.

An arm.

And it wasn't attached to anything.

-13-

In Motion
St Charles Hospital

"This is... odd," said Courtland as she tapped on her earbud for the fifth time.

Without looking up from his laptop, Church asked, "What is?"

"I can't get Gekko on the comms." She grunted. "No

matter. He might be down in the basement, and the signal's likely to be wonky. I'll try Grasshopper."

She tapped into the channel for Gary Larkin, head of Charlie Team.

"Amazing to Grasshopper," she said, sending the call to their comms as well.

The Charlie Team leader answered at once. "Go for Grasshopper."

"Deacon and I are on our way. We'll be onsite in five. Have someone meet us at the staff entrance."

"Copy that, Amazing. We're dealing with a small glitch, but it's being handled."

Church, Allenson, and Dietrich all looked at Courtland.

"What *kind* of glitch?"

Because the comms channel was heavily encrypted, Grasshopper gave a frank report. "One of the hostiles dropped at the warehouse turns out *not* to be dead after all. Kind of freaky. Apparently, it scared the crap out of the morgue staff. Gekko and Copperhead went down to see what's what and drop a security blanket over the whole thing."

"Grasshopper, this is Deacon," said Church. He tapped some keys and the feed from the team leader's bodycam filled the laptop screen. It showed a view of part of the emergency room, with the usual controlled chaos unfolding. Nurses, orderlies, doctors, patients, police, and a few of the members of Baker and Charlie teams. "Which hostile are we talking about?"

"Javad Mustapha. He's the one that tried to bite that blond cop. Don't remember his name. The one who kicked so much ass."

"Joseph Edwin Ledger," said Church as he toggled around from one bodycam to the next until he found one that was directed at Grasshopper. The agent was medium height, with pale blond hair and a face vaguely reminiscent of the old actor Danny Kaye.

Courtland gave Church a puzzled look. "There must be an error. Mustapha was shot and killed. It was confirmed by the head of the task force and by the EMTs. He bled out on the floor. I saw the footage."

Grasshopper said, "I know, Amazing, but I guess everyone was wrong. It's the same man."

Church said, "Grasshopper, go check on this personally. There must be a paperwork error. Even if Mustapha survived the gunshots, the loss of blood was significant. Someone over there has made an error and I need you to put eyes on it."

"Roger that, Deacon," said Grasshopper. "The gurney should be up here any second now."

"Go find it," said Church. "Do it now."

"Copy that, Boss. I'm going to— Whoa. *What?*" Grasshopper turned to look at something off camera. His face went from slack surprise to an expression of confusion and then alarm. "Holy *fuck.*"

"Grasshopper, what's happening?" snapped Courtland. "Report."

"Taurus, Lockjaw, stop that man," Grasshopper said, his voice rising to a pitch filled with urgency and alarm. There was a confusion of mingled images, static, the rustle of clothing, and then the feed went dead. Church cycled through the other body cams to get a fresh signal.

"What the bloody hell?" demanded Courtland. "Is this some kind of interference? I can't even make out what I'm seeing."

"No," said Church tersely. "This feels more like panic."

"Panic over what? I'm not hearing any gunfire."

"No."

Courtland pressed her earbud to increase the volume, her face screwing up with annoyance. "Bloody hell, there's too much yelling."

Church gave her a sharp look. "Those aren't yells, Major."

185

"Then what are—?"

The image on the laptop screen was wild and indistinct, showing glimpses of clustered agents, flashes of black, gray, and red. Voices began to yell. To shout.

"I think they're screams."

"Screams?" Courtland almost smiled at the absurdity of that statement. Of course it wasn't screams. That was what her expression said. She even began to say it, but Church turned up the volume on the laptop. The sounds tore through the utter silence of the SUV. There was a cacophony of raised voices. There were some shouted orders. There were cries of shock. Of horror.

Of terror.

"What in the...?" began Allenson, but all the life leaked out of his voice.

"Grasshopper, report, damn it," Courtland growled. Then the team leader's voice came back on, rising from Church's laptop.

"No, no, that one, god damn it. *That* one," Grasshopper was yelling. "Oh no. No, no. Oh, Christ. No! Oh god..."

Something ran at Grasshopper, but it moved too fast to be clearly seen. It *looked* like a doctor in blue scrubs, but there was another color smeared over his clothes, his hands, and his face.

A startlingly bright red.

The doctor ran right at the agent who had been facing Grasshopper and then the bodycam tilted upward toward the doctor's face. To his wide, empty eyes and the gaping, snarling, bloody mouth.

Then the bodycam winked out, leaving only a stunning darkness.

"Gus," began Church, but Dietrich's foot was already kicking the pedal to the floor.

-14-

Staff Entrance
St Charles Hospital

"Lock it down," roared Grace Courtland into her comms. "Lock the hospital down. Priority One. Lock it all down. Do it right now."

Beside her, Church was on the line with Bug and Aunt Sallie, rapping out orders, trusting that his team knew their jobs and could rise to the height of this emergency.

In the front passenger seat, Master Sergeant Allenson was barking orders to Redman, the next in the Alpha Team chain of command. "Roll the team. I need everyone at the hospital five minutes ago. Don't talk, fucking *go*."

They all finished setting the wheels in motion and were signing off when Dietrich skidded and slewed the SUV to a smoking stop six feet from the hospital staff entrance.

All four doors flew open and they ran for the door. Both Allenson and Dietrich slapped the fenders to release hidden compartments which sprang open to reveal M4A1 carbines with extended magazines. Both men grabbed one, and shoved two mags each into their pockets. Then they whirled and ran to catch up with Church and Courtland. She had her Sig Sauer in her hands, but Church did not have a firearm.

The door had a simple keycard lock. Church began to reach for a master keycard, but Bug's voice in his ear said, "Got it."

The red light beside the keycard reader flashed to green and there was an audible *click*. Church reached for the door handle but Dietrich shouldered past him, took the handle, and jerked the door open as Allenson and Courtland provided cover. There was a short hallway inside and they ran along it, with Dietrich taking point.

187

Just as they reached the inner door, the keycard reader there also flashed green. Bug had clearly used the DMS super-intrusion computer system MindReader to hack into the security system there at St Michael's. For him, something like that was childishly easy.

Dietrich leaned into the hall and froze. Church, taller than him by many inches, looked over and past the sergeant.

"Clear," he said, and they all ran down at the hall as quickly as caution allowed.

"The hell is everyone?" muttered Dietrich.

Allenson looked stressed. "Not digging this at all."

They reached a T-junction and paused for a moment. The righthand hall led to a bank of elevators and a small waiting area near vending machines. A can of Canada Dry ginger ale lay on its side in a pool of fizzing liquid. Near it was a cell phone. That was all. No people. No other signs of conflict.

They turned left. That hall ran forty feet past doors for X-ray and CT-scans. The hall was empty and ended at a pair of big doors above which was the sign EMERGENCY.

On one of the doors was a red handprint, lines of crimson crawling down to the floor. Drops of it had formed a small puddle, and three shell casings glimmered in the gore.

"Shit," whispered Allenson.

Church touched his earbud. "Deacon to Baker Team."

No answer.

"Deacon to Charlie Team."

Silence.

The truth was the whole hospital seemed weirdly silent. The air seemed oddly still, as if the building itself held its breath.

"Whatever's going on, Boss," said Dietrich quietly, "this feels wrong. Really wrong. Not liking this shit one little bit."

"No," said Church. "Nor am I."

They moved forward, careful to make no sound as they approached the door. Church nodded at Dietrich to open it and just beyond they saw three things.

Three figures.

One was a woman. A nurse, pretty, terrified beyond the capacity to move. She cowered on the floor. Her clothes were covered with blood, but it was hard to tell if any of it was her own. Her eyes were wide and staring and shock clearly owned her.

Beyond her was a uniformed police officer laying backward over a gurney, his automatic dangling uselessly on the curled finger of an outstretched right hand. His body trembled and his legs jerked with involuntary spasms as his body tumbled through pain and into a terminal shock. Even as they watched, the shudders stopped and a last breath gurled wetly from a savaged throat.

And then they all saw a small crowd of people. They knelt in a haphazard circle around something none of them could identify. Something lumpy and red and disconnected. Now that they were inside the emergency room, they could hear sounds.

Soft noises.

Quiet but so very ugly.

Chewing.

Nearly inaudible noises of people completely entranced by what they were doing. Nurses. Doctors. EMTs. Police. And...

...DMS agents from both Baker and Charlie Teams.

All of them holding cupped hands to their mouths.

As...

...they...

...ate.

-15-

Emergency Room

There was blood everywhere. It defined the tableau, painting the reality of the moment in a thousand shades of red.

Blood.

Blood and death.

Grasshopper was there. He suddenly raised his head and stared down the hallway right into Swann's eyes. He raised his dripping mouth from the red horror from which he had torn meat.

His eyes were dark, the pupil expanded to nearly obscure the iris. The sclera had turned from white to a sickly green shot through with crimson veins. But there was no emotion in those eyes. Only awareness.

Only hunger.

If there was anything human left in the man, Church could not see it. Not in that slack face, dead eyes, or busy mouth.

All Church or any of his companions could see was horror.

All they saw were monsters.

They stood frozen to the spot, frozen into the moment. Helpless, lost in this new reality. This was something from late-night horror movies. This was unreal. Surreal. Impossible. And yet real.

Here.

Now.

Grace Courtland put a trembling hand to her mouth. "God..."

Dietrich and Allenson had their rifles up, but neither moved. Neither fired. The world had been twisted out of true and refashioned into some shape that matched nothing any of them had ever seen or could easily grasp.

Not even Church, who had seen many of the world's more awful horrors firsthand. He had witnessed wars and plagues. Had stood in the ashes of burned cities and inside the fetid buildings where people had been stored like cordwood for furnaces that belched out smoke day and night. He had walked ankle-deep in blood on countless battlefields and had knelt weeping in holding facilities where madmen decided slaughter was the most efficient way of disposing of trafficked people rather than let them testify. He had seen all of that and much, much more. To a degree, he had become inured to the pain, with necessary calluses forming over new wounds inflicted on his heart.

But he had never seen anything like this.

Not once.

"Dear God," he breathed.

Then there was a sound behind him. He turned first and saw the policeman who had been sprawled over the gurney struggling to sit up. Even then, Church hoped it was a sign the officer was still alive.

Hope is a fragile flame that is so easily extinguished.

The policeman's face was utterly slack. His eyes were open but there was nothing moving inside. No obvious thought, no reaction, not even an awareness of the pain he must feel given the dreadful severity of his wounds. As he stood, the pistol's trigger guard slipped from his finger and the gun clattered to the linoleum floor. In the silence, the noise was shockingly loud.

Courtland, Dietrich, and Allenson all turned to see what made the noise.

They saw.

Grace's face was gray with shock. Allenson's mouth kept trying to form words but failed every time. And Dietrich, for all of his mass and muscle and combat experience, had tears in his eyes.

There was another sound, and it came in response to

the noise of the gun falling. It was a soft sound, but not a comforting one. It was a moan.

It came from deep inside the throats of the people gathered for that grisly feast. A moan of need. A moan of desire that was too basic to carry even a trace of emotion.

A moan of a hunger that ran miles and miles deep.

And the dead policeman opened his mouth and the same cry of bottomless hunger came from his ruined throat.

Then all of the blood-spattered *things* lurched forward, hands thrust out, fingers clasping the air, mouths opening and closing as if in anticipation of breaking an aching fast with fresh meat.

"What the actual... fuck...?" breathed Allenson.

As if in answer, the bloody throng rushed at Church and his companions.

-16-

In Hell

"Boss...?" said Dietrich as he shifted to stand between Church and Courtland and the oncoming tide. The people—infected or insane—moved steadily but with an odd slowness. They staggered as if uncertain how to walk, and it all took on a dreamlike quality.

"Grasshopper...?" Allenson said. "Gary? What's going on, man?"

There was no trace of recognition in the eyes of Gary Larkin, head of Charlie Team. He still held a chunk of dripping flesh in his hands. His mouth glistened with red, and thick drops of blood spattered his chest.

"No, no, no," pleaded Allenson. "Don't do this, man. Let's not do this. Please. No."

Allenson begged his friend but nothing of Gary

Larkin seemed to live in that body. No flicker of understanding. No emotion except the hunger.

"Is this a bioweapon of some kind?" demanded Dietrich. "Christ, we shouldn't even be breathing this air."

"We don't know what it is," Courtland fired back.

"Everyone back," snapped Church. "Do it *now*."

They moved away from the crowd, guns swiveling from person to person. But no one dared fire. These were civilians and police. And people they knew. Friends and fellow soldiers.

Shambling toward the four shocked DMS operatives.

The cop was closing in behind, and Courtland raised her pistol, but Church pushed her arm aside as he moved to intercept the officer. He still held no weapons, but the Big Man moved forward without hesitation.

"Easy now," he said, hands raised, palms outward.

The officer reached for him, but Church evaded the grab. He circled sideways, looking for anything that would make sense of this. A dart stuck in the officer's neck, maybe loaded with some mind-altering chemical agent. A device attached to the man. *Anything*.

Church could see the wound more clearly and it jolted him. There were visible bite marks all around the ruin of the man's throat. The big arteries were ripped open and some of the tendons were bitten clear through, making the head sag to one side. As much as his logical mind wanted and even *needed* there to be a sane answer, reality had slipped more than a few notches.

This man could not be standing. Not with that level of obvious damage. Not with the carotid arteries and jugular vein torn completely open. That was simply not possible according to anything in medical science.

Yet this *was* happening.

He was a witness and therefore it could not be impossible. So, then, what *was* this?

193

Church had a mind like a computer – organized, rational, analytical. If this man was too badly injured to still be alive, the pragmatism of Occam's razor rose up to scream an alternative. The philosophy was steadfast in its theory construction and evaluation. Even the literary version espoused by Sherlock Holmes offered a straight truth that if one eliminated the impossible, whatever still remained must therefore be true.

The *impossible* was not that a living person could still move and act with that level of critical damage. No. That was a side-effect. It was imprecise. The impossible was that no one with such injuries could still *be* alive.

There was only one alternative to life.

Death.

A kind of living death.

Something—some unknown force—made Gary Larkin capable of walking. And the other people all showed clear evidence of wounds.

No, Church told himself. *Be precise*. Not merely wounds, but savage bites. Human bites.

They wore the bites that had killed them.

Killed. Them.

This flashed through his mind in a fragment of a second. In less time than it took Grasshopper to take a single step. And that analysis kept firing, accelerating as his need to understand pulled on every available resource.

They had spoken with members of Baker and Charlie teams seconds before entering the building. Gekko had gone to the mortuary to investigate a corpse that had seemingly awakened.

Javad Mustapha.

On the video of the warehouse hit, Mustapha had been hiding inside a large blue container. A box that Baker Team said was temperature controlled and locked from the outside, suggesting Mustapha was inside and trapped.

Or... stored?

Transported.

The interior temperature of the box was near zero. Cold storage. The way meat is kept.

The cop took another full step. Church was almost within grabbing range. The world around Church seemed to have slowed, though, as his mind raced far, far ahead.

Cold storage for what purpose?

To preserve. But preserve what? Not dead meat. Not really. Bug's research confirmed that Javad Mustapha was a known terrorist agent working with El Mujahid. If he was dead, why transport his body anywhere? If he was alive, why so low a temperature and why make it impossible for him to exit that container?

Why indeed?

It only made sense if Mustapha was a danger to his own team. To the terrorists in that warehouse who were working with El Mujahid.

"What do we do?" begged Allenson.

Church ignored the plea, needing to make sense of everything, needing another fragment of a second to understand in order to *know* what to do.

El Mujahid was a terrorist. He was smart, aggressive, ruthless, and determined. But he had no standing army, no fleet of ships, no missiles he could send across the ocean. Someone like him would understand the history of guerilla warfare, especially as it applied to the United States. After all, in centuries past when Europeans were still greatly outnumbered by the indigenous population, they found ways to even the odds, to level the playing field. The conquistadors had brought diseases with them and those germs killed many times more of the peoples living on coveted New World real estate than rifles, swords, or cannons did. The roster of those diseases tore through Church's brain like a roll-call in Hell. Smallpox, bubonic plague, chickenpox, cholera, the common cold, diphtheria, influenza, malaria, measles, scarlet fever, typhoid, typhus, and pertussis.

Once the incoming tsunami of settlers came on their wooden ships and some among them realized that the First Peoples had no natural defenses against such diseases, there was a determined and well-documented shift to using an early form of biological warfare. Blankets were an excellent medium for transferring diseases to the enemy, especially with the pretense of affable exchanges of goods. Millions of indigenous people in South, Central, and North America died.

El Mujahid would know this.

Blue boxes designed to keep contaminated vectors stable for transport was hardly a stretch of credulity. Detective Ledger had encountered one of those vectors in the form of Javad Mustapha. The man had tried to bite Ledger. Bite. Such an ugly and accurate term.

Ledger shot and killed Mustapha.

Mustapha was transported to the hospital. Maybe being in a zippered body bag slowed the process of his...

His what? What was the word? Resuscitation? Resurrection? Reanimation?

Then in the mortuary, Javad Mustapha must have awakened and completed the task for which El Mujahid had him sent.

The chain of logic click-click-clicked along, faster and faster as the stalled time struggled to catch up.

Church spoke aloud the horrified thought that bloomed like a mushroom cloud in his mind.

"If this gets out..."

And then the dead policeman grabbed him with bloody hands.

Part Three
Heaven Falls

"Here is no choice but either do or die."
William Wallace

-17-

St Charles Hospital

Time snapped back with all the shock and force of a bullet.

There was no process of getting up to speed. On one side of a fragile second, Church was immobile, caught inside his need to understand the crisis unfolding around him; and on the other side of that moment, he was in motion.

He slapped at the hands that held him, doing it with such force that the impact half-turned the dead officer, ruining what little balance the man—the *thing*—had, causing it to slam into the gurney. The wheels were not locked and it rolled away, sending the officer crashing to the floor.

Before the cop was down, Church wheeled, grabbing for Courtland and Allenson, pulling them back and pushing them behind him. Dietrich had stepped toward the oncoming things, but Church darted forward, grabbed him by the shoulder, spun him, and shoved him back the way they'd come.

"Move," he roared.

Even then they were slow to react. They stared, either at the fallen officer who was now trying to rise, or at the crowd of bloody people. Church took Allenson, who was closest, wheeled him around and slapped him across the mouth.

"Move," he yelled.

That blow—the shock of it, more so than the pain—snapped Allenson out of his trance. Courtland seemed jerked awake, too, as if she had also been slapped. She blinked and gave Church a desperate stare.

"Fall back," ordered Church, and he herded them away. They stumbled clumsily at first, but then their training kicked in and they ran. Dietrich, too, though he kept looking over his shoulder. The door to the ER had swung shut behind them.

"What's happening?" gasped Courtland as they reached the T-junction again.

"Infection," Church said quickly. "It shuts down higher function in favor of a drive to attack."

"Attack *why?*" demanded Allenson. "They're trying to bite us."

"Serum transfer infection. The bites spread it."

"You can't know that."

"I *don't* know it," Church said sharply. "But that is how we're going to react until we know more."

"They were *eating* people," Allenson said, one hand pressed to his bruised cheek, and his voice cracked and broke all the way down to something close to a child's. Confused and frightened. The weight of what he was saying threatened to break him.

"Yes," said Church with brutal coldness, "and we need to stop the spread of this. Master Sergeant Allenson, are you going to help us?"

That snapped Allenson into a different mindset. He stiffened, looked wildly around for a moment, then dragged in a deep chestful of air, held it, nodded to himself, and let it out. Then he nodded again, this time at Church.

"Say it, son," Church told him.

Allenson licked his lips. "Yes, sir. Whatever you need."

Church looked at Courtland. "Major?"

"Whatever we need to do."

Dietrich nodded too. "Anything," he said. "Everything. Just... tell us what we need to do."

"Good. Keep your comms on." Church looked around to orient himself. He pointed to a glowing EXIT sign. "Those are fire stairs. The mortuary is one level down. We need eyes on what's happening there."

"On it," said Allenson.

"Gus, go with him."

"What do we do if there are more of those... things?"

"There are no established rules of engagement for something like this. By any legal or medical definition, I think these people are dead."

"How, though?" begged Dietrich.

"A disease of some unknown kind. Possibly a parasite. We don't know and don't have time for that kind of analysis. We need to do whatever it takes to keep this contained to the hospital. Find any exterior doors you can and lock them."

"Lock the doors?" echoed Courtland. "But what about *un*infected?"

Church's face was as bleak as a winter landscape. "Listen to me, all of you. There was one infected person brought here. Javad Mustapha. He woke up how long ago?"

Dietrich glanced at his watch. "Jesus. It's not even four minutes."

Everyone looked at their watches, all of them hoping that count was way off, but Dietrich was right.

"In four minutes not only has Mustapha spread it to whomever was in the mortuary, but those people have become vectors."

"That's... that's too fast," stammered Allenson.

"Check my math," said Church. Allenson merely stood there shaking his head. Not in denial but in horrified acceptance.

"I'll contact Dr Hu at the Warehouse. He may have something useful to tell us. But he also needs to be informed in case whatever this is becomes airborne."

"Why?" asked Allenson, but then he got it. They all did. If it was airborne, then all of them were potential vectors.

"What happens if we get bitten?" asked Dietrich.

"If that happens and you feel yourself slipping. About to pass out or maybe changing how you think—" Church began, but Courtland cut him off.

"Meaning if we start getting hungry?" From her expression, it looked like the question caused her physical pain.

"Yes. If that happens, then lock yourself into a room and give your status and location to the TOC. If rescue is possible, then you will be exfiltrated."

That was a sobering thought.

"What do we do if those things trap us?" asked Dietrich. "They're people. I mean… it's not just Gary, but I saw Billy Walker and Jen Dellacourt back there. I know them."

"You *knew* them, Gus," said Church. "Mourn them later, but take whatever action you need to take to avoid contamination. Now go."

The two soldiers shared a brief look, searching for connection, for understanding. Finding enough of it. They wheeled and ran.

-18-

When Church was alone with Courtland, he stepped close. "Are you here with me, Grace?"

She swallowed and nodded. "This is…" But she left the rest unsaid because it could not be quantified.

Behind them, hands began pounding on the closed

door to the ER. It was strange, though. They were not sharp blows. Heavy, yes, but soft. Unemphatic, delivered with slack hands. That added another layer of unreality to what was happening.

Church tapped into the TOC channel.

"Go for Auntie," came the reply. "What the hell's happening there, Deacon? The team channel seems to be picking up some weird interference."

"Get Dr Hu on the channel and I'll explain."

A moment later, Hu, the head of the DMS medical division, said, "What's the crisis this time?" His tone was lazy, amused.

Church told them. He gave them everything that had happened and shared his own assessment of the situation.

When he was done, Hu responded at once with, "No. Whether this is viral or bacteriological, nothing spreads that fast. Not in nature. Not unless it's some kind of neurotoxin, but that wouldn't rewire brain chemistry to do what you're describing."

"Doctor, if we survive this, I would be quite happy to put you in a room with one of these infected. Afterward, if you're able, you can tell me what is and is not possible. Until then, you will accept that what I have described *is* happening." Hu's reply was a sullen grunt.

"What can we do to help, Deacon?" asked Aunt Sallie.

"I need this hospital locked down. Do whatever it takes to make that happen."

"On it," she said, and Bug's voice echoed her promise.

"Second, send the rest of Alpha Team to my location. They are not to enter the hospital until Major Courtland or I give that order. Bug can finesse the jurisdictional knots, but I need this to happen right now. Confirm."

They promised to make that happen, too.

"What else can we do?" asked Auntie.

"Tell Alpha to bring as much CX-127 as they can pack into their vehicles in under five minutes."

There was a profound moment of silence, then Auntie said, "Repeat that order?"

"I want all the CX-127 they can bring. Do it."

And he disconnected.

Grace Courtland stood there staring at him in total horror.

"It may come to that, Grace," Church said gently. "The rate of infection is already greater than anything I have ever seen. Faster than anything I've even heard of."

"Yes, but it's only a handful of people. Surely, we can find some way of containing them."

Church shook his head. "You are not thinking this through, Major."

"What am I missing?"

"Where are the rest of the staff members?" he asked. "Where is the rest of Baker Team? Of Charlie? Why are they not scrambling through this building to establish that containment? Why is this hospital so quiet?"

"But... but it's only been a few minutes."

"Yes," said Church. "There is some hope that on the upper floors there are pockets of resistance, but we've heard no gunfire. We've heard no screams."

She stared at him with wide, glassy eyes.

"The math is against us. Javad Mustapha was in the mortuary with a nurse and a doctor and Gekko. One vector infecting three through bites, or some mix of that. Then four vectors go out of the mortuary. If each one bites just one person, and the speed of infection and — to use the only word that seems to fit — *transformation* is only a few seconds, then the spread is exponential. Four bite four, then eight bite eight, and so on. And we're only talking about the lowest possible number of enforced infections." He pointed to the closed ER door. "There were doctors, nurses, hospital staff, civilians, police, and our own people in there. Four minutes since the first known bite."

She shook her head, not wanting to hear this but unable to detach from his truth.

"Now," said Church, "consider the reaction. Consider *our* reactions. We froze. All of us. Even me, and I have been through more outbreaks than you. We froze because of the absurdity of it, the unreality of it. What's happening in this hospital is beyond our conscious acceptance. It doesn't matter how many monster movies anyone has seen, no one would expect something like this to ever be real. Even our best agents would hesitate. They would not fire on the infected because that's not what civilized people do, and certainly not in the first moments of an inexplicable and unexpected outbreak. Tell me, Grace, what would you do if Allenson or Redman or any of Alpha Team came toward you bleeding from a wound, especially in a non-combat situation? Would you draw and fire or try to offer aid?"

It wasn't a question requiring an answer. A tear broke and rolled down her cheek.

"No one is ever ready for something like this," said Church gently, "because there never *has* been something like this. Not in my experience, and I have been in this game for a very long time."

Church walked toward the ER door. The pounding was clearly louder now, as if more and more limp fists were pounding on it. He stopped and half turned to her. "We don't even know *how* to stop these people. These *vectors*. Grasshopper's throat was torn out, his veins and arteries ripped open, and yet he was ambulatory. He came after me. What aspect of our training has prepared us for that?"

He shook his head and came back to her. "This is not the war we have been trained to fight," he said. "If this disease, or whatever it turns out to be, escapes from St Charles, what will stop it? Maybe the Atlantic and Pacific can stop it. But what if the infection spills over into airports or ships? A thing like this—unless I am reading this entirely wrong—isn't just a threat to us here in this building. If this gets out, Major, then I do not know that it *can* be stopped."

"I—" began Grace, and then they heard two new sounds. From the stairwell, punching into the hall. The roar of gunfire and the shrill shrieks of people in absolute terror.

-19-

They rushed to the stairwell.

Courtland cut Church a look. "You don't have a gun."

He shook his head, opened his suitcoat and withdrew a slender device about the thickness and length of a robusto grande cigar. With a supple snap of his wrist he shook the device toward the floor and an inner core telescoped out, tripling its length with two inner layers of diminishing girth. Church held it up and thumbed a small button. A bright arc of electricity crackled at the end.

She nodded, and he opened the door.

Grace Courtland went through the door with her gun in a two-hand grip, the barrel tracking with her sightline. The screams were intense, but they did not funnel up from the basement level. Not Dietrich or Allenson.

Inside the fire tower they could better hear the gunshot signatures. Church mouthed, *nine-millimeter. Police?* A raised eyebrow made it an open question. Grace nodded and began to climb. Church followed, watching how her professionalism rolled over her fear and made her make all the right choices. She crouched and turned at the landing, aiming up toward the second-floor landing, clearing it, and moving upward.

He followed.

The shots were coming from the third floor and with each step they took, the sound of violence and terror increased.

They found a body on the third landing. A doctor, his clothes torn and soaked with blood, his arms and face marked with half a dozen bites. The name CHAN was stenciled in white thread on his blue scrubs. They recognized him as the pathologist from Gekko's bodycam footage. The doctor who had been about to perform an autopsy on Mustapha.

While Courtland kept her pistol aimed at the door on the landing, Church quickly examined the body. It was entirely slack. Inert.

Very dead.

He saw several places on the man's body and limbs where bullets had torn into him. From the resulting drip pattern of blood, it was obvious Chan had been upright and ambulatory after his infection. And yet now he was clearly dead. The screams and shots were constant on the other side of the door, but Church lingered, knowing there was something important to learn here. After reanimation, what had then stopped this man?

Then Church brushed aside the doctor's thick black hair and saw another bullet hole two inches above his left eye.

"Grace," he said softly. She turned and looked at the wound he indicated. "This is what killed him."

She almost smiled. "Head shots tend to work on anyone or anything."

"Let's learn from that."

He rose and got ready with his shock rod in one hand and the doorknob in the other. She nodded and set herself. Church opened the door and went into the hall, shifting right. Grace followed and went left, flattening out on the wall as they took in the scene.

It was a bloodbath.

There were two people at the end of the hall. Both of them wore DMS combat uniforms. A man and a woman. The man was tall and olive-skinned with a buzz cut and a black beard. Youssef Bayesh, a corporal belonging to Charlie Team. The woman was Lilah Daniels, one of the most junior members of Baker Team. Bayesh had a rifle and Daniels a pair of Glock 17s.

Several people, most of them wearing hospital johnnies, huddled behind them.

Between them and where Church and Courtland crouched were at least forty of the infected. Patients, several nurses, and a man in street clothes – likely there to visit a sick friend or relative.

The infected moved with that same relentless slowness, shuffling forward into the hail of bullets. The civilians screamed and screamed. Bayesh and Daniels fired.

Grace held her gun in one hand, cupped the other around her mouth and yelled at the top of her voice. "Baker, Baker, Baker!"

The gunfire drowned it out.

She tried again with, "Charlie, Charlie, Charlie! Friendlies on the field."

Bayesh stopped shooting for a moment as he squinted past the oncoming infected.

"*Major!*" he cried.

The rearmost of the walking dead turned toward the newcomers. With no change of their empty expressions, five of them began lumbering toward the stairwell. Grace scuttled against the wall so that her line of fire did not endanger the surviving team members. She opened up, hitting the two closest creatures center mass.

"The head, Major," bellowed Church. "Aim for the head."

She corrected and kept firing. Her next two rounds punched into one infected, but they went through the mid-face, off center. The impact made the creature judder but not fall. Her third shot took them just below the hairline. A bloody piece of scalp slapped the wall and the infected's legs lost what little control they had. The creature fell, and two others tripped over it.

Courtland steadied her gun with both hands and kept firing. This time she hit the forehead of a middle-aged woman, and the monster simply dropped to the floor.

Bayesh and Daniels opened with renewed vigor, and though her shots were accurate, Bayesh was on the edge of panic and wasted nearly a whole magazine shooting into the mass of infected. Only one of them dropped and stayed down while the others pressed forward.

Courtland edged along the wall until she reached a doorway of a patient room, and she paused there, using it as cover because Bayesh's rounds were flying everywhere. One bullet hit the metal doorframe and the major flinched back from metal splinters. When she rose and continued firing, the slide locked back after two rounds. She cursed and ducked back to swap magazines.

Church took that opportunity to move. He ducked low and ran at an angle that kept the main mass of infected between him and the DMS shooters. The two who had fallen over their comrade were halfway to their feet and they lunged at Church, clawing at him with pale fingers. He jabbed one on the throat with the shock-rod and it immediately began thrashing as its central nervous system went into overload. The second grabbed Church's cuff, but the Big Man kicked the creature in the forehead with such force that there was an audible *crack*.

Then he was moving again, passing the doorway where Courtland was emerging with a fresh magazine in place. She fell in behind him, careful to stay out of Bayesh's wild line of fire.

They quickly established a rhythm. Church moved much faster than Courtland expected a man of his size could do. He plowed a path through the infected, who—alerted by movement and the sound of Courtland's gun—were turning to focus on closer targets. He used the shock rod over and over again, but its battery was not meant for a prolonged battle, and soon he switched to using it as a club. His hand was a blur and he hit everything he swung at. Courtland was amazed because this was the first time she had seen her boss in combat.

She was a skilled fighter. Superb, efficient, and deadly. But Church was in an entirely different class. He wasted no movement. A deep knowledge of martial arts was evident in the strikes and kicks he used, but none were fancy. They were not pretty or ostentatious, but merely the most practical in each separate instance. He broke legs and broke necks. He knocked them aside, spinning them in a way that made them easy targets for Courtland.

There were so many of the dead, though. And more came out of patients' rooms. Courtland could not tell if the noise of battle drew them away from dreadful feasts or if they were just now reanimating. There were a lot of them though, and soon the hall was choked with the things. They completely blocked her view of Bayesh and Daniels, and when their gunfire faltered and fell away, she feared they were being overwhelmed.

The moaning, soft as it was, came from so many throats that it eventually drowned out the screams from the huddled survivors.

Or so she thought.

Then she saw a figure stagger toward Church, grabbing him from behind.

It was Lilah Daniels.

And she was a monster.

That broke Courtland's heart.

Church whirled to face his new attacker, and though he did not pause in shock, Courtland saw recognition and then grief carve lines into Church's face. He stepped into her pull. He no longer had his shock rod and instead took her chin in one palm and a handful of her hair in the other. He made it quick and then Daniels was falling, her neck loose and her newborn moans stilled forever.

Then Church was backpedaling, moving away from the milling creatures. Courtland put a foot up on a plastic chair outside of one of the rooms and looked over the heads of the crowd. Bayesh was gone. Dead or fled, she never did know. Near the back of the crowd were the people the two DMS agents had tried to save.

Tried.

Courtland wanted to weep and cave and fall into the well of her grief. But then a voice spoke in her ear.

"Alpha on deck," called Sergeant Redman.

A hand reached out of nowhere and caught her under the armpit. Church. He pulled her violently forward and half pushed, half dragged her toward the stairwell.

"Time to go," he snapped.

"Alpha is here and—"

"I know." He shoved her into the stairwell. Then he turned and looked down the hall, which was filled now with the walking and the fallen, and all of them dead in one awful way or another.

She saw the slump of his shoulders as he accepted the reality of it all with terrible acceptance. Pain was written into every line of his face.

"We lost," he said brokenly. "The hospital is lost."

He turned toward her and Courtland saw something she never imagined she *could* see on Mr Church's face.

Tears.

"You wanted to know why I asked that Alpha bring the CX-127?" he said in a voice filled with all the bitterness in the world. "You tell me why."

They fled down the stairs, both of them staggering under the weight of an unbearable defeat.

209

They stood outside beneath gathering clouds.

The day had grown old and crumbled to nothing as the clouds thickened to purple-black fists. Thunder rumbled in the southwest.

There were police barricades everywhere. Red and blue lights slashed back and forth with relentless vigor while all of the gathered thousands merely stood in shocked silence.

Watching St Charles burn.

Watching the hospital writhe inside a tumult of angry orange and yellow flames.

Watching as the place died, taking with it the infected. Burning them to ash, erasing the knowledge of what each person in the place had become. It was a secret the watching crowd would never know.

Or so Grace Courtland hoped.

She had a blanket draped around her shoulders, but it offered no real comfort.

Mark Allenson and Gus Dietrich sat together on a curb. Redman and the rest of Alpha Team sat in their cars.

Mr Church stood between the commissioner of police and the mayor. All three men were grim-faced and silent. The two officials had to know what Church's official federal rank was, because there had been deference in their manner despite the shock.

She wondered if Church told them what he had done.

She had aided and abetted, as had Dietrich, Redman, and Allenson. As all of Alpha Team had. Hurrying to place the cannisters of CX-127 at every entrance, in every stairwell, in the elevator shafts. Everywhere they could work without being overwhelmed by the hundreds of infected.

There was no way to know if there had been any uninfected anywhere inside. Probably not, given the speed of the spread and the aggression of the vectors. But she didn't know. None of them knew.

And that thought would haunt her. She had no doubt. And the burden of it would be something each of them would carry to their personal Golgotha when that time came.

Before he triggered the detonators, Courtland had begged Church to reconsider. She almost drew her weapon to stop him.

Church had turned and come to stand very close to her, and held out his hand. "Give me your sidearm, Major."

After a long few seconds, she did. It was loaded and there was a round in the chamber. Church eased back the receiver to verify that. Then he stood, weighing the pistol in one hand and holding the trigger device in the other.

"Major," he said softly, "tell me what other option is left to us."

She said nothing. He waited her out, giving her time. When she did not speak, Church nodded. A sad, small nod.

"A very long time ago," he said, "I found myself in a moment like this. In a situation close enough to this to have forced me to make a decision I did not want to make. I am not a madman. I am not heartless. But..."

"But what?" she demanded.

"But I am a monster," said Mr Church. "I know that I am."

"What does that even mean?" The mockery and anger in her voice tasted like hatred on her tongue.

"It means that when faced with such a terrible choice, I *could* choose. When there are no good choices then the only rational answer is to make the choice that is less horrible. Less... cruel."

"And this is the less cruel choice?"

"Yes," he said. "And you know it is."

"Bullshit. Allenson and Dietrich found Javad Mustapha. He was trapped inside the mortuary. Someone closed the door and he couldn't get out. They tied him up and brought him out so Dr Hu can dissect him and study him and do all his Frankenstein shit with him. And you dare stand there and tell me that saving him and letting all these people burn is the right choice?"

"It is the only choice."

"I can't accept that."

"Yes," he said, "you can. You will. Otherwise, you'd have shot me to stop what I am about to do."

He held out the gun. "You still can. Take the gun. It's yours. It's the one you used to kill some of the infected inside. Take it and shoot me and then explain to whoever survives what will come that yours was the better choice. If there *is* anyone left."

His hand was rock steady as he held the pistol handle toward her.

She took the gun.

She pointed it at him. At his heart.

He showed her the trigger device.

"That time long ago, I told someone that I would burn down heaven itself to stop the spread of that disease. I meant it. And that plague is nothing compared to this. That would have wiped out most of Europe. This one will kill the world."

She looked up into his eyes. They were hard to see through the tinted lenses of the glasses he wore, but she saw enough to see his hurt. And his resolve.

"Nature could not have made what we saw in there," said Church. "Someone made this. Someone dreamed it up and designed it. Built it. And sent it here. Stopping this is a single step in a march to war. And we are at war, Major. We need to go to war to stop the people behind this. You are one of the finest soldiers I have ever known, which means you know that we have to take up our swords and shields and go to war."

212

She pressed the barrel against the center of his chest. "Please," she begged.

"I will burn down heaven itself to stop this bioweapon," said Church. "If God exists and if I have a soul, then I know what penalties I will have to pay. I have many, *many* marks against that soul. But the war is the war. It won't stop for me, and it will not stop for you. And so, yes, I will push this button. That is what I am willing to do."

He leaned his body against the cold barrel of the Sig Sauer.

"Tell me, Grace... what are you willing to do—even at the cost of your soul—to save eight billion people?"

Grace Courtland was crying now. Weeping openly. Sobs racked her body but she still held the pistol steady.

Church nodded. Tears ran down his cheeks and fell onto his bloodstained tie.

He pushed the button.

-20-

Joe Ledger and Grace Courtland
The Warehouse
DMS Baltimore Field Office

I sat with Grace in my little bedroom in the newly commissioned office on a wharf by the harbor.

A bottle of very bad bourbon and eleven empty bottles of very good beer stood around us like tombstones.

Her story about what happened in St Charles was done, but her tears were not. Nor were mine.

She lifted her bottle and I picked up my glass. There was one good sip left in each. The last of what we had to share. We were both drunk. And we were both crying.

We touched glasses.

"To heaven's ashes," she said.

I took a steadying breath and then we nodded.

We drank.

Over the last few weeks, we both spent time recovering from injuries sustained in the war. Not just Mr Church's war, but the war we all shared. El Mujahid was dead. So was the crazy witch Amirah who had cooked up the Seif al Din pathogen in her lab. So were all of the people infected with it. All dead.

Along with Allenson and Redman and a lot of others.

Victims of the war. Maybe our comrades were in Heaven. Or Valhalla. Or wherever. We—Grace and I—survived. Being deserving was never part of it. Ask Church, he'll tell you.

The battle was won. That bioweapon was done.

But the war was still raging. Here and there. The war was the war, and it was always the war.

It was raining again in Baltimore. As it had rained that night at St Charles. I hadn't been there then, but I went there as Grace told me the story. Thunder boomed and the force of it punched the roof and the walls and echoed in all the empty chambers of our broken hearts.

THE RED PHONE

Dylan Demasi

His life was tied to a telephone.

So were the lives of about 5,419 others.

The muted TV flickered with a local news broadcast. A field reporter stood shaking in front of a collapsed security fence, barbed wire sprawled across the road. Mascara streaked her cheeks. The brunette. Will always figured she was headed for a national network.

In the chaos behind her, red and blue lights flashed across patrol cars, officers with guns drawn, aimed toward a gate or guard booth.

The focus shifted. The reporter glanced back as something caught the cameraperson's eye.

A distorted figure charged the cops. Fast. Erratic. Movements all wrong.

Muzzle flashes flared then vanished as the camera view followed the reporter who dropped for cover.

All of it played in silence, like an old movie. Volume wasn't allowed. Sound might interfere, even for a second, with the call that defined his entire purpose.

And then it rang.

The red phone shattered the silence.

Will's hand was on the receiver in half a second, cold plastic pressed to his ear. Just under expected response time.

He repeated the code he'd memorized and recited every shift.

Rewritten weekly.

Delivered Mondays.

Then shredded.

Then burned.

"Bravo. Lima. Alpha. Charlie. Kilo. Sierra. Kilo. Yankee."

A pause. Then, the voice on the line gave one final order and something close to a sentiment.

"Yes, sir."

Will placed the red phone back in its cradle. Without hesitation, he picked up the green-painted one beside it. "Black Sky is a go. Sunset Ride to follow," he said, urgent but clear.

He waited.

A single word came back, rough and low from the smoker's voice just three stories down and one room over.

Then the green phone returned to its cradle, never to be touched again.

Will's hands flew to the keyboard. The coordinates flashed. Numbers that had been seared into his brain, too crucial to trust to just memory. A glance at the county map on the whiteboard confirmed it. The grid, the square, everything aligned.

A switch flicked. Somewhere else, a small bulb came to life.

He shifted to the weather terminal. Wind, temp, and precipitation. All sent with a keystroke. Another switch hit.

Will stood, staring out the wide watchtower window. Below, the clearing stretched empty except for the dark, monstrous mound at its center.

PFC Morales and PFC Lee were already on the move. Boots crunching over dirt, they pulled free the ground spikes from around the boxy mass. Geared up in dark, matte CVC helmets, they were indistinguishable – just two smooth domes with dangling cords, nodding in silent sync.

With well-practiced ease, they tore away the foliage-covered netting. The special-model artillery rocket system emerged, mounted to the back of a rugged M1140 flatbed. Its battle-hardened face stared forward like a welder's mask dipped in olive drab.

Will watched them slip into their roles, preparing the launcher to wake from its slumber. Sgt Carter appeared in a blur, climbing into the cab the moment the door was free. He was always first. Crew Chief. The one who answered the sister to the green phone. The only one still assigned to the post from its earliest days. Geared up like the rest but carrying a weight that only came from decades of desert boredom punctuated by nights of bullet hell.

The others followed him into the armored vehicle's operations bay. Will couldn't see the interior from the tower, but he knew it by heart.

Two blinking yellow lights on the console meant the intel had come through. A piece of tape beneath them reading '*Mother's Permission*' in Lee's jagged handwriting.

Morales would be handling the headings. Lee, the elevation. Carter reviewing the mission printouts like scripture.

They'd seal the cabin. Engage the air system. Triple-check everything.

Some things, you just can't check enough.

Twenty seconds. That's all it took. From the moment they helped the truck shed its disguise to the hydraulics groaning as the back end tilted skyward. The launcher module rotated a few degrees, locking into place.

The radio crackled from atop a dented filing cabinet full of old ranger logbooks. Will answered with a brief acknowledgment, listening as Carter's voice—steady and final—confirmed settings, status, and readiness.

Civilians would call it overkill. They called it necessity.

He said the fateful words one last time. "Black Sky is a go."

The afternoon was ripped apart by a deep, rattling thunderclap from the launcher. The truck and surrounding forest vanished into an ocean of smoke, the trees shuddering, the air left on edge.

He scanned the clearing for signs of the crew or the machine. Pointless. He knew they were fine.

Training overruled concern. He turned west.

His free hand found the binoculars, always within reach for this exact moment, and directed them to the valley below.

An arc sliced through the overcast sky, zeroing in on a pale block in the distance.

One blink and the block vanished, consumed by a flash that swallowed the horizon.

A lightning strike from hell.

A blinding fireball clawed upward as a low, rolling roar came back up the mountain like a predator's growl, reminding them of the fury they had unleashed.

Thirty-two miles away, the five-hundred-pound warhead had found its soulmate.

The Plant Germplasm Inspection Station in Davisville, WA, had been erased from Earth.

The burning in his lungs tore through his locked focus, and with a sharp gasp, he finally remembered to breathe.

Pulling his eyes from the optics brought comfort. The view confirmed the real distance, restoring the emotional disconnect he needed.

That was the job.

At least, that's what the psych eval claimed before plucking them from their units. Lee and Morales from the 17th Field Artillery Brigade right there in Washington. Carter and Will from the 75th at Fort Sill.

The mix-and-match team made no sense, but when did a government plan ever?

He held down the PTT button on the radio, his eyes flicking to the TV.

The silent film was over, replaced by the harsh glow of emergency broadcast color bars.

His voice delivered a simple, cold status update on the target. With that, the tools of sight and sound were put away. He moved around the tower's top square, flipping off every switch from computer to surge protector before heading to the stairs at the room's center.

'All Personnel are Required to Sign In and Out.' The clipboard dangled from the top railing, tethered by a short chain.

Will grabbed it, part habit, part drilled-in protocol.

SPC Will Powell – Thursday – 4:05 PM.

A sharp checkmark in the Signing Out box. The clipboard still swayed as the sound of his boots echoed down the metal stairs.

Descending the winding steps, Will realized he'd never touched the red phone until today, not once in his two years and three months. Not even during drills, just in case the real call came.

His life had revolved around something that lasted less than thirty seconds.

Will stepped out the exit and crossed the gravel, past picnic tables, and toward the main lodge. It still wore the skin of a ranger station – weathered wood siding, green metal roof, and an antenna jutting skyward. The fire tower sealed the disguise.

Inside, the quarters doubled as an ops center, a wide-open room with bunks and computer stations. Down the hall, a kitchen, bathroom, and armory.

He went straight to his cot, pulled out a black footlocker, and shed the NPS outfit of gray shirt and green pants.

Clandestine cover was pointless now.

He suited up in his real uniform: combat boots, fatigues, tactical vest, and helmet. Will pulled his dog tags free from under the collar and glanced at the park service badge in the locker before shutting it away.

Now, finally, he felt like a soldier again.

The door slammed open.

Private First Class Ricardo Morales. The youngest of the crew, still catching his breath even when things were calm. He moved like he was bracing for an aftershock that hadn't yet hit.

Private First Class Randall Lee followed close behind, grinning like he'd just won a game instead of launched a missile. The kind of soldier who whistled through firing drills. Two years older than Morales and twice as reckless.

Sergeant First Class Carter walked in last, voice gravel-thick and short as ever. "Pack it up. Fast." Crew Chief. Only ever Carter or Sarge. If he'd ever had a full name, no one alive knew it. His beard was always well-trimmed but carried the smell of smoke, be it tobacco, burn pits, or maybe war itself.

Duffels were dragged from under bunks as the weight in the air finally caught up to them.

Will moved to the armory, grabbing the approved evac loadout: four pistols, two rifles, comms, and a light stack of mags. He laid them out on the central table, every move well-rehearsed. By the time he looked back, the firepower rush had drained from their eyes. Now, they were just soldiers, trying to forget what they'd done by focusing on what was next.

Lee had, of course, already swapped his helmet for that damn cowboy hat. It grated on Will, but not enough to waste a second on it.

A ten-year-old Tacoma waited, always parked facing a getaway. Dark-gray, dinged-up, and streaked with dried mud, it was the perfect choice for blending in with the area. Just another truck on grocery runs and bar nights, though its real purpose was clear: drive away, no looking back.

They tossed their duffels into the bed, scanning the area for anything out of place. Carter's and Will's hands rested on their M17s, while Morales and Lee gripped their short-barreled M4s. Their brigade's motto in mind like a joke: *Miles away or millimeters, artillery hits its mark.*

Carter climbed into the driver's seat, his claim on the truck unquestioned. Will took shotgun, Morales and Lee in back.

"Sarah didn't work today, right?" Morales asked as the locks clicked shut.

No one answered. Saying anything would only make it worse.

Sarah was a cashier at the grocery store, a block from the Inspection Station, well inside the blast radius. She sang country songs on karaoke nights at their usual bar.

They all liked her.

But Morales *liked* her.

"No," Morales said to his reflection in the window. "She didn't have shifts on days starting with T... I'm pretty sure."

Carter shifted into gear, and the truck rumbled down the dirt road.

The trees closed in, thickening with each bend. As the main road neared, Carter took the turns harder, pushing their pace.

There was no need for logistical talk. Codes might change but the mission never did. Evac point, radio check-in, pickup ETA. They all knew the steps. No words wasted.

Lee cleared his throat, stalling to find the courage to express a fear started by his seatmate. "Hey, Will... they confirmed to you that it was in fact an outbr—"

The sergeant yanked the wheel.

The Tacoma skidded hard around the last bend.

THUD.

A sickening, meaty impact slammed into the grille. An orange blur flew backward, crashing with a lifeless bounce into the dirt yards away.

"Shit!" Carter slammed the brakes. Tires locked, dirt and gravel spraying wide.

Will caught himself on the dash, his other hand already on his sidearm.

The backseat doors burst open in unison.

Boots hit the ground.

Rifles raised.

As the two soldiers regrouped at the front of the truck, those remaining inside scanned the mirrors. Sides. Rear. Nothing. Just the engine's low idle echoing off the trees.

Lee's eyes, half-hidden beneath the brim of his hat, glanced at the front of the vehicle. "You tagged something alright, Sarge. Got blood on the grille."

He and Morales stepped forward, approaching the crumpled figure in the road. Limbs bent at unnatural angles.

It wasn't moving. Not anymore.

"I know those boots..." Lee muttered, eyeing the yellow outdoor pair now speckled with blood. He raised his voice just enough for the others to hear. "Pretty sure that's Frank Maurice. Asshole with the hunting cabin up the road."

Morales froze a step away, brain struggling to register what he was seeing. His mouth hung open, rifle wavering.

Lee didn't stop. He moved up beside the body, gun lowering slightly as he stared down.

Carter watched through the windshield, foot poised on the gas.

Will's mind raced. "Frank Maur... Sarge, isn't he the shift supervisor at the Inspection Station?"

Lee's head snapped back, his face vaporized in an explosion of bone, teeth, and tissue.

His body staggered, boots scraping against gravel, a gurgling noise escaping from him. He collapsed backward into a twitching heap of flesh that didn't know it was dead yet.

His cowboy hat landed softly beside him.

Smoke curled into the air from the end of Frank Maurice's left arm… or what used to be one. Not a limb anymore. The flesh was stretched too thin, tendons and veins pulsing as they tried to wrap around something metallic.

The assumed-corpse sat up, a blood-soaked orange hunting vest clinging to its frame, eye sockets sealed with melting flesh while its peeled-back lips revealed a skeletal grin.

Bullets tore through the infected Frank, ripping into his chest and kicking up dirt behind him. Morales stumbled back, still pulling the trigger in a panic, each shot fired without aim or thought.

Will popped out of the passenger side, pistol drawn, and calmly went for a headshot.

"Get in the truck!" Carter yelled to Morales, who was backing himself into the woods.

Someone's bullet remade one of Frank's eye holes as he slowly rose to his feet. The wound brought his left arm back to life.

They could all see it clearer now.

The front half of a hunting rifle had replaced his forearm, half covered by sinewed flesh. Even his clothes—from boots to vest—were being consumed and changed into some ungodly fusion of skin and fashion.

The rifle barrel pointed at Will the moment his last shot went wide.

He dove behind the open truck door as the .308 round smashed through the window just above his head.

Little cubes of glass fell onto him as Carter revved the engine. Will crawled in and pulled the door shut just as Morales hopped in the back seat.

They all looked forward as Frank's wounds filled with raw, red tissue; fresh pink skin stretched over it in unnatural patches. He was no longer recognizable as human.

His legs trembled, moving in sharp, jerking steps. Each one punctuated by the wet crack of shifting bone.

The rifle arm leveled, aiming straight at the Tacoma.

"Fucking go!" Morales shouted.

Carter stomped the gas. The truck lurched forward, gravel spraying as the tires clawed for traction.

The grotesque thing fired.

A round punched through the windshield, spider-webbing the glass, missing all three passengers by inches.

Then the bumper hit. Hard.

The impact snapped Frank backward with a sickening crunch. A squishy, grinding of bone and metal filled the air as the truck rolled over the infected thing, crushing the remains beneath a half-ton of steel and rubber.

Carter didn't stop. He knew they couldn't. Knew they shouldn't.

"What about Lee?" Morales asked, breathless in the backseat, eyes fixed forward, trying not to look back.

"What about him?" Will replied coldly. It sounded like a question, but it was the only answer Morales would ever get.

Ten seconds later, the truck skidded to a stop.

They'd reached the iron gate marked: *PRIVATE PROPERTY.*

"Will," Sarge said with no urgency, just quiet command. They were the only ones still holding it together.

Will jumped out, ran to the gate, and pulled the key from his vest. He jammed it into the padlock, turned until it clicked, and tossed it aside. One hard push and the gate swung open under its own weight.

They turned onto the paved freedom of I-4, and the watchtower shrank behind them until it was a memory that could be denied.

"W-what happened to him?" Morales' voice cracked, breath struggling. "Was that what we were supposed to stop?" His hands shook, clutching his rifle like a security blanket he wished to hide under. "So how the hell did it get up here? We did our job... right?"

Morales' chest rose and fell in sharp bursts, eyes starting to fill up. "We fired. We dropped it. We wiped half that town off the map!" One hand left the barrel to claw at his scalp. "Oh god... we killed all of them. For nothing."

Will dropped the empty magazine to the footwell. Pulled a fresh one out of his pocket, loading it with a sharp click of frustration. He racked the slide, trying to ignore the realities being brought up as Carter decided to shut down the breakdown in the backseat.

"Our mission was to terminate the source of an outbreak incident," Sarge said. "Cleaning it up is someone else's job. We don't know what that was, we don't know why that was, and frankly, we don't need to know. We get to the LZ, meet our ride, and let them take us to wherever base camp is. We debrief and get reassigned. Any other focus is a waste of energy. Get it together, soldier."

The Sergeant's eyes stayed locked on the road, voice steady. The conversation was over.

Will sat back, heart exhausted from trying to deal with the past hour. "We did what we were supposed to," he said, quieter, with a fading confidence.

The next few miles passed in silence as the sun started to disappear behind the mountain.

Through the growing shadows, a battered green sign emerged, announcing their destination was within reach.

Sarge eased off the gas, letting the Tacoma crawl forward.

A utility truck lay jackknifed across both lanes, crashed into a telephone pole. Its shattered windshield and dangling door revealed an empty driver's seat, while the aerial lift stood half-raised, its bucket suspended in the air. Glass, debris, and fluid streaked the pavement, trailing to the other side of the road.

The yellow warning lights pulsed above the cab, their rhythm now a grim warning.

"Accident or blockade?" asked Will, his SIG in the process of leaving its holster as he scanned the scene.

The top of the pole was a smoking mess of broken wood and snapped cables. Night dropped like a curtain, as if the darkness conspired against them.

"I don't plan on investigating either way," Carter said, switching on the headlights. "Morales, rifle up. We're going around."

Morales swallowed the prayer lingering on his tongue. He slid to the right, shouldering his weapon and angling it out the window. Fear kept him moving as much as it kept his boot tapping.

The truck crept left, crossing the solid lines into the oncoming lanes. Will joined the defense, steadying his pistol out the window, bracing for whatever waited on the other side of the crash.

Tires crunched over pieces of metal and loosened rock as they edged around the utility truck. Knuckles white on all three of them.

"Does it smell like burning plastic to you," whispered Carter, leaning forward over the wheel to look deeper into the dark.

Morales glanced at his Sergeant, but Will kept his position.

Then the sky screamed.

A thick electrical wire whipped down from above, crashing onto the hood with a violent hiss. White-hot arcs of energy clawed across the metal, leaping toward the windshield in jagged bursts. The Tacoma shuddered, its lights flickering wildly before the dashboard went dark.

Carter slammed on the brakes instinctively as his hands went up to protect himself from the blinding sparks.

The sudden stop jolted Will, his handgun tumbling down the side of the passenger door to clatter to the pavement. He looked at his empty hand with disbelief and self-criticism.

An enraged shriek tore through the night.

Will and Morales both snapped their heads up.

From the bucket of the aerial lift, a shape rose.

The flashing lights caught glimpses of a body crammed with hand tools. Pliers twisted through the forearm, a wrench buried deep in the side, cable strippers fused into a sixth finger. A scorched clamp meter with a cracked display was slowly being pulled into the chest by fleshy tendrils. Another shriek, louder this time, came from its warped, offset jaw. The cracked shell of a hard hat still clung to its skull, revealing glimpses of bone between the breaks.

Its body spasmed again, shrieking. The soldiers didn't move. Too shaken to think tactically. None of them considered there might be another.

The cable on the hood was whipped away into the shadows behind the crashed vehicle. Carter put his hands down just in time to see it coming back. Fast.

The windshield exploded inward.

The thick, blackened cable moved like a viper out to get him, shattering glass in a spray of shards. The interior now a blur of sparks and sharp debris. Will ducked as Morales threw his arm up. Carter took the windshield fragments to the face.

And then the second one stepped out of the shadows. The owner of the sparking cable.

It was a hulking mass, six and a half feet of twisted flesh, fabric, and wiring. Shreds of an orange utility jacket embedded in its skin like a grotesque patchwork. Its face a bloody crater, crushed inward and regenerating in all the wrong ways.

But the real horror was the large, cylindrical transformer fused to its back. Attached was a thick, coiled power line that weaved through muscle and bone, snaking down its arm like a parasitic vine that exited the palm and dragged behind, the end still spitting sparks.

The cable snapped forward with a crack. Sparks ignited the night as it slammed into the truck's hood, leaving a deep dent.

Even bloodied with broken glass, Carter didn't hesitate. "Out! Now!"

He threw his shoulder into the driver's side door, boots hitting the asphalt as he drew his pistol in a single, fluid motion.

Will and Morales scrambled out the other side, Will cursing as he fumbled for the dropped sidearm. He found it just as the first infected worker from the bucket crashed down in front of him. Will registered the bad tactical luck immediately. One monster to each flank. Carter was pinned on the left side of the Tacoma with the cable-whip brute, the transformer fused to its spine powering the attack. Meanwhile, he and Morales were stuck with the tool-pierced screamer.

The cable lashed again, ripping the driver's side mirror clean off.

Carter fired twice, center mass. The rounds hit with dull, wet thuds, like slamming into thick mud.

The lineman surged forward. Too fast for something that should've been dead.

Carter didn't flinch. "Come on, then," he growled, bracing for a fight.

He didn't just shoot; he moved. Ducking and weaving as the live wire whipped around him, always inches from frying him to a crisp. His pistol barked with each step, rounds tearing through flesh and insulation.

The grim master of the electrical vine slowed as the sergeant circled, hammering it from every angle.

Click.

The slide locked back.

No time for a reload as his attacker reared its arm back. Carter slammed his shoulder into it, driving the creature against the dead Tacoma. He brought the butt of his empty gun down hard on its head. Once. Twice. A sliver of hope; maybe a few more blows could crack its skull wide open.

Until the cable twitched.

Carter didn't even see it move until it was coiled around his throat.

He gasped, dropping his gun to claw at the cable, the damaged wire searing into his skin as the open end fired arcs of blue energy into his neck.

"Sarge!" Will shouted over the gunfire he and Morales poured into the second utility nightmare.

The electrical lineman yanked the cable back, lifting Carter clean off his feet.

Sarge hit the ground hard, rolling through debris until he stopped, barely moving. Smoke curled from blackened burns on his throat.

The monster stepped over to Carter's head, raised its burned, flesh-wrapped boot...

And brought it down.

Will didn't need to see it. The sound was enough. The sick, wet crunch of bone giving way. Carter was gone.

Morales let his rifle drop to his side, stunned. "He's dead... Oh God, he's—"

Will grabbed the kid's vest and yanked Morales back to reality. "Stay with me!" he ordered, pointing at the remaining threat. "The joints. Shoot 'em!"

He shoved Morales back and snapped into a textbook stance, two hands on the grip, feet solid.

The pistol cracked off clean, controlled shots.

Moments later, Morales joined in, his rifle thundering in fast, rhythmic bursts.

Both kneecaps exploded. The lineman collapsed, the display fused to its chest flickering as it measured the current running through its own body. It writhed on the asphalt, trying to drag itself forward.

They scrambled behind the Tacoma.

Will's mind raced, flipping through every scrap of training, every battle manual.

Then his eyes locked on inspiration by the name of 'R. Lee'.

Will reached into the truck bed and pulled a duffle bag close. He tore it open, digging with dying hope.

Then broke into a smile.

Two M76 frag grenades. Leave it to the rule-breaking son of a bitch cowboy to bring home some deadly souvenirs.

Will tossed one to Morales, who caught it, hands trembling. With a nod to take the right side, the remains of the squad split.

In the middle of the road, the cable-wielding lineman pressed its boot deeper into Carter's remains. Flesh slithered into the caved-in skull, spreading its infection.

Will exhaled. "Sorry, Sarge."

They pulled the pins.

Two grenades arched through the air.

Will barely heard the first blast before diving into the dirt trench on the side of the road, it came with echoes of shattered glass and rocked suspension.

The closer, second explosion followed with a concussive roar that ripped through the night, sending debris, charred flesh, and smoke raining down.

Neither wanted to think of what exactly was landing on their shoulders.

Will opened his eyes, arms still shielding his head, and saw Morales a foot away doing the same.

They climbed back onto the I-4, brushing off dust and debris and meat as metal groaned around them from two wrecked vehicles settling after being dragged through hell.

Morales panted and spoke with surprise. "We won."

Will stared at the wreckage and let his ammo hit the ground, he pulled out his last mag. "No." He exhaled. "We walk."

☣ ☣ ☣

Easton Four Corners lived up to its name, a crossroads of the multilane I-4 and Shady Knoll Road, which was more dirt path than pavement, frequented mostly by trucks with anti-tax bumper stickers. Each corner held a single building: a gas station/general store stubbornly clinging to its decaying 1950s design, a rustic deli, and two small houses for the shop owners. Most days, the mountain town's stillness felt quaint. That evening, it was nerve-wracking.

Only the gas station had power. Its retro neon sign buzzed above the pumps, defiantly proclaiming *Prunier's Market – OPEN*.

The other corners sat in unnatural darkness, save for one car idling in a driveway, its headlights cutting through the gloom. Will wondered if the utility monsters they'd left in pieces had been through here.

The soldiers walked side by side down the middle of the road. Morales had his bag slung across his back, rifle raised, flashlight attachment glowing. Will kept his SIG drawn, his other hand gripping the AN/PRC-148 tactical radio he'd ripped from their abandoned squad truck. No personal items. Nothing to slow him down.

"Can't we make the call now?" asked Morales as they passed through the car's headlights. With its trunk open, luggage waited beside it, but no sign of their owners.

"No. The determined zone remains the same. We take a right on Shady and go up a ways to the parking lot of the abandoned resort build. Wide-open lot for proper landing and clear ground visibility."

Morales shook his head with desperate frustration at being told something he already knew. "Or we could call *here* and get picked up *here*. The intersection is good enough for an LZ."

"Those aren't our orde—"

Their souls jumped at the harsh wooden rattle of a screen door. A distorted shadow scraped at the blue home's entrance, then vanished as Morales snapped his light and aim toward it. Seconds passed, enough to decide that whatever it was, if it hadn't attacked yet, it wasn't going to. They exhaled—

The door exploded into splinters. A dark blur lunged out, clearing the porch steps in one bound, and landing on all fours. Aggression dripped in green-black saliva.

The German shepherd stepped into the beam of the rifle light, now a fused abomination of fur and metal. Its spiked collar had sunken into a pulsing neck, steel studs erupting through raw, infected flesh. Patches of fur gave way to unnatural, bubbling skin.

A rusted chain dangled from its collar, wrapping around a front leg before snaking up its back, absorbed into flesh and forming a grotesque, exposed steel spine.

Its mouth split too far, stretched back unnaturally, and held together by wriggling, fur-covered tendrils.

Morales fired. The rifle spat brass and fury but the hound moved with uncanny speed, dodging left, right, always one step closer.

Will holstered his weapon, slapped Morales's shoulder, and broke into a sprint. "Run!"

Will's boots pounded the pavement as a warped howl came from behind them. Morales threw off his duffle bag at the sound to gain more speed and catch up.

The light glowing from the market's front door called like a savior as Will jumped the curb. He sprinted past the pumps as he heard a burst of fire. Will didn't stop to look; he didn't dare. Survival first. He hit the door and wrenched it open, turning just in time to see Morales hit the ground. His spent rifle skidded across the asphalt with harsh abandon.

Will figured the kid's boot must have caught the raised edge of the pump island while focused on firing one last, desperate shot. He watched Morales finish sliding hard across the concrete, the back of his tactical vest scraping against it.

Air and sense ripped from him, Morales shook the daze from his head, hand grasping blindly for his carbine but it was nowhere near.

A growl snapped Morales back. He sat up just in time to see the horror in mid-air.

Will's hand froze on his holster, fear of hitting Morales locking his muscles. Just for a second. But a second was too long.

The infected hellhound slammed into the fallen soldier, driving him hard into the pavement.

Morales clawed for his sidearm, fingers brushing the grip...

The creature's extended jaw, lined with jagged teeth, tore into his neck. Morales screamed, the sound frighteningly raw, but it was cut short by a wet, choking gurgle. The dog pulsed unnaturally, its body twisting like something half-formed. Its paws pinned Morales' arms, starting to merge with the fabric of his army green sleeves. Its jaw clamped down again.

The struggling stopped.

Will shuddered and stepped softly backward until he was inside. He gently shut the door. With a click, the lock turned into place.

Outside, the dog chewed and tore tendons, which

were now starting to mix into the mutating skin around its mouth.

Will kept backing away, breathing hard. Aside from the store's buzzing fluorescents, all he could hear was his heartbeat pounding.

He was alone now.

No more unit. No more secret mission. Just a desperate, by-the-books soldier, a pistol nearing uselessness, and a radio to far-away angels.

All against a devouring night.

☣ ☣ ☣

The stench of sugar and rot hit him before he saw it.

To his left, at the end of the snack aisle, a slushie machine gurgled weakly with red and blue syrup swirling in lazy circles.

Fused into the machine was a body, violently missing its legs. A teenager, or what used to be. His torso had melted into the plastic shell, flesh stretched tight like a skin-toned casing.

One arm dangled, fingers becoming one with the dispenser lever, releasing a slow, sticky stream of cherry slush that mingled with blood on the linoleum below.

The kid's face was twisted in a silent scream. Will's stomach turned.

Morales was right; Will needed to get the hell out of here.

He backed up through a swinging door into a narrow hallway lined with closed doors. He raised the radio, fingers aching; he'd been gripping it so tightly the buttons had left deep imprints in his hand.

The screen lit with a dim amber glow. The presented digits changed with the push of a few buttons until they reached the right combination for an open line.

His pulse raced, but his voice came steady. Calm.

Controlled. The voice they trained into him. "Echo-Actual, this is Rootwatch-Twelve. Request immediate EVAC, priority one. Be advised, not at designated LZ. Current position is a civilian gas station, Prunier's Market, Easton Four Corners, unknown grid. Situation critical, hostiles in the vicinity. Confirm Copy."

His finger left the speak button. His eyes stayed on the swinging door, wondering if the front windows were bullet-resistant and, even if so, was that strong enough to stop the monster shepherd.

A burst of static cut through, followed by a calm, detached voice that offered no comfort. "Rootwatch-Twelve, this is Echo-Actual. Solid copy on your EVAC request. Coordinates confirmed. ETA fifteen mikes. Signal with light for visual. Radio confirm LZ secure. Over."

Will's hand shot to a vest pocket. Chemlights. Still there, all three of them. The plan had been daylight evac; Morales and Lee were carrying the smoke. With them gone and night already settled in, he silently thanked God for the standard gear loadout.

He set the timer on his watch, clipped the radio to his belt, and scanned for a way to the roof.

Three doors in the hallway. Not counting the back exit. He hoped it wouldn't come to that.

Sidearm drawn, he moved to the first door.

Storeroom. Cramped aisles and boxed inventory. He decided to save that for last.

The next door had a gold plate: Manager's Office.

Worth a shot.

He gripped the knob, finger tightening on the trigger.

Will burst through the door, gun raised, but a sudden sting came faster than his eyes could register the threat.

A flash of silver bit deep with pain. His gun clattered to the floor. A yelp escaped his lips as he stumbled back, clutching his bleeding hand.

A woman lunged forward from the shadows, her chest heaving, eyes wide and wild. Something sharp gleamed in her hands, the tip stained dark.

Will's instincts kicked in. He caught her wrist mid-swing, the blade stopping inches from his neck. The metal trembled, not with rage, but raw panic.

It was just scissors. Held normally. No fusion. No mutation.

"Stop!" he ordered, straining against her. "I'm not one of them!"

She twisted, trying to break free but he held firm. With a shove, he sent her stumbling into a desk. Papers and framed photos scattered across the floor.

The woman kept the improvised office weapon raised, ready but unconfident. Not infection, just fear.

"Stay back!" she snapped, eyes darting over him, searching for signs of immediate horror. "Are you turning?"

Will looked at the wound on the back of his shooting hand, catching his breath. "I'm military. Not infected. Just cut."

The woman's eyes flicked to the red dripping to the floor. Her expression of suspicion softened, but only a little. "Prove it," she whispered.

Will leaned against the doorframe, cradling his bleeding hand. "That's not gonna be easy exactly," he said, voice low and steady, glancing at the pistol on the floor, then back to her. "But all my parts are where they're supposed to be. My gear's still gear. Nothing's... fused."

He nodded to his uniform, dirt-stained with glass shards in the sleeve but looking legitimate. "I'm with a unit or... I was. We were en route to respond to the outbreak in Davisville."

She hesitated. Her breath slowed. The scissors lowered a few inches. "This started in town?"

Will gave a single nod.

"I was just visiting my brother. He owns the deli... I was helping out for a few days."

Her eyes drifted past him, distant, clearly watching the memory unfold. "Two guys came in around early afternoon. Sweating, shaking. Their clothes were stuck to them like their skin didn't want to let go. One collapsed. We called an ambulance, but... no one picked up."

Will knew why.

"They attacked him." Her voice cracked. "The phone lines were dead. My cell too. No police. No help. My brother..." She shook her head. "He didn't last long. I ran."

Will swallowed hard, the weight of the story closing the distance of that disconnect he held to so tightly. He knew what had happened. Standard containment. Cut the lines, jam the signals, and seal the town while the infection was dealt with.

"I'm sorry," he said, the words offending his conscience.

She blinked hard, pushing the memory down. The scissors dropped to her side.

Will studied her. Tired, shaking, just a soccer mom with streaks of gray in her tied-back hair, wrapped in a stained apron that read Easton Corner Deli in faded print.

Only the artillery unit was cleared for evac.

He started crafting the lie, already hating it. He'd go get help. That's what he'd say.

"You can come out now, Brooke."

The words stopped Will cold.

From behind the desk, a small face appeared – pale, wide-eyed, cheeks streaked with dried tears. A girl, maybe ten. She clutched a screwdriver tight to her chest, her shirt printed with a kitten batting at a jack-o'-lantern.

The air shifted. Something in Will cracked; his heart shed the last piece still clinging to protocol.

Fuck orders.

"A helicopter's coming," he said, straightening. "I'll get you both out."

☣ ☣ ☣

Door number three was the winner. Supply closet with a ladder headed up.

The roof hatch flipped open and slammed down with a heavy bang.

A wrapped hand rose first, pistol ready as Will climbed up just enough to scan the roof. Under the neon glow of the gas station sign, the flat surface looked clear.

With some effort, Sarah and her daughter followed. Will kicked the hatch shut behind them and led the way to the center. The roof was cracked and aged with years of soggy, northwestern weather, the faint buzz of the large sign humming through the night.

He checked his watch. ETA: Two minutes.

Reaching into one of his vest pouches, Will pulled out three chemlight sticks. He kept one and handed the other two to Sarah and Brooke, who was tightly wrapped in the arms of her mother.

"When you see the chopper," Will said, trying to present himself with no worries, "crack these and wave 'em high. It'll help the pilot spot us."

Sarah nodded, though her hands trembled. Brooke simply clutched hers, eyes to the ground.

"What happened? In town?" Sarah asked, voice low.

Will hesitated, scanning the eastern sky for white taillights. "Outbreak. Something bad. Might've started at the plant inspection station, but…" He shook his head. "It was destroyed early this afternoon."

Sarah frowned. "That wouldn't have mattered. Most of the workers, hell, half the town, were probably already gone by then."

Will blinked. "What?"

"It's October twelfth," she said, like it explained everything. "First day of deer season. A lot of locals skip work or leave early. My brother was going on about it this morning."

Will just stared. Then, he laughed; a short, bitter sound with no joy in it. "Millions of dollars. Full force of the government. Plans, drills, contingencies," he said with growing venom. "And not one general, politician, or agency director thought to factor in fucking deer season."

He shook his head. Even if they'd executed perfectly, Operation Black Sky was doomed from the start.

The distant sound of rotors cut through the night. Relief sparked in Will's chest but was short-lived as a low growl came from below.

He spun towards the edge of the roof, dread rising fast, trying to smother what little hope he had left.

Reaching the ledge, he scanned the lot below, expecting the dog's mutated form.

What he saw instead turned his stomach to stone.

The thing at the door was no longer just a dog.

The bloodied body of Morales had become part of it, a grotesque fusion of man and beast. The monstrous, teeth-filled canine head, now even more distorted, jutted from the hunched shoulder of what remained of his friend. Patches of fur grew out of the torn uniform as his arms—stretched and warped—bulged with unnatural muscle, his fingers curled into claw-like extensions. His shredded tactical vest had become darkened by the German shepherd's mutated skin, giving it a new fleshy covering. The rusted collar chain snaked down the chest, dead center, like a symbol of the Frankensteined terror.

The thing slammed its massive fists against the door. BOOM. BOOM.

Up above, the sound of rotors grew louder. Sarah and

Brooke snapped their chemlights, green glow spilling across their hands as they waved desperately at the sky.

But Will couldn't look away from the thing below.

It stopped.

The beast jerked its head upward. Its sunken eyes locked onto him. Not human, not animal, just hunger.

And then it grinned.

A snarl rumbled up from its chest. Its next hit wasn't to slam the door. It was to find a hold to pull itself up. The abomination was climbing.

Will raised the pistol and fired. Every shot was pure panic.

Then, the problematic click.

Empty. He already knew. No spare mags. No rifle. Nothing left.

At the edge of the lot, shapes staggered into the light. Infected. Drawn to the beast's howls. More twisted bodies, ruined lives.

He stumbled back, a choke rising. "Jesus Christ."

Turning, he scrambled back to the others at the center of the roof.

The helicopter came into view, sleek, soulless, and clearly military. It slowed to a hover above the gas station, rotors slicing through the dark.

Will pulled out the radio, heart pounding.

Behind him, the sound of claws and weight scaling the building grew louder. Closer.

"Drop the ladder!" Will yelled into the radio.

Static cracked, then came the pilot's voice, "Area secure?"

"Just pick us up!" Will shouted, frustration bleeding into panic. "There's a civilian and her kid up here!"

The helicopter hovered, rotors chopping the air. No reply.

An airman stepped into view at the side door, looking down at the rooftop, then the lot below, where infection seemed to be spreading like wildfire.

Brooke and her mother waved desperately, chem-lights glowing in shaking hands, tears cutting down their cheeks.

Will held his breath as the airman turned, raised a hand, and signaled.

The chopper began to rise.

Slow. Deliberate.

Then it turned.

And flew back the way it came.

Sarah froze, her face collapsing into confusion and panic. "What are they doing?" she screamed, clutching Will's arm. "Where are they going?"

Will didn't answer at first. His eyes drifted to the edge of the roof where a pulsing, clawed hand gripped the ledge, dragging up the grotesque, canine-like head, twisted with fur and flesh and what was left of Morales.

His voice was low. Final.

He pictured a red phone sitting patiently in some distant tower.

"To make a call."

NECROTIZING

Mark Oxbrow

Zero Three Fifty – 23 S MMCMLIV
Exoplanet: TRAPPIST-1e – 40 light-years from Earth

Sergeant Aoki Ito hit the dirt, his tactical armour deadening the impact. "Kuso," he cursed. Too many descents. The cartilage in his knees was fucked, bone grinding on bone.

Ito raised his head. The squad had dropped into an endless field of black flowers.

"Jesus Christ!" Bordel hollered. "You see this?" He reached down with a heavily-gloved hand, picking a black poppy. "Thousands. Hundreds of thousands of poppies." Bordel slowly shook his head. "This is worth millions. Jeez."

Black poppies. When TRAPPIST-1e was colonised, Vǫlundr-Myrka Corporation sent xenobotanists to study and cultivate the alien flowers. They named the flower Xeno Papaver Elysium, as it resembled Earth's opium poppy. The poppies thrived in arid soil under the intense UV radiation of its M-dwarf star.

The black poppy was intensely psychoactive, altering perception, mood, and consciousness. TRAPPIST-1e's psychedelic flowers produced vivid hallucinations and intense feelings of euphoria. Within a season, opium from the alien flowers was trafficked across the galaxy, and the rival Godthåb Corporation sent troops to take the planet.

"Millions..." Bordel gazed at the black flower. "Unbelievable..."

243

For a moment, the poppy lit up, illuminated by a ghostly green light.

The sniper fire hit Bordel's body armour, knocking the breath out his lungs. He reeled back.

"Down!" Ito yelled.

His squad bolted, scrabbling for cover.

The second bullet tore a hole through Bordel's neck, ripping open his carotid artery. He blinked, blood gushing from the wound. The third bullet cracked his helm and split his skull. It lodged an inch beneath his left eye. A split second later, the bullet detonated and Bordel's head exploded in a mess of brains, bone, and blood.

His body slumped.

"Kutabare," Ito screamed, blindly returning fire as he ran for cover. He threw himself into the shadow of a fallen mecha. It lay motionless, rusting in the field.

A drone smacked into the mecha, erupting in a massive glut of fire and inky smoke.

Ito saw the objective up ahead. Godthåb's troops took the village at nine-thirty. Six hours, twenty minutes ago. They had time to dig in and fortify.

He triggered the HUD in his helm, zoomed in close to the village perimeter. Three civilians were hanging from an industrial harvester. Their bodies swayed as the wind caught them. Hands tied behind their backs. Steel cables around their necks. The corpses were misshapen, rotting. Too much decomposition for six hours.

Ito pushed the zoom, trying to focus. A Godthåb marine broke cover, running close to the harvester. The bodies juddered. Backbones arched; legs flailed. A lifeless head twisted, jaws gaping, neck ripping. Sinews and muscles tore, discs and ligaments severing as the vertebrae broke apart.

The body fell to the ground, the decapitated head following a moment later. An arm moved, shifting to prop up the corpse as its neck split open, as ribs broke and burst through its chest.

Ito stared. "Kuso."

☣   ☣   ☣

Doctor Nita Torres tore off her bloody scrubs and dumped her blue surgical gloves with the hazardous waste. She reached up, hit the eject button and yanked her Medical-AI drive out of its slot.

"Harvest blood, plasma and organs," she growled.

The surgery-bot wheeled into action above the dead scientist. Tubes syphoned the blood from the body. Robot arms danced, slicing with lasers and scalpel blades: peeling back and collecting layers of skin, harvesting eyeballs, heart, liver, lungs. Hands were cut free above the wrists and prepped for transplant. Nothing was wasted.

"Who's up?" Nita sighed, snatching a clean set of scrubs.

"Here," Combat Medic Elia called out.

Nita swerved around a pool of blood and vomit, striding across the battlefield surgery to the next bay. She shoved her Medical-AI drive into its docking station. She'd scribbled her AI's nickname on the side of the drive: Shock. A sticker of a Murakami kawaii flower grinned at her as she pushed the play button.

"Hey, Shock, you there?" she said.

"Confirmed, Doctor Torres," Shock replied.

Nita had selected Shock's voice from a library of hundreds of languages and thousands of accents. Had tweaked the speed, pitch, volume and timbre of his voice to suit her specific needs.

She pulled on clean scrubs and surgical gloves.

Elia hovered close to the gurney. "This is Te Ariki Kauri, docking bay supervisor. Human versus loading-bot. Traumatic brain injury. Tachy one-twenty. Pulse oxygen ninety."

"Ok." Nita let the mask zoom in and focus. "Shock, four of morphine, four of ondansetron. Confirm depressed skull fracture?"

"Confirmed depressed skull fracture, Nita. Bone of skull vault depressed into cerebral parenchyma," Shock replied. "And—"

"And hyphema," Nita said.

"Correct," Shock said. "Hyphema. Grade Four. Blood is collecting in the anterior chamber of the eye, between the cornea and iris."

"Groovy." Nita leaned in. "Shock, administer anaesthetic and commence debridement of the skull fracture."

Shock's AI triggered the surgery-bot's robot arms. It began to clean blood and skull fragments from the wound.

"Nita!" Diggory shouted across the surgery. "You got to meet my new friend!"

She glanced over. Diggory was a grease monkey, a tech head who repaired the surgery-bots with whatever he could scavenge. He stood beside a massive hulking robot: a patchwork of automatous weapons and junked bots.

"This thing malfunctioned." Diggory tapped the robot with a wrench. "Nearly took that guy's head off in the loading bay. It's a decommissioned Dreadnaut. You ever seen one? The 'E, A' in Dread stands for energy autonomous. No power needed. They fed on whatever organics they found."

"Yeah?" Nita frowned.

"Hell, yeah." Diggory grinned. "Back on base, in Reykjavík, we used to feed cats to these fuckers!"

"Va te faire foutre," Nita muttered, shaking her head. Diggory laughed.

"Te Ariki?" Nita said. "You with me?"

"Yeah, hey doc," Te Ariki said.

"Ok, buddy, you have an eight-ball hyphema. Blood pooling behind your eye. I am making a small incision to drain the blood and relieve the pressure."

Nita raised the scalpel, slicing through the swelling. Blood ran down Te Ariki's face. Something moved under his skin. Writhed. A tiny, translucent worm squirmed out of the incision. Its blind head twitched, its bloated body wriggling.

"Woah. Ok." Nita leaned back. "Shock, extract the parasite."

"Parasite?" Te Ariki flinched. "Upokokōhua."

A robotic arm flicked around, minute forceps snatching hold of the worm, dragging it out of the wound. "Confirmed."

"Incinerate," Nita said.

Shock rotated the parasite to the biohazard waste unit. A red light blinked as the unit burned the worm to ashes.

"Te Ariki, did you drink the water?" Nita said.

"What?"

"The water. On this planet. Did you drink it?"

"Yes?"

"Shock, run full body scan," Nita said. "Searching for parasitic organisms."

"Scanning."

Nita looked up at the screen. Dozens of tiny, white shapes squirmed throughout Te Ariki's body.

"Ok. So, Te Ariki," Nita said. "You got alien worms eating your brain."

"What the *fuck*?"

"Never drink the water, Te Ariki," Nita said. "Never drink the fucking water."

Sergeant Ito raised his Heckler & Koch HK-MXL six-barrel rotary machine gun and pulled the trigger. One-hundred-and-ten rounds per second. It cut over the field, tearing across the harvester like a scythe.

The Godthåb sniper staggered back, ragged holes in his body armour, bullets shattering bones, punching through heart and lungs.

But Ito was aiming for the revenants that burst out of the village. Two hundred and four men, women, and children. Unrecognisable. Wretched things. Slick with some inky-black oil. Limbs contorted, writhing, bones broken and fingers clawing. Abominations.

The Godthåb marines ran. Laying down supressing fire as they fled. They'd rather face Ito and the Vǫlundr-Myrka squads than the things that came screaming from the village.

"This is Sergeant Aoki Ito, come in," Ito yelled into the comms.

Static.

"Base," Ito repeated. "This is Sergeant Aoki Ito, come in."

He cursed under his breath.

Comms shrieked and cleared.

"Sergeant Ito, this is Base. Receiving."

"Base, I need an airstrike. Danger Close. Five hundred metres northeast of my position." Ito gritted his teeth.

Static.

"Repeat. Sergeant Ito, repeat."

"Kuso," Ito swore again. "Base, I need an airstrike *now*. Danger Close. Five hundred metres northeast of my position. Bomb that fucking village with everything. Incendiaries. Daisy-cutters. Anti-Mecha. Every ATS missile you have."

Static.

Ito waited. Muttered a prayer.

"Base confirming. Airstrike imminent. Blessings to you, Sergeant."

Ito leaned back against the fallen mecha. He breathed deep. Taking a moment's peace before the Hell storm.

"Äksä Squad, this is Ito." He tightened his grip on the machine gun. "Mother of all bombs about to fall. Hunker down and if any of those fucks survive, they do not get past us. I repeat, nothing is getting past us."

He heard the missiles overhead. Unearthly screeches and high piercing whistles.

For a split second, the fields fell silent.

"Shinee," Ito growled.

Bombs thudded down into the village, detonating in colossal explosions that splintered the prefabs and shipping containers. The fireball blossomed in the night sky, bursting out into the fields, burning marines and flowers and the contaminated.

The ground ruptured, roaring, dirt and black poppies rippling up as the force of the bombs blew a hole in the face of the planet.

Ito curled himself up tight. Wrapped an arm around his knees, shielded his eyes. He felt the fires scorch his armour, paint peeling from his helm. He wanted to scream but the risk of burning his throat kept his mouth shut.

A high-pitched shriek sounded in Ito's left ear.

The ground had stopped moving.

He cautiously opened his eyes, felt the sting as he looked out from around the mecha.

It was gone. Everything was gone.

Fires burned. The air was scorched, blazing with fireflies. Barely a half dozen tangled harvesters and wrecked mecha remained. The ground was bare and blackened. The village, erased. Men, women, children. Gone.

Ito's helm couldn't filter out the smell: burning flesh, diesel, sweet-scented opium.

Spot fires sprung up among the surviving black flowers. Seeds germinated in the flames, cracking, releasing spores that drifted with the smoke in the hot wind.

249

Ito raised his hand. Black snow. Petals and burning embers falling.

The squads of Vǫlundr-Myrka troops edged out of their cover. Twenty-three five-soldier squads had dropped into the fields. Ito didn't want to count the survivors.

Black fungal spores swirled and spiralled through the filters in his helm, blurring in front of his eyes. He panicked, clawing at his visor, breathing them in. Deep down, into his lungs. Fungal particles hit his face, burrowing under his skin.

"Kuso…" Ito felt his skin burning. "Fuzakeru na."

Around him, the troops fell to their knees, screeching, clawing at their faces.

Nerves shredded, bones split, spilling marrow. It slid an inky tendril around Ito's heart and squeezed. His blood felt frozen in his veins. Pain arced through his body.

"Medic!" Ito screamed into the comms. "Medic!"

☣ ☣ ☣

"We have wounded incoming," Shock said.

"How many?" Nita hid in the meds store, surrounded by thousands of pill boxes, injections, and artificial blood packs.

"Unknown," Shock replied.

Unknown was never good.

Nita sat back on a crash cart and took out a bag of drugs. Black poppy opium. Her personal stash. It dissolved in seconds. An inky wisp swirling in the vial. She shook it, pushed it into the syringe and jammed the needle into the socket in her arm.

Her breath shuddered as the drugs hit her bloodstream and spiralled through her body. Her skin prickled, pupils dilated. Intoxicating. Ecstatic. She touched a finger to her lips, shivering as the hit seethed through her.

"Wounded arriving in two minutes," Shock said.

"Iteq." Nita steadied herself, taking a step toward the door.

The surgery was a riot of noise after the quiet of the meds store. Nurses and combat medics were clearing the bays for the incoming casualties, wheeling gurneys out to the loading bay, ready for evac to the ships in orbit.

Nita slotted Shock into a surgery-bot. She grabbed clean scrubs and gloves, and waited.

"Twenty seconds," Shock said.

Nita stretched out her back, rolled her head around on her shoulders.

The surgery doors burst open. Combat medics wheeled gurneys in, two at a time. The troops were strapped down, thrashing against their restraints.

"Holy fuck," Diggory muttered.

Blood dripped from the gurneys. Black as ink.

"Shock, we need armour removed in all bays," Nita yelled over the clamour. "Can't see what we're looking at."

"Confirmed," Shock replied.

The surgery-bots moved in parallel. Robotic arms synchronised as they cut through ceramic and steel armour. Discarded pieces clattered to the floor.

Nita leaned close, reading a set of tags: Äksä I Sergeant I Ito.

She stared at Sergeant Ito's skin. Thread veins crept across his face, a sickly dark purple. They seemed to devour all colour from his flesh. Ito's skin appeared as translucent as the worm.

"Lock down now," Nita yelled. "Full quarantine. I want everyone in biohazard gear, now!"

Nita grabbed a yellow biohazard suit, barely breathing as she shoved her arms into its sleeves. "Shock," Nita shouted. "Initial thoughts? Run gamut of tests." She fought to get the biohazard hood over her head.

"Tachy one-thirty. Blood oxygen average seventy-five percent. Body temperature's forty-two degrees and rising. Majority of patients in hyperpyrexia. Appears as necrotizing soft tissue infection."

"Ok, Shock." Nita stepped back into the bay. "I want you to…"

Ito's skull cracked open. The skin of his face separating and tearing as his jawbone broke loose and his body spasmed.

"Le Fort fracture. Type three," Shock said calmly.

"Fuck!" Nita reeled back as blood splattered across her biohazard suit. "Shock, harvest organs and incinerate!"

"Please confirm, Doctor Torres," Shock said.

"Override safety protocols, Shock, now!" Nita screamed. "All infected."

Robotic arms moved, scalpels cutting through rotting skin. Layers of putrefying nerves and tissue, liquifying fat.

Ito's arm jolted against the restraints. Bones snapped, muscle and flesh ripped.

"Radius and ulna severe fracture," Shock said.

Ito's body tore his hand off, leaving it secured in the restraint as he slid from the gurney to the surgery floor.

He stood, silent, impassive.

Ito's revenant grabbed hold of a robotic arm and wrenched it out of the surgery-bot.

"Fuck." Nita slipped in black blood and bile as she slithered around the gurney.

She fumbled with the biohazard suit, stabbing at the eject button with her gloved finger. "C'mon, damn it!" She hit the button again.

With a gentle whirr, Shock's AI drive ejected.

Nita cut a hole in her suit and snatched the drive.

"Diggory!" Nita yelled. "Where the fuck are you?"

A moment later, Diggory's head popped up from the far side of the surgery.

Robotic arms sliced through the revenants, cutting limbs from bodies and peeling back infected skin. Veins and arteries blistered and burst. Contaminated blood smeared across the surgery floor.

Black flowers blossomed out of Ito's broken skull. They skittered, spidering on eight tiny, sharp legs. Petals fluttered like butterfly wings as the black poppies juddered and flew.

Nita ran.

She couldn't think about the things she saw. Nothing could stop or slow her. Her feet slid. She trampled over bodies. Felt her ribs crack as she smashed into a gurney.

"Diggory!" she screamed.

"Here!" He reached out to take her hand.

She held him an inch from her face. "Where's the loading-bot?"

Diggory pointed. "There."

Nita staggered over to it. The bot was slumped, lifeless. An empty shell. She wiped a layer of dust and grime off its front array. There was the docking station.

"Got ya." Nita jammed Shock's AI drive into the Dreadnaut's dock.

A red light blinked. On and off.

"C'mon, you fuck," Nita screamed at the bot.

Lights flickered.

"You there, Shock?" Nita leaned against the bot.

The revenants shrieked behind her, nurses screaming then falling silent.

"Confirmed, Doctor Torres," Shock said.

The Dreadnaut growled, huge metal limbs straightening as it activated.

"Shock," Nita said. "I need you to eat those motherfuckers."

"Confirmed."

The Dreadnaut was relentless. It stomped forward, raising its arms as it crashed across the surgery, loader claws closing around a revenant.

It fed the infected thing into its body. A thousand razor-sharp blades whirled. The meat grinder cut through skulls and bones, eyes, faces, muscle and viscera.

The Dreadnaut fed on flesh. An autonomous machine powered by organic tissue.

Ito's jawbone cracked, teeth splintering. His eyeball locked gazes with Nita as the Dreadnaut consumed it.

"Yeah," Diggory smiled.

"Va te faire foutre, motherfucker," Nita yelled. "Go fuck yourself!"

CONSENSUS BREAK

R.P.L. Johnson

Its official name was Sub-Level 2 of the Bear Island Naval Hospital, but everyone just called it The Hole.

Aiden Cooper didn't know what you had to do to find yourself in The Hole. Actually, scratch that; he knew exactly what you had to do: join the US Navy straight out of high school as a Hospital Corpsman, keep your nose clean for a few years, even earn a pretty good rep. Then kill your CO with an overdose during what should have been a routine procedure. His options after that had been pretty limited, but the Navy had determined he was just stupid and not traitorous.

A job as an orderly on Bear Island had sounded better than the brig, just about. The pay was bad and the working conditions even worse, but at least he wasn't an inmate. Those guys were really fucked.

The inmate currently strapped into the wheelchair was a typical example. Aiden didn't know his name or any details about his condition. The name tape on the guy's coveralls read EX1242. That was who he'd been sent to get. And so that was who he got. Then the wheelchair broke.

Aiden looked at the man. He was old, or maybe just looked old after years of captivity. Like all the inmates Aiden ferried around the facility, EX1242 was blinkered. The micropore tape that sealed his eyelids was just visible as ragged tags across his cheeks under his tight-fitting leather hood. His mouth held a rubber bite guard secured with leather straps, looking strangely medieval as they passed around the man's head under a pair of very modern Bluetooth headphones.

They weren't supposed to let the inmates out of their chairs. They were to be delivered, pre-packaged, every time one of the doctors upstairs wanted to see them. But there was no way Aiden was going to fix the chair with the man in it. Aiden wasn't worried. He'd played center in his high school football team and the Navy had kept him fit. This guy looked to be about a buck-fifty of grey, mystery meat.

"You're going to have to get up," Aiden said as he removed the patient's restraints. Then realized that the whole point of blinkering the inmates was to cut out any external stimulus.

He took off the man's headphones. "Get up," he said again, and the man flinched. Aiden could hear the hiss of white noise leaking from the cup of the headphones.

For a couple of seconds, the man didn't move, and Aiden began to wonder if he could. Then, as if suddenly remembering that movement was possible, the inmate placed his bare feet on the flagstones and stood.

Aiden kept one eye on the man before dropping to one knee in front of the broken wheel. It looked fixable: a nut had come off the spindle allowing the wheel to work itself loose. The nut was lost, there was no way Aiden was going to be able to find it in the dark corridors of The Hole, but he managed to get the wheel back on and secured it temporarily with a bent paperclip from his patient requisition forms.

"Jesus, Coop, Pavulon? What were you thinking?"

Aiden looked up. The patient had managed to work his bite guard loose and stretched his leather hood up so he could stare at Aiden with one deep-set eye.

"The fuck you say?" Aiden replied.

"It's not even close. You fuckin' killed him, man," the patient said.

"Sir, you need to sit your ass back down," Aiden said and reached for the man's shoulder, but the inmate stepped backwards.

"I understand what they see in you," the man said, keeping the wheelchair between himself and Aiden. "You are defined by death. It clings to you, and yet you can't see it."

"Sir, you need to sit down." Aiden tried to grab him again, but the patient danced around the wheelchair with surprising agility for his age.

"Matter cannot be created or destroyed, only reimagined. There is so much you don't understand. So much you fail to see. Even the gods fail to squeeze meaning into so narrow a man. You are not worthy. YOU ARE NOT WORTHY!"

"Shit. Fuck."

Aiden grabbed the auto injector from his belt and stabbed it into the patient's scrawny upper arm. EX1242 struggled against the sudden sting but almost immediately his knees buckled and by the time Aiden had manhandled him back into the chair, his head was lolling to one side, and he was snoring gently.

Aiden quickly re-fastened his restraints and replaced the bite guard and blinkers, but after using the injector there was no way he could hide his fuck up. Doctor Hoffman was likely to notice when he was delivered a sedated patient.

☣   ☣   ☣

"And that's when you used the auto-injector?" Doctor Hoffman asked. "When the patient tried to remove the blinkers?"

"Yes, Doctor," Aiden replied. It took every ounce of his resolve not to say 'Sir'—the docs didn't like it—but the questioning was bringing back memories of his Court Marshall, and Navy habits died hard.

"Just to be clear," Doctor Hoffman continued, "—at no time did he succeed in removing his blinkers?"

"No, Doctor."

"Didn't say anything or write anything?"

You fuckin' killed him, man.

"No, Doctor. The chair broke and I stood the patient up for a second and he just started to react. I realize it was an error, but I thought it was safer than leaving the patient unattended. I administered the sedative, fixed the chair and then brought him up."

Aiden wasn't sure why he was lying. Only that letting a patient remove their blinkers was an even graver crime than sedating them. Then there was the patient's outburst: not the mad, stream-of-consciousness rambling, but what he'd said before.

Pavulon was a muscle relaxant. In small doses it was useful in relaxing the throat when a patient needed to be intubated. In larger doses it shut down breathing so effectively that it was one of the cocktail of drugs used for capital punishment. Thirty-six sleepless hours into an exercise, his CO had been brought to the sick bay after a bad fall and Aiden had got the dose wrong by a couple of orders of magnitude.

"Jesus, Coop, Pavulon?" his buddy had said when he'd seen the dosage. "It's not even close."

He'd never told anyone about that detail. As far as he knew, it didn't exist in any official report. And yet EX1242 had repeated it like it was tattooed across Aiden's forehead.

Doctor Hoffman nodded thoughtfully. "A difficult situation," he conceded. "You did what you could. He'll be out for a while. Better take him back to The Hole and maybe check all the other chairs."

Aiden left, glad to get away from any further scrutiny. He found another wheelchair and took EX1242 back down The Hole and handed him back to the duty nurse with a quick scribble of paperwork, avoiding her inquisitive stare.

At the end of his shift, he walked home through the darkening streets.

Jesus, Coop...

You are not worthy!

Was that tattooed across his forehead too?

That night, he lay in bed idly scanning through social media on his phone. He had briefly tried searching the various military news sites, checking to see if any of the old reports about his case had been updated.

Jesus, Coop... How the hell had the patient known that?

Without finding anything, he slipped into idly surfing YouTube and watched a procession of videos from his usual sites without really taking anything in —

he recognized the voice immediately. It was patient EX1242.

Aiden expanded the window and studied the man's pale face. He looked very different: fuller featured and with a healthy tan, although the eyes were still the same – deep set and dark with an unwavering focus.

The site was called *Shadow Narrative*, a paranormal channel Aiden followed, mostly for stories about UAPs and ancient secret societies. He enjoyed conspiracy theories, the weirder the better, anything to distract him from the mundanity of his normal life. He didn't actually believe any of them. After all, he spent most of his waking hours inside a Naval Intelligence black site. He was inside the conspiracy, and he knew for a fact there were no grey aliens or reptilian pre-cursor species inside The Hole, just madmen, presumably ex-government types whose mental states meant they could no longer be trusted with the contents of their own minds. Still, he treated the stories as enjoyable fictions and followed the various leaks and whistleblowers as avidly as an old abuela following the convoluted plot of a Mexican soap opera.

"The human eye only sees a fraction of the electromagnetic spectrum," EX1242 said. The caption under him read Professor Charles Carter, Brown University. *"And of that data, the vast majority is not perceived. Saccadic masking, change blindness, even the simple act of blinking: all these mechanisms conspire to blind us. Even our best scientific tools can only perceive five percent of the universe. The vast, unseen majority is put down as 'dark' matter and 'dark' energy."*

"You believe there is more to our world than what we perceive?" said the unseen interviewer."

"I don't just believe," EX1242 continued. *"I have seen it..."*

Aiden turned off his phone. This was just too weird. Sleep wasn't going to come easily, so he dressed and decided to take a walk to clear his head.

Like most of the hospital staff, Aiden lived off base. Bear Island was one of many old whaling towns scattered along the New England coast like the bones of the creatures they once hunted. There was still a small community that made its living from the sea, but most of the small island's industry now revolved around the base, and most of the Navy personnel lived in the island's sprawling terraces of old clapboard houses, now refitted as apartments.

Aiden walked down to the 7-Eleven at the end of his block. It was late, and the convenience store attached to the island's lone gas station was the only thing open. He bought a disposable vape and planned on walking until it was used up. Then he saw the car.

It was an old car. Really old. From the time of curved steel rather than injection-molded plastic. Chrome bumpers underlined glossy, black curves gleaming in the moonlight, but he hadn't heard it pull up even though it would had to have driven right past the 7-Eleven.

The car's occupants were at the intercom to his building. One was so tall he had to stoop to access the call panel below the door's camera. They were wearing dark, formal suits with a shirt and tie and both figures wore wide-brimmed hats that looked to be of the same vintage as their ancient car. Something about them raised red flags. They were too tall, too thin, too formal: certainly too formal for the local PD that were rarely seen out of a polar fleece and a pickup. They didn't look like any kind of military either. Aiden was sure they had come to speak to him, but he was equally sure he wanted no part of that meeting.

After receiving no answer to the bell, the two figures seemed to confer, leaning so close the brims of their wide hats touched. Aiden waited until they got back in their car and it moved away, soundless on the quiet street – some kind of electric resto-mod engine inside that old chassis, Aiden guessed. He walked to the corner of the block and peered around the intersection, but the car and its strange occupants had already disappeared.

☣   ☣   ☣

He was still staring down the road when a second car rolled up behind him. A white Chevy Tahoe. No fancy electric resto-mods here, the SUVs were practically standard issue to Navy brass and senior medical personnel, so he didn't take any notice until its driver got out and called his name.

"Mister Cooper?"

Aiden turned. The speaker was a woman in a dark pantsuit. The broad collar of her white shirt was fanned out across her lapels, stylish business casual rather than creepy Amish. Her partner lumbered out of the passenger side door: old muscle and thinning hair. Cops. Navy cops.

"Mister Cooper, my name is Special Agent Tally, this is Agent Crowe." She flashed a badge, Naval Intelligence. "Sorry it's so late, but we need to ask you a couple of questions."

"I get it," Aiden said. "I gave your men in black the slip, so now you send in the goon squad."

"What did you say?"

"The Goon Squad. You know… like in the movies."

"You said *Men in Black*."

The partner, Crowe, stiffened.

"Different movie," Aiden said, confused. "What are you guys doing here?"

"What did you see? Be precise."

"I don't know. Two skinny dudes in a black car. Old timey hats like they was Amish or something, except they wouldn't be driving, I guess."

"Did you talk to them? Take anything from them?"

"Nah. I was just coming back from 7-Eleven. They didn't see me, I don't think."

"When was this?"

"Right before you rolled up."

The woman immediately spoke into her radio. "Control, we have possible papillae on scene." She turned to Crowe. "Find me a sanctuary."

"What's up? Ain't those dudes with you?"

"Mister Cooper, we're going to need you to come with us."

Agent Tally had her hand on the butt of the pistol at her hip, but she didn't seem to be threatening Aiden. She seemed distracted, scanning the street in the direction the old black Lincoln had taken. Crowe looked worried too. He was scrolling through a street map on a tablet, brow furrowed.

"Crowe, where's my sanctuary?" Agent Tally asked.

"Nothing close," Crowe replied.

"Those the guys you lookin' for?" Aiden asked, pointing. The black Lincoln had appeared under the streetlights at the end of the block.

"Shit, Crowe, give me something." There was an edge to Tally's orders now.

"It's a quiet neighborhood," Crowe replied. "Nothing within a half-mile."

"What are you looking for?" Aiden asked.

Tally stared at him for a minute. "OK," she said. "You live around here. Is there a mall or a twenty-four-hour Walmart or anything nearby? Anything likely to be busy? Lots of people?"

"Nothing like that on the island," Aiden replied. "Closest thing would be the 7-Eleven."

"Five hundred yards," Crowe confirmed. "We can make it."

"Make what?" Aiden asked, but Tally had already grabbed him by the elbow and was ushering him back down the street in the direction of the 7-Eleven. "Hey," Aiden protested. "I ain't going nowhere until you tell me what's going on."

"Believe me, it's best if you come with us. It's for your safety."

"A 7-Eleven?"

"It's a public place. It's safer. Trust me."

Something about the agent's voice told Aiden they weren't messing around. Down the street, the Lincoln seemed to have edged closer, although he still couldn't hear an engine.

"Pap's closing," Crowe said.

"I see it," Tally replied. "Hold your fire."

Aiden remembered the word the agent had used on the radio.

"What the hell is a papill-eye?" he asked.

"They're the bad guys," Tally replied. "That's all you need to know right now."

"Two hundred yards," Crowe said.

Aiden could see the light from the 7-Eleven spilling out onto the street, although he wasn't sure what safety the store could provide that two heavily-armed agents couldn't.

"Papillae is following but not closing," said Crowe.

"That's something at least," Tally replied. She spoke into her radio. "We have confirmed contact with a stable papillae."

"Do we have a breach?" Came the response from the radio.

"Not yet. Single papillae. Class two maybe three," Tally replied. "Small, but highly agentic. It's hitchhiking on the target. We are headed towards an improvised Sanctuary: a 7-Eleven on Woodside Avenue."

"Confirmed. Authority to engage at Sanctuary threshold."

"Jesus," Crowe said. "Only if it breaches the threshold? If it gets that close, we're fucked anyway."

Before Aiden could ask what the threshold was, he was bundled through the doors of the 7-Eleven. Agent Tally ordered the terrified clerk to hunker down behind the counter while Crowe crouched behind a freezer of ice cream, gun drawn, eyes on the door.

"Nobody else here," Tally said. "Just the clerk."

"Damn," Crowe said. "I hate small towns."

"Shouldn't we lock the door or somethin'?" Aiden asked.

"They don't do locks," Tally replied.

"What the fuck does that mean?"

But Tally was already behind the counter turning up the volume on the TV that hung from a steel bracket on the ceiling.

There was a soft 'ding' as the glass doors slid open.

Crowe raised his pistol, but for the moment no target presented itself.

"Not unless it crosses the threshold," Tally reminded him. "We got sanctuary. Stay cool, we got this."

A slender figure walked into the light. He was impossibly tall. He would have to stoop to enter the store, but for the moment he showed no sign of attempting to do so. Just stood there, painfully thin like a cancer patient or concentration camp survivor. His black suit was cut to fit his thin frame, but it didn't hang right. Aiden couldn't quite put his finger on it, but the fabric seemed to move with its wearer as if it wasn't just clothes. He seemed more like an action figure with fabric and flesh molded together.

"Papillae at Sanctuary threshold," Tally said into her radio.

"Copy that," came the response. "QRF two minutes out."

"Two minutes?"

The figure, the papillae, extended a long-fingered hand, but stopped at the plane of the open doorway. It spread its fingers like a mime examining an invisible wall. The lights flickered and the sounds from the TV slid in pitch, like someone was playing the audio with a wah-wah pedal.

"It's not going to hold," Crowe said.

"It'll hold if you believe it'll hold," Tally snapped.

The figure at the door stooped below the lintel and for the first time, Aiden saw its face.

It was blinkered.

Leather straps below its chin held a light-fitting leather mask that covered eyes and ears under the black felt of its hat. Unlike the patients in The Hole, its mouth was free and set in a constant smile of broad, yellow teeth like the cracked keys of an old piano.

It pushed against the invisible threshold.

Aiden felt a weird kind of pressure, like he was inside a balloon and the thing at the doorway was squeezing it from the outside.

The figure stepped away from the doorway into the darkness and the pressure disappeared.

"What the fuck was that thing?"

"Better you don't know," Tally replied.

"No way that was human. What the fuck is going on?"

"Tell him, Tally," Crowe said, his Beretta semi-automatic still trained on the doorway.

"Are you nuts?" Tally replied. "It's hitchhiking on him."

"He's seen it now; you've got to tell him the truth. If he believes, it could strengthen the Sanctuary."

Tally looked as if she was struggling with something: as if trying to explain a difficult concept or maybe trying to decide on a lie. "Imagine you flip a coin," she said eventually. "While it's still in the air, is it heads or tails?"

"What the fuck has that got to do with anything?"

"Heads or tails?" Tally repeated.

"Neither," Aiden replied.

"Exactly. You don't know the call until you catch it. Reality is like that. I don't know the science behind it, just generalities, not the math. But at the most basic level, observation determines reality. The universe is just an immense field of possibilities. Nothing really happens until it interacts with a conscious mind. Scientists call it collapsing the wave function, but you can think of it as catching that coin."

Aiden had heard something like that before in a physics class. "Like Schrodinger's cat, right?" he said. "You put a cat in a box along with some poison that has a fifty-fifty chance of killing it. The math says the cat is both alive *and* dead until we open the box and look. Always sounded like bullshit to me."

"It's a very rough approximation," Tally replied, "—and it's not bullshit. But that's not all. The world, everything you see around you, only exists this way because we want it to. Millions of people, billions of observations defining how the world should act. It's kind of like a shared dream. We call it the consensus. We think the world should act a certain way and so it does. Think of it like we're the cat and the box is the known universe."

"So the world is a shared dream?" Aiden said. "What the fuck was that thing? Some kind of nightmare?"

"No. The papillae are real."

"So where do they come from?"

"We're not the only cat inside the box," Tally said.

The pressure returned and suddenly the balloon burst.

The figure, the papillae, was back at the doorway, reaching inside, impossibly long fingers grasping.

The 7-Eleven's fluorescent lights flared white then died and the darkness was lit by muzzle flashes from Crowe's Beretta and the thundering concussion of rounds fired in a confined space.

The figure staggered backwards and fell into the road.

"Crowe! What the fuck?" Tally shouted.

"It was through. Didn't you feel it?" Crowe's voice carried the edge of panic. Aiden felt it too. But Crowe's shots had put that thing on its ass. Surely, the agents had the upper hand?

The thing in the road moved.

"The Sanctuary's been breached," Crowe said. "We need to go. Now!" He grabbed the back of Aiden's jacket and bundled him out of the door past the long figure that was struggling back to its feet.

"What are you waiting for?" Aiden shouted. "Finish it the fuck off."

"Doesn't work like that," Crowe replied. "We run now."

The papillae struggled to its feet, shadows clung to it like tattered scraps of a cloak, melting into its dark suit as if the streetlights weren't sure where the thing ended and the shadows began. The second figure sat in the car across the street: a ghost of teeth and white shirtfront, unmoving behind the steering wheel.

"Let's go, before it sees us," Crowe said.

"Before it sees us? We're right here."

"There's no light on its side," Crowe said, as if that explained anything.

The papillae moved impossibly fast. Suddenly, it was in front of Crowe, long fingers in the agent's eyes as it lifted him off the ground.

Crowe's fist twitched against the trigger of his Beretta as he died. Rounds sparked off the pavement. Aiden fell, scrambling backwards, unable to take his eyes off the thing that still held Crowe's twitching feet above the concrete.

The Beretta fell from Crowe's limp fingers. The Navy cop sagged on the papillae's long-fingered hand. Aiden could see pale fingertips through the thinning, dark hair on Crowe's scalp. The man's head started to flow through the papillae's fingers as if his skull was made of wax. The big Navy cop's weight dragged him down: skin and bone and grey matter oozing until he fell to the sidewalk, his head a red fan of fleshy strips.

Suddenly, Tally was behind Aiden, grabbing him by the hood of his sweatshirt and dragging him away. He could hear her shouting into her radio.

"Crowe is down. Where's the fucking QRF?"

With a roar of powerful turbodiesel engines, two armored cars thundered onto the street: boxy, utilitarian slabs of black and green steel with powerful lights blazing behind black crash bars. It was the quick reaction force, in two Bearcat armored cars.

The newcomers were major-league door kickers. Cleanup specialists. They didn't ask questions; they just deployed from the Bearcats and started shooting.

Aiden and Tally dived to the ground.

"Do these guys know we're on their side?"

"Stay out of their way," Tally shouted above the gunfire. "They're CBIRF: chemical weapons rapid response team. Marines out of Fort Devens. Usual briefing is to take out a homegrown terrorist with a weaponized hallucinogen. Helps to explain away some of the weirdness and maintain the consensus."

The Marines were taking no chances. They had M27 automatic rifles, their faces anonymous within JSLIST chemical warfare suits with integrated gas masks.

Automatic fire hammered into the figure standing above Crowe's corpse, tracer rounds like lightning under the thunder of half a dozen automatic rifles.

The papillae fell awkwardly, legs folding beneath it in unnatural angles as if it was double-jointed.

The second papillae was still inside the car. Aiden saw rounds spark off the hood and windshield. The Marines seemed to take it in their stride. They approached the car in two fire teams, one covering while the other advanced. Efficient, deadly.

The second figure unfolded itself from the car. No human could have withstood a couple of dozen hits of 5.56mm, but the thing wasn't human. The gun in its hand wasn't produced by any human hand either.

The first round went through the lead BearCat like an armor-piercing shell from a canon. Aiden felt a pressure similar to when the first figure had forced its way into the 7-Eleven, and the Bearcat tore itself apart, strange gravities bursting it up and out in a bloom of twisted armor plating.

One of the marines threw a grenade. The red canister

landed inside the Lincoln and exploded in a flare of detonating thermite.

Both papillae screamed as if the flames were licking at their own flesh. The closest one turned and gripped the roof of the car and stood there as if welded to it. The incendiary grenade was still burning. Aiden could feel the heat thirty feet away. The entire interior of the car was consumed, and the roof was sagging, but it didn't burn. Even the black paint on the old steel was unaffected. The car ran like wax: glass and steel sagging like the center of a candle around the flame of the burning grenade.

The papillae was on its knees. It was part of the car now: black steel and black suit indistinguishable as they melted together, gleaming in the last flickers of expired thermite.

"What the fuck!" Aiden exclaimed.

The Marines had stopped firing. They also seemed confused. Some were checking their masks. Others were salvaging what they could from the ruined Bearcat.

The Papillae flailed and screeched like a beast caught in a pool of burning tar. Its hat and suit were gone. Not burned, just changed. As if the rules of combustion worked differently in its reality, as if it didn't know how to burn.

The other one, the one that had killed Crowe, lay slumped a little way off. Not dead, it flopped ineffectively on jagged spurs of elbows and knees as if remembering how to walk through reconfigured bones.

"Now's our chance," Tally said. "I need to get you out of here." She was looking along the street at apartment lights flickering on. Aiden guessed that even the darkened windows were filled with people watching the commotion, they were just sensible enough not to make a target of themselves.

"What the fuck is going on?" Aiden said.

"We need to go."

"I'm not moving until you tell me what the fuck those things are."

Crowe might have been able to manhandle him, but Aiden was pretty sure Tally didn't have the muscle for it. He wasn't moving until he got some answers.

"Remember what I said about the consensus?" Tally said. "There are other observers, other consciousnesses. Beings with a very different understanding of the world. They can push through where our consensus is weak. We call those protrusions into our reality, papillae. On our side they have to abide by the rules of our consensus. That's why they look humanoid and drive cars, or look like drones or lights in the sky. But they don't understand our reality, not really. So they're all fucked up."

"So why the guns? If these things are just projections into our reality, how come you can shoot them?"

"They have to abide by our rules. They only have a limited ability to push against our consensus. If they stray too far, act in a way that is too different from the consensus, it will snap back and throw them out. So when we shoot them, they pretend to get hurt.

"Trouble is, the weaker the consensus, the more they can ignore it. That's why you need to believe. Our reality might be a shared dream, but it's just as valid as theirs. You need to know that."

She looked again at the apartment blocks lining the street. "Shit... Too many witnesses here," she said. "It's fixed on you. We need to get you away from here into a real sanctuary."

"Another fucking 7-Eleven? No way!"

The burning papillae started to rise. The remains of the melted Lincoln were draped across it like wings of tar pulled across bones of unholy black iron. Its hat and blinkers were gone. Its eyes were a mass of writhing cilia. Its mouth a furnace lit by other suns.

The Marines opened fire again. The creature shrieked

fit to break glass, the first noise Aiden remembered either of the papillae making, but it continued to grow.

It raised one clawed finger and Aiden saw something flash across the street, a flicker of color he could barely describe – a lightning bolt frozen in time and glittering with dark prominences like whiskers of a new reality. Marines caught in its path bloomed and burst like abyssal fish pulled into the sunlight of a new world. The dark light crackled between gas pumps at the station outside the 7-Eleven, rubber and steel and gasoline burning and changing and decomposing as this finger of new physics tore their elements apart.

Aiden saw one of the CBIRF Marines drop to their knees, scrabbling frantically at their mask. Others opened fire, but this reborn papillae seemed immune to small arms.

The Marines were retreating now. About half managed a disciplined bounding overwatch while the remainder turned tail and ran.

Aiden saw shapes at the windows on the far side of the street. "It's not working," he said.

"No," Tally agreed. She, too, was looking at the witnesses in the windows above them. Roused from sleep, half-dressed and half dreaming in that liminal world between sleep and true wakefulness. "The consensus is breaking down," Tally said eventually. "The more people see it, they more they question and the more the papillae can push through."

"What happens then? What happens when the consensus breaks down?"

"Nothing good."

They ran back to Tally's car.

The streets were quiet except for the muted clatter of gunfire and even that started to fade as a heavy fog fell across the island.

"Where are we going?" Aiden asked.

"You ever wonder why a foggy path through the forest at night feels different to a busy city street?" Tally replied. "It doesn't just feel different. It *is* different. There are places where the consensus is weak. Some are natural. Others, like the hospital you work in, are man-made. Too many people with too much knowledge of how the world really works. Too few believers in the consensus. We need to get away from here, back to a sanctuary where the consensus is strong. Hold out 'til dawn."

Suddenly, it made sense: The Hole, the blinkers, the white noise through the headphones. The facility wasn't a hospital. It was an isolation ward for ideas, an asylum for those who knew the truth.

"There's a truck stop on Route One," Aiden said. "Big place. Open all night. If you want busy, that's the closest option."

"How far?" Tally asked.

"Across the causeway then north, about fifteen minutes."

Lights blazed through the fog as a vehicle charged towards them. It was another CBIRF Bearcat closely followed by a wedge-shaped armored personnel carrier on eight huge balloon tires with the thick barrel of a Mark 19 automatic grenade launcher mounted on a rooftop weapons pod.

"Do you think they can kill it?" Aiden asked.

"Literally kill it? No," Tally replied. "Drive it back? Maybe."

"What happens if they can't?"

"It follows us and beats itself to death against the walls of a sanctuary."

More lights: above them this time. For a second, they were outlined in a blazing halo of light A marine helicopter, but it wasn't alone. The sky was filled with lights: white orbs glowing like stars, metallic reflective spheres and blinking red and green lights that Aiden might have mistaken for aircraft navigation lights until they started to spin across the sky. Any civilian aircraft running those lights would have to be turning cartwheels. They weren't aircraft. Each one was a probing finger pushed through the membrane that kept realities apart.

There were lights in the houses too. People woken by the thunder of midnight traffic on the usually quiet road.

"Shit!" Tally swore as she slammed on the brakes. "They've closed off the causeway."

The near side of the long bridge that linked the island with the Massachusetts coast was ablaze with light. Two huge APCs blocked the road under the tall pylons of work lights in front of a queue of civilian vehicles.

"They'll let us through, right?" Aiden asked.

Tally was already talking into her radio. "I need a clear path to Route One north of Rowley. I have the target." She threw the radio down in disgust.

"What's wrong?"

"Stay close," Tally said. She got out of the car, badge held high. "Naval Intelligence," she shouted as he pushed past a small crowd of bemused civilians towards the Marines. "I need to speak to your CO."

The crowd was growing, more and more vehicles backing up as panicked locals tried to get off the island. Others spilled out of the nearby houses, pointing their phones at the sky or just staring slack-jawed at the light show. They should still be asleep. In a few hours, they should be waking to their alarm clocks and the dawn of another day safe in the shared belief that the world was still sane. Instead, they stared at the blockade of armored vehicles and the alien suns bursting into existence above them and marveled at the strangeness they were witnessing. And with each broken routine, each furrowed brow and fleeting speculation that perhaps there was more to this world than they had imagined, the consensus grew weaker.

"It's spreading," Aiden said.

"I know," Tally replied.

Aiden looked up at the sky. There was a blur of motion above the drifting fog. Another helicopter, perhaps, but there was no noise.

"One of yours?" Aiden asked.

Tally shook her head.

Maybe it was that knowledge or maybe just its visibility started the change. Too many people could see it. Too many people who'd watched too many TV shows about abductions and alien autopsies, about Roswell and Atlantis, about cryptids, the Anunnaki or just harbored the desperate need to believe that there was more to life than the nine-to-five, ten days paid vacation, and unlimited refills at Taco Bell.

The people were primed. They stared up at the sky and started to believe.

The consensus was breaking down.

The whirling in the sky grew larger: a dark rotation of spindled arms turning against the stars, as if the sky was being pinched and twisted between great fingers.

Too many people saw too much of the unreality as it unfolded across the island, and with every person whose worldview was shaken, the breach grew.

And with every new growth, more people were turned.

The contagion was spreading.

The thing in the sky grew more and more solid. The spiral twisting of space became great arms radiating from a shapeless mass of a body.

Something streaked across the sky and slammed into the spiraled nightmare above. Aiden tracked the missile back to a helicopter, a real one this time, coming in low using the buildings as cover. It was small and agile. A two-seater attack helicopter with stubby wings bristling with armament pods: an Apache, or maybe a Viper.

Another sidewinder streaked from the gunship's port wing. It slammed into the papillae with a concussion that drove Aiden to his knees. He scampered into cover behind a parked car as burning chunks of flesh rained down around them and turned the air foul with a rancid stench.

The giant papillae fell to the ground, arms flailing. The thing was a mass of whip-like tentacles. Any earlier resemblance to a helicopter lost in a writhing mass of arms, some as fine as hairs, others fit to throw buses around like toys. The concrete under the creature blacked and cracked, disintegrating into a drift of black sand. It seemed more solid now: less dreamlike and more definite. Aiden could feel the pressure again as the creature stretched the limits of what their world could accommodate. Perhaps that made it vulnerable. Perhaps that meant it would need to submit to this universe's rules on high explosives.

The gunship's pilot seemed to sense some advantage too. It circled closer and opened up with its twenty-millimeter cannon.

The rounds tore through the thing, blowing out great chunks of flesh in horrific exit wounds and slamming into the crust of transformed concrete below, raising clouds of black dust. The creature's wounds pulsed, and new eyes grew to peer through the flaps of burst flesh like bloody eyelids.

The pressure was back. That sense of the other pushing against his reality. The air shimmered as the new papillae twisted the world around itself. Aiden panted ragged breaths as if even the oxygen around him had lost its potency.

The noise from the helicopter's engines rose in pitch as reality changed around it. The balance of forces that kept it in the sky stuttered and failed in the alien reality around the papillae. Metal shattered like ice; layers of carbon fiber and polycarbonate cracked and splintered. The helicopter folded around its cockpit, rotors flung away in centrifugal swarms of deadly hypersonic shards.

The papillae roared in victory, great arms writhing, trailing corruption as the consensus broke down.

They were trapped. Trapped in a liminal space between warring realities, between the Island and the mainland, between sanity and madness, between earth and water and the stinking corruption of bastardized physics that followed every movement of the huge papillae like slime after a snail.

One arm passed through Tally as if she was a shadow. In its wake it left death. Instant cellular death. Her skin turned grey and flaked away like sand. Blood and tissue simply ceasing to function in the altered physics of the alien papillae.

The grey skin started to weep a foul-smelling ichor of necrotic tissue. Her right leg crumpled under her, bones suddenly turned friable, snapping under her own weight, muscle turned to dead sacs of stinking jelly.

Her untouched head and left shoulder sagged against the ruin of her chest as the halves of her tried to slide apart.

"Go," she managed through what remained of her lungs and fell forward onto the concrete.

☣   ☣   ☣

Aiden backed away. He looked at the papillae and a hundred eyes stared back at him.

"You are defined by death... It clings to you."

He ran back to the car and snatched up Tally's radio. "Tally's down," he said into the radio. There was no answer. He didn't even know if anyone was listening. He pressed the button again. "Everyone is down. You can't beat this thing. All you can do is... restore the consensus. No witnesses, you understand? I don't know if it's still hitchhiking on me. Maybe it's too big now. But I'm headed to the hospital anyway. You know what to do."

There was dead air for a second and then.

"See you on the other side."

Aiden dropped the radio and set off towards The Hole.

☣   ☣   ☣

FROM: ########
SENT: ####
TO: #####
SUBJECT: Potential   Consensus   Break/Ref: 00046738XX

We may have a problem...

TRANSCRIPT BEGINS:

Welcome back to Shadow Narrative and boy do we have a show for you tonight.

It's just two months since the explosion at the Bear Island Naval Hospital. The community is still reeling from the resulting fire that took out half the island and led to most of the population of that small town being resettled.

If you're listening to this show, I'm sure you've heard the rumors: the F-35s seen taking off from Barnes Air National Guard base just minutes before the explosion, the closed-door hearings and media blackouts. But today we have eyewitness testimony from someone who was there that night, and they're bringing the receipts. Never before seen video of what really happened out there and, according to them... it was no gas explosion.

If this is your first time listening to the podcast, let's just say tonight's interview is going to make a believer out of you. It's going to turn your world upside down."

PLAGUE PIT

Charles R. Rutledge

I knew something was wrong when the train began to slow not long after we had left Goodge Street Station. A collective groan went up from my fellow passengers. Like me, they probably thought we were about to have one of those delays familiar to anyone who has spent much time on the London Underground.

If only.

"I can't believe this," a very blonde young woman in a fashionista raincoat said. "I have an appointment in twenty minutes."

She ended up missing that appointment as almost half an hour later we were still stuck in place. Up above it was late March and cold, but down in the tunnels the air was warm and becoming close. I heard a murmur pass through the car and, looking out the window, spotted flashlights bobbing up and down in the darkness from the direction of Goodge Street.

A couple of moments later, the train doors opened and two people clad in the familiar uniforms of the London Transport Authority stepped inside.

"Very sorry," one of the Transit people said. She was an attractive, middle aged Black woman. "We've had some trouble on the line and can't get you to Warren Street. Come with us, please, and we'll guide you back to Goodge Street."

"You mean we have to walk?" the blonde woman said.

The second Transit employee, a red-haired youth, said, "I'm afraid so, ma'am. It's only about a five-minute walk."

The blonde woman managed to look very put-upon, but she followed instructions, and the passengers began a more or less orderly exit from the train. I'd had to walk out of the underground before, so I knew there was a narrow walkway along the tracks, mostly used by workmen.

The Transit folks herded people to our right, but I glanced to my left as I stepped off the train and saw more flashlights, and something I wasn't expecting – a group of United Kingdom Special Forces, wearing flak jackets, and carrying Heckler & Koch MP5 submachine guns.

"You must have been expecting trouble from this lot," I said to the Transit lady.

She said, "Nothing to do with us, sir. Please keep moving."

I would have been more than happy to comply with her request. Whatever the Spec Ops guys were doing, it was none of my business. Until it was.

I heard shouts from the soldiers and then one of them began firing his weapon. The others focused their flashlight beams down the tunnel, and I saw something rushing toward them.

At first glance, I thought it was an enormous spider. It had an assortment of mismatched limbs arrayed around a central mass, and it didn't seem able to coordinate the movements of those appendages as it lurched our way. A thick layer of black slime covered the entire body. It glistened darkly in the emergency lights.

The bullets from the MP5 ripped through the thing, but it was still coming. The other ops began to fire. The sound of the submachine guns was deafening in the tunnel. Behind me, the train passengers screamed. I pushed past the Transit lady and headed toward the soldiers.

The creature reached the ops and landed on one of them, its slimy body hiding him from view. The man screamed for a moment, then went silent. The other men stopped firing and rushed up to the thing, attempting to wrestle it off their comrade. Various limbs whipped out to grasp the soldiers and I was stunned to see the familiar outlines of human hands.

Another man fell, and some of the black substance from the creature covered his head. The other two ops were still struggling but I could see more of the black slime crawling over them with questing tendrils as the gunk-covered hands clutched at their uniforms.

Grappling with the thing was obviously a bad idea, so I held out my hand and called the sword. It appeared in my grasp, three feet of gleaming steel with two razor edges. Being careful of the flailing soldiers I hacked into the slime-coated monstrosity.

The thing sent pseudopods of slime my way, but I chopped through them and the reaching hands that followed, continuing to cut away big chunks of the creature. I got another shock, as under the slime I recognized the structure of at least three human bodies that had been melded together in some obscene conglomeration.

I finally cut off enough of the thing that it stopped attacking me, though I could see it still was moving feebly. The two living soldiers managed to pull away from the creature, flicking away stands of squirming slime. They both moved to help their fallen friends, but a second later they recoiled and backed quickly away.

"Good God, it ate part of Paul," one of the men said.

I stepped up to see what he was looking at. Where the black slime had covered the other fallen man's head, the skull had caved in, and his eyes were gone.

I said, "Let's move away from this thing. And get your flak vests off. You don't want any of that stuff clinging to you."

"More of them!" Someone shouted.

The top-mounted lights on the MP5s showed half a dozen writhing, slime-coated things lurching our way.

All of them seemed to be composed of at least two melded human forms, and one monstrosity was made up of what looked like four unfortunate people. What were these things?

"Don't let them out of the tunnel!" the spec op guy closest to me said. "Where the hell are the flame throwers?"

Behind me, the train passengers continued to scream. I turned and saw at least one of the things had already gotten past us and had grasped two passengers in its glistening tentacles. It had four legs and the same number of arms and was using all those limbs to crawl.

I hadn't released the sword, and I hurried toward the creature and its prey. The smartest plan seemed to be to limit its mobility, so I cut through two of its legs, causing it to topple to one side. It pulled its two victims with it as it fell, and now I saw one of them was the blonde woman who had missed her appointment. She'd be missing all future appointments as the thing had already eaten half her face.

I continued to cut into the mass, though it fought back with appendages both human and slime. I dismembered it sufficiently to get clear of its grasp and stepped back. There was nothing I could do for the two people now.

Unfortunately, there was something they could do for, or rather, to me. The blonde woman sat up; her one remaining eye had gone as black and as soulless as that of a shark. She lurched to her feet and staggered toward me, her hands twisted into claws. The black slime flowed over her body and sent wiggling tendrils my way.

I had no illusions about the woman still being alive. I cut off her head, then split her torso from shoulder to waist. As near as I could tell, whatever intelligence the slime possessed, it was animating the bodies using the corpse's muscles, nerves, and such. Do enough damage and the body couldn't function.

Filaments of slime had stretched from the woman to the fallen man. I didn't wait for the other passenger to come at me. I hacked into him just as he began to stand. If I sound cold, it's just the way things are. I've been killing monsters for centuries.

The tunnel was filled with the sounds of gunfire and screaming. I turned back and saw not only had more soldiers arrived, but men wearing hazmat suits were milling about the train and the frightened passengers. Whatever the hell was going on, it was seriously bad.

A trio of spec ops hurried past me, carrying flame-thrower units. Some of the first group of soldiers had delt with the attack and escaped, but others lay struggling on the ground, covered in the black slime. As they began to rise with jerky, unhuman life, their former comrades shot them until they stopped moving. Then the flame-throwers did their gruesome work. I wasn't the only one who could see there was no saving the fallen.

Two of the men in Hazmat suits approached me. One of them said, "We'll need you to come with us, sir."

I said, "Unlikely."

"It wasn't a request, sir."

"Then it's even less likely."

The two men started toward me but one of the spec op boys stepped between us.

"Leave him," the op said. "He killed as many of those things as my men did and he hasn't got long. Go get the civilians, God help them."

I said, "Thanks for stepping in, but what do you mean I haven't got long."

The guy looked at me. He was probably about fifty and in good shape. "What's your name, son?"

"Gavin."

"Okay, Gavin. I'm Carver, and I'm sorry, mate. That stuff touched your skin. You've been exposed to an unbelievably deadly strain of bubonic plague."

"Come again?"

"The black death. That slime carries it. That's why we can't let it out of the tunnel."

I didn't tell him that I seem to be immune to disease. In the fifteen hundred or so years I've been alive, I haven't had so much as a head cold. "Even if that's true, the plague can be cured now with antibiotics."

"Not this strain. I'm truly sorry. You've got maybe an hour or two."

"What about you and the other soldiers?"

Carver shrugged. "We all volunteered. We know where this is probably going for us but that's the job, innit?"

I looked around at the weirdly lit tunnel and at the train passengers looking lost and afraid. "How did this happen? What is that stuff?"

"Long story, that. Why don't you come with me and the squad. I've got to get my team through this tunnel to Warren Street Station. I'll tell you what I can on the way. We can use you and that sword."

I'd forgotten I was still holding the sword. I opened my hand, and the blade vanished. "What sword?"

Carver grinned. "That's a good trick, but I hope you can bring it back."

"Guess we'll see. I'm still waiting for an explanation."

"You'll get one. Let me get this lot moving."

Carver called his men, and we started creeping down the tunnel. He offered me an MP5, which I declined, and a flashlight, which I accepted. I added my own beam to those of the ops. There were nine of us in total.

"Here's what I know," Carver said as we walked. "Late last night, a maintenance crew was replacing some rail segments in the tunnel near Warren Street. They had finished up and were on their way out of the tunnel. One of the workmen was walking on the side of the tracks when the ground collapsed, and he fell into a deep hole."

Carver shook his head. "He was injured, and the rest of the crew got some ropes, and someone went down to get him. They saw the hole was filled with human skeletons. They'd obviously been down there a long time."

I said, "A plague pit. A remnant of the plague of 1665. London is riddled with mass graves like that."

Carver gave me that expression that means I must be smarter than I look. I get that a lot. Thing was, I'd been in London during that plague.

"That's what the Government men tell me," Carver said. "But there was something else in the pit. A black ooze of some sort. Something that had evolved maybe, down there in the dark for all those years. When the workmen dragged their two friends out of the hole, they were covered in it. Within minutes..."

The soldier to my left suddenly leaned forward and vomited. The others moved away from him. They were tough men, but I could see fear on their faces.

Carver said, "You know we can't stop, Davey. Just sit down. It won't be long now."

"I'm sorry, Sarge," Davey said. "I guess I got too much of that stuff on me."

"Nothing to be sorry about. Not likely any of us are walking away from this."

Davey leaned against the wall and slumped down. The rest of us moved on toward Warren Street.

I said, "It acts very quickly."

"Horrifyingly so."

"The original plague did too. People used to say 'You could have breakfast with a loved one and bury them at supper', and that was true."

"Yes, well this is even worse. The people who came to help the work crew are all dead. Fortunately, one of the first responders recognized a potential outbreak and contacted his superiors.

"It was approaching rush hour by the time all this played out. They got the station shut down, but not before one train came through the tunnel. The one ahead of yours. A train load of people is dead now, along with everyone who was in Warren Street Station before it was sealed off."

We were quiet for a moment. Then I said, "What about those things we killed?"

"Creatures like that started coming out of the tunnel shortly after my people arrived. They killed the first team we sent in."

"The ooze appeared to be animating and controlling the bodies."

Carver nodded. "Yeah, though we don't know to what degree. It doesn't always take over the corpses. We think it may take a certain quantity of the slime to animate them, but hell, who knows?"

"Is that why you just left Davey?"

"Yeah. If he's lucky, he'll just die quietly. If not, the rear guard will finish him."

I said, "Any indication it's airborne?"

"Fortunately, no. Like traditional bubonic plague it seems to require contact with contaminated fluid or tissue. Of course, the problem is, the ooze is a mobile fluid. It's literally a crawling plague."

Up ahead came a wet, squelching sound. We all turned our lights down the tunnel. More slime-covered human 'meldings' were lurching and shambling our way.

I called the sword and got ready. "Carver, have your men focus their fire on the creatures on each side of the tunnel. I'm going up the middle to try and minimize your team's contact with the slime."

Carver said, "You're crazy, mate, but I can't argue with your tactics. I saw what you can do."

As the crew fired, I charged. The meldings flowed around me and I hacked and cut in every direction. The problem with the things was whatever intelligence was animating them was in the slime, not the corpses. Cutting off their heads wouldn't help. I had to keep hacking until they were too butchered to move.

Just using the flamethrowers wouldn't work either, because the things would keep coming until the fire did enough damage, so we'd have been fighting flaming foes, which didn't seem like a good idea. Once they were immobilized, both the body and the slime could be burned.

I was starting to think we were making progress and then something huge reared up out of the darkness, almost filling the tunnel. A great clot of mangled and melted flesh, coated in slime and flowing toward us like a foul river. Carver had told me a train full of people had died. Here were twenty or more of them, merged into a nightmare mass of writhing limbs and gnashing teeth.

I had no choice but to backpedal. It was that or go down beneath a flood of dead matter and slime. As I retreated, I continued to cut, hacking off arms, hands, and gleaming tentacles. Around me, a cacophony of soldiers firing and shouts of panic.

A trio of faces appeared in front of me out of the wall of flesh, with vacant eyes and snapping jaws. I hewed into them, detaching the half-melted heads from the mass. It didn't do much good, but at least I didn't have to stare into those faces anymore.

It took a long time, but eventually the sword and the MP5s wreaked enough havoc that the writhing serpent of melded dead things stopped advancing. I turned back to Carver and his squad. We had been eight after losing Davey and now were five. The remaining soldiers were spattered with gore and flecked with slime.

I said, "Get that gunk off your bare skin as fast as you can. As near as I can tell, the black ooze seems to be acting like a giant bacterium. It feeds on organic material and absorbs it."

"What does the bloody thing want?" Carver said.

"It appears to want to do what all bacteria want," I said. "To feed and multiply. We can't let it get out of the tunnels. It's limited to what raw material it can find down here, but if it gets to the streets above..."

Carver said, "That was the plan when we came down here, Gav. Find the source on the far side of Warren Street station and burn it. Hopefully, that will stop the spread. And speaking of burning, everyone move past this mess so we can light it up."

We continued on toward Warren Street, pausing only for two of the men to set fire to the pulsating mass. The stench of burning flesh followed us to the end of the tunnel. We stepped into the light of the station and climbed up to the platform.

I was expecting more creatures to attack as we emerged, but apparently the giant mass of them in the tunnels had exhausted the bacteria's reserve for the moment.

Or so I thought.

Without warning, a soldier I'd heard the others call Ron turned his head and expelled a stream of vomit and blood. When he turned back to us, his eyes were black, and his face seemed to be melting. Whatever the necessary level of contact was, he'd made it. He lunged at one of the other men, bearing him to the tile floor and tearing at his throat with his teeth.

Carver grabbed Ron by his shoulders and pulled him off the other man, sending Ron rolling away. I went after him, and as Ron scrambled to his feet, I cut off his head and hacked though his arms and legs. The fallen limbs and torso twitched and spasmed, but at least they couldn't ambulate.

Unfortunately, Ron's teeth had severed the main arteries in his comrade's neck. The man bled out before we could do anything. That left Carver, one soldier, and me.

The fallen man had been carrying one of the flame-thrower units. Carver unfastened the harness and slung the unit over his shoulder. "Like I said, we aren't getting out of this alive. The side tunnel is in the short junction between the Northern and Bakerloo lines. We have to reach it and damn quick, before we end up like Ron."

We followed the 'Way Out' signs along the passage between tunnels. Our footfalls echoed in the empty spaces. But when we reached the next platform, the space was no longer empty. Three good-sized meldings stood at the tunnel mouth. Whether they sensed or saw us, they started our way.

I didn't wait but leaped from the platform and into the midst of them, slashing and cutting all around. One of them that was only made from two corpses, latched on to me, clawing at my face. I shoulder-blocked it, shoving it away, and then cut through one of its legs.

From the platform, Carver and the other guy, whose name I hadn't learned, made controlled shots at the thing farthest from me. I continued cutting at the other two until they were down.

Carver and Other Guy climbed down, and we started into the tunnel. Carver said, "The hole the slime came out of should be a couple hundred yards ahead, Gav."

We continued down the tunnel. Between the emergency lights and our flashlights, I could finally make out a ragged opening in the floor off to the right. There it was. The plague pit. I didn't see any sign of meldings. That was good news.

The bad news was something else was climbing out of the pit. There were doubtless a couple of dead workmen in the massive form clambering from the ground, but it was mostly mud, muck, and bones, mixed with the ever-present slime. These were the original inhabitants of the pit. A stench rolled off the thing like an abattoir in summertime.

"Jesus, God," Other Guy said.

"Yeah," I agreed.

The thing was almost shapeless, having just enough semblance to human or animal form to have limbs for motion. It was going to be a lot harder to hack it to pieces than the meldings. I caught a glimpse of something glittering in the dark mass. For a moment, I thought it was just a reflection, but then I saw it was something generating an eldritch glow of its own.

I said, "There's some sort of artifact in that thing, Carver."

He didn't answer. I turned to see him down on hands and knees, retching his guts out. He looked up at me, with black slime dripping from his lips.

"Don't let it take me, Gav," Carver said. "I don't want to end up like that."

"I won't," I said. Then I stepped up and cut off his head.

I looked at Other Guy and he gave me a quick nod. He was a soldier. He understood what I'd done.

I said, "Empty your magazine at that thing. Aim for the limbs and do as much damage as you can."

Other Guy did as I asked, firing away at the things. I let the sword go, picked up Carver's MP5, and did the same. We managed to do some damage but not nearly enough. When we were both out of ammo, I told Other Guy to get one of the flame units ready. Then I called the sword and turned back toward the crawling plague.

It was, without doubt, one of the most stomach-churning things I'd ever seen, a great mass of dark, viscous matter with hundreds of bones and skulls sticking out of it. The plague-carrying slime writhed around on its surface like many, black, glistening snakes, and waved ebon tentacles in the air.

The artifact, whatever it was, was wedged in the 'front' of the thing, and I got the feeling that it could 'see' me. It was my primary target, and I rushed in, aiming the sword at it.

But one of the big appendages swung toward me and I was forced to block. Ancient jagged and broken bones slashed at me. I kept it from hitting me, but the impact knocked me backwards and I fell.

Other Guy pulled his sidearm, a Sig Sauer 9mm and emptied it into the thing. It didn't bother it much, but it turned from me and started toward the soldier. Other Guy tried to angle to one side, but in the tunnel, he didn't have much room to maneuver, and the plague creature slammed into him, dozens of sharp, ragged bones impaling him and pinning him to the tunnel wall. The thing scraped him along the wall for good measure, before scrabbling back my way.

Other Guy's blood soaked into the monster's hide as it lurched toward me. One of its pseudopods reached for me, but I leaped over it and drove a hard, downward cut at the edge of the artifact. It broke loose from the thing's surface and clattered to the floor.

The crawling plague beast stumbled for a moment, then toppled to one side and lay still. As I watched, the black slime, so hideously active moments before, flowed from the creature sluggishly and seemed to be stretching out feelers for the artifact.

I rushed in and snatched the object away from the ooze's grasp. I took several steps back and looked at the artifact. It was an amulet, mostly gold, with a single, large emerald in its center. The gem gave off a baleful glow. Carved into the gold above the jewel were some words in Latin.

'Exurgent mortui et ad me veniunt'

The necromancer's chant. Translated loosely to English: the dead will rise and come to me.

I looked down at my feet. The slime had almost reached me. I took another step back and placed the amulet on the floor. Then I raised the sword and used the hilt to smash the jewel and crush the gold with its carved words.

The slime stopped moving.

I stood and released a long breath. How had a necromancer's amulet come to be in the pit? Perhaps the plague had taken some unknown magus back in the 1660s, and his body had been tossed into the mass grave with the rest. I'd likely never know. But somehow, the relic had kept the plague alive all those years, waiting down there in the dark. And perhaps it had sustained something of the will of the necromancer as well.

I picked up one of the flame throwers and tossed it into the pit. Then I used Carver's sidearm to shoot it, sending up a great explosion of flame. I used the other unit to burn the inert mass of muck and bones, and the bodies of my two fallen comrades. I was taking no chances.

The heat forced me to step out of the tunnel and back into the station. Wearily, I dragged myself up to the platform, then began the long walk back to daylight.

ONE BULLET

Aysline McGrath

Mission Briefing

The tactical display cast light across scarred knuckles and calloused hands. Captain Marcus Reyes studied the holographic projection of Research Station Delta, three miles beneath the Pacific. Around the briefing table, his handpicked team ran final equipment checks.

"Run it again," Reyes ordered, his voice carrying the weight of fifteen years in Special Operations. "Thompson?"

Private Jessica Thompson, fresh from Force Recon's advanced combat diver school, pulled up the sonar readings.

"Last transmission at 0300 hours, sir. Seismic activity followed by multiple hull breaches. Security feeds showed..." She hesitated. "Movement patterns inconsistent with known marine predators."

"Show them," Admiral Chen commanded from the shadows.

The hologram shifted. Security footage showed a research team member moving through a flooded corridor. The timestamp jumped – same corridor, same angle. Something else moved through the frame. The analysts had enhanced it: elongated limbs, too many joints, a face that wasn't quite human anymore.

"Jesus," Corporal David Lee whispered, checking the seals on his modified HK416 for the third time. The weapon had been specially adapted for extreme depth operations – pressure-compensated action, UV-enhanced rounds, and an integrated sonar targeting system.

"Twenty-eight personnel unaccounted for," Sergeant Sarah Kim reported, her marine biology credentials evident in how she analyzed the creature's movements. "Sir, these biological readings... they're showing rapid cellular reconstruction."

Admiral Chen activated another display. "Three previous attempts at contact have failed. Last rescue team..." The footage showed armed divers entering the station. Static. Then screaming.

"We're running a full tactical loadout," Reyes began, moving to the equipment table. "Pressure-rated combat gear, modified for three thousand feet. Primary weapons: HK416s with UV rounds. Sidearms: modified FN Five-sevens with thermite tips. Kim, you'll carry the sonic deterrent package."

"The LRAD might work," Kim agreed, checking the Low-Frequency Resonance Acoustic Device. "Deep sea creatures are sensitive to certain harmonics."

"Thompson, you're our demo specialist. We're carrying enough thermite to melt through the station's core if necessary."

"Understood, sir." Thompson patted her explosive charges. "These babies burn hot enough to cut through anything. Even underwater."

"Lee, medical kit plus emergency mutations protocol gear. The CDC provided experimental counter-agents, but they're untested at these depths."

Lee nodded grimly, checking his medical pack. The syringes inside glowed faintly; experimental bioweapons designed to combat mutation.

"Questions?" Reyes surveyed his team. Their faces showed appropriate concern, but no fear. Not yet.

"Sir," Thompson spoke up. "Rules of engagement regarding infected personnel?"

The room grew colder.

Admiral Chen stepped forward. "These were taken

twelve hours ago." New images appeared: twisted forms moving through dark water. "These aren't personnel anymore. They're biological hazards with military training. Terminate on sight.

"There's more," Chen continued. "The research team found something in a sixteenth-century Portuguese wreck. An artifact. Our orders are to secure it or destroy it. Nothing reaches the surface without authorization."

Reyes studied the tactical overlay again. Three miles of ocean above them. Pitch black. Crushing pressure. And somewhere in that darkness, things that used to be human. "Gear up," he ordered. "We drop in thirty minutes. Whatever's down there, we end it. Understood?"

"Yes sir!" The response was automatic, trained. They were professionals. They'd handled black ops, wetwork, things that never made official reports.

But as they moved to the armory, Reyes caught their subtle tells. Thompson double-checking her magazine count. Lee's fingers brushing his cross. Kim's eyes lingering on the creature footage.

They were the best. But they were about to face something worse than their worst nightmares.

Descent to the Depths

The military submarine Nautilus cut through the Pacific waters like a bullet through midnight. Reyes watched the depth gauge tick steadily downward: five hundred feet... a thousand feet... fifteen hundred. With each hundred meters, the darkness outside the reinforced viewport grew more absolute.

"Anyone else feel like we're being swallowed alive?" Thompson's attempt at humor couldn't mask her unease. The rookie's fingers drummed against her tactical vest, a nervous rhythm that echoed through the cramped cabin.

Sergeant Kim adjusted the sonar display, her face bathed in its ghostly green glow.

"There's something beautiful about it," she mused, "knowing we're heading into one of Earth's last unexplored frontiers—"

A series of strange pings interrupted her reflection; sound signatures that didn't match any known marine species.

"Beautiful isn't the word I'd use," Lee muttered, checking the seals on his medical kit for the fourth time. "My grandfather was a deep-sea fisherman. Used to tell stories about things down here that..." He fell silent as a massive shadow passed overhead, visible only as a momentary eclipse of the submersible's external lights.

The vessel creaked under the increasing pressure. Two thousand feet now. The water outside took on a strange quality; patches of bioluminescence pulsed in patterns that seemed almost calculated, like distant morse code signals.

"Anyone else seeing this?" Thompson pointed to a cluster of lights that definitely wasn't following natural movement sequences. The lights swirled, converged, then scattered like startled fish.

"Maintaining course," Reyes announced, his steady voice an anchor in the growing tension. But even he couldn't ignore the way the submersible's metal hull groaned, as if something out there was testing it.

A haunting sound filtered through the hull; a low, whale-like moan, but distorted.

Sergeant Kim's instruments spiked. "That's impossible," she whispered. "That signature is similar to human vocal cords but..."

The words hung unfinished as they passed through a cloud of debris. In the beam of their lights, they could make out fragments of metal and what looked like shredded diving suits.

"Three thousand feet," Reyes reported. "Research Station Delta should be visible soon."

As if on cue, their lights lit up a massive structure looming out of the abyss. But something was wrong with its silhouette. Sections of the station's outer hull appeared warped, as if something had tried to force its way in... or out.

"Welcome to the bottom of the world," Reyes said softly. "Keep your weapons close."

Arrival at the Research Station
The airlock cycled with a hiss, releasing stale air that carried a faint, unfamiliar odor. Something between rotting seaweed and copper. Captain Reyes led the team into the station's main corridor, their helmet lights cutting through the darkness. Emergency lighting cast sporadic red pulses across water-stained walls.

"Power's still operational," Kim noted, checking her tablet. "But these readings... make no sense."

They passed a common area that told its own story of chaos. Half-eaten meals lay moldering on tables, chairs overturned. A coffee mug lay shattered, its contents long dried into a dark stain that trailed across the floor like something had been dragged through it.

"Signs of struggle," Lee observed, kneeling to examine scratch marks on the metal flooring. "These aren't from furniture." He ran his gloved finger along the grooves. "Whatever made these was sharp."

Thompson discovered a personal tablet, its screen cracked but still functioning. "Sir, look at this." She played the last recorded video entry. A panicked researcher appeared, his skin bearing strange, iridescent patches.

"*...changing us... the samples... don't let them...*" The video dissolved into static.

The containment lab doors stood partially open; their emergency locks apparently overridden. Inside, the team found a batch of specimen tanks. Most were shattered, their contents long gone, but one remained intact. Within it, something pulsed with an unnatural blue glow.

"My God," Kim breathed, examining the specimen. "The cellular structure... it's attempting to mimic and modify other organic material." She pointed to a nearby microscope display, still active. "These aren't just mutations. They're transformations."

Captain Reyes discovered a research log, its pages water-damaged but legible. His flashlight revealed hurried notes:

Day 47: Specimen shows unprecedented ability to alter host DNA

Day 48: Crew experiencing unusual symptoms

Day 49: Morrison's transformation... God help us... they're still conscious after...

A distant metallic clang echoed through the station's corridors. Followed by what sounded like wet footsteps. The team's lights snapped toward the sound.

"We're not alone," Reyes whispered and raised his weapon. "Form up. Thompson, watch our six."

The emergency lights flickered, and in that moment of darkness, something moved in the corridor behind them.

"Split up and search the station," Reyes ordered, his voice tight. "Kim, check the research labs. Lee, medical bay. Thompson, with me to the crew quarters. Stay on comms."

Corporal Lee made his way to the medical bay, his flashlight beam revealing overturned equipment and scattered supplies. In a corner desk, he found a leather-bound journal, its pages filled with increasingly erratic handwriting.

"Captain, you need to hear this," Lee's voice crackled over the radio. "The station's chief medical officer documented the infections. Listen: *'Patient zero showed signs within hours. Shimmering patches spreading across the skin, followed by severe muscle spasms. By day three, the skeletal structure began to realign.'*"

In the research labs, Kim discovered computer logs detailing genetic analyses.

"These readings are impossible," she muttered. "The organism doesn't just alter DNA. It rewrites it completely. Like it's trying to return human cells to some prehistoric state."

Thompson and Reyes encountered their own horrors in the crew quarters. Personal effects lay scattered; family photos, letters home, daily routines interrupted mid-moment. Thompson's light caught something on a bathroom mirror: a handprint, but the fingers were stretched out and webbed.

"Sir," Lee's voice trembled slightly. "The journal's final entry... *The screaming is the worst part. They scream, not only out of pain, but because they feel their thoughts changing, their memories slipping away. Morrison recognized me yesterday. Today, he tried to tear my throat out.*"

A sudden power surge caused the lights to flare. In that brief flash, they all saw it; dark stains on the walls; trail marks. As if something had been crawling across the surface.

A wet slithering sound came from above. Thompson's light caught movement – a flash of pale flesh disappearing around a corner. The emergency lights pulsed red, turning the corridor into a strobe-lit nightmare.

"Movement!" Thompson called out, weapon raised. "Eleven o'clock, upper level!"

The creature struck before they could react. It dropped from an overhead vent, its mutated form a horrific fusion of human and marine anatomy. What had once been a crew member now moved with grace, its long limbs ending in webbed talons.

"Contact!" Reyes opened fire, but the creature moved like mercury, each bullet missing as it ricocheted off walls. Kim dove for cover as claws raked through the air where her head had been, leaving deep gouges in the metal wall.

Lee scrambled for his med kit but froze as the creature landed between him and his gear. Up close, they saw the full horror of its transformation. Flesh rippled with bioluminescent patches, jaw distended to reveal rows of needle-like teeth. Its black eyes reflected their terror back at them.

The thing moved, testing their defenses. It feinted toward Kim, then suddenly changed direction, launching itself at Reyes. He barely managed to dodge, feeling talons slice through his tactical vest like paper. The creature's inhuman shriek reverberated through the metal corridors as it rebounded off walls.

"Fall back!" Reyes commanded, laying down suppressing fire. "Main lab! Go!"

The creature retreated into a ventilation duct, metal groaning as it contorted its mutated form through the small space. The sound of its movement echoed all around them, making it impossible to track.

They regrouped in the main lab, sealing the doors.

Kim shared her findings, voice shaking. "The organism appears dormant in cold temperatures, but once it makes contact with a host..." She swallowed hard. "The transformation seems to follow a pattern: skin changes, skeletal reconstruction, organ adaptation for underwater survival."

"And the mind?" Thompson asked quietly, keeping her weapon trained on the ventilation grate above them.

"According to these notes," Lee answered, examining Reyes's skin, and breathing a sigh of relief when he found no injury, "that's the final change. But the victims remain conscious throughout the entire process. Aware of everything they're becoming."

A low, gurgling sound echoed through the ventilation system. Something was moving through the station's arteries, hunting them.

"We need to find out what happened here," Reyes said grimly. Cold sweat broke across his forehead as he realized how close he'd come to sharing the fate of the transformed crew members. One scratch was all it would take.

The Pressure Builds

The first tremor hit without warning. Metal groaned as the entire station shuddered, sending equipment crashing to the floor. Emergency sirens blared to life, their wail mixing with the sound of straining steel.

"Status report!" Reyes shouted over the noise.

Sergeant Kim rushed to the nearest terminal, fingers flying across the keyboard.

"Seismic activity on the ocean floor. The pressure differential is—" Another violent shake cut her off. "Sir, the main communications array just went dark!"

"Surface link?" Reyes demanded.

"Nothing. We're cut off."

Thompson stood at a viewport, her face pale as she watched massive air bubbles rise from somewhere beneath the station. "Those old shipwrecks are shifting on the seafloor."

"We need to evacuate," Lee insisted, gathering their medical supplies. "Whatever happened to the previous team, we've seen enough. We can come back with a larger force—"

"Stand down, Corporal," Reyes ordered. "We're not leaving until we understand what we're dealing with. If this contagion spreads to the surface—"

"With all due respect, sir," Lee shot back, "we're not equipped for this. Did you see those transformation records? We're sitting in a trap, and now we can't even call for backup!"

The pressure gauges on the wall climbed, their needles trembling in the red zone. A distant part of the station creaked dangerously.

"He's right," Thompson added, her confidence cracking. "We're not containment specialists."

"We're what's standing between this thing and the rest of the world," Kim said. "The quarantine protocols in the research logs... they tried to contain it but failed. We might be the last chance to stop it here."

Another tremor rocked the station. Somewhere, metal shrieked against metal.

"Listen to yourselves," Lee said. "We're trapped three miles under the ocean with something that turns people into monsters, and you want to stay?"

"That's enough!" Reyes's voice cut through the argument. "This isn't a democracy. Our orders are to investigate and contain. Until we know exactly what we're dealing with, no one's going anywhere."

The lights flickered, and in the short darkness, they all heard it; a wet, sliding sound in the walls. Then a laugh, distorted and bubbling, echoing through the ventilation system.

They weren't just trapped in the depths. They were trapped with something that was waiting for them.

First Signs of Infection

"Don't touch anything without gloves," Kim warned, her voice echoing in the containment lab. The tremors had knocked over specimen containers, their contents forming iridescent puddles that seemed to pulse in the emergency lighting.

Thompson cataloged the damage, her helmet camera recording. "Most samples appear to be..." She trailed off, distracted by movement in one of the puddles. The liquid wasn't just spreading; it was moving against gravity, creeping up the sides of broken containers.

"Thompson?" Reyes said.

"Just thought I saw..." She shook her head and stepped forward.

The floor was slick. Her boot slipped.

Time slowed. Thompson's hand shot out instinctively to catch herself. The broken tank's edge sliced through her glove. For a moment, no one moved. They all stared at the small cut, watching as drops of her blood mixed with the sample.

"Med bay," Lee said quietly. "Now."

The first hour was deceptive. The cut was cleaned, bandaged. Thompson's vitals remained stable but she couldn't stop staring at her hand.

"The rate of transformation correlates with exposure type," Kim explained, studying the medical readouts. "Direct contact with pure samples causes rapid mutation. Secondary exposure is slower, more gradual."

"It feels wrong," she whispered. "Like something's watching me from inside."

Kim noticed it first. Thompson's veins near the cut were turning black, pulsing with a faint light. When Thompson's nose began bleeding, the drops glowed on the med bay floor.

"My skin," Thompson's voice cracked. "It's too tight. Like something's trying to..." She clawed at her arm until Reyes grabbed her wrist. Where her nails had broken the skin, the wounds shimmered.

The scanner in Lee's hands screamed alerts. "Her cellular structure is... Jesus Christ."

Thompson convulsed. The sound that came from her throat wasn't human but a wet, clicking noise that made the others instinctively back away. Her spine arched, pressing against her skin from within.

"Help me," she begged, but her voice was already changing, developing harmonics that hurt their ears. "I can feel them. In my head. So many voices... so hungry..."

Her transformation wasn't just physical – they watched awareness drain from her eyes like water. When her bones began to crack and reform, her screams carried both agony and ecstasy.

Blood vessels burst beneath her skin. Her fingers elongated with wet, tearing sounds, bones splintering and reforming into talons. Through her stretching skin, they could see her muscles unknitting and reweaving themselves into inhuman configurations.

"Hold her down!" Reyes ordered, but Thompson's strength had become monstrous.

She threw Lee violently across the room. The impact left a dent in the metal wall.

Thompson's jaw dislocated with a sound like breaking ice. Rows of needle-teeth punched through her gums in waves. Her eyes... her eyes were the worst. They didn't just change color but transformed into something that shouldn't exist in nature, depths that seemed to go on forever.

"The water calls," she gurgled through a throat that was more gills than vocal cords. "We've been waiting so long..."

Her ribcage exploded outward, shredding her uniform and rupturing skin. Internal organs hung suspended in the cavity, pulsing and writhing against gravity as if held by invisible strings. Everyone stared, frozen, at the glistening collection of organs.

When she lunged, it wasn't the attack that horrified them most, it was the grace. Every motion perfectly adapted to an environment humans were never meant to inhabit.

"Seal the med bay!" Kim's hand slammed the lockdown control. But Thompson's body flowed through the narrowing gap like water, leaving trails of blood.

They ran, pursued by sounds no human throat could make. The station's lights flickered, and in the darkness, they caught glimpses of her. Now a perfect fusion of human and deep-sea horror.

At the main junction, they finally saw her fully transformed. Thompson's new body rippled with bioluminescent patterns that spoke of abyssal depths. Her black eyes found them through the pressure door's window.

When her distended jaw split into a smile, they saw not just teeth, but a hunger older than humanity.

And in the darkness behind her, other lights began to answer her call.

Psychological Breakdown

An oppressive silence hung in the control room. Captain Reyes stared through the reinforced glass at the section where Thompson—or what remained of her—had disappeared into the darkness. His hand hadn't left his weapon since their retreat.

"We need to check ourselves for contamination," Lee said, voice trembling as he pulled out his medical scanner. "Any cuts, any exposure..."

Kim's hands shook as she removed her gloves, examining every inch of skin. "I keep feeling... itching. Like something's crawling under my skin." She scratched at her arm until Reyes grabbed her wrist.

"Stop," he ordered, but his usual authority wavered. "We can't give in to paranoia."

A distant screech echoed through the station's corridors. The lights flickered, and in that moment of darkness, Lee swore he saw something move across the ceiling – a shadow with too many limbs.

"The water pressure's affecting the hull integrity," Kim reported. "Or maybe... they're trying to get in. The transformed crew, they could be anywhere in the station's infrastructure by now."

Reyes found himself drawn to his reflection in a darkened monitor. For a moment, he thought he saw his pupils expanding, becoming black and endless like Thompson's had. He blinked hard, and his normal eyes stared back.

"Captain," Lee whispered, "I think I'm seeing things. The walls are pulsing like they're breathing."

"It's just stress," Reyes insisted, but even he couldn't

ignore how the shadows seemed to writhe at the edges of their flashlight beams. "We need to stay focused."

Kim suddenly doubled over, gagging. "The smell... Can't you smell it? Like rotting fish and copper..."

But when the others checked the air quality monitors, they showed normal readings.

The station groaned under the immense pressure of the depths. Or was it something else moving through the structure? The sound of dripping water echoed from multiple directions, making it impossible to tell what was real and what was imagination.

"We should separate," Lee suggested, his eyes wild. "If one of us is infected... we can't risk it."

"No!" Reyes slammed his fist on the console. "That's exactly what it wants. Division. Isolation. We stay together."

A wet laugh echoed through the ventilation system, Thompson's voice, but distorted, inhuman. *"Together... yes... join us..."*

Kim screamed, pointing at the viewport. For a split second, they all saw it; a mass of twisted forms moving in the darkness outside, faces pressed against the glass. Faces they recognized from the crew manifest.

"They're in my head," Lee moaned, pressing his palms against his temples. "I can hear them."

"Listen to me," Reyes grabbed both Kim and Lee by the shoulders. "Whatever this thing is, it's playing with our minds. We have to stay rational."

But as another tremor shook the station, they all heard it; a chorus of voices rising from the depths, a siren song of transformation and surrender. And somewhere within that symphony, Thompson was calling their names.

Through the viewport, the ocean's darkness seemed to pulse with bioluminescent light, like a heartbeat growing stronger, drawing them deeper into madness.

Discovering the Truth

"There has to be more," Reyes muttered, forcing open another sealed door in the research wing. The emergency lights cast a glow across rows of abandoned equipment. Behind him, Kim and Lee moved in tight formation, jumping at every shadow.

"Wait," Kim called, her flashlight beam catching a keypad hidden behind a loose panel. "This isn't on any station schematic."

The hidden door slid open, revealing a laboratory that made their blood run cold. Specimens in various stages of transformation floated in preservation tanks. Charts and diagrams covered the walls, documenting the progression of change.

"My God," Lee whispered, examining a series of microscope slides. "The organism... it's not just changing them physically. Look at this cellular structure. It's complete genetic rewriting."

Reyes found a terminal still running on emergency power. His fingers flew across the keyboard, accessing research logs. "Listen to this: *'Subject zero made contact with artifact recovered from wreck site Delta. Initial transformation occurred within hours. Subsequent infections spread through direct fluid contact and... environmental exposure.'*"

"Environmental exposure?" Kim's voice cracked. "You mean just being here..."

"No," Lee interrupted, studying a contamination map. "It needs a medium. Water. Specifically, water that's been in contact with infected tissue or the original source." He pointed to notations on the chart. "That's why the pressure suits protected the recovery team initially."

Reyes continued reading, his face growing darker. *"'The organism appears to possess both biological and psychological vectors of infection. Subjects report shared consciousness, compelling urges to spread the contagion. Attempts at containment have failed as transformed individuals demonstrate unprecedented ability to adapt to aquatic conditions and...'"*

"What?" Kim demanded. "What else?"

"*'They're not just surviving in the deep pressure,'*" Reyes read slowly. "*'They're thriving. Evolution accelerated beyond anything we've seen. And they're all connected, part of something larger, something old.'*"

A crash echoed from the corridor. Through the lab's observation window, a massive shape moved past. Far larger than Thompson had been.

"We need to contain this," Reyes said, downloading the research data. "If any of these creatures reach the surface..."

"The whole coast could be infected within days," Lee finished grimly.

Kim's hand brushed against a damp surface, and she jerked back with a gasp. In the dim light, tiny luminescent spots had already begun appearing on her skin. "We're running out of time."

The Infected Team Member

Kim's scream shattered the tense silence. The spots on her skin spread like wildfire, pulsing with an otherworldly glow. She clawed at her throat as gills split open beneath her jaw.

"Hold her!" Reyes commanded, but Lee hesitated, remembering Thompson.

Kim's spine arched unnaturally, her uniform tearing as ridges erupted along her back. Her eyes, already clouding over with a pearlescent film, locked onto Lee. "I can hear them so clearly now," she gasped, her voice distorting. "The others... Thompson... they're all connected. So beautiful..."

"Kim, fight it!" Reyes raised his weapon but couldn't bring himself to pull the trigger. Not yet. Not while there was still something human in her eyes.

The transformation accelerated. Kim's skin sloughed off in wet sheets, revealing iridescent scales underneath. Her fingers elongated, webbing spreading between them as curved talons erupted from the tips. The sound of cracking bones filled the lab as her jaw dislocated, reforming into something better suited for the depths.

"Captain?" Lee backed away.

The thing that had been Kim moved with impossible speed. She slammed Lee against the specimen tanks, shattering them. Preserved mutation samples spilled across the floor, their stench overwhelming. Lee screamed as the contaminated water soaked through his uniform.

Reyes opened fire, but Kim was already moving again, her new form fluid and deadly. She crashed through the observation window, disappearing into the darkness of the corridor. Lee's screams turned to gurgles as his own transformation began.

"I'm sorry," Reyes whispered, and fired twice. Lee's body slumped; the change halted permanently.

A wet, scraping sound drew his attention back to the corridor. Kim wasn't alone. Thompson's massive form emerged from the shadows, even more mutated than before. Where Kim's transformation was sleek and predatory, Thompson had become something brutish; layers of muscle and armored scales, massive claws dragging against the metal floor.

They had him cornered. Kim circled to his left, Thompson to his right. In their inhuman faces, he could still see traces of his team members, but their eyes held nothing but alien hunger.

"Your turn, Captain," Kim's voice was a wet rasp. "Join us in the deep. Become part of something greater."

Reyes backed against the lab controls.

Thompson lunged first. Reyes dove, rolling under her massive arm as claws tore through the space where he'd been. Kim's talons raked his back, drawing blood. The burning sensation told him he was already infected.

In desperation, Reyes triggered the lab's emergency protocols. Decontamination sprays hissed from the ceiling, filling the room with caustic chemicals. The creatures shrieked, their modified flesh sizzling.

Reyes used the distraction to break free, sealing the lab behind him. Through the broken window, Kim and Thompson thrash in agony before retreating into the ventilation system, their inhuman howls echoing through the station.

Blood trickled down his back, each drop glowing faintly when it pattered to the floor. He could feel it; a whisper in his mind, calling him to the depths. His hand shook as he checked his weapon's ammunition.

Four full mags. And one bullet left in his sidearm. But first, he had to finish this. Had to find a way to stop the infection before it reached the surface. Before what remained of his humanity slipped away completely.

The station groaned around him, and somewhere in the darkness, his former team members waited.

☣   ☣   ☣

Reyes stumbled through the corridor, each step a battle against the transformation spreading through him. The infection from Kim's attack burned like ice in his veins, and the whispers in his mind grew louder with each passing minute.

Through the haze of pain, he forced himself to focus on the station schematics displayed on his tablet. The nuclear reactor that powered the facility lay at its heart. Enough raw power to sterilize everything within a half-mile radius. Including the ancient artifact that had started all of this.

"You can't stop evolution, Captain," Thompson's voice echoed through the ventilation system.

His fingers trembled as he input commands into the reactor control terminal. The station's warning systems blared to life, but he could barely hear them over the roaring in his ears. In the reflection of the screen, he watched in horror as his eyes began to cloud over with that familiar pearlescent film.

"Override code: Alpha-Seven-Delta," he growled, his voice already beginning to distort. "Initiate core meltdown sequence."

The terminal flashed red: *WARNING–CONTAINMENT BREACH IMMINENT – 15:00 MINUTES TO CRITICAL*

A brutish tremor rocked the station. Through the viewport, dozens of transformed creatures converged on the facility; former crew members, now part of something larger, something ancient that had waited centuries in these depths.

"We feel your change, Captain," Kim's voice joined the chorus in his mind. "Why fight it? The deep is calling..."

Reyes collapsed against the console as another wave of transformation wracked his body. His uniform was already splitting as ridges formed along his spine. But he wasn't finished. Not yet.

He forced himself up, checking his weapon one last time. One bullet remained. He held tight to that information. His last resort if the reactor failed. Through the pain, he plotted his course to the artifact chamber. He had fourteen minutes to reach it before the core went critical.

Somewhere in the darkness ahead, he heard the wet slither of mutated forms moving through the corridors. His former team members were determined to stop him from destroying their newfound evolution.

"I'm sorry," he whispered, though he wasn't sure if he was apologizing to his team or to whatever remained of his humanity. The transformation continued its relentless advance, but he had to finish this. He had to reach the artifact before the deep claimed him completely. *One bullet left.*

The station groaned under the weight of the ocean, and Reyes began his final mission.

The Confrontation

The reactor's warning echoed through the corridors as Reyes fought against his own body. Each step toward the artifact chamber sent waves of agony through his transforming muscles. *One bullet left.* Behind him, the timer counted down: 12:47 until meltdown.

The passage to the ancient shipwrecks had collapsed, forcing him through flooded maintenance tunnels. His flashlight beam caught movement in the murky water; twisted shapes that might once have been human. The infection heightened his senses; he could feel them watching, waiting.

"You're one of us now," Thompson's voice resonated in his skull. "Why deny what you're becoming?"

Reyes pressed on, even as scales erupted along his arms. The maintenance tunnel opened into a vast chamber where the Portuguese shipwreck lay preserved in the station's artificial environment. Ancient timber, black with age, rose like ribs of some prehistoric beast. The dark water swirled around his stomach.

Kim emerged from behind a rotted mast, her transformed body now a horrific fusion of human and deep-sea predator. "The artifact calls to us, Captain. It chose us to evolve, to adapt."

"It's killing us," Reyes growled, his voice gurgling as gills tried to form in his throat. "We're not evolving. We're being consumed."

More shapes slithered from the darkness. Former research team members, now monstrous parodies of marine life. Their bodies pulsed, casting sickly light across the chamber. Thompson's massive form crashed through a rotted hull section, now more creature than human.

"Remember Panama?" Thompson's distorted voice carried a hint of her former self. "When you left Jackson behind to complete the mission? You're always willing to sacrifice others, Captain. But can you sacrifice yourself?"

The words hit harder than any physical blow. Reyes stumbled, memories of past failures threatening to overwhelm him. The infection seized the moment of weakness, sending fresh waves of transformation through his body.

"I made mistakes," he admitted, fighting to maintain control as his fingers began to web together. *One bullet.* "But this isn't about me. If this infection reaches the surface..."

Kim lunged with inhuman speed. Reyes barely managed to dodge, but her talons raked his side. Fresh blood clouded the water, glowing with infection. The other creatures moved closer, drawn by the scent.

Through the pain and guilt, Reyes saw the artifact chamber's entrance beyond the wreck. But Thompson stood between him and his goal, her massive form blocking the way. In her mutated features, he saw accusation – for all the times he'd chosen the mission over his people.

"I'm sorry," he told his former team, raising his weapon. "For everything."

The creatures attacked as one. Reyes fired, each shot finding its mark but doing little damage to their mutated flesh. He fought hand-to-hand as his ammunition ran out, using their own momentum against them. Kim's talons missed his throat by inches. Thompson's massive arm shattered a support beam where his head had been moments before.

The reactor warning flashed: 10:00 minutes remaining.

In desperation, Reyes triggered emergency charges he'd planted during his approach. The explosions sent timbers crashing down, momentarily separating him from the creatures. He used the chaos to break for the artifact chamber, Thompson's roar of rage following him through the darkness.

Blood trailed in his wake, each drop glowing brighter as the infection spread. His fingers brushed his sidearm. *One bullet.* But ahead, through the chamber doors, he caught his first glimpse of what they'd found in the wreck; an object that pulsed with light, calling to the monster he was becoming.

Destroying the Artifact

The reactor warning flashed 6:13 as Reyes established his final defensive position. Years of CQC training told him the artifact chamber's architecture was a tactical nightmare: multiple entry points, poor visibility, and too many angles of attack. He set up his last UV flares in a defensive perimeter, creating zones of illumination that would reveal incoming threats.

Contact, multiple vectors. His enhanced senses picked up movement from three directions. Kim emerged from an overhead vent, her mutated form now perfectly adapted for three-dimensional combat. Thompson's massive bulk crashed through the main doorway, while transformed research team members slithered through flooded maintenance ducts.

Reyes's tactical assessment was automatic:
   - Primary threat: Thompson, heavy assault capability
   - Secondary: Kim, speed and maneuverability
   - Tertiary: Research team, overwhelming numbers
   - Mission critical asset: Artifact control terminal
   - Time constraint: 6:08 to reactor critical

"You taught us this formation in Panama," Kim's voice carried underwater.

The transformed crew was moving into a pincer pattern. A standard Special Forces encirclement tactic.

Reyes deployed his thermite charge, creating a barrier of superheated water between him and the western approach.

"And I taught you its weakness," he growled, triggering his modified depth charge.

The concussive blast disrupted their formation, but they recovered with inhuman speed. Thompson charged through the thermite barrier, her mutated flesh burning but regenerating. Reyes met her with his combat knife – the same CQC sequence he'd drilled into her during training.

But Thompson's new form turned familiar combat moves into something horrific. Her long limbs allowed for almost impossible angles of attack. Where there should have been predictable strike zones, there were now writhing tentacles and razor-sharp talons.

The research team attacked from above, their bodies moving as a coordinated hunting pack. Reyes rolled under a swipe that would have taken his head off, coming up firing. UV rounds illuminated the chamber in strobing bursts, revealing twisted shapes moving through the water.

5:45 to critical.
Kim struck from his blind spot, exactly as he'd trained her. Her talons raked his back, accelerating his own transformation. But the mutation had an unexpected advantage; enhanced strength and reflexes kicked in as his muscle structure began to change. *One bullet.*

Reyes used Thompson's massive bulk against her, executing a modified judo throw that sent her crashing into the advancing research team. But Kim had already outflanked him, moving with predatory grace to cut off his access to the control terminal.

"Remember close quarters protocol seven?" Her voice carried a hint of her old self.

"Yeah," Reyes activated his last UV strobe. "Never let the enemy predict your pattern."

He broke protocol, charging straight into Kim's attack zone. It was exactly what she wouldn't expect – no

trained operative would willingly enter a superior oppo-
nent's kill zone. The gambit worked. Her strike missed
as he slid past, combat boots finding purchase on the wet
floor.

4:50 to critical.
Thompson recovered, her massive form now between
Reyes and the artifact. He was running out of options
and ammunition. The mutation was spreading through
his body, making each movement a battle.

"Last mag," he announced to no one in particular,
slamming fresh UV rounds into his weapon. "Make it
count."

The transformed crew attacked as one – a coordinated assault that demonstrated their retained military
training combined with their new predatory instincts.
Reyes met them with everything left in his arsenal: UV
rounds, thermite charges, and CQC techniques modified
for his partially mutated state.

The fight became a blur of tactical responses and
mutated flesh. Thompson's claws shattered his armor.
Kim's speed made her nearly impossible to track. The
research team moved like a single organism, filling any
gap in his defense.

3:30 to critical.
Blood clouded the water – some his, some theirs, all of it
glowing with infection. Reyes fought through the pain of
transformation, each movement bringing him closer to
the artifact controls. His partially webbed fingers found
the emergency release sequence.

"You trained us too well, Captain," Thompson's
voice resonated through the chamber.

"No," Reyes slammed the final sequence. "I trained
you to complete the mission. Whatever the cost."

The artifact containment field collapsed as the
reactor warning reached critical levels. In the chaos that

followed, Reyes saw his training reflected in every move his transformed team made but it wasn't enough to stop him from finishing the mission.

Some lessons, it seemed, went deeper than even genetic mutation.

Escape and Extraction

The emergency pod's metal groaned under intense pressure as it ascended through dark waters. Inside, Reyes watched his surviving team members; their bodies twisted by permanent mutations, but their minds their own again. Thompson's massive frame barely fit in the cramped space, while Kim's newly formed gills struggled to process the recycled air.

"Surface contact in five minutes," the pod's computer announced.

Reyes touched the rough patches of scales on his neck, a permanent reminder of how close he'd come to complete transformation. The reactor's explosion had severed their connection to the artifact but couldn't undo what they'd become.

"What do we tell them upstairs?" Kim asked, her voice carrying a slight underwater echo. "About the others? About us?"

The question hung in the pressurized air. Below them, the research station was now a radioactive grave for those who hadn't made it; scientists and soldiers whose bodies had been too far gone to save.

"The truth," Reyes finally answered. "Some of it, anyway. They need to know what's down there. What's still down there."

Thompson shifted uncomfortably.

"They'll quarantine us. Study us. We're walking biological hazards now."

"Better than the alternative." Reyes remembered the visions the artifact had shown him; ancient civilizations transformed and consumed by the same force they'd encountered.

The pod shuddered as it hit warmer waters. Sunlight began to penetrate the darkness, making their mutations more visible. In the light, Reyes could see the toll their experience had taken – not just physically, but in their eyes. They'd all left pieces of themselves in the abyss.

"I'm sorry," he said quietly. "For leading you down there. For not seeing the signs sooner."

Kim reached out with her webbed hand, touching his arm. "You saved us, Captain. What was left of us, anyway."

The surface grew closer. Soon they'd face debriefings, quarantine, and endless tests. Their military careers were over; their normal lives were over. But they were alive, and more importantly, still human enough to remember why the artifact needed to stay buried.

"Whatever happens up there," Reyes told his team, "We stick together. We're probably the only ones who understand what's really at stake."

The pod breached the surface with a splash, bobbing in the morning sun. As rescue helicopters approached, Reyes saw his reflection in the pod's window; a face caught between human and something else, marked by both victory and loss.

They'd survived the depths, but their war against the abyss was far from over.

Uncertain Future

The quarantine facility gleamed white and sterile, a stark contrast to the dark waters they'd left behind. Through reinforced glass, doctors and scientists observed their mutations with poorly concealed fascination. Three weeks had passed since their rescue, but the questions never stopped.

Reyes sat in his isolation room, watching the sunset

through specially treated windows. His latest blood test results lay on the table. Pages of anomalies and inexplicable genetic markers. The mutations had stabilized, leaving them as hybrids, but the doctors remained baffled by their condition.

A soft tap on the glass drew his attention. Kim stood in the connecting observation area, her gills fluttering slightly. She held up a tablet displaying classified satellite images. New thermal readings from the explosion site.

Something was moving in the debris field.

"They're planning another expedition," she said through the intercom. "Different agency, different team, but same objective. They think there might be more artifacts."

Reyes felt a familiar chill. In his dreams, he still saw those ancient underwater cities. The artifact they'd destroyed wasn't unique. It was just one piece of a larger whole.

Thompson joined them, her massive shadow falling across the room.

"They found traces in our blood work," she reported quietly. "Microscopic structures, still active."

The implications hung in the filtered air. The infection hadn't just changed them; it was still changing them. In their bodies, something was learning.

"How long until they notice?" Kim asked, unconsciously touching her gills.

"They already have," Reyes replied. "Why else keep us in isolation this long?"

Through the facility's windows, he could see the ocean in the distance. Sometimes, late at night, he felt it calling to him. To all of them. The doctors blamed it on psychological trauma, but Reyes knew better. Whatever they'd encountered in the depths had marked them. In those moments, he would silently repeat, *one bullet,* the words that had tethered him to his humanity. Those two words still anchored him, but he wondered for how long it would be enough.

And it wasn't finished.

"We need to be ready," he told his team. "For when they go back down there. For what they might wake up."

Kim and Thompson nodded, their altered bodies casting shadows in the setting sun. In their eyes, Reyes saw the same knowledge that haunted him. The abyss had given them a glimpse of humanity's true place in the world's history. They were not the first dominant species on Earth.

And if the things sleeping in the deep had their way, they wouldn't be the last.

As darkness fell over the facility, Reyes felt the familiar pulse in his modified DNA; a beacon calling out to something in the depths. Somewhere in the dark waters, ancient things were stirring, drawn by the signal in their blood.

One bullet.

A CASE OF THE GIGGLES

Benjamin Spada

I

This is the way the world ends.
Not with a bang.
Not with a whimper.
It ends with a laugh.

II

'*ve gotten used to the sounds of combat from running and gunning with the Black Spear initiative. We were the blackest of America's black-ops, which meant I was more than familiar with hearing all the noises war had to offer. The crack of gunshots, cries of the injured, and skull jarring booms of explosions. Laughter, though? That's a new one. And not some sad giggle of a poor soul who'd simply cracked. No, at least that would've made sense. This was a whole-bodied laugh that echoed throughout the halls from behind doors.

And it wasn't alone.

It was an utter choir of madness. I aimed my weapon down the apartment building hallway. My two teammates, Billy and Tag, did likewise. The three scientists we escorted shrunk back like scared children. Doors on either side of the hall rattled in their frame as their occupants beat against them. I told myself that none of us would hesitate to shoot once those doors broke down. The three of us had walked through the fire together and been singed by unworldly nightmares more times than I can count. Cutting-edge military tech straight out of science fiction, and insane bioengineered pathogens ripped from horror movies were our bread and butter. We'd seen it all. Killed it all. We didn't hesitate. Why would a little fungus be any different?

The first door broke outward into the hall, and its occupant spilled into view. Despite our training, every last damned one of us paused.

Hemorrhagic Anthropophyte. That's what our scientists called it. A parasitic fungus that rooted into its host's nervous system to hijack their bodies and puppet them around so it could spread. The skin of the infected went deathly white as the fungus soaked up nutrients, red fungal growths swelled their noses to the point of bursting, and sickly blood leaked from their eyes and mouth. The fungus had a rather unique way of spreading the infection to others. It forced a carrier's mouth impossibly wide and triggered a violent spasm in their diaphragm to launch the spores airborne. In short? Hemorrhagic Anthropophyte twisted its carriers' flesh until they resembled nightmarish clowns, then made them laugh so hard their cheeks split open. Their very laughter was quite literally infectious.

"I fucking hate clowns..." Billy said.

The moment of hesitation passed. I sent a bullet through the closest clown's bulbous red nose. The bullet cratered out the back of the skull, sending bloody chunks to splatter the hallway. Fungal infection turned the innards of the clown's skull into a gross mismatch of yellows, reds, and blues. It looked like wet, gory confetti bursting out the back of its goddamn head. These weren't zombies, and headshots weren't required, but goddamn did they work faster than center mass.

Only twelve hours had passed since the fungus manifested on the top story, and it had already spread down through all thirty floors of the apartment building and infected every occupant. A little thing like locked doors didn't keep it from creeping in. If we didn't stop it here, the rest of the city was next. After that? Well, you get the picture.

More doors splintered as the clowns crashed into the hallway. The fungus turned them violent, but they retained some level of intelligence. I saw a portly clown in a wife-beater wielding a great big wrench. Another was a woman in a blood-stained nightgown, a steak knife in either hand. An elderly clown at the rear of the hall hefted a rolling pin in her wrinkled hand, already slick and red from a previous victim.

"Captain West," the lead scientist, Doctor Nolan, said behind me, "minimize the damage, please."

Billy, Tag, and I each exchanged a look. Then we promptly opened fire. We put them down hard and fast. Our bio-suits and masks would prevent spore infection, but I wasn't keen on giving any clown a chance to get close and tear a hole in my gear. The walls were painted with multicolored blood as we gunned them down. By the time the last laugh went quiet, it looked like some teenagers had shot paintballs up and down the corridor.

"They're all yours," I said politely. "Take as many samples as you want."

Nolan glared at me from behind his suit's protective visor. His two fellow scientists clung close to him as if waiting for a go-ahead to move past.

Doctor May Parks was a short woman with wide, eager eyes; the other, Doctor Jim Baker, was skittish and seemed way out of his element in this type of fieldwork. I gestured to the dead bodies like an usher at a theater, and Nolan begrudgingly waved Parks and Baker forward.

There had only been one previous incident with this fungus, in an isolated Idaho town that was contained with a firebomb before it could spread. Nolan's research team hadn't gotten there in time and were clearly looking for a second chance here. I was more concerned with the size of bomb it'd take to cover *this* up if the fungus got loose in the city.

"Clowns," Parks said, her voice dripping with fascination. "Level 1 HA infection."

Remind me to track down whoever thought that abbreviating the name of a fungus that mutates people into psycho clowns to 'HA' so that I can introduce their teeth to my boot.

It was theorized the fungus possessed something akin to a hivemind, and this hivemind determined what forms the infected developed into for the collective need. Each had delightfully frustrating names. Level one base infection had Clowns, while level two included Marionettes and Harlequins. The level three tier was populated by truly monstrous strains like the Jesters. Lastly, level four's sole occupant was the hulking Punchline.

The mission dossier had also been frustratingly bare-bones on the HA variants. All we had from the Idaho incident were secondhand witness testimony, some questionable sketches, and a couple blurry photos. It was like having a catalog of freaks without any context of what they could do. We didn't know for sure *how* the different variants formed. Was it length of infection? Would a single person progress from level one all the way to four if given enough time? Jury was out, but Nolan theorized it had more to do with proximity to the hivemind.

The reason only three Black Spear operatives were escorting Nolan's team instead of a full squad was because we were plan B. Plan A was Beowulf Squad, who were supposed to insert via helicopter on the roof to establish a foothold before clearing the building. Yours truly and my two favorite Black Spear buddies were only intended to be security escort once Beowulf had done their part. That plan went to shit when mechanical failure crashed

Beowulf's helicopter right into the rooftop where the hivemind was supposedly rooted. Their whole squad was assumed dead.

I reached the stairwell at the end of the hallway and eyed the building's floor plan next to the door. It was a sobering reminder of how far we had to go.

Thirty floors, countless infected, and just three operators. Yeah. These were fun odds.

III

"You should've let me bring a rocket launcher," Billy grumbled.

"Sure," I said. "You, big explosive weapons, a high-rise with tight corridors, what could go wrong?"

We were on the fifteenth floor. Halfway there. Twice now the way was blocked off by barricaded furniture—either emplaced by desperate survivors or by infected at the Hivemind's behest—and forced us to cut across hallways to reach the alternate stairwells. This would be the third time. The higher we went, the less it resembled an actual building. Mold spread along the walls in huge patches, wispy roots stretched out from large mushroom cap growths, and the floor was carpeted with a thick mushy layer of bright rainbow-colored fuzz and more crisscrossing roots. A real fixer-upper.

I pay close attention to mission briefs because relevant intel tended to keep you alive. That's why I knew that what spread all along the walls and floor was called 'mycelium'. The intricate lattice-like network of roots was the fungal equivalent of a massive nervous system. Mycelium networks spread for miles beneath forest floors and contained *trillions* of branching fibers. This network slithered throughout the building like an early warning system for the Hivemind. I didn't like that one bit.

Billy snorted. "Everything I learned about facing biological weapons I learned from half-assed, on-the-job training, and *Resident Evil* games," he said as we trudged along the slime-slicked floor. "And if the latter taught me three things, it's this: always shoot them in the brain, the monsters always get worse the deeper you go, and always—I cannot stress this enough—*always* bring a rocket launcher."

"You're lucky he let you keep the grenades," Tag mused.

Billy touched the frags on his vest like an older woman clutching her pearls. "I bet Beowulf Squad brought rocket launchers." He snorted again. "I liked you more when you weren't in charge. Cole West was way more fun than Captain West."

"I'm a delight," I retorted.

Billy turned back to me, incredulous. "Knock-knock," he said.

"No."

"Come on, Cap," Billy pleaded. "Knock-knock!"

I checked behind me to make sure Tag wasn't allowing the science team to get too distracted and fall behind. The big man just waved me forward. Footfalls thumped on the floor above. Deranged laughter drifted down the hallway, but the acoustics of the building were playing tricks on me. It was impossible to tell where it came from.

A door next to Doctor Jim flung open, and a Clown tumbled out, stabbing wildly with a metal spatula. I thought about how absurdly random a weapon it was when the Clown thrust it at Jim's throat. Tag stepped in, parried the spatula with a sharp chop of his forearm, and palmed the Clown's entire head. A vicious laugh ripped up from the Clown's throat and forced its mouth open wider.

Spittle pelted Tag's visor. Disgusted, the man turned the Clown around and slammed it face-first into a wall. Its swollen red nose pulped with a burst of brightly colored blood, unveiling twitching fungal tendrils underneath. Tag grimaced and smashed the Clown twice more to finish the job.

The spatula clattered to the ground.

We stared back at Tag, the brief but brutal outburst momentarily silencing us.

Billy finally broke the quiet. "Tag," he said slowly. "Knock-knock."

I rolled my eyes and pushed forward. The mission was to locate and eliminate the Hivemind source, and to keep Nolan's team alive. While the former task was mandatory, the latter was more of an 'if possible'.

As if on cue, the door to the stairwell behind us rattled, and then a Clown eased it open. A cacophony of laughter rose behind it, filling the hall as Clowns scrabbled over each other to get to us. The staccato chatter of our rifles greeted them. Bullets ripped through pale white flesh and sent rainbow-tinted blood splashing across the crowd.

"Move, move!" I yelled.

Tag took point, practically dragging the scientists with him towards the opposite end of the hallway. They were latched onto each other's wrists like a daisy-chain.

"Aren't you glad I brought these?" Billy asked, removing two frags from his vest and pulling the pins.

"Aren't you glad I let you keep them?" I answered, taking out a grenade of my own.

We waited until Tag got the scientists through the door. Billy and I rolled the grenades down the carpeted hallway. Rolled, not threw. Didn't need to ding a Clown in the face and have the grenade bounce back in our own direction.

The mob of infected neared. Each of their faces was twisted with insane glee. The grenades passed underfoot, and Billy and I slammed the stairwell door shut behind us. Tag braced against it. There was a muffled *BOOM-BOOM-BOOM* that shook the walls, and then nothing but a handful of slowly dying giggles.

We caught our breath as best we could. I allowed everyone just a moment to pause, to make sure none of the doors from the floors above crashed open with infected coming to investigate the explosion, but all remained quiet. I signaled Billy to move up.

My breathing was loud within my suit. And the more I heard my own breath, the more convinced I was that I was missing something. I slowed, focused my awareness.

There it was. A strange stretching sound. Almost like rope being pulled taut. But no laughter. So, at least we had that going for us.

I gestured to Billy, who nodded. He'd heard it too.

That stretching sound came again. From high above. Tag, ever the sentry, held the three scientists back with a muscled arm. Parks fought against him. Her eyes went straight to the unseen ceiling as her curiosity beat out her sense of preservation. Jim would've bolted if Tag's steely hand hadn't clamped onto his shoulder.

"What is it?" Jim hissed. "What's up there?"

The flashlight illumination from Billy's rifle barely pierced the dark above. He scanned the light back and forth, trying to find the source of the rope-like noise.

"What's up there?"

"Damn it, Jim, I'm a soldier not a scientist," whispered Billy, craning his neck.

A giggle from the floors below us had Jim whirling around. We'd missed some Clowns. He put his back to the stairwell handrail and pointed his own flashlight into the shadows behind him.

"Steady," I urged, training my barrel towards the lower floors.

More giggles crept up the lower steps. More stretching noises from above.

"Could be a Harlequin," said Parks. Her voice was all fascination, no fear. "Or even a level three variation?"

Two things happened next. First, a hard, violent laugh fell fast to our floor as if someone had leapt to their death from above. Second, I learned why level twos were called Marionettes.

The man had black fluid dripping from his eyes, more across his lips. A mime. Long, putrid stalks stretched out from his back and limbs like puppet strings, trailing up to the ceiling far above. It dangled in the air just the other side of the handrail.

Jim didn't even have time to turn around before the Marionette wrapped both arms around him and launched a full-chested laugh straight into Jim's visor. The mycelium strings pulled back with a sudden, elastic *SNAP* not unlike bungee cords. Jim was yanked up to the darkness of the ceiling like some perverse magic trick. He didn't even have time to scream.

Laughter fell around us as two more Marionettes descended like spiders lowering on their webs. Their pale hands reaching, threatening to snatch us up into the dark like they'd done Jim, but I was too busy shooting to be scared.

The rapid shots from my rifle lit the stairwell up like a strobe light. A Marionette leaned closer to me in horrifying still images. Descending. Reaching. Its face blasting apart beneath my gunfire.

Billy kicked the second one away before it could touch him. It bounced off the far wall with a puff, jettisoning spores, then went spinning and tangling itself in its own grotesque strings. Billy followed up with a three-round burst, turning its head to black-tinged mulch.

The two Marionettes hung from their strings, twitching with death spasms. Pale fingers clenched erratically as their limbs jerked about, and I realized that somehow *neither* of the now headless Marionettes were actually dead. The HA was still rooted throughout their bodies and trying to claim more victims, but without the aid of eyes to find anyone—

The door to the fifteenth floor pulled open and giggling Clowns tumbled into the stairwell. Some bore the maimed limbs and bloodied flesh from the earlier grenades, while others were unscathed – newcomers to the frenzy.

Tag turned to cover our rear, quickly gunning down four of the cackling freaks as they climbed the steps after us. The big man's aim was steady, certain. Bulbous noses popped like ripe tomatoes, flinging rainbow-tinted fluids in every direction. The first line of Clowns went down. Those following behind, tripped and tumbled to the steps. Easy pickings for Tag.

As Tag worked, a third Marionette dropped to Doctor Parks and gripped tight to her face and shoulder. Tag spun around, drew a large knife, and cut right through the Marionette's strings. The severed tendrils recoiled upwards on a grotesque wail that went on and on. The Marionette slumped at Tag's feet.

Huh. Unlike Clowns, whose mushroom-like clusters on their red noses acted as a sort of exposed brain, the Marionette's strings were their literal connections to the Hivemind.

So much for Billy's rule of always shooting them in the brain.

"Cut 'em down!" I ordered as the other two beheaded Marionettes kept blindly fumbling about for us. Billy and I fired in tandem. Our bullets tore through the mycelium strings, the bodies bouncing off the handrails as they fell into the darkness far below. The severed cords squealed, spurted ichor in every direction like cut water hoses, and coiled back to the top floor.

I aimed upward into the shadows, waiting for more freaks to come. The stairwell was filled with gun smoke, and HA spores danced in the air. We waited.

None came.

I looked back to tell Nolan and Parks that we were moving, but found they were too busy examining the dead Marionette on the steps. Parks prodded at the spots where the strings rooted into the flesh, and I was not at all comfortable with the excitement on her face. The fact that Jim had just been killed didn't seem to put a damper on her curiosity one bit.

"Fourteen floors to go," I said, putting a bit of edge to my tone. "I'm sure the higher we go, the more interesting specimens there'll be for you to examine."

My gibe seemed entirely lost on her because she stood, slid a small sample into a pouch, and gave me an enthusiastic thumbs up. Parks' disregard for Jim's passing rubbed me the wrong way, so I pushed up past Billy and took point. He kept uncharacteristically quiet. This wasn't the time for jokes anymore. This job wasn't fun to begin with, but even his gallows humor had run its course.

We cleared another seven floors before our next roadblock. An immense collection of growths had formed like a ceiling and barred further progress. It was there that we found the 'hand' from which the Marionettes had been strung. Shriveled stalks fell from the fungus, and suspended below it was the first Marionette along with the late Jim Baker.

Jim's face-shield was broken. White filaments reached out from the fungus and were rooting into his face through his eyes, nose, and mouth. His body shook horrifically, but I found myself unable to look away. The Marionette, however, was very still. As if the mycelium strings had no more interest in puppeteering one corpse when they had a fresher one to play with.

I raised my rifle, lining up a shot at Jim's face. "What do you think?" I said harshly, finger curling along the trigger. "Wanna stop and take some more samples?"

IV

I'm usually a glass-half-full kind of guy. But when that half is in reference to our remaining ammunition, I get a little antsy. There was no positive spin I could put on it: we were running low. Earlier, Billy had joked that in videogames the deeper you went, the worse the monsters got, and I found myself wishing he'd brought that rocket launcher along after all.

The hallways on the twenty-fourth floor didn't even resemble an apartment building anymore. More like we'd stumbled into some nightmarish alien nest. The floors, walls, and the doors to the apartments had all been overgrown with fuzzy, purple mold. Mushroom caps of various sizes sprouted everywhere. Dense, calcifying plates grew from the walls and narrowed the passage. We were forced to go single file. Thick clouds of spores puffed out from bulbs lining the halls. I got the sense I was trapped within an enormous, disgusting petri dish.

Between the wet pop of the swollen bulbs, the squelch of the moist fuzz under our feet, and the quiet gurgle of fluids seeping throughout the corridor, I almost missed the maniacal laughter rather than this nauseating ambience.

The quiet was unsettling. Like a pause before the next cruel joke the world was ready to play on us.

There weren't any Clowns up here, but it was hard for me to be grateful for that. My mind went through the catalog of HA variants, of those yet to appear, and my anxiety rose. It did me no favors that the outcroppings of large fungal plates had the walls quite literally closing in. They reminded me of coral, and I struggled to avoid touching their hard calcified edges. I wasn't about to risk tearing my suit. One glance behind me at Tag's massive frame told me he was having a similar problem.

The scientists—far smaller in stature—were looking around in wonder at just about everything. Had it not been for Tag pushing them along, I'm sure they'd spend all day studying the developing growths.

I stepped carefully. "Let me be cliché and say it: it's too quiet."

"Oh, I can solve that," said Billy. "Knock-knock."

I shimmied further down the narrowed hallway.

"Aw, come on, Captain," Billy pleaded. "Knock-knock!"

Despite the tight passage, and fully disregarding the slight risk it took to do it, I shifted around to give Billy a hard stare. His sheepish grin didn't falter for an instant.

Tag sighed from the rear, "I'll play his game, Cap. Go ahead, Billy: hit me."

Billy perked up, "Finally! Okay. Tag: knock-knock."

Tag's scowl turned into a big shit-eating grin. "Come in."

Billy's defeated cursing brought a smile to my own and made the remaining trudge through the cramped passageway that much easier. The plate-like growths widened out as we rounded a corner, the hallway opening up enough for two of us to stand shoulder to shoulder. It also freed up space for me to have an overdue conversation.

I waved Nolan forward. "Doctor, when Beowulf Squad went down, why did command send my three-man team in, instead of waiting for proper reinforcements?"

His eyebrows scrunched up with confusion.

Still, I held his gaze. "I already know there's a clock ticking, but I'm thinking the countdown's lower than what I was briefed."

Nolan's eyes betrayed nothing. Until my glare finally broke him.

"Propagation," said Nolan. "Per Idaho witness statements, it's the final stage of Hemorrhagic Anthropophyte.

Once the Hivemind has infected enough hosts and gathered enough biomass, the matured colony will jettison its collective biomass as spores into the airways."

"We've been dancing in spores all day," I said. "What's different?"

"The individual hosts expel hundreds of spores in their immediate vicinity, but those won't travel." He licked his lips. Nervous. "We're talking about *billions* of HA spores released into the atmosphere."

My eyes drifted from Nolan to the spores suspended in the air. I felt a stone plummet in my gut. Billions. This was no video game, but that was game-over, plain and simple.

"It's why my team's here," Nolan said. "We need to collect as much as we can on the infection and the Hivemind. We still understand next to nothing about it!"

"We're here to kill it," I said. "We get to the top and you—"

The wall behind Nolan *moved*.

It played out in slow-motion like a re-creation from *Aliens*. A portion of the fungal plates along the wall shifted, and a figure separated from it. The hard, chitinous plates formed out of its skin had acted like camouflage as it nested itself into the wall.

The thing turned in our direction, squatted low on its haunches. Its lanky body and long limbs were covered entirely with the purple, velvety fungus. More of the calcified HA adorned its shoulders and arms in thick patches. Stalks of the fungus had burst out the top of its skull and developed into petals that hung around its face. The entirety of its flesh was discolored, making it impossible to tell where the host's flesh ended, and the plant-like growths began. The way the petals fell around its face, reminded me of the floppy hat of a—

"*Jester!*" Parks shrieked.

I fired three rounds before she screamed. I was an

ace shot as it was, and the Jester was barely twenty feet away. Easy game.

Except there was a muted *THOP-THOP-THOP* as the bullets thudded into the thick layer of fungus of its upper body. The HA plates weren't just a form of camouflage. The purple fungus effectively acted almost like a carapace. Natural body armor.

"Pour it on!" I ordered and Tag stepped up to my side to shoot.

Our combined gunfire rattled against the Jester's hide. It cowered, hiding its face with a long, purple arm. Some of our bullets punched through softer sections unprotected by the plates, but instead of blood we were rewarded with the slow drip of yellowish ooze from the wounds. The trickle slowed before hardening like resin. Just like that, all the bullet wounds plugged up, and the Jester attacked.

I couldn't see eyes behind the petals, but it knew where I was. It swung one of its unnaturally long arms our way. The Jester sported similar hardened growths along the length of its forearms. Unlike the carapace-like armor, the hardened mushroom plates along its forearm were jagged and narrow like blades. The Jester giggled low and quietly, then bounded toward us with explosive speed. Its arm blade whistled through the air and I retreated, nearly tripping over the mold-covered floor underfoot.

The Jester lunged, but I stopped it dead in its tracks with a mighty boot planted square in its chest. The blow forced a hard laugh from the Jester's lungs, and I followed up with a downward swing of my rifle's buttstock. Crashed right atop the petals of its pseudo-hat. Purple and yellow fluid pulsed from its wounds. The Jester's head canted unnaturally to the side. A broken neck.

But it didn't die.

It writhed on the ground like a headless cockroach. Limbs twitched and spasmed, the arm blade slashed uselessly at the floor. Just as I took aim to finish it off with a round or five through its head, it sprang to its feet as if yanked upright by invisible strings. The crusty blade of its arm sliced frantically while it stumbled awkwardly forward. The fungus rooted throughout its body struggled to puppet its host despite the damaged nervous system.

I spared a glance behind me to Billy, who gave me an unsurprised shrug.

Deeper you go, the worse the monsters get.

"Stay behind us, Docs," I muttered to Nolan and Parks.

The two scientists cringed backwards. And then the wall cackled.

Three more Jesters separated from the fungus. Strands of yellowish ichor trailed behind their bodies, and the madness of their giggles carved across my ears like knives.

Tag and I couldn't turn around fast enough, Billy wasn't close enough to pull them away. The scientists could only scream as the scythe-like arms fell upon them.

Right before the first blade met flesh, Nolan stumbled to the floor, and whether intentional or not, it left Parks the only one within immediate reach. There was a split-second of indecision as her eyes flicked backwards to where Nolan lay. Then a blade chopped into the flesh between her neck and shoulder as brutally as a meat cleaver. A second blade slashed low into her side, stopping only when it struck her spine. The third Jester giggled as it planted its blade high in her back between her shoulder blades.

We shot the three Jesters, and they didn't stop.

Chopping.

Stabbing.

Slashing.

They butchered Parks before we could do a damned thing.

Billy unleashed a colorful string of obscenities as he opened fire on the trio of Jesters. Yellow ichor splashed outward from the superficial wounds, slowed, hardened.

Nolan did his best impersonation of a flat sheet of paper on the floor while the bullets passed overhead. The Jesters, unfazed by the assault, bent over and snatched up all the pieces of Parks.

I shook my head. "The fuck is that all about—?"

The first Jester with the broken neck was in my face.

I didn't have time to level my rifle to its head, and was forced to shoot low. The round punched through its kneecap and exploded out the back. The Jester fell to the mold-laden floor, its grotesque movements even more erratic.

The Jester might be human shaped, might even laugh like one, but it wasn't human anymore. It was a network of fungus wired around hijacked flesh. It didn't need a brain. There were no vital organs. Wasn't even a circulatory system for it to bleed out, and whatever holes we punched into them quickly clotted over with that yellow resin. If it didn't have a weak point, or any sort of vulnerability, then there was only one option left on the table.

Dismemberment.

I squeezed off two shots at each knee and elbow. If I couldn't kill it, then at least I could sever its arms and legs, immobilize it. Its stumps still twitched in an impossible effort to attack us, the threads of mycelium coiling grossly from the wounds.

Tag nodded his understanding of the new strategy on deck, and we both turned to face the remaining three Jesters.

Billy dragged Nolan backwards by the wrist as we backpedaled down the hallway. The scientist screamed unintelligibly as the fungal mutants approached. They stalked like predators, melting into the shadows of the dark hallway, giggling low and cruelly all the while.

They were toying with us.

"Let's *go!*" I shouted.

We shot controlled bursts behind us to keep the Jesters at bay, but they were a goddamned durable bunch. Our bullets kept *THOP*ing into their armor plating. I urged Billy and Tag to move while I covered the rear.

Ammo count was swirling the drain. I finally cracked the closest Jester with a shot through the knee. He went sprawling, still giggling.

I took another step back when an iron-firm hand planted itself on my back.

"Watch yourself," Tag said.

I'd very nearly stumbled into an open elevator shaft. A thick cable dangled above the pit. My stomach launched up into my throat at the realization that I'd come that close to falling to my death. At least it would've been an easier ending than hacked to pieces. As if to make that thought clearer, the bolt of my rifle locked back on an empty chamber.

"Shit."

The Jesters' head petals twitched slightly, like they understood what the noise meant. They discarded their slow, methodical approach and charged down the hallway. One ran on all fours like an animal, another clung to the wall like some grotesque overgrown bug, and the third with the hobbled knee, reached up to the mushroom-capped ceiling and swung itself forward with its long blade arm.

I braced myself for the creature's impact, but Billy pulled me out of the way. The two able-bodied Jesters collided with him. He pushed one back with the muzzle of his rifle while firing a point-blank burst into its face, then sank his knife into another's neck between its armor plates.

The third leapt down from the ceiling and landed amidst the frenzy.

All four of them fell through the open elevator doors.

Nothing but their laughter and Billy's surprised gasp, trailed behind.

"No!" I shouted.

I tried to look for my friend down in the dark but a tearing sound from behind me stole my attention. Four more Jesters ripped their way out from the camouflaging walls.

Tag's hand pulled at my shoulder, "We've gotta keep moving, Cap!"

I took one last look at the elevator shaft. "Saved my ass," I muttered. "He's always doing something stupid."

V

Here we were at last: the door to the top floor. Home of the apartment building's pool, a skylight ceiling, and one Hivemind.

The laughs of the Jesters had hounded us all the way up and gave my legs the extra oomph I needed to power up the final steps.

I patted the magazine of my rifle—my last—and tried to draw some reassurance from its solid feel. Thirty rounds left, thirty floors up. Maybe there was a sign somewhere in there that things would work out in our favor. A good omen of sorts. But I was probably jerking myself off mentally.

I glanced at Nolan. "How difficult do you think it'll be to locate the Hivemind?"

"I believe it'll be fairly easy to find."

I gave him a begrudging nod and turned the handle. The door only budged a few inches in its frame at first. HA spores drifted out of the crack and danced in the air. My visor fogged. It was like a sauna on the other side of the threshold. The dense spore cloud had me wonder how close we were to propagation, and game-over.

Tag moved up to lend a hand and after one, two, three heavy pulls we managed to wrench the door open.

Nolan's estimation that the Hivemind would be easy to find was a bit of an understatement. The thing stuck out like a sore thumb. A gargantuan cluster of pink and grayish fungus stalks rising up to the skylight above, its mycelium roots crawled out with a million tendrils into the large pools and drank their waters. The stalks coiled together into a huge bulb of quivering matter, easily a hundred feet in circumference, with a wrinkled pink surface. It very much looked like an oversized moldy brain, and I suppose that's pretty much what it was.

"The Hivemind..." Nolan marveled.

Tag and I didn't exactly mirror his enthusiasm.

"Tag, we definitely don't have enough bullets," I said. "Help me find a way to kill it, and let's get the hell out of here."

It'd been a fight every step of the way here. Clowns, Marionettes, the Jesters... and yet here in the equivalent of the Hivemind's throne room, it was unguarded.

Nolan approached the Hivemind while Tag and I scanned the room, looking for some way to destroy it.

My gaze locked on to what had to be the remains of Beowulf Squad's helicopter. It'd crashed through the skylights above and come to a rest with its nose at ground level. HA had rapidly grown over most of the chopper, along with the hole it had punched in the skylight. There were no signs of our comrades. Likely already absorbed or warped into clownish mutants and sent after us.

I cocked my head at the wreckage, and Tag nodded. There could be explosives within the helicopter.

The tip of my boot brushed against something, and my aim snapped down on reflex.

A severed arm. Matter of fact, it was a pile of severed limbs. A thin layer of purplish fuzz had grown over it and blended them into the rest of the floor, but right at my feet was a macabre collection of butchered body parts. Legs, heads, hands. It struck me as odd, and then I recalled what the Jesters had done with Parks just a couple floors below.

They were collecting the parts...

A squelch of releasing gases came from behind me. I turned to find an even larger pile. A mass grave of massacred victims. White mycelium roots grew across the accumulated corpses like a delicate net. Upon closer inspection, it wasn't just draped over the bodies, but growing into them. My eyes locked onto a decapitated head piled among other heads. Their flesh had gone soft and clay-like. In certain spots, it was hard to tell where the flesh of one face ended and another began.

"Unbelievable," Nolan said, pulling my attention from the mass grave. "They destroyed the first Hivemind before we could extract anything of value. Antitoxins, vaccines, priceless research that could be used to make the next penicillin. I kept dreaming we'd get a *second* chance, Captain."

My patience withered, and when the scientist gently pressed a palm against the brain-like surface of the Hivemind, I had to fight back a cringe.

"*Doctor*," I said. "We need to—"

A wet squelch behind us.

I turned slowly, grimacing as I did because I already knew I wouldn't like what I saw. The pieces of all the gathered corpses quivered and twitched as one. Then, a groan like a house settling came from deep within the pile.

It rose. A disgusting amalgam of corpses, a golem of disparate hunks of flesh conjoined into one being, stitched together through the impossible black magic of the Hivemind's infection.

Its monstrous chest formed of a dozen separate torsos, hulking arms grafted from countless limbs twisted together and ending in more of those chitinous growths, though this time the growths were round rather than sharp. It had two clubs for hands and two legs thick as tree trunks. Where a head should be, there were instead many. A cluster of white-skinned, red-lipped, grinning clown faces laughed as one. One face stood out amongst the collection: Parks.

Again, Billy's words came back to me. '*In videogames the deeper you went, the worse the monsters got.*' What stood before me would undoubtedly be what Billy would've called the Boss Round.

Level 4 infection: a Punchline.

If I'd had a hundred magazines, it wouldn't have been enough, but here I was down to my last. Like the Jesters, there was no visible weak point. No Achilles heel for this laughing titan of mushrooms and clownish faces. I fired every bullet I had. Thirty rounds gone in the span of two breaths. Five of the clown heads burst, revealing the wispy, white HA threads within.

The Punchline only laughed harder.

It smashed its club-like arms into the floor again and again, trying to crush me into paste. The room shook with every blow as I dodged. Tag yelled something through the radio in my ear as a volley of gunfire tore into the Punchline's face-cluster. Vibrant rainbow blood oozed down its chest. The Punchline's laugh became a roar that reverberated off the walls, nearly toppling me.

Tag waved to me from the door to the stairs, beckoning me closer. Nolan was rooted to the floor in terror. I ran for him. Grabbed his wrist. Then the Punchline's mallet-fist smashed the doctor into the ground.

His death was instant, though no less horrible. There one instant, fleshy chunks the next.

The deep-pitched giggle from a dozen infected throats rose behind me as the Punchline lumbered closer.

"Knock-knock…" a familiar voice said over our radio.

It stiffened, slowly turning as if to ask who was there. "Caw," the voice said.

The Punchline's laugh quieted into an almost curious murmur. And then a rocket streaked across the area, punched into the monster, and exploded.

The roar of the explosion silenced all laughter. Pale flesh and scorched fungus rained down as the Punchline was blown clean in half. Its lower body was erased while an arm and its torso splattered down next to me and Tag. The smoke trail from the rocket led back to Billy. Holding a rocket launcher.

"Ka-*BOOM!*" he said with a giant grin.

I just stood staring in disbelief. "How…?"

"Turns out gnarly blade-arms aren't too good at grabbing hold of elevator cables. Also, I *told* you Beowulf Squad brought rocket launchers," he said, gesturing triumphantly to the nearby helicopter he'd pilfered it from. "They were generous enough to leave us not one, but *three* rockets!"

His smile vanished when the Punchline roared and lurched upright. It swung its remaining mallet-fist and nearly took me and Tag out.

Billy reloaded the rocket launcher, fired. Missed. The rocket sputtered out and exploded across the room. The walls rattled. Debris and fungus on the ceiling came down in huge chunks, large blades of glass from the skylights came with it and threatened to slice us open.

"Spores…" I said, eyeing the broken ceiling.

Again, the Punchline roared its impossibly deep laugh, and this time an answer came from the stairwell.

Tag whirled around as a pack of giggling Jesters bounded for the door. He put his considerable weight behind slamming it shut in their faces. One of their blades stuck through the door frame, slashing as it tried to get at Tag. The man strained, but when he tried to brace his feet, the moldy floor offered little purchase.

The mangled Punchline crawled towards us; rainbow blood gushed from its wounds. Its massive arm raised once more to deliver the killing blow. Death before us, death waiting on other side of the door, and nowhere else to go.

It dawned on me how right Billy had been the entire time about everything. The monsters getting worse, his whole point about Beowulf being fun enough to bring rocket launchers, and the very first thing he'd said.

Always shoot them in the brain.

I ran for Billy, snatched the rocket launcher away, dropped to a knee, and brought the weapon to my shoulder. The Hivemind's pulsating pink mass was lined up in the launcher's sights. One last shot.

I took it.

The rocket hit dead-center.

The explosion was blinding, brilliant, and absolute.

A shockwave burst outward from the Hivemind, flinging the scorched fungal matter in every direction. The ringing silence that followed was matched only by an utter stillness in the room. Nothing moved. Not the lumbering Punchline, not the Jesters on the other side of the door, not even the millions of mycelium strands around the room.

Then, it all fell apart. The invisible stitching that had tied the Punchline together from its many corpses simply unraveled. The pieces splattered to the floor. The masses of mushroom clusters along the walls and up to the ceiling collapsed on themselves. Every single one of the Hivemind's infected mutants dropped dead.

Our victory was so sudden I had trouble accepting it. The colorful mold on the floor blackened and shriveled up as the infection receded. Tag stepped away from the door, and the pack of Jesters fell dead into the room.

It was over.

"Any last lessons from your fucking videogames?"

I sighed as I dropped the spent rocket launcher to the ground.

Billy's smile faded, and his gaze turned upwards. I followed his line of sight to the broken skylights above. A strong wind was blowing, and for the life of me, I didn't have an answer on whether or not HA spores were carried upon them.

"Yeah..." said Billy as he stared into the open sky. "Always be ready for a sequel."

OUTPOST ZERO

Subham Rai

The chopper's blades sliced through the frigid Newfoundland air, but Captain Mara Vigneault already knew they were too late. Outpost Zero was a graveyard, and her squad was flying straight into its open jaws.

The distress call had come in twelve hours ago – garbled, panicked. "Containment breach—", then nothing. Now, as the chopper descended, the silence below felt heavier than the storm clouds rolling in.

Mara's squad—five Canadian Armed Forces soldiers, each handpicked for this rapid-response unit—readied their gear. Sergeant Leo 'Bear' Tremblay, Mara's second-in-command, checked his 12-gauge shotgun, his broad frame steady despite the turbulence.

Corporal Elise 'Sparks' Gagnon, the comms expert, adjusted her headset, her sharp eyes scanning the horizon. Privates Ryan 'Doc' Carter, the medic, and the sharpshooter, Zoe 'Hawk' Bennett, ran through their pre-op checks with practiced precision.

They were a tight unit, trained for the worst, but nothing had prepared them for this.

The chopper touched down on the icy helipad, and Mara led the squad out, boots crunching against frost. The outpost's main gate loomed ahead, its steel doors ajar, swaying in the wind.

No guards, no lights, just an eerie stillness that made Mara's skin prickle. "Bear, Sparks, on me," she ordered, her voice low through the comms. "Hawk, Doc, cover the rear. Stay sharp."

They moved in formation, M4s up, sweeping the perimeter. The air stank of salt and something fouler – a damp rot that clung to the back of Mara's throat.

As they breached the gate, the interior courtyard was a mess: overturned crates, a jeep on its side, and blood smeared across the concrete in long, dragging streaks. Fungal growths, pale and glistening, crept up the walls, their tendrils pulsing faintly like veins under the skin.

Mara's stomach churned. The fungus wasn't just growing, it was consuming. Tendrils pulsed where they touched blood, and the air shimmered with spores. One breath, one open wound, and you'd join the infected.

"Sparks, any signals?" Mara asked, scanning the shadows.

Elise shook her head, her comms unit crackling with static. "Nothing, Cap. It's like the whole place went dark."

Bear kicked at a patch of fungus on the ground, his boot leaving a wet smear. "What the hell is this stuff? Looks like it's growing."

Before Mara could respond, a low, guttural snarl echoed from the main building. The squad froze, weapons snapping toward the sound.

The double doors at the far end of the courtyard hung off their hinges, the darkness beyond a gaping maw. Something moved inside – fast, jerky, unnatural.

Mara's pulse quickened. "Positions," she hissed. "Bear, with me. Sparks, Doc, hold the gate. Hawk, eyes up."

Zoe fanned out, taking up a sniper position on the far side of the courtyard, her rifle trained on the doors. Mara and Bear advanced, their steps silent, breathing steady despite the adrenaline, M4s at the ready.

The snarl came again, closer, followed by a wet, scraping sound. Claws on concrete. Mara signaled Bear to flank left as she took the right, her M4's muzzle steady.

The first infected soldier lunged from the darkness, a nightmare in tattered fatigues. Its body was a grotesque mockery of humanity – fungal tendrils sprouted from its shoulders, writhing like snakes, and its face was half-covered in pale, pulsating growths.

Spore clouds puffed from its mouth with each ragged breath, the air shimmering with a sickly green haze. It moved fast. Too fast. Its clawed hands slashing as it charged Mara.

"Contact!" Mara shouted, squeezing the trigger. Her M4 barked, rounds tearing into the creature's chest, but it barely slowed.

Bear opened fire with his shotgun, the blast shredding its arm, fungal goo splattering the ground. The creature screeched, a sound that clawed at Mara's ears, and kept coming.

Two more infected burst from the doors, their movements erratic, bodies similarly mutated. One had a fungal growth exploding from its back, tendrils whipping the air, while the other's arms were elongated, talons dragging sparks across the concrete.

"Hawk, take 'em down!" Mara yelled, diving behind a crate as the first creature swiped at her.

Zoe fired, sniper rounds punching through the infecteds' skulls. The creatures staggered but didn't drop, their fungal growths pulsing as if absorbing the damage.

"Aim for the tendrils!" Zoe called, adjusting her shot. Her next bullet severed a cluster on the second creature, and it collapsed, spore clouds billowing from its corpse.

Mara rolled out from cover, unloading a burst into the first infected's legs, bringing it down. Bear finished it with a shotgun blast to the head, the fungal mass exploding in a wet spray.

But the third creature reached the gate, where Elise and Doc held position. Elise fired her pistol, but the creature was on her too fast, its claws raking her arm.

She screamed, stumbling back, as Doc dragged her behind the jeep.

"Elise, status!" Mara shouted, sprinting toward them.

"Spores—got me!" Elise gasped, her arm already showing faint fungal veins creeping under her skin. Doc injected her with an anti-fungal from his medkit, but her eyes were wide with panic. "It's spreading, Doc. I can feel it!"

The creature turned on Doc, but Mara slammed her M4's butt into its skull. It staggered, and Bear's shotgun roared again, blowing its head apart.

The courtyard fell silent, save for Elise's ragged breathing and the distant howl of the wind.

Mara knelt beside Elise, her heart sinking. The fungal veins had reached Sparks' shoulder, the comm's expert's skin turning pale and waxy. "Doc, can you stop it?"

Doc shook his head, his face grim. "It's too fast, Cap. We need to quarantine her. *Now*."

Elise grabbed Mara's arm, the grip weak. "Don't let me turn, Cap. Please."

Mara's jaw tightened, and she nodded to Bear, who handed her his sidearm. "I'm sorry, Sparks," she whispered, pressing the barrel to Elise's temple.

The shot echoed across the courtyard, a stark punctuation to the chaos. The squad stood in stunned silence, the reality of the fungal threat sinking in.

"Secure the gate," Mara ordered, her voice hard. "We're going in. Whatever did this, we end it."

The gate to Outpost Zero slammed shut behind them, the steel groaning under Bear's weight as he secured the lock. Mara wiped Elise's blood from her hands, the image of her friend's fungal-veined arm seared into her mind.

The courtyard was a graveyard now. Three infected soldiers lay in pieces, their fungal growths still twitching, spore clouds dissipating into the frigid Newfoundland air. But the main building loomed ahead, its broken doors a black maw promising worse horrors within.

"Form up," Mara ordered, voice steady despite the ache in her chest. "Bear, take point. Hawk, cover our six. Doc, stay close. We're not losing anyone else."

The squad nodded, their faces grim but resolute. They were down to four, but they were still a unit, trained to fight through hell.

They moved into the main building, M4s up, flashlights cutting through the darkness. The corridors were a maze of concrete and steel, but the fungal growths had taken over, coating the walls in a pale, pulsating mass.

Tendrils hung from the ceiling like vines, dripping a viscous slime that hissed faintly on the floor. The air was thick with the stench of rot, and every step echoed with a wet squelch.

Mara signaled for a tactical formation: Bear and Mara at the front, Doc in the middle, Zoe at the rear, her sniper rifle scanning for threats.

The first attack came without warning. Two infected soldiers burst from a side room, their bodies grotesque with fungal mutations—tendrils sprouted from their spines, and their mouths were gaping holes emitting spore clouds.

"Contact," Bear roared, firing his shotgun point-blank as one lunged, its claws slashing while the other charged Mara.

Bear's blast tore through the creature's chest, fungal goo splattering the walls, but it kept coming, vines whipping toward his face.

Mara dodged her attacker's claws, her M4 barking as she unloaded a burst into its legs. The creature stumbled, spore clouds puffing from its wounds, the air again shimmering with that sickly green haze. Mara drove her combat knife into its skull, severing a cluster of tendrils.

Its screech echoed down the corridor, and it collapsed, body oozing a black sludge. Bear finished his target with a second shotgun blast, the monster's head exploding in a spray of spores and gore.

"Clear!" Mara called, her heart pounding. But the screech had drawn more attention. Footsteps—too many, too fast—thundered from deeper in the corridor. "Move, now!" she shouted, leading the squad forward at a sprint. They rounded a corner, the fungal growths thicker here, spore clouds sparkling.

Mara pulled her scarf over her mouth, motioning for the others to do the same. "Don't breathe this crap in!"

They reached a security room, its door half-open, papers scattered across the floor. Mara kicked it wide, sweeping the space with her M4.

Empty, but the fungal growths had crept inside, coating a bank of monitors in a glistening sheen. A desk in the corner held a stack of classified files stamped with the Canadian Forces insignia.

Letting her M4 hang from its strap, Mara grabbed the files, flipping through the pages as the squad secured the room. The words jumped out: Project Mycelium. Deep-sea fungal sample. Enhanced soldier program. Unstable mutations. Containment failure. Last entry: *If containment fails, sterilize the site—personnel are expendable.* Signed by Director Kessler.

"They were experimenting on soldiers," Mara said, her voice tight. "This fungus, it's from the ocean floor. Meant to make super soldiers. But it got out of control."

She stuffed the files into her pack, her mind racing. The outpost had to be destroyed – no way this infection could reach the mainland.

Bear read her expression and nodded, pulling a satchel of C4 from his gear. "We set charges, blow this place to hell. Main lab's gotta be deeper in, where the distress call came from."

He started rigging the explosives to the room's support beams, his hands steady despite the distant snarls growing louder. Before he could finish, the floor shook, a deep rumble that sent dust cascading from the ceiling.

Something massive was coming.

"Positions!" Mara barked, taking cover behind the desk. Zoe aimed her sniper rifle at the door, Doc crouched with his pistol, and Bear readied his shotgun, the C4 half-set.

The creature that smashed through the doorway was a nightmare. A brutish mutation, easily eight feet tall, its body a mass of fungal growths. Its arms were thick with muscle, tendrils sprouted from its shoulders, and its chest pulsed with spore sacs that burst with every step, clouding the room in green.

It had once been a soldier, but now it was a monster, its eyes glowing a sickly yellow through the fungal mass covering its face.

"Fire!" Mara shouted, unloading her M4 into the creature's chest. The rounds sank into its fungal flesh, but it didn't slow, charging straight for Bear.

He fired his shotgun, the blast tearing a chunk from its arm, but the creature roared, slamming him into the wall with a sickening crunch. Bear grunted, blood trickling from his mouth, but he rolled free, drawing his sidearm and firing into its spore sacs.

Zoe's shot cracked through the air, hitting the creature's head, severing a tendril cluster. It staggered, spore clouds erupting, and Mara switched to her flamethrower attachment – a last-resort weapon.

Flames roared, engulfing the creature, its fungal growths sizzling and popping as it screamed. The fire slowed it but didn't stop it. Claws slashed through the desk, forcing Mara to dive aside.

Doc fired his pistol, but a spore cloud hit him square in the face. He coughed, eyes watering. Fungal veins crept up his neck.

"Doc, no!" Zoe yelled, but it was too late. His body convulsed, tendrils sprouting from his arms, and he spun, lunging at Zoe with a guttural snarl.

She fired, center mass, the round punching Doc through his chest, and he collapsed, ichor pooling beneath him.

The brutish creature roared again, its burning body still advancing. Mara grabbed a grenade from her belt, pulled the pin, and tossed it into the creature's spore sacs as she dove for cover once more.

The explosion rocked the room, chunks splattering the walls. The creature finally fell, its body a smoldering heap. But the spore clouds were thicker now, the air unbreathable.

"We can't stay!" Mara shouted, grabbing Bear's arm. He was limping, favoring his ribs, but he nodded, scooping up the C4.

Zoe covered their retreat, picking off smaller infected that emerged from the shadows, their tendrils whipping through the haze. The squad sprinted back down the corridor, the fungal growths pulsing faster, as if the outpost itself were alive and angry.

They reached a stairwell, the infected close behind, their growls echoing in the dark. Mara slammed the door shut, leaning against it until Bear found a pipe to wedge through the handle.

"Downstairs, main lab's our target," she said, her voice hoarse.

The squad descended, the stairwell walls slick with fungus, the air growing colder, heavier. They'd now lost Doc. The outpost was a death trap, but Mara's resolve hardened. Whatever was down there, they'd face it.

And end it.

The squad descended into the bowels of Outpost Zero, each step colder, the growths thicker, their pale tendrils glowing faintly in the dark. Captain Mara Vigneault led her dwindling squad through the suffocating air, their weapon-mounted flashlights barely piercing the spore-laden gloom.

The classified files had pointed them here, to the main lab, the epicenter of the outbreak. Mara's grip on her M4 tightened, the loss of Doc and Elise fueling her resolve.

Whatever was down here, they'd finish it, even if it meant not all of them would make it out.

The stairwell opened into a cavernous lab, its steel walls overtaken by a pulsating mass. Bioluminescent growths cast an eerie green glow, illuminating shattered equipment – smashed monitors, overturned tables, and glass vials leaking a black sludge.

In the center of the room stood a massive containment chamber, its reinforced glass cracked, the interior a writhing nest of tendrils. Something moved inside, a hulking shadow that made Mara's blood run cold.

"Positions," she whispered, her voice steady through the comms. "Bear, left flank. Hawk, high ground. We take this slow."

Zoe climbed a scaffold, her sniper rifle trained on the chamber, while Bear moved to the left, shotgun at the ready, the C4 satchel slung over his shoulder. Mara advanced cautiously, her M4 sweeping the room.

The air was thick with spores, the stench of rot overwhelming, and every sound echoed with a wet, organic pulse. She reached the chamber, peering through the cracked glass, and her breath caught.

Inside was the spore mother – a former soldier, now a fungal monstrosity, easily ten feet tall. Its body was a mass of pulsating growths, tendrils sprouting from its back like a spider's legs, and its face was a gaping maw, spore sacs pulsing within, emitting clouds of green.

Its arms were thick with muscle, fungal veins glowing beneath its skin, and its eyes burned a sickly yellow… staring directly at her.

"It sees us," Zoe hissed over the comms, her voice tight.

Before Mara could respond, the spore mother roared,

a sound that shook the lab. The glass chamber shattered outward, shards flying like shrapnel.

Mara dove behind a steel table, glass cutting her cheek as the creature emerged, its vine-like tendrils whipping the air.

It was a hive mind, controlling the infected, and its roar summoned them. Dozens of fungal-infected soldiers poured from the lab's shadows, their bodies grotesque with tendrils and spore-emitting growths, their movements jerky but fast.

"Open fire!" Mara shouted, her M4 barking as she targeted the nearest infected. Rounds tore through it, spore clouds puffing from its wounds, but it kept coming.

Bear's shotgun roared, blasting another infected apart, fungal goo splattering the floor. Zoe's sniper shots cracked through the air, severing tendrils with precision. The infected swarmed, a relentless wave, their screeches echoing as they closed in.

Mara switched to her flamethrower attachment. Fire roared as she swept the infected, their fungal growths sizzling and popping. The flames slowed them but the spore mother advanced, its massive form shrugging off Zoe's sniper rounds.

It slammed a large tendril into the scaffold, sending Zoe crashing to the ground, her rifle skidding across the floor. "Hawk, move!" Mara yelled, but Zoe was already up, drawing her pistol and firing at a lunging infected.

Bear tossed a grenade into the swarm, the explosion scattering the infected, fungal chunks raining down. But the spore mother was undeterred. Its sacs burst, filling the lab with a thick green fog.

Mara's scarf did little to filter the air, her lungs burning as she coughed, her vision blurring. "Bear, the C4! Set it now!" she ordered, knowing they couldn't hold this position much longer.

Bear nodded, limping quickly to plant the explosives on a support pillar near the lab's center. "Timer's set.

Five minutes!" he shouted, but an infected tackled him, its claws raking his chest.

He roared, slamming the creature into the pillar, and fired his shotgun point-blank, its head exploding in a spray of spores. But the spore mother's tendrils whipped toward him, one piercing his shoulder, pinning him to the ground.

"Bear!" Mara screamed, sprinting toward him, but the spore mother turned and spat a spore cloud at her. She dove behind an overturned table, the haze so thick she could barely see, her flamethrower running low on fuel.

Zoe reached Bear, dragging him free, his blood mixing with fungal sludge as she fired her pistol at the creature's tendrils.

"We're out of time!" Zoe yelled, her voice hoarse.

Bear, clutching his wound, looked at Mara, his eyes hard. "Get Hawk out," he gasped, pulling the C4 detonator from his belt. "I'll finish this."

"No, Bear, we're not leaving you!" Mara shouted, but he shook his head, his face pale but determined.

"You have to," he said, coughing blood. "This place goes down, or the mainland's next. Go!"

He pressed the detonator into her hand, his grip firm, and pushed her away, staggering toward the spore mother, shotgun in hand.

Mara's heart shattered, but she grabbed Zoe, pulling the sniper toward the stairwell. "Move, Hawk!" she ordered, tears stinging her eyes as they ran, the lab shaking as Bear fired his last rounds.

The spore mother roared, its tendrils slashing.

Mara heard Bear's final shout—"Hoo-rah!"—before an explosion rocked the lab, the C4 detonating in a fiery blast.

The shockwave threw Mara and Zoe into the stairwell, flames licking their heels. A fused mass of soldiers—

three bodies tangled in fungal vines—lurched from a side corridor.

Their combined mouths emitted a wet, harmonized scream as spore sacs bulged from their ribs. Mara torched them with the flamethrower, their melting flesh popping like overripe fruit.

But through the smoke, the spore mother emerged, its body scorched but alive, fungal growths regenerating as it charged. The explosion had weakened it, but not enough.

Mara shoved Zoe up the stairs, turning to face the creature alone. With her M4 empty, her flamethrower spent, she only had her sidearm and combat knife left.

She squared her shoulders and drew her knife, the blade glinting in the flickering light. "Zoe, get to the chopper!" Mara yelled, her voice raw. Zoe hesitated, her face streaked with soot and tears, but nodded, sprinting up the stairs to radio for extraction.

Mara faced the spore mother, its sacs pulsing as it loomed over her. She had no weapons left save her knife, sidearm, and her will to protect the last of her squad.

The creature lunged, tendrils slashing. Mara dodged, her knife slicing into a spore sac, green cloud erupting. She rolled under its arm, stabbing its fungal mass, each cut releasing more spores, her lungs burning as she fought.

It slammed her into the wall. Pain exploded through her ribs, but she drove her knife into its eye, goo spraying as it screeched. The creature staggered, its tendrils flailing. As much as Mara wanted to draw her sidearm, she was still a long way from the chopper, so she used the spore mother's staggering moment to grab a broken steel pipe from the debris, ramming it into its maw with all her strength.

The spore mother thrashed, its body convulsing, and Mara twisted the pipe deeper, fungal growths bursting around her. With a final, guttural roar, the creature collapsed, its massive form slamming into the ground, spore sacs deflating in a final, toxic cloud.

Mara stumbled back, coughing, her body screaming with pain, but the spore mother was down – she was pretty sure for good this time.

There was no time to confirm it. The lab was collapsing, flames spreading. The outpost's destruction was imminent.

Mara staggered up the stairs, her vision swimming, Bear's sacrifice a weight heavier than any wound. She'd lost her second-in-command, but she'd protect Zoe, the last of her squad, no matter the cost.

Behind her, the lab was a hellscape – flames licking the walls, fungal growths sizzling in the heat, and the air thick with spore clouds that burned her lungs with every breath.

Her ribs ached from the creature's blow, her hands slick with goo and her own blood, but the spore mother was down. She'd driven the pipe through its sacs, severing the hive mind's control, and the infected soldiers throughout Outpost Zero had collapsed mid-step, their tendrils going limp.

But the victory was hollow—Bear's sacrifice, the C4 detonation he'd triggered, echoed in her mind, a wound deeper than any physical pain.

The lab shuddered, a deep groan reverberating through the concrete as the explosives' aftershocks began to tear the outpost apart. Cracks spiderwebbed across the ceiling, chunks of debris crashing down, and the flames spread faster, fueled by the fungal sludge coating the floor.

Mara snapped out of her daze, her soldier's instincts kicking in. Hawk was the last of her squad – still out there, racing for the chopper. Mara had to get to her, had to make sure Bear's death wasn't in vain.

Her boots slipped on the slime, the heat searing her back. A fuel line ran along the wall, its valve hissing, a faint whiff of gasoline cutting through the rot.

An idea sparked. Mara grabbed her combat knife, still slick with fungal goo, and slashed the line open. Fuel sprayed out, pooling on the floor, and she pulled a flare from her belt, striking it against the wall.

The red flame hissed to life, and she tossed it into the pool, charging back up the stairs as the fuel ignited with a whoosh. The explosion roared behind her, a fireball engulfing the lab, incinerating the spore mother's remains and the fungal growths in a cleansing blaze.

The shockwave threw Mara hard against the stairwell wall, her shoulder taking the brunt, pain lancing through her. She gritted her teeth, pushing herself up, the outpost collapsing around her.

The stairs buckled, concrete slabs falling, and she leaped over a gap, catching the edge of a broken step. She hauled herself up, muscles screaming, and kept climbing, the heat and smoke chasing her.

The fungal growths on the walls withered in the fire, their tendrils curling like dying spiders, but Bear's C4 had been set to bring the whole outpost down.

Zoe's voice crackled through her comms, frantic. "Cap, I'm at the courtyard! The chopper's inbound, but this place is coming apart!"

"On my way, Hawk!" Mara shouted, coughing as smoke filled her lungs. She sprinted down the corridor, dodging falling debris.

The infected soldiers they'd killed earlier lay charred and scattered—

A new sound stopped her cold.

A guttural snarl, echoing from the shadows ahead.

A final wave of infected emerged, their bodies less mutated – freshly turned before the spore mother's death. Five of them, their tendrils shorter but still deadly, their spore sacs puffing weakly as they charged from a side passage.

Mara drew her sidearm, firing as she ran. The first infected took a bullet to the chest, spore clouds erupting, and she ducked under its claws, slamming her knife into its throat.

It screeched, fungal goo spraying, and she kicked it into the flames, its body igniting.

The second infected lunged, its tendrils whipping, and Mara rolled aside, the fronds slashing the air where she'd been. She fired two shots into its spore sacs, the creature staggering, and finished it with a headshot, its fungal mass exploding.

But the other three were closing in, their claws scraping the concrete, and Mara's ammo was running low. She holstered her pistol, grabbing a broken pipe from the debris, and swung it like a bat, cracking the third infected's skull.

It collapsed, but the fourth slammed her to the ground, spore clouds puffing into her face.

Mara's vision blurred, her lungs burned deeper, but she drove the pipe into its spore sac, twisting until the creature screeched and rolled off. She staggered to her feet, coughing, and saw the fungal veins creeping up her arm from the exposure.

The fifth infected charged, but a sniper shot cracked through the corridor, the round punching through its head. Zoe stood at the far end, her rifle smoking, her face streaked with soot.

"Cap, let's go!" she yelled, waving Mara on.

Mara ran, her arm throbbing, the fungal infection spreading, but she pushed through the pain. They burst into the courtyard, the gate hanging off its hinges, the helipad just beyond.

The outpost was an inferno now, flames roaring through the main building, the concrete walls collapsing in a cascade of dust and fire. The chopper hovered above, its blades roaring, and a rope ladder dangling from its side.

Zoe grabbed the ladder, climbing fast, and Mara followed, her injured arm screaming as she hauled herself up.

A final explosion rocked the outpost, the C4's chain reaction reaching its peak. The helipad cracked, the ground splitting, and flames erupted, consuming the last of the fungal growths.

Zoe pulled Mara inside, and the pilot banked hard, soaring over the cliff as Outpost Zero erupted in a massive fireball, the shockwave shaking the chopper. The infection was contained, the fungal nightmare reduced to ash, ensuring it wouldn't spread to the mainland.

Mara collapsed against the chopper's wall, her breath ragged, the veins on her arm pulsing faintly.

Zoe knelt beside her, her sniper rifle across her lap, her eyes red but fierce. "We made it, Cap," she said, her voice hoarse. "Bear... he'd be proud."

Mara nodded, her throat tight, Bear's final "Hoo-rah!" echoing in her mind. She grabbed the chopper's radio, her voice steady despite the pain.

"This is Captain Vigneault, requesting immediate extraction and quarantine. Outpost Zero is down. Fungal outbreak contained. Two survivors."

She paused, her gaze hardening. "And I want intel on who authorized Project Mycelium. Someone's answering for this."

The radio crackled with a response, confirming their pickup coordinates, and Mara leaned back, staring at the burning wreckage below. The chopper lurched as the fuel tanks below erupted, a fireball licking at its skids.

The outpost collapsed into the sea.

Mara clenched her infected arm, veins dark. The chopper's interior smelled of sweat and smoke, the hum of the blades a steady rhythm against the chaos they'd left behind.

She could feel the infection creeping, a cold, itching sensation that snaked up her forearm, but she forced her focus outward—Zoe's steady breathing beside her, the pilot's clipped updates over the radio, the faint glow of dawn painting the horizon red. They'd survived Outpost Zero, but the cost was etched into every scar, every memory of her fallen squad.

"Cap, your arm—" Zoe started, her voice tight with worry, her sniper's eyes narrowing as she studied the fungal veins. She reached for her pack, pulling out a field dressing, but Mara waved her off.

"Save it, Hawk," Mara said, her tone firm despite the tremor in her hand. "We're not out of this yet. Quarantine first—then we deal with me." She met Zoe's gaze, a silent promise passing between them: they'd face whatever came next together, just as they'd fought through the nightmare below.

The pilot's voice crackled through the comms, cutting through the tension. "ETA to extraction point: ten minutes. Hazmat team's on standby, Captain. They're ready to lock you down tight."

"Good," Mara replied, her jaw clenching. She glanced at the files tucked into her pack, the words of Director Kessler burning in her mind: *personnel are expendable*. The betrayal stung deeper than the infection, a cold fury settling in her chest.

The contagion was contained, the spore mother destroyed, but the fungal veins on her arm whispered a truth she couldn't ignore: the nightmare wasn't over. Not for her. Not yet.

Someone had known what Outpost Zero held—known, and sent her squad in anyway. She'd make them pay, even if it was the last thing she did.

MOLOTOV ANGELS

Martin Livings

The makeshift Soviet base was nestled in the foothills of the Hindu Kush mountain range, some eighty miles from Kandahar. It had been built quickly some months ago according to local witnesses, springing up almost overnight in the autumn of 1983. Nobody seemed to know why they had built it; it had no strategic or logistical value, and, apart from a small airfield, it was largely an inaccessible and inconvenient location. Nevertheless, there it was. And, if they had simply minded their own business, kept to themselves, there it would have remained.

But, typical of the invaders from the distant north, they had not minded their business. They had not kept to themselves. Far from it.

And so, the Molotov Angels had come.

Imama led her squad to the tall razor-wire fence that encircled the base, wrapped both in night shadows and her late husband's robes. Her Enfield bolt-action rifle was slung across her shoulders, the bite of the leather strap on her flesh a familiar friend now, after all the years carrying it. She moved, low and silent, keeping out of any of the pools of light cast by the sparse lights the Soviets had placed along the base's perimeter. Imama looked closely, alert to any sign of patrols or guards, but there were none. She frowned, dark eyebrows furrowed beneath her headscarf. Long experience had taught her to distrust when things seemed too easy, a lesson that had kept her alive when so many others had perished at the hands of the infidels.

Finally satisfied, she waved the other Angels over.

365

Zaafirah came first, stepping through a thin layer of snow and ice, filled with her usual confidence and her usual fury. She was dressed similarly to Imama, as all the Angels were. Women wearing men's clothing, an unforgivable sin in normal times. But these were not normal times. Zaafirah flashed a harsh grin at Imama, exchanged a silent nod, and moved into position to cover through the fence, peering down the length of the AKM assault rifle with an under-slung GP-25 grenade launcher she had liberated from cold dead Soviet hands years before.

Behind her came Mehrbano and Sumbul, looking for the world like mother and daughter despite Mehrbano being only a few years older than Sumbul. Like all the Angels, they were women left behind by a murderous war, wives to husbands lost, sisters to brothers lost, daughters to fathers lost. Mothers to daughters lost.

Imama gestured to Sumbul, then to the fence. The young woman moved up silently, reached into her pack and pulled out the bolt cutters, heavily rusted by years of use in the elements but still sharp enough for their purpose.

It was the work of less than a minute to open a hole in the fence large enough for the Angels to get through. Imama hunched down and slid through the opening Sumbul had created for them, then shuffled to the side to let Mehrbano through. Zaafirah remained at her post at the fence, keeping a close eye on the small airfield beyond, rifle at the ready, until she was satisfied that it was safe. Then she crawled through and joined the others.

The airfield was almost empty, the only craft being a huge cargo plane that sat between them and the rest of the base. A Russian-made beast of an aircraft, it dwarfed the tiny, inadequate runway it rested upon, barely more than a silhouette against the star-filled sky. Mehrbano grunted with approval. She was a pilot, not by trade but necessity, initially trained by her late husband's brother. He was dead too, now. Mujahideen rarely lasted long in this war, and the ones that did became legends, boogeymen for the Soviets.

Like the Angels.

"Ilyushin Il-76," Mehrbano smiled, admiring the plane as they approached it. "Must have used it to ship equipment in."

"Engines are on," Sumbul pointed out, her voice quiet as always. It was just her nature, Imama mused. Sumbul lived quietly, and would most likely die quietly.

Mehrbano nodded. "It's been prepped for take-off. Rear door and ramp is open. The pilot is probably inside. Be careful."

Without a word, Zaafirah disappeared, running low to find a vantage point. She climbed onto some empty cargo crates, swung her rifle around, peered through the sights at the cargo plane. Then, less than a minute later, she shouldered her weapon and returned.

"All clear," she grunted. "Empty."

Mehrbano frowned. "But where are—?"

"Wait," Imama hushed, one hand raised. "Listen!"

The Angels went quiet. In the distance, raised voices. Shouts, guttural and panicked, in that ugliest of languages, Russian. Gunshots.

Screams.

"Wh... what is that?" Sumbul asked, sounding once again much younger than her years.

"Move out," Imama ordered. "The mission remains the same."

The others nodded, unslung their weapons, and advanced towards the sounds of conflict. They kept to the shadows, moved forward in two groups, Imama and Zaafirah together, then Mehrbano and Sumbul, each stopping and covering the other before continuing with a caution born of long, painful experience.

They soon reached the first bodies. Two Soviet soldiers, both gripping their AK-74 assault rifles in their dead hands.

They lay on the ground, dusted with a light smattering of snow.

They had been burned to a crisp.

Their limbs had contorted, ligaments and tendons contracted violently into unnatural postures. Their uniforms were virtually unrecognisable, charred cloth and melted metal. Strangely, their boots were intact. Their eyes, though, were gone, as were their lips, leaving nothing but a ghastly rictus smile on the face of each of the dead men.

"Ah zuma khdaya," Imama murmured, looking away from the bodies and shaking her head. The others remained silent, except for Sumbul, who allowed a horrified sob to escape her lips. She had not seen many of the things the others had.

"What... what happened?" Sumbul asked.

"Flamethrower," Mehrbano replied, patting Sumbul on the shoulder.

"No," Zaafirah grunted. "No flamethrower. The eyes."

Imama did not want to look at those terrible, missing, ruined eyes. But she was their leader, and a leader leads through example. She looked at the bodies, at the melted faces. At the eyes. It took long moments before she realised what Zaafirah was saying.

Their eyes had exploded. From the inside.

They left the twisted, burnt bodies behind them, proceeded towards the centre of the camp. There were more bodies as they advanced, all charred and contorted. And the same eyes. They ignored them, continued forward.

"Look," Sumbul whispered, pointing to their left. Imama followed her gesture, and at first only saw more of the burned bodies. Then she saw slight movement there. She gestured to the other Angels, and they approached the bodies, weapons raised. Imama stepped forward, spoke in the Russian she'd learned during the years of occupation and conflict.

"Stand up. Hands where we can see them."

From amongst the bodies, a man clambered to his feet, hands in the air. He was well-dressed, a white coat over an expensive looking suit.

"Scientist?" she asked the man, pistol aimed square at his chest.

He nodded, swallowing nervously.

"Name?"

"K-Kozlov," he stammered. "Pasha Kozlov. Doctor Pasha Kozlov."

"What are you doing here, Doctor Pasha Kozlov?" Imama asked him.

"Research," he told her cagily.

"Research? Research into what?"

"That's classified," he told her with a sudden and ludicrous arrogance, possessed by that entirely unmerited confidence that seemed so prolific in such deeply mediocre men. "You don't have clearance."

She raised the pistol to point at the Russian's face. "What about now, Doctor Pasha Kozlov?" she asked, eyebrow raised. "Is this high enough clearance?"

The scientist shrank back, his misguided defiance evaporating as quickly as it had appeared, leaving nothing but the pathetic creature he truly was. "Please!" he cried. "Get me out of here! I'll tell you everything, but we need to leave! Now!"

"No," Imama told him. "We are here for someone. Once we find them, we leave."

"Someone?" Kozlov asked, incredulous. "You mean one of the test subjects?"

"I mean one of your prisoners," Imama said through gritted teeth. "Is that what they are to you? Test subjects?"

"You're insane," the scientist sobbed. "There's nobody left! They're all dead or..."

"Or what?"

"Or worse," Kozlov concluded. "Please! We must leave!"

Imama turned, gestured for the others to join them. They marched over, weapons at the ready. Mehrbano seemed particularly keen, the barrel of her Enfield aimed squarely at the man's head.

Imama looked back at the Russian scientist. "Where are they kept?" she demanded. "The prisoners? The test subjects?"

Koslov pointed towards the sounds of screams and gunfire, lessening now. "The main building," he told her. Then he pointed back, toward the airfield and beyond. "But that way," he told them, "is where we should be going. The other way is a death sentence."

Imama shrugged. "If you try to run," she growled, "then we'll shoot you in the head. *That* is a death sentence. Do you understand?"

He swallowed once, hard, and nodded.

"Good," Imama grunted. "Now, move." Then, in her native tongue to the Angels, "Come on."

They advanced slowly, weapons hot. Imama remained beside the Russian scientist, her pistol jammed into his side, urging him forward. His eyes were wide, panicked. She realised that this was no act, no ploy to distract them. Kozlov was genuinely terrified, no doubt.

But of what?

A hundred feet or so away, a panicked Soviet soldier emerged from around the corner of one of the rough tin and fibro structures. He ran towards them, screaming.

"Pomogite mne! Radi Boga, pomogite mne!"

Mehrbano immediately raised her rifle, but Imama waved the girl back. There was something wrong. The soldier was unarmed, for one thing, and begging them for help.

Imama saw a burst of bright light on the approaching man's shoulder, as if a flash camera had gone off. The man stumbled a little, his eyes filled with fear.

A moment later, his shoulder burst into flames.

The man did not scream, there was no time. The fire on his shoulder spread so rapidly, like he was doused in petrol. In less than a second, he was engulfed entirely. A pillar of fire, just as the Quran described. The gates of hell.

The burning soldier fell to his knees, his arms drawn up tight to his chest like a boxer ready for a bout, fists clenched. His mouth opened, but no sound emerged, just more fire. He looked at the Angels, looked unseeing.

Then his eyes exploded.

Sumbul screamed. Imama did not, but that was more from sheer shock than courage. She watched the man burn, the flames dying down as rapidly as they had appeared.

Mehrbano approached the still smouldering body, walking as if in a trance, mesmerised by the impossible sight.

"Nyet!" the scientist, Koslov, screamed at her in Russian. "Stay back! It's not safe!"

She froze, not understanding the words but grasping the meaning.

"What do you mean, it's not safe?" Imama asked him.

"It spreads," he told her, shivering. "It spreads through the flames."

"What? What spreads?"

"Imama!" Zaafirah barked, raising her huge Russian anti-tank rifle. "There!"

Imama turned from Koslov and looked. There, where the soldier had emerged, another figure was visible. This one was an old, bearded Afghani man, dressed in nothing more than a torn and tattered blue hospital gown. He walked towards them without hesitation, without fear. His eyes were closed.

"Sir?" Imama called to the man, concerned. He looked so frail, dressed in those rags. "Are you alright?"

The man stopped, smiled with his lips closed tight. Opened his eyes.

They were filled with fire.

Imama gasped, staggered backwards, as did the other Angels. Even stoic, unflappable Zaafirah was frozen in place. Flames flickered within the old man's eye sockets, slithering across his brows. His smile grew wider, and his lips parted to reveal fire there too, inside his mouth. A tongue of flame brushed across his face. His whole body gave off a thin mist of smoke. He held one hand out towards them, as if in greeting, and his fingers caught alight, burned like kindling.

"Kill it!" Koslov screamed. "Kill it!"

Zaafirah broke herself from her trance, aimed her grenade launcher. Pulled the trigger.

The sound of the 40mm grenade firing was anti-climactic, but certainly effective. The shell streaked through the air and caught the old man square in the chest, the explosion opening up a hole as big as a man's fist in his rib-cage and blowing his back out. There was no blood, though, only more fire, catching on the remnants of his hospital gown and setting them ablaze. He stumbled backwards, but that fiery smile never wavered. He raised his hand again, still aflame, and this time pointed a burning finger at her.

A stream of flame emerged from his fingertip, strafing across the ground towards Zaafirah, leaving a trail of fire in the snow behind it. The flames reached her feet, set her boots alight.

"No!" Mehrbano yelled, and pushed Zaafirah out of the path of the fire. The Angel collapsed to the ground, feet still burning. Mehrbano fell to her knees beside her, grabbed her shoulders, and rolled her back and forth in the snow, dousing the flames.

Now the old man was making a strange noise, a popping almost-laughter, like wet wood burning. The flames in his eyes intensified, twin columns of fire shooting up over his forehead and into his sparse grey hair, setting it ablaze. And still that that awful smile. Imama was frozen, looking at the old man, at her fellow Angels rolling in the snow.

Snow angels, she thought distantly. She looked back at the old man. There were flames on his body now, rising from his shoulders, his ruined chest, his arms and legs. He was no snow angel.

He was a fire devil.

A single shot rang out, and the devil's head snapped back. He stood there a moment longer, expressionless, the inhuman laughter gone all at once. Then the flames in his eyes flickered and died, and he collapsed, a single, neat hole between his hollow eyes. He was just an old man again, a burned, thin, dead old man. Imama looked to where that single shot had come from.

Sumbul had her Enfield at her shoulder, a curl of smoke still visible at the mouth of the barrel. Her young eyes were wide, panicked. But her hands, Allah be praised, were steady as a rock.

Koslov turned to Zaafirah, still lying in the snow with Mehrbano by her side. His eyes were wide, frantic. "Are you burned?" he demanded of the prone woman in Russian. "Are you burned?"

Mehrbano and Zaafirah looked up at the man, unfazed. "Imama," Zaafirah said, "what is he saying?"

"He's asking whether you've been burned," Imama replied.

"Why?"

A cold feeling crept across Imama's spine. Koslov's earlier words came back to her. *It spreads through the flames.* "Are you burned, Zaafirah?"

She examined her feet. "No," she said. "Just my boots."

"Only her boots," Imama told Koslov in Russian. He breathed a sigh of relief.

"What's going on, Imama?" Sumbul asked her shakily. "What was that... thing?"

"That," Imama replied, "is a very good question." She turned back to Koslov. "Start talking," she demanded. "What were you doing here?"

Koslov hesitated. "This is not the best time to…"

Imama raised her pistol, pointed it between Koslov's eyes. "Talk or die," she said simply.

Koslov blanched but stood his ground. "If I talk, I'm dead anyway. Or if I don't. Unless we leave now, we're all dead."

Imama pondered this for a moment. "Fair." She lowered her pistol, aimed it at his stomach instead. "But if I shoot you in the gut, you will survive long enough for those things to find you. Not all deaths are created equal."

"Fuck," he spat. "Fine. I'll tell you. What harm can it do now?" He closed his eyes for a moment, finding the right words. "Have you heard of spontaneous human combustion?"

She shook her head.

"Really?" Koslov asked, incredulous. "Jesus, you people really are savages, aren't you?"

Imama cocked her pistol. "Get on with it."

Koslov blanched, continued. "There have been cases of this throughout history, people simply burning alive with no real explanation for it. Polonus Vorstius in the late fifteenth century, Countess Cornelia Di Bandi in the eighteenth. Robert Francis Bailey in England in 1967, Ginette Kazmierczak in France in 1977. Usually, the body appears to have burned from within, with parts untouched. Often, nearby objects are completely unscathed. I know the British have been investigating it, their E-Branch has done multiple inquiries into their cases, never with any results though. Primarily because they have treated it as some kind of chemical reaction." He smiled proudly. "But we posited that it wasn't chemically-induced combustion, not as such. No, this was something else."

"What?" Imama asked, impatient. She looked around, for signs of any other combatants approaching. There was no-one, but still in the distance there was gunfire and screams, becoming more sporadic.

Koslov virtually beamed when he responded. "A virus," he said. "A virus unlike any other. A pyrovirus, carried upon the flames of its infected victims." He waved his hand, gesturing at the prefabricated buildings around them. "Brezhnev ordered us to analyse the virus here, far from civilisation. Somewhere our citizens would not be at risk. Somewhere we could find..." He trailed off then, suddenly uncomfortable.

Imama knew what he was about to say. "Somewhere you could find test subjects." Her finger tightened against her trigger reflexively.

"Please," Koslov begged, hands raised. "I was just following orders! We're not soldiers, not killers. We're scientists!"

"A bullet or a virus," Imama snarled. "What is the difference?"

"Brezhnev wanted to deploy it here," Koslov continued desperately. "Not to kill, not as such, but to destabilise. To terrify a population still largely superstitious and backward. He wanted to release it immediately, but we refused. We refused!"

"Why?" Imama's gun did not waver, and nor did her voice, despite everything.

Koslov hesitated. "Because it was wrong," he said at last, but his eyes did not meet Imama's.

She lowered her gun further and pulled the trigger. The report was shockingly loud, and a bullet tore into Koslov's foot, sending a spray of bright red blood across the scattered snow. He screamed and staggered backwards.

"Do not lie to me, Pasha," she told the shrieking Russian, her voice still preternaturally calm. "The next one will be in your knee. Then your stomach."

Koslov regained control, tears streaming down his ashen cheeks. He took a few deep, gulping breaths, then looked at her, eyes filled with terror and agony.

"W-we refused," he told her, "because the results were

not as we'd hoped. Unpredictable. Some went up in an instant, others burned for hours. And some... some didn't burn at all." He sighed. "We refused because something had gone wrong, and by the time we knew what it was, it was too late."

"What was it?" Imama asked him. "What went wrong?"

"The virus was affected by each infected person's genetics," he told her. "And each time it infected someone, found itself in a new genetic environment, it mutated, adapted. *Perfected* itself." He shook his head. "Soon, some of the subjects stopped dying. They simply burned and burned and burned. Which delighted us, to be honest," he confessed. "I mean, a virus that kills the victim immediately has no chance of spreading." He frowned. "Then there was test subject fifty-two. Something about that one was the perfect storm, the perfect environment."

Imama eyed the scientist. "What happened, Pasha? What happened after test subject fifty-two?"

He snorted. "What happened is that we lost control of the experiment. It wasn't our project, not anymore. No, it was hers! And we, we became the test subjects!"

"Hers?" Imama's free hand shot out, grasped the Soviet scientist by the neck, fingers digging deep into the soft flesh there. "Hers? Who is she?"

"Imama," Sumbul called, pointing. "There's more of them!"

Imama looked away from Koslov's reddening face, and saw them, coming from the direction of the screams and gunfire. Two more burning men, these ones in military uniforms. No, three, another coming around the corner of the buildings ahead of them. All three had flames flickering across their flesh, and their eyes were like burning coals embedded in their sockets, red hot and smoking. She released the scientist, allowed him to fall to the ground.

"Advance!" she barked at the Angels. "Take them down!"

Mehrbano stepped forward, helping Zaafirah to her feet before aiming her rifle and firing. She caught the lead burning soldier in the chest, but that did not slow it down, not at all.

"The head!" Imama yelled, aiming her own weapon now. "Go for the head!"

Mehrbano calmly released another shot, this time taking the top of the burning man's head clean off. He dropped to his knees and collapsed, the flames dying away. Imama shot the second with her pistol, the bullet entering his fiery eye-socket, felling him. And Zaafirah, on her knees now, aimed her GP-25 at the third approaching creature, which opened its mouth to release a jet of flame. She fired, and the shell went straight into that hellish maw. His entire head exploded in a spray of blood, brains and fire.

"Go!" Imama told them, as the third soldier crumpled to the ground. "We need to get to the main building."

"What did he tell you?" Mehrbano asked her as they all moved forwards, weapons raised, eyes darting about for any sign of a threat. Any sign of a fire devil. "The Russian? What did he say?"

"A virus," she told her, and the others. "In the flames. Do not get burned." She chose not to tell them the rest. There was no point. They had to keep moving.

There were no more of the flaming creatures between them and the main building, which looked more like a gymnasium than a military installation – a large, tall structure that stood out from the rest of the buildings there. There was no screaming now, no gunshots. Just an eerie silence, with a strange noise lurking in the background. It took Imama a few moments to recognise it.

It was the soft crackling of a burning fire.

Imama glanced at Zaafirah and nodded once, then she and the other Angels fell in on either side of the double doors that led into the main building, in a formation never taught but simply learned through years of deadly experience.

Koslov was shoved to the side roughly. Zaafirah remained in front of the doors, dropping to one knee and readying her AKM rifle. She nodded back at her commander.

Imama counted down from five silently on her fingers to the Angels, then after one she reached out and pulled one of the doors open, careful not to leave herself exposed, ready for whatever might emerge.

Nothing did. Just that crackling noise, which grew louder.

She looked over at Zaafirah, who still knelt at the entrance, motionless as a stone. The woman's eyes were wide, horrified, and the rifle slowly lowered to the ground, barely held in hands gone suddenly numb.

"Zaafirah?" Imama asked in a whisper. "Zaafirah, what is it?"

There was no reply.

Mehrbano and Sumbul stepped into the doorway, weapons raised. Sumbul screamed and fell to her knees, while the others simply looked on in shock.

Then Imama took a single step into the doorway, one hand grasping Koslov's upper arm tightly, the other holding her pistol. They both looked inside.

The building was one gigantic open space, set up with dozens of sealed, transparent cubicles, glass perhaps, or more likely plexiglass, each with a hospital bed and equipment inside. There were airlock-style doors leading to each one, and ventilation ducts emerged from the rear of every cell—for cells they were—and snaked away into the roof. It must have been a very impressive setup at one point, when it was still intact.

No more. All of the cells were half-melted and charred, the once-clear walls smoky and grey. The beds were scorched and ruined, many with twisted, burned bodies still in them. Imama could see that more than a few contained nothing more than a single leg or arm, strangely untouched by the flames. Scattered about were also many bodies of Soviet soldiers, all burned, still clutching their weapons, surrounded by abandoned ordnance.

But it was not the cells that caught her attention. It was what lay beyond them.

At the far end of the building, down the corridor formed by the wrecked cubicles the Soviets had set up for their inhuman experiments, there were perhaps two dozen or so people gathered. They were aflame, some in tattered and burned hospital gowns, others in military uniforms. They knelt in a wide semi-circle all facing away from the entrance, the air around them shimmering with heat haze.

And, beyond them...

"Oh," gasped Koslov. "My, how she's grown!"

The creature was easily three metres tall, maybe four. It was human-shaped, yes, but definitely not human, not anymore. Most of its enormous body seemed to be composed of pure flame, just preternatural ropes of fire curling around one another like seething eels, eels with no heads, no tails. But there was flesh there too, yes, in various places, as if torn apart by the flames themselves, suspended in them, stepping stones in that violent fiery river. Fingertips at the ends of the impossibly-long fingers of fire. Patches of burned, peeling skin where it should have been consumed by flame.

And, worst, the face was almost entirely intact, though the hair had mostly burned away, leaving the scalp a patchwork mess of blackened flesh and exposed bone. The face that, despite the distortion of the fire around it, was still instantly recognisable.

Hooriyah.

She had come to Imama over two weeks ago, told her the rumours she had heard. A Soviet base in the mountains. People going missing from the surrounding villages. She had suggested the Angels check it out, but Imama had refused to act on such weak intel. They had bigger fish to fry. Hooriyah, furious, had declared she would go alone if need be. Imama had ignored her foolishness.

379

And now...

"No," Imama sobbed, and lowered her gun. "Please, no..."

"What are you doing?" Koslov yelled in her ear. "Shoot it! Kill it!"

Zaafirah loaded another round into the GP-25's muzzle and raised her rifle again, her expression resolute.

"No!" Imama screamed, but too late, Zaafirah had already pulled the trigger.

There was a bright flash in the air around the creature's head, Hooriyah's head. But nothing more. Zaafirah frowned, fired again. And again. Each time, the 40mm shell was vaporised before it could reach its target. Mehrbano raised her Enfield and fired as well, but with no more success. Sumbul was on her hands and knees, sobbing like a war widow, far too young to be crying like that.

And Imama, she just watched, frozen, as Hooriyah looked over at them with burning eyes, eyes of flame. She—it—pointed at them, and screamed, a terrible high-pitched howl that hurt Imama's ears.

The other fire devils turned to face the Angels, started to shamble towards them.

"No," Imama breathed, dazed. She raised her own pistol, aimed and fired, caught one of the approaching devils in the shoulder. No effect. The other Angels followed her lead, though, redirected their fire to the creatures coming towards them, cutting them down one by one, each headshot extinguishing their flames forever.

Not enough, though. Too many.

"Hell with this," Mehrbano grunted, and ran to one of the fallen Soviet soldiers nearby – the charred body beside a small, stout-looking weapon on a tripod with a dark green drum attached to it. She shoved the corpse aside, aimed the weapon at the oncoming horde, and fired. It discharged with a muffled thump, and a large projectile arced from the gun into the creatures. A split second later, there was an explosion, and three fire devils were blown to pieces, bodies shredded into ribbons of flesh, blood, and flame.

Imama looked over Mehrbano, stunned. She smiled back grimly. "Plamya," she told her. "Portable belt-fed grenade launcher. They had these when they attacked my village." She fired again, and another group of creatures was obliterated.

The huge fire devil at the back, Hooriyah, screamed again. She stepped forward on long, spindly legs made mostly of flame, then reached down and grasped one of the smaller creatures in her nightmarish hand. It burst into flames upon her touch. She—*it*, she reminded herself again—raised herself up, looked directly at Imama for a moment. Smiled, a horrible, fiery, malicious smile.

Then she threw the fire devil at Mehrbano.

"Look out!" Imama yelled, but too slow, too late. The burning body struck the ground just short of the grenade launcher and exploded, sending plumes of flame in all directions. A moment later, the launcher itself exploded, the remaining grenades detonated by the intense heat and fire. Mehrbano was thrown back, her robes on fire, screaming in pain. Sumbul screamed as well, started to run to her, but Koslov grabbed her upper arm viciously. She turned to look at him, tears and fury in her eyes. He shook his head. Imama looked back to Mehrbano's fallen form. She had stopped screaming, stopped moving, just lay there, still ablaze.

Then one of her arms raised up, flames licking at the rough cloth that covered it.

"Let me go!" Sumbul cried. "She's alive!"

"No," Imama said through numb lips. "No, she's not. She couldn't be."

Mehrbano sat up then, turned her head to them. Opened her eyes.

They were fire.

Imama raised her pistol, pointed it at Mehrbano's head. But her hand shook, for the first time in so many years, shook so badly she could not draw aim. She looked past the woman she'd known for so many years, now no longer that woman but something else, something *infected*. Looked past, to Hooriyah.

She was already grabbing another fire devil to throw.

"Retreat!" Imama barked. The others did not hesitate, slinging their weapons and turning to flee. Imama helped the limping scientist out of the building and closed the doors hard behind them. Then they ran, not looking back, ignoring the sound of the doors exploding behind them, struck by another one of the hurled devils. There were explosions around them as they retreated, back past the small structures they had passed on their way towards the main building.

"We have to get out of here," Sumbul gasped as they ran. "There's nothing we can do. Hooriyah is gone!"

Imama did not respond, was too busy thinking. Thinking about Mehrbano, about all the others. Thinking about Hooriyah. She turned to Koslov, who struggled to keep up the pace the Angels set. "That is subject fifty-two, yes?" she asked him.

He nodded. "There's something in her genetics," he gasped as they fled. "She doesn't burn up. And she can control the others, it seems. But she needs fuel."

"Fuel?"

"Anything that burns," Koslov answered. "She will eat, and eat, and eat, until there's nothing left to eat."

Imama thought of the villages in the area, villages with trees, and orchards, and wooden buildings, and fuel depots. Villages, and beyond them, the cities.

And people. So many people. Her people.

"The plane," she said to the Angels. "Head to the plane."

Imama glanced behind them, saw the devils approaching, less of them now, and behind them, the huge, loping fiery form of the creature that was once Hooriyah. She smashed prefabricated buildings as she passed them with her impossibly long arms, setting them ablaze with every blow. The base was burning to the ground now, something that gave Imama some pleasure. Zaafirah halted once in a while, fired her grenade launcher back at their pursuers, took out some of the fire devils in the process.

Nothing would stop Hooriyah, though. Nothing.

They ran back to the airfield, dirt compacted into some semblance of a runway. Good enough for their purposes, Imama thought. Hopefully, good enough for the Angels' purpose as well. The Ilyushin Il-76 cargo plane loomed before them, enormous and squat. Its hull was gunmetal grey, almost black in the sparse lighting. There were flickers of orange in it too now, reflections of flames. Its engines still ran, the four jets spinning idly.

"Inside!" she ordered her soldiers, her troop, her family. "Into the cargo hold!"

Imama looked around, saw a small shed nearby. She darted across to it as the rest of the Angels and Koslov ran up the ramp into the gaping maw of the plane. Inside the shed were a couple of sizeable jerry cans, and the stench of jet fuel filled her nostrils. She holstered her pistol, grabbed the nearest can, and lugged it back towards the plane. When she reached the foot of the steel ramp, she looked back, saw Hooriyah approaching. Before her was a single fire devil, the last of them, the rest used as makeshift grenades by the monster. Imama's eyes widened when she saw who the fire devil was.

Mehrbano.

"No," she breathed, but it was already happening. One of Hooriyah's enormous, spindly claws reached down and closed around Mehrbano's neck. The woman's fire eyes flickered for a moment, a brief emotion visible there. Doubt? Pain?

Fear?

Then she was entirely engulfed in flames, all form and features gone in a heartbeat. Hooriyah lifted her with no apparent effort, flung her towards the plane. She left a trail of fire in the air behind her, then landed some ten meters away from them. She exploded on impact, the concussion rocking Imama back. The heat seared her face, and she reflexively shielded herself with her hands for a moment, dropping the fuel canister.

When she looked again, there was no sign of her friend aside from a small fire in the dirt.

"Here!" Imama screamed at the monster that wore Hooriyah's face, reaching down and opening the can of jet fuel. She tipped it a little, spilling some of the fuel, the vapours making the air around her shimmer like a desert mirage. "You want this?"

The creature howled. A fiery, crackling howl that split the still night air.

Imama grinned viciously. "Come get it!" she yelled, and hauled the canister up the ramp and into the cargo hold.

The hold was huge, nearly three meters both tall and wide, and a good twenty meters long. It was empty, any equipment taken out and deployed. It was mostly metal inside the hold, and thick canvas straps and netting for cargo hung at intervals from the walls and roof. At the far end was the steel hatch leading to the cockpit. That was where the Angels gathered, looking back at Imama, their expressions a strange mixture of horror, determination, and expectation.

Koslov, on the other hand, simply looked terrified.

Imama walked towards them, pausing about half-way into the hold to place the fuel canister gently on the metal floor before continuing to the far end. She looked to Sumbul. "Prepare to take off," she told the young woman.

"M-me?" Sumbul stammered. "But I can't..."

"I know Mehrbano was the pilot," Imama interrupted her. "I know she was like a mother to you. And I know she is dead."

Sumbul's face crumbled, tears flowing anew.

"I also know," Imama continued, "that she trained you. I know that she was a fine teacher, as well as a fine soldier. And a fine friend," she added, working to keep her own tears in check. "I know she trusted you, and believed in you. And so do I."

The young woman closed her eyes, took a deep, shuddering breath, released it. Looked up to meet Imama's gaze steadily, resolute. She wiped her tears away, and nodded, turned and opened the hatch to the cockpit, climbed inside.

"Lock the door," Imama told her. "Do not open it again until I tell you to." She reached over and tapped the intercom on the wall next to the hatch. "Do what I say, when I say. No questions. Understand?"

Sumbul nodded assent, then turned and entered the cockpit, closing the hatch behind her.

"Wait!" Koslov cried, trying to follow. "Don't leave me in here!"

Imama looked at the Soviet scientist. "What's the matter, Pasha?" she asked him with mock sweetness. "Afraid to face the consequences of your actions?" She turned to Zaafirah. "Are you ready?"

Zaafirah nodded, rifle at her shoulder.

Koslov looked back and forth at the two women, eyes wide. "You bitches are fucking crazy!" he spat.

"Possibly," Imama conceded with a small shrug. She looked back out of the cargo hold. Saw what was coming for them. "Definitely," she corrected herself.

Hooriyah was there at the gaping cargo bay door at the rear of the plane, mounting the snow-speckled metal ramp with heavy footsteps that boomed and sizzled. She snarled, like the crack of the bough of a burning tree collapsing under its own weight, sniffed the air, and turned her burning, distended head toward the fuel container that sat halfway between them. Imama could see the vapours coming out of the open canister.

The monster stepped towards it, further into the cargo hold.

Imama jabbed at the intercom. "Now!" she barked into it.

Outside the plane, the jet engines whined as they powered up, and the plane began to move, slowly at first, then faster and faster. Beyond Hooriyah, the makeshift runway blurred away from them, the snow kicked up into sizeable flurries that whirled and danced behind the plane, caught in its jet-stream. The engines screamed, deafening. Then the nose eased upwards, the deck of the cargo hold tilting back suddenly, and the plane shuddered into the air. Imama grabbed one of the cargo straps that hung from the wall and held tight. The creature snatched at the walls, fiery fingers melting holes in the metal. The plane continued to ascend, tilting upwards more and more.

The fuel canister slid towards the still-open cargo hold doors. Towards Hooriyah.

The huge fire demon saw this, and hunched towards it, still gripping both walls of the cargo hold with its nightmarishly long arms. Imama swallowed multiple times to equalise the air pressure in her ears, then turned to Zaafirah, who had one arm wrapped in a strap to keep her in place. Zaafirah nodded, braced herself, and aimed her rifle.

She fired as the canister reached Hooriyah.

The 40mm explosive slug from the launcher tore into the heavy steel fuel can and detonated, creating a massive fireball within the confines of the cargo hold. Imama momentarily felt the heat of the flames, but the fire was quickly snatched away, by the whistling wind from the open doors at the far end, but mostly by the monster. She swallowed the flames, sucking them into her maw, just a never-ending inhalation that absorbed every last trace of the fireball. All that remained was Hooriyah, who was even larger than before, swollen by the burning fuel. Her shoulders pressed hard against the top of the cargo hold, her fiery bulk filling it. She looked down the length of the cargo hold. At Koslov, and Zaafirah.

And at Imama. Especially at Imama.

The air was ice-cold now, prickling at Imama's flesh. She was dressed for the winter, for the snow, but not for this. She watched, breath caught in her chest, as the fire devil approached. Distantly, she recalled her father telling her his usual stories to frighten her into being a good and dutiful daughter, tales from his beloved Quran. About the ifrit of the jinn, formed from smokeless fire, the worst of the demons.

She had never believed them. Until now.

The creature took another step towards them, and another, ember eyes burning. There was nothing there of Hooriyah, just a devil, wanting to destroy them. Consume them. Another step. Another.

Then she faltered, eyes suddenly uncertain. Tried to take another step, but her leg gave way, and she fell to her knees. The flames that licked around the small amount of flesh of her body flickered, guttered.

Died.

Hooriyah collapsed in on herself, shrinking rapidly in the thinning air of the open cargo hold. Twenty thousand feet up, and there was not enough oxygen for fire to burn. Imama knew that, knew that fuel wasn't the only thing this thing needed. It needed air.

Of course, so did she. The breath she was holding burned her lungs, but she held on, glanced across at Zaafirah and Koslov. Zaafirah's eyes flickered as she clung to conscious-ness, rifle at her feet. Koslov was out completely. Imama's own vision was blurring, greying at the edges. But she held on. She had to.

The fires surrounding and creating the monster before them were gone, dead. All that was left was the small naked form of a young woman, scorched in places but otherwise intact. She did not move.

Imama turned to the intercom, pressed the button, and screamed as loudly as she could with her last breath.

"Down!"

She collapsed to the floor, suffocating. But Sumbul was a good soldier, good Angel. Good friend. The plane levelled out beneath her, then tilted downwards, descended rapidly. As it did, the limp body of the young woman slid along the deck. Imama, despite the pain in her lungs, crawled towards the prone form, met it halfway. Gathered Hooriyah up to cradle in her arms.

The woman's eyes flickered open. Normal eyes, dark brown, almost black. The eyes of her father. She looked up at Imama, confused. Then, in the thin cold air, she spoke.

"Mama?"

Imama embraced her daughter tightly, tears hot on her cold cheeks. Hooriyah, her headstrong, brave, loving daughter, so much like herself at her age. She clambered to her feet, helped Hooriyah to hers. Kissed her on the forehead and cheeks, again and again. Looked in her eyes.

There was a spark there, somewhere deep. Too deep for even Hooriyah to feel. Not yet.

Somewhere behind her, Koslov was speaking in a strangled voice, barking something in Russian. She did not listen, did not have to. She knew what she had to do.

"Mama?" Hooriyah said again. "Mama? What's happening? Where am I?"

"Shh," Imama soothed her, held her close. One arm was wrapped around her daughter. The other was by her side. Hooriyah's body was beginning to smoke again, and Imama felt her own flesh burning with the heat of it, blisters forming on her skin.

Her hand found the handgun holstered at her side, pulled it out.

She kissed Hooriyah again. "Mama is here. You can rest now."

She raised the pistol, pressed the barrel against her daughter's temple. Pulled the trigger.

The gunshot was strangely muffled in the still-thin air, barely audible over the screaming engines. Hooriyah's head jerked to the side, and she collapsed to the floor. Zaafirah let out a horrified wail, fell to her knees behind them. But Imama simply stood there, made herself look. Look at what she had done. What she had been forced to do.

Finally, she tore her eyes away, stepped over the body of her dead daughter, walked to the open cargo doors at the end of the plane. Gazed out at the familiar landscape passing beneath them, the vast plains and dramatic cliff faces and outcrops, the mountains in the distance.

Koslov limped up behind her, clinging to the walls. He stood next to her.

"You did the right thing," he told her.

She did not reply.

"She was a danger to humanity," he continued. "She would have eaten the world, given the chance."

"The world can go to hell," she mumbled through numb lips.

Koslov looked out of the plane, thoughtful. "Perhaps it will," he said finally. "But not today. Thanks to us."

Imama did not look at the man. She just reached out, put her hand on his shoulder. Patted it once.

Then she gripped him tight and threw him out of the plane.

She saw his face, just for an instant, an expression of utter shock writ there. Then he was gone, taken by the wind and gravity, vanished, gone forever.

"Only angels get to fly," she murmured.

She turned back to Zaafirah. The woman nodded gravely, picked up her rifle again. Imama walked back to the other end of the cargo bay, pressed the intercom button.

"Take us home," she said into it.

"Yes, Imama," Sumbul replied, though for a moment she sounded so much like Mehrbano that it shook her to the core. Sumbul had been changed by this. As had they all.

She stood there in the cargo hold, feeling the warmth come back to her chilled fingers. Warmer than she would have expected, in fact. Almost hot, like the flesh of her arms that had been burned by Hooriyah's final embrace. And, once again, she felt that familiar rage for the Russian invaders within her, not cold as it had once been, but white hot. Fire in her gut. Sparks in her veins.

Imama was a Molotov Angel, and she would watch every last one of them burn.

GOTTERDAMMERUNG

Robert Mammone

'Hell is empty and all the devils are here.'
~William Shakespeare

A half-acre of Ukrainian soil, mixed with the body parts of a dozen trench defenders, fountained thirty yards into the sky under the hammer blow of a Russian artillery barrage arriving with all the sudden fury of God's own wrath.

Fleming, standing at the highest point of the trench network to survey the lay of the land, leapt for his life as more artillery strikes dispelled the darkness in staccato bursts.

The animal screams of the injured and dying pierced the night. The earth trembled as if in the grip of a grand mal seizure. As Fleming flung himself against the crumbling trench wall, the strikes crept closer with a relentlessness that made his blood run cold.

His earpiece crackled. Lurching away from the wall's scant protection, Fleming saw a figure scramble to the top of a trench.

Striker's voice echoed tinnily in the team's comms system. "Run for your fucking lives!"

Fleming needed no encouragement. The mercenary hauled himself up the earthen wall with the agility of an ibex.

Across a lunar landscape littered with the dead and dying, Fleming ran into the darkness with the others. They clambered over a defensive breastwork and tumbled into a ditch filled with corpses.

"God damn it," Austen gasped, her Southern twang exaggerated by her foul temper. "The fucking stink." An unlit cigar jutted from the corner of her mouth.

Beneath his boots, Fleming felt soft, rotting flesh, and almost retched. Many of the dead had a single bullet hole in the back of their head.

Striker crawled to the lip of the ditch, and Fleming watched the man pull a pair of infrared binoculars from a pouch at his hip and peer towards the village. Beside Striker, almost lost in the dark, crouched an older man with a cloth cap pulled low. He had been their guide since the rendezvous six hours ago. Had watched the village with despair in his eyes.

"What's the word?" Fleming's Scot's burr was almost lost amidst the rattle of gunfire.

Beyond the ditch stood the remains of a building, roof gone, shattered walls riddled with bullet holes. Flickering flames played tricks with Fleming's eyesight. The shapes of opposing men looked misshapen before vanishing into the night. Tracer rounds lit up the ruined village, creating a stop-motion vision of Armageddon.

"Old mate Pyotr here has led us into a firefight." Striker's Aussie drawl did little to hide his disdain. "Bloody fools blueing over a heap of rubble." His eyepatch was as dark as night. "Head east along this lane, then bear north. Weapons free."

Striker beckoned him over. Fleming moved forward, his bulky MTV chafing his shoulders.

"You bring up the rear," Striker said. "Herd these sheep in the right direction."

Fleming watched Striker and the guide disappear into the gloom. A steady parade of greasepaint smudged faces followed. Federici, with his toothy grin. Austen and her fierce glower. Goldstein, cool as a cucumber and hot as Hades. Rocard, if anything, more excited than the Italian. Then Naevu, with his solemn, watchful face.

"What a shower," Fleming muttered. He adjusted the shoulder strap of his L85A2 and fell in.

An ominous vibration sounded overhead. On instinct, Fleming ducked but a hasty glance showed the drones had other targets in mind. They dominated the skies across Ukraine. Like everyone in the mercenary world, Fleming had watched the videos on YouTube and understood that war had changed yet again. Death was everywhere; as below, so above.

Shouts, in Russian. A drone changed direction. Fleming and the others hunkered beside a half-collapsed wall as the drone hit the ground and exploded. The blast tore through the patrol, leaving a stark image of a street filled with broken bodies.

"God *damn*." Striker's voice filtered through their earpieces.

Fleming crouch-walked up the line where he found Striker kneeling beside Pyotr. Blood pooled around an ugly head wound. The body convulsed then settled with a sigh.

"Shrapnel's a bitch," Austen said, voice stripped of emotion. She stared down the sights of her M4A1 carbine at anyone who might dare come anywhere near.

Federici hustled forward to examine the Ukrainian with the steadiness of a battlefield medic. He shook his head as he pressed two fingers in the crook of the man's jaw. "He's gone."

Gunfire, explosions, and shouts sounded. More drones swooped past, black smudges against a night sky heavy with clouds and the threat of rain.

"It is too dangerous," Naevu said, his face bathed in sweat. The big man crouched like a child under the cosh.

"Take it easy, Tommy," Striker snapped, flicking on his helmet-mounted torch then unfolding a map. He traced a finger along a particular line. "We're being paid too much and come too far to turn back." His surviving eye narrowed. "We go. Fifty yards north there's the old council building. The hatch is on the ground floor."

Gunfire. Endless gunfire. Drones gathered in swarms, their buzzing like screaming cicadas awakening to summer's dawn. Several plunged to the ground and detonated, adding to the chaos.

A shape bounced towards them.

"Grenade!" Striker shouted.

Like cockroaches under torchlight, the team scattered as all hell broke loose.

The grenade exploded with a sharp crack. Fleming saw one of the team stumble. Rocard gathered up the figure. Bullets ripped overhead.

Striker fired in bursts as he scuttled between piles of heaped rubble. Behind him, Austen unloaded a clip into soldiers caught in no man's land. Two fell dead and the survivors fled.

Paired with Goldstein, Fleming watched their backs. Goldstein aimed her Jericho 941, cooly picking off anyone foolish enough to draw near. A drone watched from above, camera eye focussed on her.

Fleming glanced at her. "Someone in Kyiv likes what they see."

In response, Goldstein shot a soldier standing carelessly in an upper window across the street. The despairing cry and the dull thud underscored her contempt. Looking at the drone, she grabbed her crotch with her free hand and aimed the Jericho at the camera. The drone dipped forward then darted away. In the distance, the thunder of approaching artillery strikes portended disaster.

"You talk too much." Goldstein holstered her pistol then unlimbered her carbine and scanned the area.

Rocard beckoned from the shadow of a building. Fleming and Goldstein jogged forward – they were the last through a shattered doorway into the council building.

The grand interior—marble flooring, heavy baroque architecture—contrasted sharply with a corpse slumped in a corner and picked over by animals.

There was movement down the main corridor, and Rocard emerged from the shadows. "We've found the entrance," he said, expression eager.

In a side room, Fleming heard a groan. When he looked in, Federici was tending Naevu. The Italian pulled on the lanyard attached to the MTV Naevu wore, and the component parts unlatched. Quickly, he lifted away the abdominal and groin guards.

"*Madonna,*" Federici hissed, and reached for his med kit.

Blood ran from several wounds under Naevu's ribs. The man closed his eyes and whispered a prayer while Federici probed with forceps.

"Grenade fragments," Austen said. Cradling her M4A1, she leant against the wall opposite, the cigar rolling from one side of her mouth to the other. She spoke with the passion reserved for cataloguing car parts.

"Why are you here?" Fleming asked.

Austen grinned. "Same as you. Money." She hefted her carbine. "Plus, I'm American. We love shooting people. Target-rich environment Ukraine, dontcha know?"

Snorting, Fleming moved up the corridor and found Striker, Rocard, and Goldstein in a room crouched before a metal hatch with a wheel jutting from it.

"This it?"

Rocard nodded. "Oui."

"The code's not working," Goldstein said, staring in frustration at an old-style keypad and darkened analogue display.

"Battery's dead." Fleming cast a critical eye over the set up. "No surprise after forty years." He noticed fresh-looking scratches on the hatch. "It's been recently opened."

"That's impossible," Striker said.

"Look outside, boss," Fleming said. "Soldiers everywhere. Lower level's useful as a barracks."

"Russians?" Rocard asked.

Fleming shrugged. "Russian. Ukrainian. Little Green Men from Mars. It doesn't matter."

"No guards about," Rocard said.

"Locked from the inside," Fleming said. "Might be waiting."

"Get out the plastique," Striker ordered. "I want some shock and awe."

Fleming nodded. "The old-fashioned ways are the best." From his backpack he removed a canister containing a plug of Semtex. He thumbed the explosive into position around the hatch's hinges and lock. Finished, he inserted a detonator into the largest piece.

"Get back unless you want to wear the hatch like a hat." Fleming pulled a device from his backpack and switched it on.

"No wires?" Rocard asked.

"Twenty-first century, mate," Fleming said. "Bluetooth all the way."

The team backed down the corridor. As they did, Federici emerged and grabbed Striker's arm. "He's stubborn." The Italian nodded towards Naevu sitting on the floor, a blood-stained bandage wrapped around his torso.

"You're not leaving me behind," Naevu said. With effort, he climbed to his feet and pulled on his tunic.

Gunfire and shouting echoed outside. Crossing the doorway, flames streaming from it, a drone dropped at a sharp angle. It hit the ground and detonated, the sound overwhelming the screams.

"Heads down, bums up," Fleming said. He pressed a button, and a moment later, a loud bang resounded.

All that remained of the hatch was a gaping wreck.

A musky reek wafted from it.

"What's that stink?" Austen said, pressing her hand over her mouth and nose.

"Forty years of bad air," Striker said. "Give it a minute or two to clear."

Goldstein removed a drone from her backpack. She woke it with her iPad, and it buzzed into the air where its camera began livestreaming. Lights on the drone came on and it darted into the hatch.

Rocard fixed a bayonet beneath the barrel of his HK416.

"Easy," Fleming said. "This isn't Verdun."

"Give me a few minutes, mon ami, and I could make it so."

"We're in." Goldstein's eyes were intent on the iPad.

Striker called to Austen. "You and Rocard guard the entrance for two minutes, then fall back. Give anyone too nosy a reason to be somewhere else."

Austen hefted her carbine and smiled. "Sure thing."

Fleming watched Federici help Naevu down the corridor. Beads of sweat sprinkled the Fijian's face as he stumbled along, gripping his M4A1 like it was a holy relic.

"How far down?" Fleming asked Goldstein, who watched the iPad as the drone exited the stairwell into a corridor.

"Twenty-five metres."

"Who puts a facility seventy feet underground?" Fleming asked.

"Communism and paranoia go hand in hand," Striker said. "If the Soviets did anything well, it was burying their people *and* their secrets."

"What's that?" Goldstein inched the drone forward.

"Corpses," Fleming said, peering at the screen. "Soldiers?"

"Doesn't matter," Striker said. "We're going in."

Placing the drone in hover mode, Goldstein went first, Striker close behind. Naevu and Federici were next. Naevu looked stronger.

"Our friend has his second wind," Federici said, watching Naevu climb through the hatch. Federici looked uneasy. "He is running a temperature."

"Infection?"

"I gave him antibiotics. There is no reason to have an infection."

"You're our medic, Frankie," Fleming said. "Keep an eye on him."

Federici nodded as Rocard and Austen arrived. The Europeans entered the hatch while Austen waited impatiently.

"Ladies first." Fleming waved Austen forward. The American frowned as if Fleming would take the opportunity to slap a 'kick me' sign on her back. She went through, boots echoing.

Fleming eased his safety off, then descended into darkness.

☣ ☣ ☣

The corridor reminded Fleming uneasily of a killing chute. The funky smell was stronger here. "Get a grip, laddie," he muttered. Still, he felt like a gun had been sighted between his shoulder blades.

Ahead, the group clustered together. Goldstein wrestled with the hatch wheel, the drone hovering overhead. Austen was arguing. Naevu leant against the opposite wall, face bathed in sweat. He looked exhausted.

"I ain't touching them, no way, no how," Austen declared. She chewed her cigar.

Rocard rolled his eyes. "Putain de stupide Américain."

"Who you calling a fucking stupid American, Frenchie? Frog eating fucker."

Rocard's hand dropped onto the butt of his Glock 17. Austen smiled invitingly.

"Enough!" Striker snapped. "They're just corpses."

"What's that shit covering them?" Austen said.

Fleming pushed forward. A dense carpet of green filaments ran up the walls and across the ceiling, covering three bodies lying in a tangled heap. The smell that bothered Fleming was strongest here. It reminded him of his pa's compost heap.

"I don't know, Austen," Striker said, stabbing a finger at her. "Step over them. Step around them. I don't give a shit. We're going. Now."

Naevu coughed then hunched over. Federici reached for him, but on instinct, Fleming grabbed his arm. Naevu's coughing worsened. A wet tearing sound emerged, followed by a gout of brackish blood that splattered the ground.

"Get back." Fleming dragged Federici away. The Italian protested, only relenting when Naevu's back arched, smashing his head against the wall. Eyes bulging, his mouth yawned wide until the tendons stood stark.

"What's happening to him?" Austen yelled. There was a sudden racket at the bottom of the stairs. A pair of canisters trailing smoke clattered around before rolling towards them.

"Gas!" Striker shouted. Helmets were tossed as everyone reached for the masks riding at their hips. Fleming frantically pulled his on, breath rasping as it settled into place.

Through the mask's plastic eyeholes, the corridor took on a smeary patina. Gas swirled around Naevu who stood ramrod straight, viscous chunks of blood dribbling down his chin.

"Holy Mother of God." The words crackled in Fleming's earpiece.

He turned and saw the mound of corpses shift, arms and legs twitching as they rose puppet-like to their feet.

Mouths sagged open, revealing red-streaked holes burrowing deep into dried flesh. Purple spores spewed into the air. The head of one of the corpses, riddled with mould, cracked open like a budding flower. Tendrils shot forward from the veined cavity, whipping in a wild frenzy.

Naevu's face exploded. Bones, blood, and flesh splattered the opposite wall.

Fleming emptied a clip into Naevu. The Fijian's body jerked spasmodically beneath the barrage then slid to the ground. Grey stalks erupted from the ruined skull, their tips opening and closing like foul sphincters.

Shots from the stairs rang out. A ricochet showered Fleming in concrete shards. With Rocard at his shoulder, they fired on a pair of soldiers who had ventured down the stairs. The bullets struck home and the soldiers danced, then collapsed. The wall behind them was slick with blood.

A whistling noise erupted from a corpse as Striker grappled with it. A fine, cloudy mist erupted from its mouth, enveloping the Australian, clinging like a second skin.

"Get that fucking hatch open," Striker shouted, desperately holding the corpse away. A dense thicket of yellow gills grew from its wasted flesh. The mouth opened wider, skin, muscle, and tendons tearing. The jaw fell off, exposing a cavernous hole from which more spores bloomed.

Austen stepped up, shoved the barrel of her carbine into the cavity and fired. The top of its head erupted, spraying dried brains and fungal matter in a Rorschach pattern across the ceiling.

The air filled with the terrible sucking sound of tearing flesh, and as Naevu's chest collapsed, a riot of colourful bulbous caps swayed into the air. Fleming and the others watched, horrified, as the caps bulged, ready to burst.

Amidst the chaos, Goldstein, groaning with effort, slowly turned the wheel. The door opened with a squeal. "Let's go, let's go." Goldstein followed the drone as it ducked inside. More soldiers pounded down the stairs. In short order, everyone retreated into the gap.

With a thick splatter, the caps exploded as Striker pulled the door shut, spraying purple fluid everywhere. Through the glass, Fleming watched the screaming soldiers' bodies melt like heated wax.

Inside, the gloom and cold pressed close. Stunned silence as everyone took stock.

"What. The. Fuck. Was. That?" Austen said. Her eyes bulged like billiard balls.

Silence.

"Can we take these masks off?" Federici asked.

Everyone turned to Striker standing beside a narrow table. The spores that enveloped him had mostly fallen off. Those remaining were brown. After a moment's hesitation, he pulled off his mask. Austen's gun barrel tracked towards him. Everyone waited.

Striker smiled thinly. "Nothing," he said. "Happy?"

There was a rustle of movement as masks were removed.

"Look at this," Rocard said, pointing his torch at the wall. Powder-blue filaments ran up the walls and the ceiling. Despite the lack of a breeze, the filaments shivered. More growths disappeared into the gloom.

"Did you see Naevu? How could... that happen to him?" Federici said, staring through the window. Tendrils of gas swirled, but there was no movement.

"Yeah, Striker." Austen rounded on him. "What aren't you telling us?"

Striker ignored her. Clearing a table, he removed from his backpack a document pouch and took out a sheaf of paper, which he spread across the table.

"Are you ignoring me because you're scared, or are you ignoring me because you're an arrogant prick?"

Austen shouted. "This was a mission to retrieve documents. I didn't sign on for a horror show."

"'I'll take arrogant prick for two hundred dollars, Alex,'" Striker said. "You leave now and I'll shoot you like a dog. We are too close for your grandstanding to risk everything."

Austen measured Striker with a glare, then shook her head.

After a moment's hesitation, everyone joined Striker at the table, taking in the plans of the facility. Goldstein stood to one side, transfixed by a yellow device in her hand. It ticked softly, and Fleming had a bad feeling.

"This facility was built in the mid-60s and evacuated in 1986. My contact, your paymaster, found information indicating that research is here, on the third level."

"What sort of research?" Austen said.

"Officially? Fertilisers. Off the books, bio-warfare."

"And the mechanism?

"Genetic manipulation of fungus to increase the lethality of the mycotoxins produced. The Commies wanted to expand their biological warfare capabilities."

"Fungus? Mushrooms?" Austen laughed disbelievingly.

"You've led us into a trap," Rocard shouted. "Naevu became infected. We're next!"

"Not if we're careful," Striker said. "The masks work, right?"

"And those monsters?" Austen said. "Masks won't stop them eating my face."

"We're armed to the teeth," Striker said. "They die as easily as anyone. Listen. These things prove the research is unique. Rarity equals value. Or would you prefer living like a fucking redneck in Shitsville, USA?"

Austen looked ready to kill him, then she shook her head again.

"What next?" Fleming said. "Russians and Ukrainians

are duking it out up top, and we're down here with these ungodly things."

"Striker's right," Austen said. "Damn me for saying it. Shrooms or no shrooms, we blow the fuckers away. I signed on for a million dollars, and by God, I'm gonna claim it come hell or high water."

"Spoken like an American," Rocard said. He turned his head and spit.

Austen sneered. "Tell me why your President married a woman old enough to be his mother, then I'll listen to what you have to say. Otherwise, shut the fuck up."

Despite the warmth of their bodies, goosebumps broke out over Fleming's arms. He started at a sudden thud.

Naevu pressed the red ruin of his face against the window set in the hatch.

"Oh, this is too much," Austen said. Ropy tendrils slid greasily across the glass, smearing the blood. On the walls, the filaments shivered in ecstasy.

"Be quiet," Goldstein snapped. She pressed her earpiece, listening intently.

"What is it?" Striker asked.

"Russians are planning an artillery strike on the village in the next few hours, once the weather clears."

"Bunker busters?"

Goldstein shook her head. "But they have a habit of overkill."

Naevu bashed his skull against the window. A crack appeared. Tendrils tried to insert themselves into the fracture.

"We'd best hurry," Goldstein said. She held up the yellow handheld. It ticked softly.

"Geiger counter?" Fleming said. "Chernobyl was forty years ago."

"Chernobyl is six hundred kilometres to the west," Goldstein replied. "This is inside the facility."

Federici and Rocard swore.

Austen laughed. "There's a nuclear reactor down here?"

"I was told it was on standby," Striker said. "Control rods in place, coolant flowing through."

"God damn," Austen said. "What an absolute clusterfuck."

Striker moved to the interior door and cycled the handle. As the door opened, a faint musky smell, like that of the corpses in the corridor, wafted in.

"There's enough money on offer to change your lives," Striker said. "Come or go."

Austen snorted. Fleming looked at Rocard, who shrugged. Federici chewed his lip, but in the end nodded. Goldstein hung the Geiger counter from a loop on her vest. It ticked away, a sign, maybe, of things to come.

"That's it then?" Fleming said. "We charge headfirst into who knows what?"

"Sounds about right," Striker said, slapping a fresh magazine into his weapon. He slipped several more into carriers on his belt. The others rearmed.

"And to think I could've gone fishing," Fleming said, changing out the L85A2's magazine. He raised the rifle to his shoulder and led the way.

Their lights cut through the darkness. There were signs of a hasty retreat decades old. Upturned furniture. Paperwork. Even the dried remnants of a kielbasa sausage sandwich on the floor, only lightly touched by a reddish mould.

Fleming nosed open a door with the barrel of his weapon. Inside was a small dormitory. Empty. Next, a refectory. Echoes.

"What do you think happened to Naevu?" Goldstein said as she stepped into another empty room.

"Infection," Fleming said. "The Soviets' experiments are loose. And they work fast."

Goldstein grimaced. "Keep your mask close." She glanced around. "Who knows what's in the air."

An elevator stood at the end of the corridor. A delicate pattern of mould covered the doors like an intricate mosaic. Fleming pushed the call button but it remained dead.

"We take the stairs." Fleming nodded to a door beside the elevator. A now familiar sense of unease washed over him. He put his ear to the door. "Cover me."

Goldstein slipped her Jericho from its holster.

Fleming grabbed the handle. *Why was it so hot?* He opened the door.

A seething purple light spilled out of the stairwell. With it came the vile miasma of rotting flesh. A riot of hooked fronds reached for Fleming, who caught a quick glimpse of piled bodies before slamming the door shut.

"Dio." Federici crossed himself.

Rocard reached into his backpack and pulled out a bandolier of grenades.

"You're joking," Austen said. "He's joking, isn't he?" She laughed hysterically. "You're going to blow up fungus with grenades? What else have you got in there? The Rockettes?"

"If only," Rocard said. He looked at Striker, who nodded.

"Put your masks on," the Aussie said.

Masks were donned again. At the door, Fleming heard rustling sounds. Behind them, silence. Striker pointed to Austen, and they warily made their way up the corridor.

"Let's go, mon ami," Rocard said, eyes intent.

Fleming raised his weapon. Rocard kicked the door open, where it caught in something soft. He tossed a pair of grenades into the gap then stepped back.

Muffled explosions. Chunks of fungus writhed on the ground. Up the corridor, gunfire. Pounding boot-steps echoed towards them.

"Go, go, go," Striker shouted. He let Austen get past him, then he fired a long burst as a figure lurched into view.

"Naevu," Fleming said.

The Fijian staggered forward, wiry filaments rising in a crown around his shattered head. A whistling hiss issuing from the ragged hole in its face carried eerily down the corridor.

"How in God's name is he still alive?" Fleming said.

"Not God, my friend," Rocard said. "Le Diable." Hefting a grenade, he pulled the pin then tossed it down the corridor.

"Everyone, into the stairwell," Striker ordered.

For Fleming, reality smeared. The grenade ricocheted between the walls. The other mercenaries turned and charged into the stairwell as the grenade's detonation sent Naevu flying backwards, great gouts of blood spraying everywhere. An arm, torn off at the elbow, twitched feebly on the ground. Naevu, now a crumpled wreck of torn flesh and burning clothing. More tendrils burst from his smoking body, swaying back and forth as if on the scent. With his remaining hand, he dragged his body forward on splintered fingernails.

The inside of the stairwell was a nightmare of convulsing life. Corpse-flesh burst beneath their boots in a bubbling froth. Fronds and ropy tendrils groped blindly for them. Corrugated caps burst in a spray of fine green mist that clung to everything. Fleming retched inside his mask, the acid stink of bile a welcome respite from the filthy stench in the air.

With a cry, Federici slipped on the stairs and tumbled down to the landing. He lay groaning in the thick sludge. Fleming manhandled Federici to his feet, the Italian's body lolling against him.

At the turn, Fleming sensed movement and looked up to see Naevu's twitching body framed in the doorway, held upright by thick stalks emerging from his chest. Cursing, Fleming pulled his P320 from its holster and emptied the mag. The Fijian jerked backwards again and again as bullets slammed into him. There was no blood now, just a thick, green ichor spurting from the holes. Fleming abandoned the effort and followed the others down, with Federici waking as Rocard slammed shut the stairwell door.

"Anyone got a God damned flamethrower?" Austen said.

Federici coughed. It was when Fleming sat him down that he noticed the Italian bleeding from a gash in his side just below the edge of the MTV. The Italian coughed again. It sounded like wet cloth tearing. Gingerly, Fleming removed the man's mask. He swore and stepped back.

Chunks of hair came away with the mask, exposing raw scalp. Sunken, desperate eyes stared dully at Fleming. His exposed skin bulged, pulsing horribly until a carpet of mushrooms burst through the flesh. Tendrils grew from his nose, questing the air with tips that split and split again. A musky scent rolled off him. Federici bared his teeth and snarled.

"Fuck this," Austen said. She stepped forward and shot Federici between the eyes. His body went limp.

"What in God's name were they doing down here?"

A shockwave struck the facility, rocking them on their feet. Walls groaned like the damned. The wave built and built until it seemed the ceiling would collapse. Then, it stilled. In the silence, Goldstein's Geiger counter ticked like a deathwatch beetle.

"A near miss," Striker said.

"What about the radiation?" Rocard said. "You said it was safe."

Striker shrugged. "Safe enough. Either the containment shield around the reactor has been breached, or the cooling basin is losing water." He looked at Goldstein. "How many roentgens per hour?"

Goldstein checked the Geiger counter and blanched. "One hundred fifty."

Austen snorted. "You better tell me my annual mammogram pumps out more radiation." She tugged at her mask. "God damn this thing. It's humid as fuck down here." This time, she pulled the mask off.

The others waited. "Idiots," Austen shouted. "Haven't you worked out the fungal infection transmits in the blood, not by breathing it in? Naevu and Frankie were cut, remember?"

After a moment, the others followed suit.

Fleming cast his gaze around at the others. "If we don't leave in the next two hours, we'll be dead in a month." He stared hard at Striker.

"We have no choice," Striker said. His remaining eye glittered bloody in the torch light. "We're close. Like I said before. In or out."

"Out," Rocard shouted. "What's the point of all that money if I piss blood and die screaming?"

Fleming weighed the odds. "Striker's right. We're close. We can be gone in an hour."

"You're as mad he is," Rocard said. "And the Russian missiles?"

"On their way," Goldstein said. She had been checking the bandwidth for radio chatter. "The local Russian commander confirms the strike. He's asked for RBK-500U cluster bombs to be deployed in an hour."

Rocard held his head in his hands while Austen marched around in a little circle, running a hand through her hair. "Jesus fuck, Striker. What have you led us into?"

"More money than you've seen in your life. An hour is all we need."

"Christ." Austen looked at Rocard. "What about you, Frenchie?"

"Ce'st la vie," Rocard said, though he glared at Striker with murder in his eyes.

Striker looked at Fleming, who smiled lopsidedly. "Since we've become a democracy, I vote we go on. If my cells are being fried, I should get compensated for it."

They left Federici. In just a few minutes, a forest of tiny, shivering mushrooms had grown over him, distorting his features into a melted plastic mask.

Hurrying down a corridor, they checked doors and found storage rooms.

"Wait," Fleming said. Racked on shelves were dozens of foot-long cylinders, covered in Cyrillic. "Anyone read Russian?"

Striker nodded at Goldstein. "You do, right?"

Goldstein hesitated. "Acetone. Flammable."

"Acetone?" Fleming said. "Perfect. Each of you takes one. We're going to do some clearance work."

Everyone took a cylinder. Out in the corridor, Rocard called as Naevu stumbled from the gloom. Like a demented angel, fronds unfurled over his shoulders. A green miasma hung around him, spores trailing like a comet's tale.

"Whatever it is you're planning, mon ami, it had better work."

Loosening the tap, Fleming dropped his cylinder and kicked it forward. He aimed and fired. The cylinder exploded in a ball of flame, filling the corridor and igniting Naevu in a crackling rush. A terrible whistling sound escaped as Naevu disintegrated, leaving twitching lumps of smouldering flesh.

Drawn by the heat and noise, nightmare shapes coalesced out of the shadows. One man, his body grotesquely puffed up, squeezed down the corridor. His head looked like a giant, pulsing tumour thick with shivering nodules oozing a heavy mucus.

Austen swore in disgust. The creature's face split like a burst sausage, and a cloud of spores exploded into the air, covering everything in a thick, slippery goo. It felt warm on Fleming's skin, like blood. He shouted incoherently and opened fire.

There were more explosions as the team hustled through a dining area festooned with monstrously large mushroom caps. Rocard shot a creature in the guts then delivered the coup de grace with the bayonet. He then grappled a creature whose body was a network of nodules blinking in a bewildering, hypnotic kaleidoscope. Striker put an end to it by blowing its brains against the wall.

More mutated horrors from the depths of a drug addict's shattered mind appeared. Acetone canisters went up like Roman candles, the concussive blasts ear shattering. There were fires everywhere, pyres of human flesh overtaken by fungal infections.

Fleming experienced this as a series of dreadful staccato images... things that were once Russian soldiers flopping about, great rents in their bodies spewing spores that ate concrete. Austen laughing hysterically as she emptied a magazine into a pair of men joined at the head like Siamese twins, exposed brains black-veined and dripping ichor. Heads with yawning mouths and eyes consumed by terror and madness merged with the mould-riddled floors and walls.

Then they were out and in a corridor. Behind them lay a holocaust, a kiln heaped with the dead and dying, the mutated remains of men condemned to the foulest of deaths.

Austen had her pistol half out of its holster. "God damn, that paperwork better be where you say it is Striker or I'll shoot you dead myself." Striker ignored her, and she jammed her weapon back.

"Almost there," Striker coldly intoned.

Fleming gathered a pair of the remaining cylinders. Cautiously, he opened the stairwell door. Swaying on a thick stalk, a malign combination of three bodies interwoven with fungal flesh greeted him, moaning in a terrible symphony. Turning the taps, Fleming tossed the canisters inside then followed up with one of Rocard's grenades.

Multiple detonations blew the door off its hinges, sending burning, reeking chunks flying. Even with the carnage, the whistling shrieks drew closer.

"Go, go, go," Striker called, taking point.

They discarded emptied magazines as they raced down the stairwell. Writhing growths lined the ceiling, black-spotted caps thick with bony teeth snapping at their heads. The air was humid, dank with rot. Fleming heard a splashing sound ahead, then Striker cursing.

Fleming came around the final turn to find Striker knee deep in water before the open stairwell door.

"Fucking coolant leak," the Aussie said.

Goldstein's Geiger counter ticked faster.

"This goddamned mission is jinxed," Austen said. She rolled the cigar from one side of her mouth to the other, jaw clenching as she chewed on it.

They exited the stairwell into a bizarre wonderland. Distended, fruiting bodies clung to the walls and emitted a purple light that hurt their eyes. Clumps of fungus crawled across the ceiling or floated in fuzzy bergs over the water. All around, corpse-coloured caps roosted on desks or clumped together over cabinets and workbenches.

Goldstein raised the Geiger counter. The ticking was a steady, ominous drone.

"Everything in here is irradiated," she said, looking warily around. "The water, the walls, the fungus. Whatever experiments were done here have mutated over the last four decades."

"Mère de Dieu. Look at this," Rocard said. He stared through an opaque window set into a wall.

Fleming came over and began swearing.

A squat cylinder stood in a broad basin of water. Thick layers of an eerily luminescent purple mass covered the reactor, breathing like a bizarre set of lungs. The air inside the reactor area was thick with swirling spores.

Goldstein came over and placed the Geiger counter against the glass. The meter shrieked.

"Tell us what we are looking for, Striker," Rocard said, his accent thick with stress. "The sooner we find these papers, the sooner we escape this nightmare."

Striker nodded. "Look for a small safe. Inside, there's a red posey... I mean folder." Absently, he rubbed his eyepatch.

A chorus of whistling shrieks sounded as figures erupted from the stairwell. Rocard turned, firing, cutting down the lead attacker who slipped beneath the surface of the water. A sudden, violent gurgling clamoured, then a pipe set in a far wall blew out sending a stream of water arcing across the room.

"What's going on?" Austen shouted.

"Cascading failures in the coolant systems," Fleming called above the chatter of his carbine. A creature exploded from the water and he was forced to use the weapon as a club. The soldier, his entire head wreathed with thick mushrooms that deformed his features and rendered his eyes grotesque slits, skidded sideways as the butt of the carbine clipped his head. Mushrooms broke off, taking pieces of his skull. Brains dribbled from the holes even as Fleming jammed the end of the barrel under the creature's jaw and blew out the side of his head.

Rocard screamed. His magazine was empty and he was so panicked he hadn't reloaded. He swung his rifle; a caveman armed with a thigh bone. Crying for his mother, he nearly lost his balance. As he righted himself, the water bubbled around him.

A mottled curtain rose behind Rocard. Nodules spasmed open and shut, exhaling black spores. Rocard's screaming rose several octaves as his flesh sizzled. The fleshy growth fell on him and dragged him under. There was a frenzy of bubbles then the waters stilled.

Austen held her carbine in one hand and pistol in the other. Cigar discarded, she appeared in the grip of a Berserker fury; eyes wild, lips peeled, chanting words that seemed half Lord's Prayer and half demonic summoning. Creatures were drawn to her, dying at her feet even as they clambered over each other to reach her. Austen leaped onto a desk. From that vantage, she dealt death with all the fervour of a Crusader seeing Jerusalem for the first time.

Fleming and Goldstein stood shoulder to shoulder, holding off the horde with sheer weight of firepower. Fleming shot coolly while lobbing grenades salvaged from Rocard's gear. Water geysered as the grenades detonated. A corner of his mind screamed he risked a total coolant system failure with an errant explosion. The larger part urged him to *kill kill kill.*

A weight cannoned into Fleming, and he went down in the water. The grip loosened, and he struggled to his feet.

Striker roared. Fleming chanced a look and saw him tearing at his face. Yellow fluid dribbled from beneath the eyepatch. Then Striker straightened and shot at Goldstein. The Israeli staggered under the impact, saved only by the MVAT. She returned fire and Striker threw himself behind a metal cabinet.

"He's gone mad," Goldstein shouted. Her eyes widened, and she slogged over to a box sat atop a shelf. The metal band around it was bolted to the wall.

"Ring-a ring-a rosey," Striker screamed. He fired again, the shot missing Fleming and felling a creature behind him. Bewildered, Fleming held back from firing. Striker splashed towards him.

The two men went at it like wild dogs. The Australian's remaining eye was feverish, flecked with grey motes that swirled across the iris before burrowing into the white. Striker's punch whipped Fleming half around in the water. Fleming spat out a tooth then clapped both hands over Striker's ears. The man's mouth opened wide in agony.

Striker shook his head like a wounded bear. Seeing Fleming coming forward, the Australian shoulder charged. With his greater weight, Striker pushed Fleming into the water, holding him by the throat.

Putrid water filled Fleming's nostrils, worming down his windpipe and into his lungs. Sparks filled his vision as Striker's image warped and swelled as the water eddied around his face. His vision darkening, Fleming desperately reached up, fingers hooked into claws as he tore at Striker's face. The thumbs pressed into Fleming's throat went deeper, and he felt the cartilage creak. Thrashing wildly, burning the last of his oxygen, Fleming, by pure chance, hooked a finger on Striker's eyepatch and pulled it away.

The team leader's mouth opened in a soundless scream as anemone-shaped tendrils of fungus quested from the ruins of his eye-socket. Releasing his death-grip on Fleming, Striker clawed at his face. Fleming surged up, coughing up a torrent of brackish water. Then Austen shot Striker twice in the chest.

The man flew backwards and disappeared into the water.

"All right, all right," Fleming said, breathing heavily.

Goldstein beckoned frantically, and Fleming dug into his waterlogged backpack and found the canister of plastique. He shaped a charge around the safe's lock and hinges while Austen and Goldstein held back the remaining creatures with their dwindling supply of ammunition.

"Here we go," Fleming shouted, holding the detonator in his hand.

Austen put two bullets in the chest of the last creature, which sank beneath the waves in a gargling exhalation of spores. Austen and Goldstein crouched behind a shelf as water eddied around them. Fleming ignited the detonator.

The safe door came off with a sharp report. Fleming was there first, rummaging inside until he found the red folder.

"At last," Goldstein said, then pointed her Jericho at Fleming's head. "Give it to me." Austen looked sharply at her. Goldstein's Israeli-tinged English faded into something thicker, harsher.

"A goddamned Russian," Austen said in disbelief. "Thick as fleas on a mangy dog!"

"Shut up, you fucking *говнюк*, white-trash bitch," Goldstein said. She held out her hand. "Give me the folder and you will live."

A shudder rocked the chamber. Fleming hesitated as the ceiling groaned.

"Make me ask again, and I will blow your head off."

Fleming handed over the folder.

"You won't make it outside alone," Fleming shouted, as Goldstein retreated. The Geiger counter hanging from a cord around her neck, howled.

Goldstein shook her head. She reached the stairwell and backed up it. Fleming saw movement behind her. He reached for his pistol when Austen grabbed his arm.

"She wanted it," Austen said. "She can deal with the consequences."

Goldstein flinched when a fibrous tentacle flopped onto her shoulder. Suckers bit deep into her flesh and the folder flew from her spasming hand to miraculously land on a desk. She screamed as blood was sucked from the wounds, engorging the writhing limb. It flexed and tore her arm from its socket. More tentacles lifted her screaming into the darkness.

"Fuck me," Austen breathed. She darted through the water to retrieve the folder.

"Now let's get the fuck out of here."

"How?" Fleming said.

"You're the engineer. Surely, you can do something to get the elevator started?"

Fleming ran to the elevator. With Austen's help, he pulled open the doors. Once inside, he ripped away an access door and probed amongst the wiring.

Hooting and shrieks echoed. Austen stepped outside, her carbine at the ready.

"I think I can re-route some of the power," Fleming said to the clatter of tools as he rummaged through his kit.

"Damned shame you didn't think of it before," Austen shouted. Tentacles were again visible at the final turn of the stairwell. She snagged an abandoned acetone cylinder and twisted the top. Gas hissed.

"Hurry the fuck up, Fleming." Austen heaved the cylinder up the stairs, where it bounced perilously on the top step. She took aim, fired, then dove into the elevator just as she heard a ping.

The canister exploded. The cage shuddered and the lighting flickered agonisingly. The power held and the doors jerkily closed. They ascended in fits and starts. Austen slumped against the wall.

"So this is it." She held up the folder. "People died for this shit." Austen shook her head as the elevator shuddered to a stop.

The door opened, revealing a transformed Striker. One leg had thickened massively, splitting the skin and releasing a riot of colourful tendrils. Shivering nodules covered his face. A massive growth bulged from his eye socket, reaching back over his skull and down his left arm, turning flesh and bone into a profusion of black-veined, bulbous tumours.

"Ring-a ring-a rosey," Striker said thickly, the corner of his mouth pulled back in a leer revealing blackened teeth. "A pocket full of—"

"Oh, fuck you," Austen said and shot him in the face. Striker went down, fluid pumping from the hole in his head.

Fleming and Austen sprinted down the corridor, up the stairs and through the hatch into the town hall and then outside. Pitch darkness greeted them, then an artillery strike landed half a kilometre away. For a moment everything was brighter than the sun at noon. An enormous explosion rocked the village. Buildings went down like falling dominos. A blizzard of dust.

Fleming shouted. "Head north, that'll take us awa—"

Another strike landed. Windows up and down the street blew out in a flurry of lethal shards.

"Go, go, go!" Fleming said.

Together, they charged down the street. Strikes blossomed in the west. The earth trembled and ran like water. On the right, a building slid into the street in a clatter of brickwork and masonry.

"Bastards," Fleming shouted as artillery strikes continued to explode all around them. He saw Austen glance over her shoulder, then an explosion swallowed the world and punched them down into the dark.

☣   ☣   ☣

Fleming woke to despairing laughter. Groaning, he rolled onto his back. With trembling hands he patted himself down, relieved to find he was still intact. He stood, gaze drawn to his shadow sprawled starkly across the ground. Turning, he found Austen staring at the village. And then he saw the cloud.

Austen turned to him then. Tears streaked her dirty face. "We're cooked, Fleming. So, so fucking cooked."

Tendrils of a brilliantly lit, phosphorescent-purple cloud reached across the sky above the village. A flock of birds veered too late from the leading edge. One by one, touched by the spores, they fell dead to the ground.

"They've done it now," Austen shouted. "God Almighty, they've done it now."

Another artillery strike hit where the facility lay. The explosion drew more spores into the air. The cloud loomed higher and higher, a dread hand reaching up to tear down Heaven.

Fleming started laughing. He dropped to his knees and laughed and laughed and laughed as the cloud drew near.

Austen pulled her pistol out, pressed it against her temple and pulled the trigger.

The cloud. Larger now, then larger again. A rain of death turning the land brown and desolate. This was only the start. But it would soon be the end.

Everywhere.

Well, thanks for reading *SNAFU: Contagion*.

We hope you've enjoyed it as much as we did putting it together.

Please consider leaving us a review if you see fit. Any and all reviews are gratefully accepted.

I would ask please, if you DO review online, send a link to Geoff via editor@cohesionpress.com or via our Facebook page messaging system.

Thank you.

PS - Our email signup gives you a free EXCLUSIVE SNAFU volume, and we won't spam you, either.

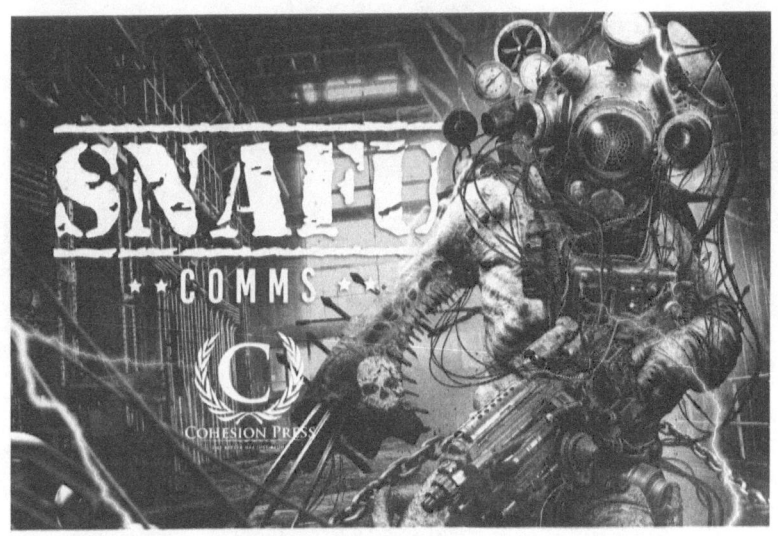

Signup form on the website.
www.cohesionpress.com

Geoff Brown/Dawn Roach - Directors, Cohesion Press.
Mayday Hills Asylum
Beechworth, Australia

Amanda J Spedding - Editor-in-chief, Cohesion Press
Sydney, Australia